SHE WAS A FIERY NOBLEWOMAN WHO
MET HER MATCH IN THE
WARRIOR PLEDGED
TO DELIVER HER
TO ANOTHER
MAN'S ARMS.

P9-DEI-959

M. KANE

"WOULD YOU *LIKE* ME TO FIND YOU DESIRABLE?" HE INQUIRED SOFTLY.

An odd, giddy rush of hot blood flooded Ariel's limbs as she found herself staring up into eyes as dark and turbulent as the sky overhead, at a mouth that offered no compromise.

"I . . . want nothing from you, sirrah," she stammered.

"Nothing?"

Ariel was stunned by the contact, stunned by the bold intimation of his hands and body. She tried to turn her head, to wrest it out of his grip, but he held firm. He crowded her even closer to the battlements, his torso an immense, overpowering wall of muscle and brawn.

His head bent toward her and she flinched back, but there was no escape. His mouth, surprisingly warm and supple, brushed over hers, taunting her with the promise of further outrage to come. She gasped again, intending to rail at him for his audacity, but before a word or breath could be uttered, her lips were no longer being merely brushed, no longer being taunted. They were being crushed, devoured, plundered by a mouth that was suddenly as ruthless and arrogant as the man himself. . . .

Through a Dark Mist, and
winner of the *Romantic Times*
Reviewers Choice Award
for Best Historical Romance of 1992

"Ms. Canham has set quill to bow and struck directly into the heart of every swashbuckling adventure lover's soul. . . . The action doesn't stop until the final paragraph with no questions left unanswered. Gadzooks! I love a good romp!"
—*Heartland Critiques*

"A medieval novel with rare authority, weaving a rich tapestry of atmosphere, action, and romance. This book is a wonderfully satisfying love story that I would recommend to anyone."
—Anita Mills

"Swashbuckling adventure. Sweeping pageantry. Lusty passions. Clever dialogue. A thoroughly engrossing love story."
—Nan Ryan

"Infectious characters, witty dialogue, thrill-a-minute intrigue and intense conflicts of the heart—Marsha Canham gives you all this and more. If you like romance; if you like adventure; if you like first-rate fiction, you'll love *Through A Dark Mist.*"
—Elaine Coffman

"A legend is brilliantly brought to life on the pages of *Through a Dark Mist* . . . unfolds with all the adventure, rollicking good humor, wildly exciting escapades, cliffhangers, and, most of all, smoldering sensuality any reader could desire. Once you begin this mesmerizing tale there is no way you will put it down until the very last page and then you can only wish for more."
—*Romantic Times*

"Well-written, passionate adventure . . . you'll love *Through a Dark Mist!*"
—*Affaire de Coeur*

Other books by Marsha Canham

CHINA ROSE
BOUND BY THE HEART
THE WIND AND THE SEA
THE PRIDE OF LIONS
THE BLOOD OF ROSES

THROUGH A DARK MIST*
UNDER THE DESERT MOON*

*Available from Dell Publishing

IN THE SHADOW OF MIDNIGHT

MARSHA CANHAM

A DELL BOOK

Published by
Dell Publishing
a division of
Bantam Doubleday Dell Publishing Group, Inc.
1540 Broadway
New York, New York 10036

ISBN: 0-440-20613-8

Printed in the United States of America

Published simultaneously in Canada

April 1994

10 9 8 7 6 5 4 3 2 1

OPM

This too, and always, is for The Chief.
It was one wager I did not want to win.

Prologue

✝ **H**e had deliberately cut the pad of his thumb open on a sharp edge of stone, then pushed tiny bits of gravel into the bleeding wound so that the slightest pressure would send sharp pains up his arm, commanding his full attention. He was exhausted, ill, weary beyond words, but he could not afford to let his concentration slip. He could not appear weak or intimidated in his uncle's presence. He could not allow the accumulated filth, stench, and despair of these past nine months of imprisonment show him to be unworthy of the noble Angevin blood that flowed through his veins.

He was Arthur, Duke of Brittany, Geoffrey's son and heir, and by right of blood succession, heir to the throne of England upon Richard the Lionheart's death.

It was said that all Angevin spawn were descendants from the witch Melusine—a sorceress who had escaped the fiery waters of the river Styx and come back to earth half-woman, half-serpent.

From the devil they came and to the devil they would return.

Yet they had been handsome men—Henry of Anjou, his sons Richard and Geoffrey. They looked the way kings were supposed to look: tall and powerfully built, as blond and bright as gold, with blazing blue eyes. Only John, the runt of the devil's brood, was set apart from the others. Stout and bullish, darker than Satan, with a sly, vulpine face, he made up in greed and ambition what he lacked in stature and appearance.

After years of living in the shadow of his warrior brother, the great Lionheart, John, as the last surviving son of Henry II, had placed the crown of England on his own head at Westminster. He had already ruled as regent for almost a decade while his brother was off leading armies and fighting Crusades, and those who supported John's continued, corrupt rule turned a blind eye to the fact that there existed another claimant, a Plantagenet prince who was as blond and blue-eyed and regal of bearing as the revered Pendragon king for whom he had been named.

Unfortunately, Arthur had been a mere boy of fourteen when Richard fell to an archer's arrow at Chalus. He was no match in terms of military strength or cunning for his uncle, Prince John. Moreover, Arthur had spent his entire life in Brittany. He had never set foot on English soil and the barons of England, even those who feared John's excesses, were more wary of the influence the French king, Philip II, had had on the young and impressionable Arthur. Even William the Marshal, Earl of Pembroke, who loathed John with the same passion as he had loved Henry and Richard, decided it was better to deal with the devil they knew than with a boy who boldly displayed the fleur-de-lys on his coat of arms.

As expected, the domains of Brittany, Anjou, Maine, and Touraine had risen in support of Arthur. Normandy's barons, those who had the strongest ties with England, supported the wisdom of William the Marshal. The Aquitaine, the rich and vast province that had come under England's rule with the marriage of Henry and Eleanor, was still and ever loyal to the dowager queen, who, though seventy-eight years of age when she had cradled the golden head of her dying Lionheart, had also known that in order to avoid a bloody civil war, she must support her son over her beloved grandson.

Rejected and betrayed, Arthur had fled to Paris to live under Philip's protection. At fifteen he had been knighted by the French monarch and wed to the dauphine, Marie. At sixteen, with the might of his father-in-law's army behind him, Arthur had marched on Normandy, declaring his intention to reinstate himself as a claimant to the throne of England. Foolishly advised, his first point of attack had been the dowager's castle at Mirebeau. Eleanor, by then a bent, frail figure who walked the ramparts with the aid of a cane, collected her defenders around her and held the castle until John arrived to relieve the siege. Arthur, who had advanced on Mirebeau with less than a third of his forces, was surprised by his uncle's swift and deadly response. Surrounded and vastly outnumbered, he had no choice but to surrender. He had been taken prisoner and held at Falaise; more recently moved to Rouen to await John's decision as to what to do with this bold and handsome young prince who reminded him all too painfully of the two great kings who had gone before him.

"Two years ago," John said evenly, "when you realized the barons of England and Normandy would never support your feeble claim, you whimpered to me on bended knee, as I recall, and pledged homage . . . *swearing* your allegiance and loyalty in exchange for my not stripping you of your rights as Duke of Brittany."

Arthur squeezed his thumb and forefinger together. In the tomblike silence of his donjon cell, he could hear the soft *pat pat pat* of blood dripping from the end of his thumb, but his face remained expressionless.

"For that I do thank you, Uncle," he said calmly. "Without those rights, I should not have been able to add to my army in Brittany."

"Army? You call that handful of ill-trained rabble you had capering about you . . . an army? Your own captain of the guard, M'sieur *des Roches*"—he spat the name with the contempt it deserved—"deserted at the first sight of armoured men along the Seine."

Several more drips were added to the crimson stain at Arthur's heels as his fair complexion turned ruddy. The air was dank and chilled, the stench of mold on the walls was ripened by the stench that came from the overflowed slops bucket in the corner. The cell was small, lit by a single smoky candle. It boasted the comforts of one scarred table and one x-chair—which his uncle now occupied—and a lumpy pile of months-old rushes that served as Arthur's bed. He had not seen the sun or filled his lungs with clean air for better than three months.

"I could have you killed," John said matter-of-factly, picking at a weal on his chin. "As a vassal rebelling against your king, your life is legally forfeit in the eyes of any court or country. I could have you killed and not a brow in the kingdom would be raised in approbation. Moreover, you attacked your own grandmother. My mother. The beloved dowager queen of England. You laid siege to an old, frail, defenseless woman—

dried teat that she may be—and by doing so, earned the scorn
and condemnation of every knight in Christendom." He
chuckled and flicked away the bit of pustule he had collected
under his nail. "I could have you executed and not even be
challenged to justify the deed."

"Then order it and be done, Uncle, for I weary of these
games."

"Games?" John launched himself out of the chair—something he had been reluctant to do since the boy was a full head
and neck taller. "You call it a game to decide your fate?"

"Uncle—" The title was used disdainfully, accompanied
by a hard glint of shrewdness in the crystalline blue eyes. "You
decided my fate the instant Richard drew his last breath. You
decided it before the barons took their puppet vote, and long
before my mother bartered a few sweaty hours in your bed for
the *privilege* of permitting me to pledge homage."

"I showed you mercy," John seethed.

"You showed me arrogance, greed, and blind ambition.
You showed me a man so twisted with corruption and jealousy
he could barely wait until his brother's blood had cooled before
he was racing to count the coins in the royal treasury. You
showed me a man with a soft sword who would pay homage to
a French king instead of recognizing him as an enemy and
driving him from the land with force, as your father did before
you, and his father before him. Softsword . . . is that not
what your loyal subjects call you now?"

"*Traitor* . . . is that not what your subjects would call
you for making your bed under Philip's roof?"

"There is a difference, *Uncle*, between cultivating an ally
to pacify him, and constantly testing an enemy to invite him to
destroy you."

The king swayed slightly under a rush of hot anger. He
bunched his fist and swung out sharply, catching Arthur's
cheek and tearing the flesh on the edge of one of his gold rings.
The duke staggered back a step, but did not fall. He straightened immediately, his eyes burning brightly, his jaw clenched
so stiffly the blood oozed from the fresh cut and ran in a jagged
streak down his neck.

"Six months ago, when I threatened to have you blinded, I should not have allowed myself to be swayed by compassion. I should have had the irons heated then and there and your eyes seared from the sockets, ridding me once and for all of your insolence. You begged me then, boy. You begged me in the name of pity to withhold the irons."

"You will not enjoy the pleasure again, Uncle," Arthur said through the grate of his teeth. "Take my eyes. Take my hands and my limbs. Take anything you wish piece by piece and see how quickly the tide of condemnation would turn. Kill me, aye, and you remove an enemy from power. Torture me, blind me, cripple me, and every knight in the realm would see you for the yellow cur you are."

"You plead an increasingly good argument for death, boy."

"By killing me, you announce to the world that you were afraid of a sixteen-year-old stripling. If my death would make such a coward out of you, then I welcome it."

John's hands were trembling with the fury that coursed through him. He turned and paced the length and width of the small chamber, his rage pounding in his temples, his vision blurring under sharp jolts of pain.

If he had hoped the deprivations of the past few months would humble his nephew, he had been mistaken. If anything, the boy had found new strength in his spine where there had been sinews lacking. Even worse, all of Brittany, Touraine, Poitou, and Normandy were demanding clemency for the brave, but misguided young princeling. Philip was using Arthur's continued imprisonment as an excuse to push his army deeper into English territory. The barons were outraged at their king's inability to drive Philip back into France, yet not so enraged that they would send another man or spare another denier to fight the French plague. John's ancestors were Norman and had conquered the English Isles, yet here he stood, on the verge of losing all of the Norman domains to a poxy French king who had been a mere vassal himself a decade ago.

Arthur. Arthur was the root of all his troubles. Arthur had tested the loyalty of the English barons, and had incited rebels into calling for a civil war, not once, but *twice!* If he was allowed to go free, the arrogant young upstart would only join forces with Philip and unite the armies of France with those of Brittany, crushing Normandy between them. Even if he kept the boy in prison the rest of his life, there would always be the threat of some malcontent breaking him free and stirring up trouble all over again. Blinding him had been an inspired notion. Whether his claim was viewed as legitimate or not, the people would never rally behind a blind king. Unfortunately, however, the moment of inspiration had passed and maiming the fool now would earn only the disgust of his nobles.

What he needed was for the boy to humble himself in front of a vast audience of witnesses. He needed the *boy* to earn the scorn and derision of his peers, to subject himself to such public humiliation that no sane man in the kingdom would look to him again as a leader or a king.

Straightening himself, forcing his anger back under control, John walked to the cell door and yanked it open. He nodded once, brusquely, to someone waiting outside and a soft bloom of yellow light came forward, the splutter of a torch preceding the low whisper of velvet skirts dragging over the rough floor.

Arthur closed his eyes. He knew who it was without looking. He knew simply by the glow that radiated long after the torch was withdrawn, by the scent of sunlight and rosewater that not even the effect of grinding his thumb could overpower.

"Arthur? Dear God . . . Arthur . . . ?"

The warmth of pure sunlight came closer and Arthur averted his face. It was a cruelty beyond belief to bring such beauty into such squalor. It was the cruelest offense of all that she should have to see him like this.

"Arthur . . ." Cool, gentle fingers brushed his jaw and forced him to turn back, forced him to face a torment almost greater than he could bear. He braced himself and looked down into clear blue eyes that were a mirror reflection of his own. The face itself bore a startling resemblance, with the same fine, straight nose, the same noble cheekbones and generously shaped mouth. In his sister, however, the fair complexion only added to her ethereal beauty; the spun gold hair became a cascade of luminous, rippling silk.

Eleanor was eighteen months older than Arthur, but equally as foolhardy, for she had insisted upon riding by her brother's side when he had marched through Brittany. She had also insisted upon remaining with him even though she had known surrender and captivity would be her only reward for loyalty.

"Dearest brother," she whispered and rose on tiptoes, pressing the clean, smooth surface of her cheek against his.

"Do you not mean ridiculous, foolish, asinine brother?" John said, pacing in front of the door. "Tell him. Tell him, by God, and we can end this matter once and for all."

Eleanor retreated haltingly, sinking back onto the soles of her feet, leaving only her hand cradled to her brother's cheek. The threat of tears was in her eyes as she noted the open sores on his skin—rat bites that had gone untreated and were festering. He was thin. So very thin. His eyes were sunken deep into their sockets, smeared with dark purple circles beneath. His hair hung in lank, greasy strings and his clothes were in tatters, crusted in filth, stained with blood and vomit. Whether by jest or torment, those clothes still included the azure blue tunic he had worn so proudly and defiantly at Mirebeau. The device of lion, griffon, and unicorn was boldly emblazoned on his chest, though all three creatures were sadly tarnished.

She turned and confronted her uncle with a fierce loathing. "Can you not see he is fevering and ill?"

John shrugged and arched a black eyebrow. "He knows what he must do. Both of you know what he must do."

"What is it he wants you to tell me?" Arthur asked on a weary sigh, for he had heard all of the bribes and promises before. The lies, the treachery . . .

The most beautiful face in all the world lifted to his, becoming even more breathtakingly exquisite as her shoulders drew back in proud defiance. "I am come to tell you you are the rightful king of England," she declared. "I am come to tell you I have refused to bow to his puny, cowardly threats and that I will continue to stand by you no matter what befalls."

   "No!" John screamed. "No! No! No! I offered exile! The two of you together! As far away as I can send you, but alive. Alive, you fools!"

   Arthur's eyes had not left Eleanor's. "You did not believe him?"

   "Did you think I would?"

   He raised hands that were shaking and bloody and laced his fingers with hers. "If I thought . . . if I truly believed I could do something to save you . . ."

   Eleanor smiled then, a loving, tender smile that he took to his heart and hoarded like a priceless jewel. "I would not love you half so much if you bowed to him now. And not at all if you bowed because of me."

   She heard her uncle's savage curse and she flung herself forward, clinging to her brother through one last, fierce hug before the guard rushed into the cell and dragged her away.

   "Believe nothing he tells you," she cried. "Believe only that I love you, that the people of Brittany love you, and that one day they will seize this serpent by the throat and grind him under their heels. On that day they will make you king. King Arthur! Long live the king!"

   "Bitch!" John screamed, pushing her out the door. He kicked the thick oak panel after he slammed it shut and when he spun back around, his fists were clenched and his face mottled with rage.

   "Will you or will you not openly pledge me homage, relinquishing once and for all any claim to the throne of England?"

   Arthur continued to stare straight ahead. He could see his uncle's shadow on the wall; John was standing beside the table, his shoulders hunched, his fists moving in spastic little punches against his thighs. The young duke bit his lip to keep his courage aloft and said slowly, evenly, "Neither chains nor prison towers nor the threat of an executioner's axe shall make me coward enough to deny the right I hold from my father and my God. This I would declare before all who would listen."

   John let the air hiss out from between his teeth. His vision danced with painful spheres of bursting light and his fist curled around the iron candlestick.

"And that is your last word?"

"With my last breath, if need be."

Arthur heard his uncle curse and experienced an explosion of pain at the base of his skull. He stumbled forward with the blow, his hands flying out in front to save him from a hard crash against the stone wall. But they also braced him upright for the next blow . . . and the next. Hot splashes of wax sprayed his hands and arms, and splashes of something else—warm and wet and red—began to spatter the rough surface of the wall. The agony in his head sent him staggering onto his knees, but the driving, thudding blows followed him down, slamming again and again into his neck and skull.

Out in the low-ceilinged corridor, the captain of the prison guard, William de Braose, heard what he thought was the wail of a wounded animal. He reached for the latch of the cell door, but on a farther thought, hesitated. He was a large, square-jawed bull of a man but he knew the king's rages all too well. To interrupt without being summoned could put him in his own shackles in his own cell with his back flayed to bloody ribbands.

So instead, he pressed his ear to the door and tried to identify the rhythmic, muted thuds. He tried for two, three minutes, his brow beading with sweat and his hands clammy with indecision. He glanced both ways down the corridor, but the other guards were long gone, dragging the weeping princess between them.

Suppose the prince had overpowered his uncle and was beating him to death? Suppose the wailing sound was the king trying to call for help? Suppose—?

De Braose lifted his ear away from the oak. The thudding had abruptly stopped, as had the eerie wailing sound. He glanced down and noticed there was no longer a sliver of light showing beneath the door . . . someone had doused the candle and thrown the cell into darkness.

De Braose drew his sword and reached for a torch smoking blackly in a nearby cresset. He adjusted his helm forward so that the steel rim was level with the slits of his eyes, and, with a caution born of many years spent as a mercenary and assassin-for-hire, he twisted the door latch and used his boot to kick the panel wide.

It was black as pitch inside the cell and at first he did not see anyone. A faint shuffling, snuffling sound was coming from the far corner and De Braose angled the torch higher to thrust the spill of harsh orange light over the disturbance.

The king was lying there, his limbs rigid and twitching like the wooden legs on a marionette. His eyes were rolled back in their sockets, his mouth was wide and flecked with foam. There was blood on his hands, blood soaking the sleeves and front of his tunic, blood splashed in his hair and in the forks of his beard, and sprayed down the legs of his hose. An iron candlestick lay beside one clawed hand, the candle knocked off the spike, the carved base clotted with gore.

De Braose edged farther into the room, the point of his sword beginning to tremble as he saw the second, crumpled body in the corner. There were dark, glistening stains on the walls and floor, and not much more than a shapeless lump of bloodied mush and shattered bone where the proud, golden head of the Duke of Brittany should have been.

De Braose, a hardened veteran of many battles and many battlefield slaughters, gagged over the sour taste of old ale that rose in his gorge. He sheathed his sword and choked back his disgust as he knelt beside the king and tried to determine, through the convulsive thrashings, if any of the blood was of royal leakage.

He had heard rumours of the king's apoplectic fits, but he had thought they were just that: rumours. He had no notion of what to do or how to help his sovereign beyond some vague recollection of ensuring the tongue was not bitten off and swallowed. As far as he could tell, there were no other physical injuries, but the stench of blood and vomit and urine was nearly overpowering.

He sat back on his heels and stared at the king, then glanced over at the lifeless body in the corner. He should fetch help . . . not for the duke, but perhaps for the king, who might need some physic or potion to calm the spasms. At the very least, he thought with narrowed eyes, he should have another witness present, for had the king not just murdered his own nephew? Bludgeoned him to death with an iron candlestick?

Maude. His wife Maude would know what best to do. She could ooze sympathy and oaths of discretion in such a way that even a king who suspected treachery and malice behind every shadow would have no cause to doubt their loyalty.

Racing along the corridor, the torch guttering and the black smoke trailing in a stinking streamer behind him, De Braose smiled and wondered just how grateful a king could be.

Pembroke Castle, Wales

Chapter 1

Lady Ariel de Clare bit down on the fleshy pad of her lip and separated the tightly woven lattice of branches as carefully as she dared. Her heart was pounding in her throat, her skin was cool and wet—not entirely the result of the too-hasty departure she had made from the bathing pond.

The glade was almost a mile from the castle, deep in the heart of a belt of gaming forest where the echo of a scream would not carry very far. She knew she had disobeyed standing orders by coming to the pond alone, but it was not the first time she had done so, nor, if her past history of obeying orders was anything to judge by, would it be the last.

The water in this particular pool was clear and sweet, held in a basin of sun-baked rock that kept it warm enough for wading even this late in October. She had never been interrupted by human company before. Deer, hare, even the odd waddling grouse had succumbed to their curiosity and crept to the edge of the surrounding thicket to accept the offerings of fennel and basil she left for them. For the most part, however, she had always been left alone in the verdant mists and dappling sunshine.

There had never been any reason to fear the isolation of the woods. The rolling fields and forests, as far as any man could see from the highest peak of the highest hill belonged to her uncle, the Earl Marshal, William of Pembroke. There had not been a poacher caught anywhere near Milford Haven over the past several years. Even the outlawed Welsh raiders, who often foraged south to harry the Marcher lords and protest the English presence on their land, stayed well clear of any estates brandishing the Pembroke lions.

Strangers in the vicinity would explain why Ariel had not been visited by any of her four-legged friends. Particularly missed had been the spindly legged fawn who had begun to come shyly up to where she sat to take the sprigs of tender herbs right from her hand. Both the fawn and his mother must

have smelled the intruders long before Ariel had heard the
heavy tramping of horses hooves scything through the thick
carpet of fallen autumn leaves.

She had fled the pool at once, her body glistening in the
sunlight, her hair a half-soaked tangle of long, gleaming skeins
that hampered her every move as she gathered her clothing
and quickly shielded her nudity. Without the benefit of a brisk
toweling, her linen bluet had stuck to her wet flesh, bunching
uncomfortably under her arms and down her legs, testing her
patience as she tugged and pulled at the folds of her woolen
overtunic. Having no time to waste on stockings, shoes, or
headdress, she had snatched up all three and carried them to
where her palfrey stood, head raised, ears pricked forward and
twitching nervously as she followed the sounds.

"Rest easy, my Beauty," Ariel whispered, pressing her
hand, then her lips to the elongated, velvety snout. "I have
heard them too. Three, perhaps four of them, would you say?
And carrying much armour for all the clanking and squeaking
they make."

She glanced back over her shoulder, the motion causing a
ripple to travel the full length of her hair. Out of its braids and
pins, it fell almost to her knees, and while the crown was
darkened to a rich auburn by the dampness it held, the ends
had begun to dry and spread into a shining cloud of frothing,
bright red curls.

Eyes as pure and undiluted a green as the forest pond
searched the banks of pine and oak, seeking the darkest, deepest cover. She gathered up the reins of the palfrey and urged
the horse into the thicker shadows, knowing there was a cavern
of rock a small distance away that would afford protection from
sight and sound. Beauty was fleet of foot and could outrace the
wind if it was asked of her, but she was also gentle-natured and
appallingly terrified of the tremendously muscled destriers
most knights rode. That these interlopers were knights, there
could be no mistake. The sound of much grating metal made
for distinctive and accurate identification over and above the
fact they were boldly mounted and not creeping through the
woods on foot.

Offering several more strokes and whispers for assurance, Ariel hobbled her mare, and, as an added precaution, withdrew the shortsword that hung in a sheath on her saddle.

"As still as still can be, my Beauty," she cautioned, then slipped back the way she had come, her head bent low and her tunic lifted high to avoid having it snagged on an errant branch.

The soil was rich and crumbly under her bare feet, cool beneath each stealthy step. She crept warily back to the verge of the glade and remained crouched behind a thicket, her gaze widening at the sight of the four mounted knights who emerged from the hazed mist of the forest and rode singly into the clearing. Unaware of any eyes watching them, they fanned out to sit abreast along the shore of the pond while their coursers lowered their heads and thrust their muzzles beneath the smooth surface of the water to drink.

The four men wore full suits of armour; hauberks of iron-link mail over thickly quilted leather gambesons. They were sworded and carried their shields slung over their backs, but only two wore gypons emblazoned with coats-of-arms. The other two were bareheaded, their mail basinets lying in loose folds around their necks, their helms hanging from hooks on their saddles. Both had full beards as black as the shaggy manes of hair that curled forward over their cheeks and foreheads; both bore the rugged, insolent look of the Welsh warlords who inhabited the wild, mountainous regions to the north.

Two Normans, two Welshmen. All four hard, seasoned veterans of the battlefield. They wore their armour like second skins, grown accustomed over the years to the hundredweight of added bulk and burden. Arms, shoulders, chests, and thighs were powerfully muscled and solid as rock. Even the steeds they rode were all steely muscle and lethal power, beasts from hell reared to respond with a unique savageness and skill to the scent of blood.

Ariel crouched lower in the bushes and hoped the slight motion of the branches lacing back together would not be detected. A woman caught out in the open, unescorted, unprotected, was fair game to any or all who might need a lusty appetite assuaged. A *beautiful* woman come upon in the sylvan isolation of a sun-drenched glade would stand little chance of escaping untouched—or of escaping at all if a like-minded knight took it into his head to throw her over his saddle and keep her for amusement.

She stared down at the sharp glint of the shortsword she gripped and acknowledged it to be a paltry defense against armoured knights with double-edged broadswords. She would have speed on her side if they dismounted, for a man burdened by layers of bullhide and chain mail moved like a lumbering ox. On horseback, however, a knight reigned supreme. In battle he could easily down ten, twelve, even a score of foot soldiers. In the forest or on an open plain, a mounted knight could run aground and prance merry circles around any man, beast . . . or woman.

Ariel tilted her face up to the clear patch of blue that showed through the gap in the otherwise unbroken latticework of soaring treetops. She had left the castle around noon and ridden without haste to the glade, stopping here and there to gather the last of the wild currants she had seen growing along the way. Bathing had taken another leisurely hour at least, for she had enjoyed the delicious privacy of floating naked in the sparkling sunlight.

"What hour do ye make it?" a gruff voice asked, startling Ariel's attention back to the edge of the pond.

One of the English knights reached up and unbuckled the leather strap under his chin, easing the conical steel helm off his head with a sigh.

"What hour?" he asked. He pushed back the mail hood and snug woolen cap he wore, revealing a damp tousle of dark reddish-blond hair, flattened and glued to his scalp from the heat and sweat. "The eleventh, I fear, with the minutes passing faster than a man could care to guess."

The Welshmen exchanged a wry glance. They bore identical pairs of ebony eyes in faces so alike, despite the bearding, there could be no doubt they were brothers. The grin on one mouth turned into a slight scowl when he saw the blond knight making preparations to dismount.

"Surely we must be close to the castle," he said. "I have been smelling the sea since we entered this part of the forest."

"Aye well, as close as we may be," the Norman retorted, "we are not close enough. Any further delay and you will smell naught but the foul mess in my chausses."

The men laughed good-naturedly and Ariel rolled her eyes skyward.

"The next time, Lord Henry," the burliest of the group advised, "mayhap ye'll not be so quick to sample a cotter's pies."

"There was nothing amiss with the pie." The unmounted knight, distracted momentarily in a search for a suitable place to squat, removed his leather gloves and set them on the decaying stump of a tree. "It was the effort of trying to swallow the king's intentions along with the pork lard that has soured my gut."

"Likewise has it caused you to drag your steps slower and slower with each league that passes?"

"If I do drag my steps, it is because I know the reaction our news will bring. I know it and I dread it and . . . *merde!*" —he groaned with relief, not a moment too soon after loosening his chausses and angling his bared rump over the log— "and I would sooner face a hoard of Infidels alone and unarmed."

"Come now, my lord," chuckled the older of the two brothers. He scratched intently in his beard, then, as an afterthought, stuck the tip of his little finger in his ear and dug ferociously after an itch. "It cannot be as bad as all that. I for one, would risk those same Infidels just to have a roof over my head and bedding that does not rustle and stir beneath me the blessed night long."

"And a wench," the heavyset knight grunted wistfully. "I would settle for a wench with stout thighs and a hearty need to clamp them around me. Nor would I care if she had fleas or not," he added sincerely.

The Welshman arched his brow, bemused by the Norman's criteria. "Just so long as she does not bleat and kick too often with her hooves? Indeed, you have mellowed over the weeks, Sedrick."

The swarthy Sedrick bristled and curled his lips back over his teeth. "At least I know what to do with a wench when I do find one beneath me. And when they bleat, they do not bleat with laughter."

"More likely with pain," the younger brother chided. "You crushed the last three whores you straddled, did you not?"

Sedrick grinned slowly. "In truth, it was the last five; the fourth and fifth being yer mother and sister."

The brothers stiffened and sent their hands to the hilts of their swords.

"For the love of Christ," Henry muttered from his perch on the log. "Can the three of you not pass a single hour without drawing insults? Lord Rhys . . . ? Lord Dafydd . . . ? My belly aches enough without having to constantly run a course with your Welsh humour."

"Neither Dafydd nor myself is smiling," the older of the pair answered blithely. "In fact, the very notion of either our mother or our sister showing such poor taste as to choose this barrel-brained Norman for a bedmate causes even the hint of mirth to vacate our heads."

"Mmmm. Perhaps not Gwladus," Dafydd objected mildly. He leaned forward to see past his brother's armoured chest and cast a slow, critical eye along Sedrick's form. "She has been known to admire any manner of long, thick objects when her husband is absent from home. Mother, however—" He leaned back with a creak of saddle leather. "Aye. I suppose I might be prompted to slit a throat or two in her defense."

The squatting knight started to respond, but a swift, cool slash of steel came out of the bushes beside him, the deadly edge of the falchion pressing a painful threat into the stretched underside of his chin.

"The only throat that will be slit here today, my lords," Ariel announced, "is the one resting over the edge of my blade."

Gold-flecked hazel eyes darted upward and widened when they saw who wielded the sword that teased his throat. The unfortunate knight opened his mouth to speak, but the blade nudged higher, forcing him to crane his neck to the limit to avoid having skin and sinews severed.

The other three men had whirled around at the sound of Ariel's voice, their weapons half out of their sheaths before her shout stopped them.

"I would not want to be the cause of so brave and illustrious a knight losing his head in such an ignoble position," she warned.

The Welshmen kept their fists curled around their hilts, but they made no further move to draw. Their faces hardened into angry masks; all traces of humour—mocking or real—vanished. Only the bearlike Sedrick remained stolidly impassive, although a close observer might have seen the grimace of disgust he directed at his blond, compromised companion.

"You seem to have us at a disadvantage, my lady," said the one called Rhys. His anger waned somewhat as he took a long and insolently frank perusal of the slender wood nymph's body. With her long red hair flaming around her shoulders and her tunic still clinging damply to shapely breasts and thighs, she made an intriguing impression on eyes unaccustomed to such delicacy—delicacy with the added pique of a sword in her hand. "Might I inquire as to how we might serve you?"

Ariel was not listening. Her gaze had fallen to the limp, flaccid body of the fawn draped carelessly over the back of Lord Rhys's saddle. She recognized the small white diamond on the snout and knew it was *her* fawn, the timid, trusting creature who had begun to answer to her whistle, and for whom she had brought the fragrant sprigs of dried parsley today. A large wound in the pale brown neck was proof of the skill with which the knight wielded the enormous longbow he wore slung across his shoulder.

The surge of cold rage that shivered down her arm caused the edge of the falchion to slice into the taut surface of her captive's neck. A curse brought his hand shooting up at once and he knocked the blade aside. His fingers grasped Ariel's

wrist and he wrenched her forward with enough force to fling
her onto her back in a crush of ferns, and moss, and thrashing
white limbs.

The Welsh brothers laughed and wheeled their big warhorses around. Sedrick scratched at his chin and shook his
head, but did nothing more than lean an arm over the front of
his saddle and observe.

The hotly flushed Norman jumped to his feet and fum-
bled to refasten his chausses. He dabbed at the cut on his
neck, cursing anew as he saw the streaky threads of blood on
his fingertips.

"By all the heavenly martyrs—! What manner of game is
this? And what the devil are you doing here"—he glanced
around as if searching the fringe of woods for more unexpected
surprises—"*alone!*"

"What matter does it make?" Lord Rhys asked with a
slow smile. "She is not alone now."

Ariel saw where his black eyes were roving and scrambled
to cover her bared limbs. She stood and brushed furiously at
the clods of earth that clung to her tunic, and when she finished, she planted her hands on her waist and ignored the
leering Welshman in favour of the knight who still tugged and
yanked at his clothing.

"A more worthy question might be: Where the devil have
you come from and why are you strayed so far off the main
road?"

The knight glared at her. "We thought to avoid any travellers who might announce our arrival in Pembroke."

"Why? What manner of heinous crimes have you committed that cause you to skulk from one shadow to the next like
. . . like . . ." She glanced at the dead fawn and the man
who had slain it. "Like the lying, thieving, cowardly vermin
who infest the nether regions of Wales?"

The piercing hazel eyes narrowed. "You have a bold
tongue in front of strangers, wench. Happens one day it might
be pulled from your head if you do not take a care."

She gave a derisive snort and bent over to retrieve her
falchion. "I should not give warnings of anything being pulled

from anywhere, my dear Lord Henry. Not if I had just been caught with my jewels hanging over the edge of a tree stump."

The Welshmen showed surprise. "You know each other?"

Lord Sedrick chuckled—a deep, rumbling sound that brought to mind giant boulders rubbing together. "Ma lords . . . ye have the pleasure of making the acquaintance of Lady Ariel de Clare, Lord Henry's fair sister."

"Sister?" Lord Rhys whistled under his breath. "He mentioned he had one, but not that she was as delectable a morsel as what I see before me."

"Take heed not to say such things too loudly to be overheard," Sedrick warned amiably. "The Lady Ariel takes poorly to compliments, regardless of who delivers them."

"Perhaps she will accept a gift then," the Welsh lord announced in bolder tones. "As an offering of peace for having obviously intruded on her solitude."

He reached around and grasped the dead fawn by the slender forelegs, lifting it from the horse's rump and dangling the soft, lifeless body for Ariel to admire. "A single arrow at two hundred paces," he boasted. "It should provide a tender meal for a maiden of such . . . tender abilities."

If the gentle mockery was meant to flatter her prowess with the ambush, it fell well short of the mark. Ariel's gaze grew even colder and harder and she forced herself to turn away from the arrogant Welshman before she gave way to the temptation to slash his grin to bloody ribbons.

She waited for Henry to retrieve his gloves before she trusted herself to speak. "Did I hear you say you brought news from the king?"

He looked up sharply and stared at her for a moment. "I, ah . . . Aye. Aye, I do have news."

"Well?"

"Well . . ." Henry's stomach responded with an audible and prolonged gurgle. "Better it should wait until we reach Pembroke. Is Lady Isabella there, or has she left for Cavenham?"

"She is still here . . . why?" Ariel grabbed Henry's arm

and blanched a shade. "Is it Uncle Will? Have you brought news of Uncle Will? He is not—? He has not been—?"

"The lord marshal is fine," Henry assured her quickly. "At least he was the last time I heard."

Ariel's shoulders rounded briefly with relief, then squared again with a return of impatience. "Then what is it? What has you squirting over logs and travelling in the company of . . . of *outlaws*?"

Henry glanced over his sister's head, but the two Welshmen had either not heard the hissed insult, or, because they were indeed outlaws and deserving of the appellation, decided to ignore it.

"At home, Ariel," he insisted grimly. "It will be best if I tell you at home."

Chapter 2

$\dagger$ The original keep of Pembroke Castle had been built thirty years after the Norman conquest of England, when the death of the great Welsh king Rhys ap Tewdwr had cleared the way for a further invasion into Wales. Initially a single square keep standing on the edge of a promontory of land, successive generations of prudent—and wealthy—lords had added towers and baileys, tall crenellated battlements and barbicans. William of Pembroke's father-in-law, the immensely powerful warlord known as Strongbow, had used this castle stronghold as his base for the successful invasion of Ireland. Upon his death and the subsequent marriage of his daughter and heir Isabella to William, work had begun on the enormous eighty-foot-tall circular tower that commanded not only the view, but the respect of several square miles of land and sea surrounding the inlet of Milford Haven. Within a hard day's ride of Pembroke there were other castles that had been raised to defend and hold this important thumb of Wales— Haverford, Tenby, Lewhaden, Stackpole, Narbeth, Martin. But none were as impressive, as important, or as impregnable as Pembroke.

To the wide-eyed child of four who had first passed beneath its enormous barbican gates, and who had clutched her brother's hand and stared up in awe at the sharpened teeth of the three separate iron portcullises, the castle had appeared as terrifying and overwhelming as the giant, lion-maned knight who ruled there.

Ariel de Clare and her brother Henry had been sent into the marshal's keeping upon the sudden death of Isabella's half-brother and his wife. Barely wed a year and anticipating the arrival of their own first child, neither the gruff Earl of Pembroke nor his dainty wife knew what to make of the two orphaned children who stood in their grimy, tattered clothing before them. Young Henry, at eight years of age, was fiercely protective of his sister, daring to challenge even the marshal at swordpoint when a casual observation was made concerning the unusual, fiery red colour of her hair. Pembroke was quick to recant, albeit with the hint of a smile lurking behind his twinkling blue eyes, and even quicker to recognize Henry's potential as a knight and vassal whose loyalty and bravery could be counted upon to the last drop of blood. As a result, the boy had not been fostered out to another household as had been William's first intent, but became page to the Lady Isabella—a very great and grave honour which he bore with the solemnity of a grown man.

The tiny Lady Ariel, with her big green eyes flashing and her jaw jutting with determination, let it be known with equal vigor that she was just as impatient to begin her own apprenticeship toward knighthood. She too looked forward to the day when she would earn the right to wear the golden spurs and smite mighty dragons in battle.

It came, therefore, as a rude and unaccepted shock when she was forced to wear gowns and girtles instead of the more practical garb of jerkins, tunics, and leggings. When Henry turned thirteen and she nine, instead of applauding proudly at his investiture as the lord marshal's squire, she launched an insurrection in the castle nursery—by then swollen in number with three of the marshal's natural children—that lasted several months and saw five nurses flee in terror for their lives. No amount of whippings or threats had any lasting effect. It took promises from both Henry and the marshal to finally restore a semblance of peace, with the one agreeing grudgingly to share every scrap of knowledge he gained during his instruction and training for knighthood, and the other agreeing to turn a blind eye to her tutoring, a promise she held her uncle to even some years later when he found her in the stable yards, bruised head to toe, but stubbornly learning how to ride and handle one of the huge warhorses.

Lady Isabella was openly horrified by the calluses on her niece's hands and the whiplike leanness of a body that should have been growing round and soft and dainty. She scolded and clucked over torn hose and soiled tunics—patches of which were left clinging to trees and pallisades that had been climbed and conquered in the heat of a mock battle. She complained often to her husband, but Ariel had long since managed to wheedle her way into a special place in his heart and he could never quite stop the smile that lit his face each time he confronted her with one of her mischiefs. Moreover, in dangerous times and in dangerous surroundings, he saw no reason why a woman should not be proficient with a sword and bow, and had, on occasion, supplemented Henry's instructions with a lesson or two of his own.

The countess, recognizing defeat when she saw it, had thrown up her hands in surrender and concentrated her efforts on grooming her own sweetly natured daughters to be the proper chatelaines and hostesses they were expected to be as Pembroke heiresses. Thus, at age eighteen, when most young women were long married or at the very least, betrothed, Ariel was still tilting at quintains with her cousins, scorning any and all advances by prospective suitors.

But because she was the niece of the Earl Marshal of England, and because there were a number of modest estates endowered to her through her mother's will, there was no shortage of two-legged bloodhounds sniffing after her skirts. From the time she came of eligible age at twelve, there was a constant flow of knights, nobles, first sons, second sons passing under those same portcullis gates that had intimidated Ariel as a child. Some erstwhile swains sought only to ally themselves with the House of Pembroke. Some were more intent upon supplementing their holdings in Wales and could not have cared a whit if her teeth were black and her body bloated with suet. Ariel had sent them all riding out again, their ears pinned to their heads and, more often than not, stinging from the vehemence of her rejection.

The countess had despaired; the earl had supported his niece's right to choose whom she would or would not marry, although he admittedly grew impatient at times with her various reasons for refusal. One had crossed eyes and breath that stank of dead rats. Another possessed narrow, greedy eyes. Yet another, she claimed, had pissed himself when she had drawn her dagger and offered to defend him from an attacking dog.

It should not have come as any surprise to hear of this stubbornness finally reaching the king's ears, since many of those first and second sons would have whined straight to court with news of the insolence of a certain flame-haired heiress. It was also well within the royal right to contract unions between one powerful house and another, and to use such contracted marriages as a means of repaying debts the crown could not otherwise raise from its depleted coffers. The fact that there were not already writs of betrothal for each of the earl's five daughters and five sons was solely due to King John's reluctance to rouse the great lion's wrath. William the Marshal, with his vast estates in Pembroke, Striguil, England, Ireland, and Normandy, was actually a far wealthier man than the king—a point which pricked the crown's patience as well as his greed. And as his ambition for more wealth, more power, grew, the king's cunning black eyes turned more and more often to Pembroke.

"Possibly, because the lord marshal is bogged down in Normandy with these futile negotiations for peace with the French, the king feels safe attempting a small display of his authority this side of the Sleeve."

The family was gathered in the great hall. Ariel stood before the hearth, a log blazing brilliantly behind her in the twelve-foot-wide fireplace. Apart from the crackle and snap of burning wood, the hall was a cavern of throbbing silence. The monstrous arched beams overhead might have formed the vaulting of a cathedral; the gloom and chill gave it the atmosphere of a tomb. Not a foot stirred the rushes. No servant or varlet dared to venture near the circle of brighter light; they moved like wraiths in the smoke-hazed shadows, with only their eyes flicking warily toward the yellow glow around the hearthside.

Henry, whose neck still stung from the slash he had earned earlier, was keeping a prudent distance from his sister and watched her guardedly each time her agitated pacings took her too near the display of crossed swords mounted along the walls. The Welsh lords, Rhys and Dafydd, maintained a similarly discreet gap between themselves and the immediate family members, although their faces were lit with ill-disguised amusement and intrigue.

"I do not believe it," Ariel seethed, the rage keeping her voice as taut as a bowstring. "I will have to see the writ with mine own eyes before I will give credence to this *news* you bring to Pembroke."

Lady Isabella twisted her hands and appealed beseechingly to her handsome nephew for guidance. Petite and showing little signs of aging or plumping in spite of the ten children she had given her lord husband over the happy years of their marriage, the countess was at a complete loss to know how to deal with her niece's mounting fury. That an explosion of Ariel's famous temper was imminent, neither she nor Henry doubted. They watched her as they would watch a pane of glass pressed to the verge of shattering, wary of uttering the breath or word that would bring the deed about.

"De Braose is a fine, respected name," Isabella offered lamely. "Why, they once held lands in Brednock, Builth . . . even Limerick. The elder Simon de Braose rode with my own dear father when he fought the Celts."

Ariel turned nothing but her head. "Indeed? Was this the same Simon de Braose who fell drunk out of his saddle and was trampled to death under the wheels of a passing dung cart? The same De Braose who squandered every single hectare of land they ever owned in Wales and England? The same De Braoses who were reduced to hiring themselves out like common Brabançons just to retain the right to keep the family coat of arms on their blazons?"

"Families . . . fall into hard times," Isabella said haltingly. "And the current lord has . . . has performed valued services to the king in his desire to restore his family's former prominence."

Ariel's eyes narrowed. "Well. He will not be restoring it at my expense. I have seen this poxy son of his. At a distance, mind, for the stench he gave off would have offended a swineherd. The very *sight* of him would have offended the swine themselves, so pocked and bloated and festered with pustules was he. He could not walk without his finger up his nose and what he found there made for most enjoyable nibblings between meals. His eyes do not look in the same direction, but go every which way as if someone is standing constantly behind him hitting him with a pan. Marry him? *Marry* Reginald de Braose?" She snorted a fair imitation of a warhorse and whirled back around to face the fire. "I would sooner marry myself to the Church . . . or to the grave."

Lady Isabella fluttered a dainty white hand to her throat and looked hopefully toward Henry. "Perhaps . . . perhaps there has been some dreadful error in understanding the communication."

Henry had been eased of his armour but had not yet been allowed the time to bathe and refresh himself from his travels. His hair stood up in tarnished spikes, glinting gold in the firelight as he sighed wearily and shook his head.

"There is no mistake. As I told you, we were delayed at Llandaff by heavy rains, and, as it happened, the king's courier had sought refuge there as well. He readily accepted our offer to share a tankard of ale by the fire, and when we asked if he had any news from Normandy, his tongue began to flap like a codfish thrown aground. Soothly, since he was ignorant of our identity—we four addressing ourselves only as Lord Sedrick or Lord Rhys or Lord Whatnot—he thought it might prickle our humour and tip our flagon more generously to hear how the king had recently taken it upon himself to contract the hand of Pembroke's niece. A few tankards more bought us the name of the happy groom."

"Happy?" Ariel grumbled. "He will be happy with the business end of a pike thrust up his arse."

Lady Isabella's hand fluttered again. "Surely there might be *some* room for error. There are fully a score of De Braoses in the king's service. Possibly more than one named Reginald, for they do tend to marry amongst themselves and name sons after fathers and brothers after uncles."

"Inbreeding and incest." Ariel spat contemptuously. "An easy guess by the squinty look of them."

"This particular Reginald is certes the son of William de Braose," Henry continued, ignoring his sister's japing. "Who, until as recently as five months ago, presided as captain of the guard over the king's citadel in Rouen."

"A prison guard!" Ariel exclaimed. "How charming. The king has pledged me to the son of a common gaoler!"

"Not just any gaoler," said Lord Rhys, venturing into the circle of firelight for the first time. Indeed, he showed a certain reckless courage by drawing close enough to Ariel that a stretch of his long arm could have touched her. "Forgive my intrusion, my lady, but I too am familiar with this particular brood of De Braoses. Some of the lands they lost to incompetence and poor defense border our own."

Ariel caught a strong drift of leather and lingering woodscent as Lord Rhys leaned casually close to the fire. Despite the immeasurable fury fomenting within her over the king's proposed attempt to intervene in her life, she could still spare a portion for the unctuous Welsh princeling.

She had recognized their names when she had heard them in the forest. The lords Rhys and Dafydd had a third brother, older by some years, who had entered into a pact with King John, granting him recognition as Prince of Gwynedd and giving him power and title over the region of Wales known as Snowdonia. In exchange for this recognition, Llywellyn ap Iorwerth had halted his raids on the border Marches and had pledged fealty to the English king, a reprieve of hostilities which allowed Llywellyn to turn his full attention on the growing power of a distant kinsman, Gwynwynwyn of Powys.

All titles and holdings were tenuous at the best of times in the wild, mountainous reaches of Wales. Dozens of self-proclaimed princes ruled dozens of self-proclaimed kingdoms, the possession of which changed constantly from one bloody uprising to the next. To contain and control the savagery of these barbaric clans, the English had erected a line of fortified castles along the border, in territory known as the Marches. The barons who ruled these Marches were often as cruel, bloody-minded, and ruthless as the men they sought to defend against, and few lived long enough to ensure the natural succession of their lands into future generations.

Ariel's father, Roger de Clare, had once held land along

the Marches—land coveted by the ambitious Iorwerths of
Gwynedd. A raid had cost Roger and his wife their lives, or-
phaning their two children into the wardship of the Earl of
Pembroke. For this, and other deeds of outlawry over the
years, it made anyone associated with the name Iorwerth . . .
including Llywellyn and his brothers Rhys and Dafydd . . .
nothing more than murderers and common thieves in her eyes.

"You say *not just any gaoler* as if there were gaolers of high
blood and gaolers of low blood."

Her voice dripped with icy sarcasm and Lord Rhys smiled.
"More like *prisoners* of high or low blood, I trow. For unless I
am mistaken—a rare occurrence, I assure you—the citadel at
Rouen was where King John held the young Angevin prince,
Arthur of Brittany."

"Guarding a prince of royal blood does not turn one's own
blood any richer a hue," she countered sardonically.

"No. But if you consider a gaoler has access to a prisoner
at any time, day or night, and is perforce the only witness to
any . . . *accident* . . . that may or may not have befallen that
same prisoner . . ." Lord Rhys paused and let his eyes rove
downward to where the firelight was gilding the outline of
firm, round breasts. "Would it not give meaning to the king's
sudden gesture of magnanimity? Surely he could have realized
far greater profits by selling your hand to the highest bidder."

In the pensive hush that followed, Ariel felt herself drawn
into the Welshman's eyes—eyes that were not black, as she
had first supposed, but so deep and dark a brown as to be easily
mistaken. They were dangerous eyes, gleaming with secrets
that did not offer too close a scrutiny. The nose dividing them
was a straight slash of authority that had somehow escaped the
usual damage and breakage of the long years of a misspent
youth. The mouth beneath was full and generous, confident of
its own sensuality and given to frequent smirks of insolence.
His age? Ariel guessed him to be nearing the end of his third
decade, although, if he were to scrape away the lush black
growth of elflock curls on his jaw, he could scrape away as
many as four or five years from that guess . . . or add as many
again by virtue of exposure.

His brother, on the other hand, was not much older than herself—twenty, perhaps—with large, expressive eyes that gave him the look of an earnest-faced puppy. No doubt he had cultivated his beard in an attempt to add substance to otherwise tender features, although to Ariel's mind, it only made him look like a wilder puppy.

"Are you implying, sirrah," she asked slowly, taking careful measure of the closed expression on Lord Rhys's face, "that De Braose was in some way responsible for Prince Arthur's death?"

"His death has not yet been confirmed," Rhys replied, treading with equal care into the lure of the emerald green eyes. "His *disappearance*, however, would seem to match the gaoler's unexpected turn of good fortune at having his lands around Radnor returned to him."

Ariel felt the skin begin to constrict in waves along her spine. He was right. The coincidence was too obvious to dismiss out of hand.

"Oh, the poor, poor prince," Lady Isabella said, sinking weakly onto a chair, "if such was indeed his fate. And it is no secret the king rewards his assassins with great prizes."

"It is even less of a secret," Henry said bluntly, "that our valiant king demands hostages from those he suspects of plotting against him. Hostages in the form of brides and grooms wed into households of his choosing."

"Plot against him?" Isabella whispered. "But my William made him king. When Richard died and the crown could have gone to Geoffrey's son—"

"*Should* have gone to Geoffrey's son," Lord Rhys interjected quietly.

"My lord husband swayed the barons' vote in support of John over Arthur," the countess concluded. "He has no reason to suspect William of treachery."

"The king has a notoriously short memory," Henry said dryly. "And a distinct distrust of men who hold more wealth, command more respect, wield more influence than he does. Lackland would plot to have the lord marshal discredited outright if not for fear of turning the entire barony of England against him in open rebellion."

"The whole world could rise against him in open rebellion," Ariel cried, flinging her arms wide in exasperation, "and it would be too late to save me from this wretched writ he has imposed upon me!"

She paced a quick, hot path to and fro the length of the hearth. Her skirt dragged the surface of the stone floor, collecting and discarding bits of rushes and dust as she walked, brushing Lord Rhys ap Iorwerth's booted foot each time she passed. She had not taken the time nor trouble to braid her hair upon returning to Pembroke Castle and the firelight was playing havoc with the foaming red curls, shooting them with threads of gold and amber and bright russet.

Dark Welsh eyes followed her every movement, speculative eyes that roved with increasing interest over curves and angles, noting a firmness here, a softness there. He was growing rock hard himself, and it was a true test of mettle to look away and try to concentrate on what Henry de Clare was saying.

"We have a little time, at least. We have preceded the messenger by a day or two, for he comes by way of Kidwelly and Carmarthen, where he had other correspondence to deliver."

"Good," Ariel declared, swirling to a halt. "Then we have time aplenty to lay an ambush. The forest road, methinks. It should be an easy enough task to make it look like the work of outlaws."

"Ambush the king's messenger?" Isabella looked up aghast. "Surely you cannot be serious."

"What would you have me do?" Ariel asked. "Greet him at the gates? Plan a fête in his honour and actually *acknowledge* the charter he carries?"

"We can acknowledge it without accepting it," the countess pointed out primly. "And perhaps, if we send him back to the king with our felicitations and gratitude for the concern he is showing in your future welfare, we might win the time needed to send a dispatch to your uncle and apprise him of the situation."

"Think you the king will not have taken measures to guard against just such a ploy? Supposing his writ includes instructions for me to hasten at once to Radnor to take my place beside my groom? Under threat of arms if necessary!"

"Oh, I do not think—"

"Henry—" Ariel interrupted her aunt's protest and cast a narrowed glance at her brother. "Was this harbinger alone or did he travel with an escort?"

"An escort," he conceded grimly, lanced on the other side by Isabella's gaze. "Six or more men-at-arms made their beds in a nearby stable."

"Six men-at-arms," Ariel repeated in disgust. "And there is still doubt he means to carry me away, willing or not?"

"I doubt nothing at all," Henry declared, lifting his arms in supplication.

"And?" she demanded.

"And . . ." He shrugged his big shoulders and offered a crooked grin. "I would gladly, for the sake of your virtue, set upon them in their beds and throttle the lot, if you asked it of me."

Isabella sighed and glared at her nephew. Henry had proved to be an invaluable asset in helping to oversee the vast Pembroke holdings during her husband's prolonged absence in Normandy. He had, in the beginning, resented being left behind, although she could not see where he could complain of having spent these past eleven months sitting lax and inactive. There were constant raids from the north to be dealt with and the guilty parties caught, the stolen properties returned or recompensed; constant peacekeeping missions to mediate between the two rival Welsh warlords, Gwynwynwyn of Powys and Llywellyn of Gwynedd.

Only this past fortnight, one of Llywellyn's vassals had taken it in his head to lift a herd of some one hundred cattle from a demesne bordering Snowdonia. The two black-haired, black-eyed princes had accompanied Henry back from his investigation in order to convey Llywellyn's personal apologies for the affront. Not that the culprit had been caught or the cattle returned. And not that it could not be proven absolutely that Lord Rhys himself had not been responsible for the original raid.

Cows and diplomatic platitudes were the furthest thing from Lady Isabella's thoughts at the moment. She was relieved Henry was home, relieved there was someone with whom she could share the burden of responsibility in dealing with King John's connivings. After all, he *was* Ariel's brother, and he *was* Lord de Clare, with estates and responsibilities of his own. All the same, "throttle the lot" was not the kind of levelheaded advice she was seeking.

"We could always hide you," the countess suggested. "Steal you away in the middle of the night and keep you moving from castle to castle so the king's man could not deliver his wretched charter. How quickly can a missive be sent to my lord husband?" she asked Henry, who considered his answer for a moment before replying.

"At last word, he was still in Rouen. If so, three days . . . four perhaps, if the tides are with us and the roads clear."

"And if he is not in Rouen?" Ariel snapped. "Or if the tides are against us and the roads a quagmire of mud and offal? Or if we cannot keep the king's man riding in circles for the required number of *weeks* it might take to return with advice from my uncle . . . what then? Will you all think kind thoughts of me as I am dragged away toward wedded bliss?"

"We cannot ambush the king's messenger," Isabella insisted calmly. "We are not murderers, nor do we wish to give the king any reason to challenge your uncle's loyalty."

Ariel stamped her foot and whirled to begin pacing again, but scattered only a few footfalls of dust before she found herself standing face to face with the indolent and watchful Lord Rhys ap Iorwerth, Dark Prince of Gwynedd.

As much as she despised who he was and where he came from, there was no denying he was a man who would not stand on convention to get what he wanted. She could believe he had wanted one hundred of Pembroke's prime cattle and had taken them without a care to the consequences. His princely brother had commanded him here to make humble amends for the deed, but it would be done, she suspected, with his tongue firmly thrust into his cheek.

It made her wonder what else he would do if the mood . . . or the incentive . . . suited him.

"How much have you come to offer my aunt in reparation for the cattle your tribesmen stole?" she asked bluntly.

Lord Rhys, standing with a shoulder leaned casually against the stone mantel, examined the splayed fingers of one hand with exaggerated interest.

"I know nothing of any *stolen* cattle, my lady," he mused. "There was some question of a *discrepancy in numbers*, and in a gesture of good will, my brother has sent me to offer—"

"Yes, yes, yes," she said impatiently. "Penitent words and a handful of copper coins, no doubt; neither of which would equal the value of one hearty bovine."

"Ariel!" The countess gasped.

"You have some other suggestion to make?" Lord Rhys asked blithely. "Some other method of repairing any damage this sorry misunderstanding might have caused?"

Isabella started to protest again, but Ariel's habit of voicing a thought the same time it sprang into her mind cut her aunt short.

"My lord," Ariel said, her eyes leaf-green and sparkling with conspiracy as she addressed the tall Welsh prince. "You have seen this messenger and you know what he looks like? What road he is likely to travel?"

Lord Rhys nodded, vastly amused by the wench's audacity. More than that, he was finding it increasingly difficult to concentrate on what she was saying when all he could think about was the way those sweetly shaped lips would feel beneath his. She was a magnificent beauty: high-spirited, hot-tempered, yet as supple and silken as fresh, warm cream. It was no great stretch to envision her naked on a bed of dark furs, or to imagine the heat of her body wrapped fiercely around his. So strong was the picture he formed, so real and so exciting, he felt fine beads of moisture forming across his upper lip.

"Would it not be child's play," she was asking, "for a man of your considerable . . . *talents* . . . to waylay this rogue and carry him north into your own lands, there to hold him as your, ah, guest . . . until such time as a suitable ransom could be squeezed from the king for his safe return? Is that not a common method employed by your kinsmen to prick the royal temperament? Common enough he would not suspect the deliberate selection of one courier over another?"

Lord Rhys returned her stare for a long moment, then slowly, slowly gave way to the smile that had been toying at the edges of his mouth. "Of more appeal is our fondness for stealing away heiresses the king has designated for his lackeys, and to marry them out from under the royal nose without a care for writs or charters."

Ariel's heart skipped a beat, but she stood her ground and submitted to the boldness of his gaze moving speculatively down the length of her body. She could sense movement beside her and knew that Henry was not reacting quite so calmly to the Welshman's impertinence, but she managed to catch his eye and discourage him from displaying any errant gestures of protectiveness. She could handle this brigand herself.

"I do not believe my uncle would take too kindly to that particular solution to the problem. It could, in fact, lead to an unpleasant urge to retaliate."

"The beauty of a deed that has been done is that it cannot be undone."

Ariel's skin began to burn, as if she was standing too close to the fire, but she suspected it was the heat of his eyes searing her, his lust blazing as bright and hot as any flame.

"By the same token, my lord . . . would you not prefer my uncle's gratitude instead of his enmity?"

Rhys waited, curious despite himself, guessing what was about to come from between the vixen's luscious lips, but never in his wildest imaginings believing he would hear it.

The objects of his focus required a liberal moistening before she could dare voice the absurdity herself, but she did it, keeping her face straight and her voice steady all the while.

"An alliance between our two families would not be entirely without advantages."

"An alliance, my lady?"

"Yes. A . . . a matrimonial alliance. Assuming the proper candidate could be found, of course."

"Of course. Would I do?"

Ariel blinked. "You?"

"Assuming I was interested, of course."

"Of course," she murmured. "Well—" Her composure suffered a small stumble and she lowered her lashes in an attempt to appear modestly embarrassed. "Naturally, my uncle would have to sanction any proposed union, but . . . if he could be convinced it was not entirely to my disliking . . ."

Lord Rhys's pulse beat visibly in his temples. He was no fool and knew it was only a ploy to buy time, but by God's teeth, the idea was not without enough appeal to send a shiver of awe down his spine. He had raged at Llywellyn a full week before grudgingly bowing to the command to present himself at Pembroke Castle, there to grovel in mock vassalage while the self-declared Prince of Gwynedd feasted on the roasted spoils of his labour. Returning to the forests of Deheubarth with the lion's niece bound to his loins, willingly or not, would more than make up for the humiliation. He would not only be able to thumb his nose at his lordly brother—who had been trying for years to win the marshal's favour—but quite possibly be in a stronger position to challenge Llywellyn for control of all of Snowdonia.

His dark, gleaming eyes studied the lowered sweep of Ariel's lashes a moment longer, not yet trusting his voice to conceal his excitement. While it was barely conceivable that William the Marshal would sanction a union between the House of Pembroke and the Dark Prince of Gwynedd, it was equally doubtful he would agree to bind his favorite niece to the loins of a common gaoler's son. The proposed union was itself an outright slap in the face for the old warrior—an insult to his integrity and popularity with the people. If he was presented with a viable alternative, however farfetched, but delivered with honour and sincerity—not to mention a promise of

extended peace along the Welsh Marches—by God . . . he
might just take it.

He might just take it!

Rhys's gaze slid past Ariel's shoulder. Lord Henry de
Clare's handsome face was without expression save for the
tension keeping the muscles in his jaw strained and jumping.
It was plain to see he was fighting the urge to grab his sister by
the shoulders and shake her until her teeth rattled. Both Rhys
and Dafydd had acquired a healthy respect for the tawny-
haired Norman as well as for the hulking shadow of Lord
Sedrick of Grantham. The pair had ridden boldly and without
escort into the heart of Gwynedd, and had ridden out again,
their skins intact, their dust cloying the throats of the two
Welsh princelings forced to follow like humblies in their wake.

A debt was owing there too, Rhys determined. A debt that
could be avenged with the greatest pleasure each time the
sister's bared thighs spread beneath him. In the meantime, the
De Clare scion would require careful handling. A hook, perhaps. Something of distinct benefit to himself that might make
him regard the proposed union as being more than a bad jest.

His humour restored at the thought, Lord Rhys smiled
again. "I certainly have no qualms about extending an invitation to the king's man to be our guest for as long as you wish it.
But would it not be easier to simply run the harbinger through
and leave him for the sheriff's men to find at some future
date?"

"*Benedicite,*" Isabella groaned and covered her face with
both hands.

"As my aunt has already made clear," said Henry evenly,
"we are not murderers, nor do we condone murderous acts."

"We merely wish to have the delivery of the king's writ
delayed," Ariel added.

"To what end?" Henry demanded, his patience with his
sister's madness drawing dangerously near an end. "The king
will only send another and another. Suppose our uncle does *not*
see any merit in this"—he wanted to say *crackbrained scheme,*
but checked himself at the last instant—"this *proposed union*
. . . and sees instead that he must obey or run the risk of

defending a charge of treason? How do you explain this waylaid messenger then?"

Ariel squared her shoulders. "The king is at war with
France. He is in jeopardy of losing control over Normandy. In
his absence, his child bride has been swivving every courtier
and bull-hung mountebank who catches her fancy—"

"*Ariel!*" Isabella gasped.

"—while the barons plot and scheme behind his corpulent
buttocks at every opportunity, searching for ways to curb his
powers and limit his authority. Think you he will notice the
delay of a betrothal charter to an obscure province in Wales?"

The younger Welsh lord, Dafydd, gaped at the fiery-
haired damosel in open astonishment. In his experience with
the Norman savages, it was his understanding that women
were generally regarded as being little more than receptacles
for the breeding up of heirs. Unlike Welsh women, who contributed much to the planning and executing of raids and clan
warfare—some even riding into battle alongside their men—
the Englishry were not credited with possessing many abilities
or desires away from the bedchambers and cook fires. The idea
that one would concern herself, nay, understand matters of
politics and warfare was uniquely intriguing and he could see
why his brother's interest (along with other things) had been
roused.

Henry was equally intrigued, but more over the knowledge that his sister was aware of the queen's sexual appetites.
Royal whores aside, it was a preposterous notion to suggest his
uncle would agree to a marriage between Ariel and Lord Rhys
ap Iorwerth. He knew it, Ariel knew it, and, to judge by the
cunning look in the Welshman's dark eyes, Lord Rhys knew it
too. If it was a gambit to buy time, it was a careless and reckless one to make, for it was indeed an altogether too common
practice for these northern outlaws to simply steal a bride of
their choosing—the nobler the better. And if the thought had
not occurred to Rhys before, it was certainly spinning merry
cartwheels through his brain now. An alliance with the House
of Pembroke would double his prestige and power almost
overnight, not to mention increase the wealth and holdings

that would come under his control the moment the marriage was consummated. His present domains were not nearly as extensive as his brother Llywellyn's, but he would add considerably to his territories that stretched from Deheubarth to Cardigan.

A second shock, as icy and hard as a sharp slap in the face caused Henry to turn and stare at Rhys ap Iorwerth. Not surprisingly, the Welshman's eyes were waiting for him.

Cardigan Castle had once belonged to the De Clare family. It was, in fact, the place where Henry had been born and lived the first two years of his life before his father had been forced to abandon the castle and flee east to more protected territories along the Marches. The chance of returning the De Clare name to Cardigan was not something to be lightly dismissed, as loathsome as the method might first appear to be.

Lord Rhys smiled faintly. "Is it possible, my lord, you might also begin to see some benefit to this union?"

Henry released the breath he had been holding, mouthing it around a soundless curse. Was the bastard actually going to suggest he do nothing to discredit Ariel's lunatic proposal . . . encourage it, even, in exchange for Cardigan?

"Henry, please—" Ariel's voice tore her brother's gaze away from Iorwerth's penetrating stare. "Speak to me."

"What would you have me say?"

"Say you will help me. One of Uncle's ships—the *Etoile*— is anchored in the Wogan taking on provisions. She could be ready to sail on the morning tide and we could be in Normandy before week's end."

"*We?*" Henry's brows were startled upward, as were everyone else's.

"You surely would not leave me here, at the mercy of the king's spies, who you know peek from every crack and crevice in the castle walls! What is more, if I were with you and if we were in Normandy, then we truly could claim we knew nothing of any messenger from the king, naught of any betrothal charter, and certes that we were blissfully ignorant of any mishap befalling Lackland's courier."

Isabella made a choking sound and reached for her goblet of wine.

Sedrick stared.

Henry, accustomed over the years to hearing, even to participating in some of his sister's more ludicrous schemes, pursed his lips and made a slow, careful study of each of his blunted, calloused fingertips.

"If," he said at length. "And I say again . . . *if* I were to decide to go to Normandy in pursuit of this . . . this venture into futility . . . how far do you suppose I—or we—would actually get? This is not exactly the time or political climate for a caravan to be traipsing through the provinces."

"I do not recall saying anything about a caravan."

"I beg your pardon?"

"Speed, dearest brother, would be of the essence, would it not? Who would pay heed to a knight and his squire carrying letters to the earl marshal from his beloved wife?"

The countess cradled her brow in one hand and refilled her wine goblet with the other. "I am not hearing this. Jesu, Mary, and Joseph . . . I am *not* hearing this."

Lord Rhys folded his arms across his chest and leaned against the wall. He was truly beginning to enjoy himself. The wench had more nerve and more spirit than a hundred Englishmen thrown together. Disguise herself as a squire? Run halfway across the Continent to find her uncle? Christ, but she was magnificent! Far too magnificent for anyone but himself to possess, by whatever means or method.

"William," Isabella continued, more to herself, but loudly enough for the others to take heed, "would be furious. No. No, he would be more than furious; he would be in a rage. And doubtless, he would blame me for contriving the whole affair."

"Do you not think he would be more furious if we did nothing and allowed the king to proceed with this travesty?" Ariel asked. "Surely he would want to know how Lackland is seeking to manipulate and undermine him. He would want to know, dear Aunt . . . *if only to safeguard his back and ready himself for the next assault.*"

Isabella looked up. "The next assault?"

Ariel took shameless advantage of her aunt's confused state and went down on her knees before her. "Are you forgetting you have children of your own in the nurseries above us? If the king succeeds in shackling me to this gaoler's son, what is to stop him from binding sweet Matilda to a Flemish foot soldier, or Sibilla to a lust-mad fishmonger, or Eva, Joanna, and Isabella to—"

"Stop!" the countess gasped, her hand covering her mouth. "Oh, my poor dears—the king would not do such a thing . . . would he?"

Ariel's response was a dramatic sigh, rife with pity and melancholy.

"Oh." Isabella's huge, swimming eyes looked to Henry for guidance. "What shall we do?"

The word *applaud* came wryly to mind as Henry assessed his sister's performance, but it was Sedrick, quiet until now, who stepped forward and bowed solemnly before the countess.

"Forgive ma boldness, Lady Isabella, but as much as I am loathe to say it, there is some merit in what the Lady Ariel says. Lord William should be told what is happening in his absence. He should be told of the king's connivings and he should be told without delay. I, in ma humblest capacity, would be more than willing to carry the news to Normandy . . . and to carry aught else ma lady deems necessary under the protection of ma sword."

Ariel glanced up from beneath the thick sweep of her lashes, but Sedrick would not meet her eyes. He was the eighth son of a noble who had had very little to begin with, and nothing at all after deeding lands to his other seven sons. Sedrick had, if castle gossips were to be believed, at one time intended taking the cross and shaving his head in the tonsured style of a penitent. His plans went awry when several women in the village near the abbey where he was studying to take his vows gave birth to by-blows who bore a striking resemblance to the swarthy-skinned Celt.

Undaunted and secretly relieved to be off his knees, Sedrick of Grantham had quite happily taken up a cross of a more violent nature. He had answered the Lionheart's call to join the Crusades, and, because of his size and ferocious appetite for battle, had soon joined the ranks of Richard's personal guard.

Serving thus, he had made the acquaintance of William the Marshal—not only met him but managed to save his life by thwarting the aim of an assassin's sword meant for the earl. Sent back to Milford Haven to recuperate from his wounds, he and Henry had struck up a friendship which had remained solid to this day. Despite his years of service to Pembroke, he still felt like a shy, cumbersome creature when he was near the dainty Lady Isabella and seemed always to be balancing on a bed of eggshells in her presence. He had, however, proven his bravery and loyalty to the House of Pembroke too many times to have his opinions or his concerns waived lightly.

"You think we should send word to William?" Isabella asked.

"I think ye cannot take a chance on the king's moods these days."

"You may also count upon me to help in any way I can," said Lord Rhys. "From waylaying a dozen couriers, to conveying my own sincere application for the Lady Ariel's hand in marriage."

"Henry and I will present your offer in the best terms possible," Ariel assured him, barely glancing up.

"I have no doubt you would," Rhys agreed affably, his teeth appearing in a white slash through the parting of his beard. "But since it would be an honour beyond my ken to have the lord marshal even consider me a candidate, I could not do him the disservice of approaching the matter with anything less than personal representation. My brother Dafydd will accompany you to Normandy, with my signed and sealed offer of good faith."

Henry and Ariel both stared at the Welshman.

"Your brother?" they asked in unison.

"Being somewhat more scholarly inclined than myself"—meaning he could read and write, where Rhys could not—"Dafydd is far more capable with pen and ink negotiations than he is with bow and arrow . . . which is not to say he suffers any lack of skill or enthusiasm with either. In fact, it would further ease my mind to know there was another stout sword arm at your disposal."

"It . . . is a generous offer, my lord," Ariel stammered, "but—"

"You object to his company?" Iorwerth asked lightly.

Ariel looked askance at Henry, but for the moment he appeared content to let her stew in the juices of her own concocting. "N-no, of course not, but . . . surely you cannot expect to kidnap the king's man and six of his guards on your own?"

The gleaming slash of teeth broadened. "Surely not," he agreed. "There are a dozen of my men within sight of these castle walls even as we speak. For unlike your brother, my lady, I travel without the Pembroke lions on my shield to guarantee me safe passage through unfriendly lands."

Henry, clearly startled to hear that Iorwerth's men had been following them, exchanged a hard glance with Sedrick. Neither the glance nor the insult to their powers of observation went unnoticed by Lord Rhys.

"And now," he stated evenly, "if there are no further objections, my brother and I have quite a few things to discuss before morning. Lady Pembroke, Lady Ariel . . . my lords . . ."

The two Welshmen offered a formal bow and excused themselves, striding out of the ring of firelight, then out of the room entirely, leaving utter silence in their wake.

Ariel, still on her knees by her aunt's chair, frowned after them, wondering how such an inventively clever plan had flared so completely out of control. She had no intentions of marrying Rhys ap Iorwerth. She'd had no intentions of even putting him forward as a candidate in her uncle's eyes—a conclusion the outlaw had obviously determined and countered with the offer of his brother's "company." His brother's watchful eye, more's the like.

"Well." Lady Isabella waited until her niece, nephew, and husband's liegeman gave her their full attention. "It seems as though this Welsh renegade is familiar with the game of chess.

If I am not mistaken, he has just placed us in check. William," she added curtly, "will not be impressed."

Ariel refused to be daunted. "He will recognize a desperate measure when he sees one."

The countess sighed and rubbed her aching temples. "I suppose, if I were simply to forbid you from leaving Pembroke Castle, you would not heed me."

"Sweet Aunt . . . I do not want to hurt you, or anger you, or ever disobey you," Ariel insisted, "but this is my *life*. My *future*. My very *destiny* being decided. I would sooner perish on the road to Normandy than tolerate one moment of hellish exile in Radnor."

"But the dangers—"

"I will have Henry and Sedrick to watch over me . . . and the Welsh pup, for what he is worth. I have made the crossing before, Aunt. I know the road to Rouen well."

"Aye, and what if the road back leads to Wales?" Isabella asked gently.

"Well—" Ariel bit the soft pulp of her lip and gave the possibility—however remote it might be—a moment of thought before she offered a quick, too-bright smile. "At least the rogue has no pocks and smells reasonably clean."

Lady Isabella sighed and stroked a hand down the shiny red ripple of Ariel's hair. "Nor is he a man to trifle with. You have offered him something of great value which he will not lightly dismiss."

"Offering and actually *giving* are two very different things, Aunt."

"Sometimes a woman has no choice. Sometimes . . . a man can do things that render a woman senseless and without a will of her own."

Ariel sat back and frowned in bemusement. "I should like to meet the man who could render *me* without a will of my own."

"I recall saying much the same thing before I met William," Isabella murmured despairingly. "And all it took was one glance. One moment in his presence . . . and I was lost."

"Well, I have glanced at this rogue and I have been in his

presence, and I can promise you I am still in full possession of my senses." She saw her aunt give rise to another spasm of anxiety and sought to comfort her by adding, "I will also promise, if it will ease your mind to know, that I will accept Uncle Will's judgement in this, whatever it might be."

"And God's," the countess whispered. "That He should not forsake you now."

"Have you forsaken all your senses?" Lord Dafydd asked his brother, well out of earshot of those in the great hall. "Sending me to Normandy? Proposing a marriage between you and Ariel de Clare?"

"Do you doubt you can put an eloquent enough pledge in the marshal's ear?"

"I could put it to the pope himself, for all the good it would do."

Rhys grinned and pulled on his gloves, tamping each finger snug to the joint. "You do not think the old lion will see any benefit to allying himself with Gwynedd? God's blood, man, he will see the proposal with a warrior's eye, if nothing else. Access to Snowdonia gives him access to Ireland as well as half of northern Wales. And did you see the brother's eyes glisten when he thought of Cardigan? I could bed the wench tonight and the brother would cheer us on."

Dafydd reached out a hand and hooked Iorwerth's arm, halting the echo of their heavy bootsteps in the stone corridor.

"You are not thinking of—"

"Lying in wait for the fair demoiselle and ravishing her to seal our pact?" Rhys laughed and started walking again. "In truth, the thought occurred to me. I'm hard enough to ride a brace of maids, top and bottom, and still have leavings for a slut or two. But no. You may rest easy on that count, little brother. Your tender morals are as safe as I will expect you to keep hers on the way to Normandy and back. It is important to make no mistakes, to present our intentions in the best, most honourable light. I want her to come to me willingly and pure. I want no taint of corruption or coersion to shadow this marriage."

"In this quest for purity . . . are you forgetting you already *have* a wife?"

Rhys stopped suddenly enough and angrily enough to send Dafydd's brows arching upward.

"I am not forgetting. How could I forget a spindle-legged, gap-toothed weanling who weeps ceaselessly whenever I am lucky enough—or sodden enough—to succeed in prying her knees apart?"

"Nevertheless—"

"Nevertheless," Rhys interrupted with a scowl, "I have tried a thousand times over the past seven years of our wedded ordeal to plant the seeds of an heir in her womb . . . to no avail. The bitch is barren. It will take no great effort to be rid of her, which is why I am returning to Deheubarth and you are travelling to Normandy. You will seal this alliance with the old lion, promising him anything if need be, so long as you return with his sealed contract before Llywellyn sniffs anything in the wind."

"What about the king's men?"

"What about them?"

"How can you kidnap them, hold them to ransom, then send them back to John *without* Llywellyn catching the scent?"

"It takes a grievous long time for the odour of corpses to rise up through the earth," Rhys said matter-of-factly. "By then, my new bride will be queen of Gwynedd."

He glared his declaration into Dafydd's eyes a moment longer then turned and ducked through an arched doorway, leaving the younger man staring after him, his expression carefully guarded against the disdain he was feeling.

It was typical of Rhys to expect the world to bend to his designs. Typical of him to think the marshal would welcome him eagerly to the House of Pembroke. Typical to think a woman like Ariel de Clare would be as easily crushed under his thumb as the other cows he normally took to his bed.

But if he thought Llywellyn would simply stand by and do nothing while he raised the Pembroke lions over the battlements of Deheubarth . . .

Dafydd almost chuckled to himself. Indeed, it would be

his pleasure to escort Lady Ariel to Normandy and plead his
brother's case to the Marshal of England. It would be equally
pleasurable to bring back an echo of the lion's laughter, or,
should the heavens split open and gold florins fall from the
sky, to bring him back his new bride and stand aside while
Rhys and Llywellyn fought each other over possession of
Gwynedd.

For with any luck at all, they would kill each other and he
would be free of them both.

Château D'Amboise, Touraine

Chapter 3

✝ It was the blade of sunlight that disturbed him. A single bright beam of light had found a narrow chink between the wooden shutters and had crept slowly across the width of the bed, stroking a path of lazy warmth across the faces of the two recuperating occupants.

The first had tiny beads of dampness glistening on her brow and throat. She looked and, indeed, was utterly drained and depleted by the activities of the hour preceding her collapse. The raw potency of the energies she had expended softened the lines of her face and showed in the swollen redness of her lips. The mottled pinkness across her breasts and belly kept her warm and scorned the need for any covering or blanket.

She dozed with her head cradled on a muscular shoulder, her body curved against another of immensely powerful proportions. A soft white arm was flung limply across a chest thickened and plated by years of wielding heavy swords and lances; a pale limb was hooked over a thigh that might have been carved from marble. The hand of her companion was broad and callused, and rested in the tangled, damp nest of her hair; another cupped the plump white flesh of her rump and periodically moved through a stretch or a vague restlessness to pull her softness against him.

The blade of sunlight spilled its liquid gold over the man's strong, square jaw, lighting a mouth that had, until a sennight ago, been issuing battle orders and shouting words of encouragement to fellow knights as they fought a bloody melee with King Philip's army at Blois. The rout had been a complete success, but the knight had been wounded slightly in the crush of steel and armour, and the ragged cut on his arm still glowed an angry red between the barber's row of knotted threads.

It was only a trifling wound and the memory of earning it had probably already been lost amongst the scores of other

scars, some big, some small, that marked the powerful muscu-
lature of his body. One of the cruelest scars he bore disfigured
his left cheek. It was not so hideous as to make a maid faint
outright from the sight, but it was shocking enough to draw
stares and sighs of pity, for without the flaw, he would have
been handsome enough to leave women swooning and gawk-
ing for very different reasons.

It was just as well, though, for he had little time or interest
to spare on women. He liked them well enough and used them
often enough to bolster his reputation for being more than just
a champion in the lists. For the most part, however, he preferred to release his tensions on the battlefield or the practice
yards, leaving the wenching and whoring to those who thrived
on it.

At twenty-six, he was in his prime as a fighting man and to
his credit had amassed a respectable personal fortune on the
tournament circuit, winning prizes of armour and horseflesh
from his defeated opponents, then ransoming them back for
double their original worth. He had never suffered the igno-
miny of a loss himself. He could, in fact, boast of being split
from a saddle by only one man—coincidentally the only man
who could have won a rueful smile as a result of the ungallant
tumbling. That man was his father, Randwulf de la Seyne Sur
Mer, Baron d'Amboise, Scourge of Mirebeau, champion to the
dowager queen, Eleanor of Aquitaine.

The sunlight continued to pour its golden heat across the
thick crescents of chestnut lashes and Eduard FitzRandwulf
d'Amboise was forced to open them. He squinted up into the
brilliant shaft and the smokey gray of his eyes was seared
almost colourless. His annoyance brought a muffled curse to
his lips and he turned, pressing a kiss into the crown of the
woman's head. A yawn and a phantom itch gave him an excuse
to untangle his arms and limbs and start the process of extricating himself from the bed, but the wench knew his tricks and,
in a move so subtle it impressed the breath from his lungs, she
parted her thighs and shifted herself sideways, drawing him
slowly up and into her sleek warmth.

Half asleep, wholly focussed on the swelling spear of turgid flesh within her, she roused herself with sinewy, catlike stretches, waiting until his blooded fullness was as thick and deep as she could coax it before she lifted her head and purred.

"You were not thinking of leaving me just yet were you, my lord?"

The husky, throaty sound of her voice washed over him, and his hands moved of their own accord to fill themselves with the incredibly ripe, round globes of her breasts. "I confess . . . I did not want to trouble you further."

She looked down to where the dark red discs of her nipples had stiffened against his fingers, forming two jutting peaks, hard as berries, tempting as sin.

"When I want you to stop troubling me, my lord, I will tell you plainly enough. Listen—" she whispered, leaning over to nip the lobe of his ear between her teeth, "and tell me what you hear."

Eduard sucked at a breath and his hands grasped hold of her hips as she began to move over him. Diamond-shaped flecks of blue altered the pewter gray of his eyes, the blue becoming darker and deeper with each stroke of sliding heat that engulfed him. The strong, supple limbs gripped his thighs like a vise and as the greedy fist of her womanhood became more and more insistent, his hips began to surge upward, answering the determined tug and pull of her flesh.

Gabrielle was blissfully aware of the mighty tremors building and gathering in the rock-hard flesh beneath her and she braced her hands on his chest, letting each thrust carry her to a new peak of sensation. He was by far her most virile lover, although his visits came so infrequently she wondered how he could survive with all this pressure stored up inside him. She would never dare ask, but she often wondered why he came to her when there were so many other, younger, prettier maids within the castle walls who would have spun rainbows to please the son of La Seyne Sur Mer. There was only one possible reason she could think of, for she did not flatter herself that her lovemaking skills were any more or less astounding, given the prowess of the man who sought them. Rather, she suspected it had something to do with the fact she was barren, and, being a bastard himself, he had no desire to father another into the world.

Whatever the reason, she was only glad to know that when he did feel the need to release himself, he did so with her.

And did it so splendidly.

A groan shivered in Gabrielle's throat and she urged her body through a blurred frenzy of ecstasy, not slowing or stopping until the last drop, the last shudder had been wrung from his flesh. Only then, limp and laughing from sheer exhilaration, she collapsed in a weak, trembling heap in his arms.

Eduard held her that way until his own senses were restored, then chuckled softly as he tilted her face up to his. "Why are you always determined to see me hauled back to the castle in a trundle cart?"

Gabrielle smiled so deeply a dimple appeared in each cheek. "It is always a challenge to see if I can keep you here an hour more."

"An hour more and they will be searching the baileys and bothys for my sapless corpse."

"Nonsense. A man finds his strength in a woman's womb. And you, my lord, have never run short of sap yet."

As she spoke, Gabrielle ran her hand across his chest, combing her fingers through the luxuriant mat of crisp chestnut curls. Her fingers snagged briefly on the gold ring he wore suspended from a leathern thong around his neck, but she passed it by without a thought, continuing to trace lacy patterns down onto the lean, flat plane of his belly, then lower still to the coarse, dark nest of hair at his groin.

They both smiled at the immediate response she won when her hand curled around the thick shaft of his flesh, and, with a sigh, she set her lips and tongue to following the same meandering path her hand had taken downward.

"Will I see you again before you return to Blois?"

"I cannot say for certain," he admitted honestly. "We have been gone from camp a week; too long for a troop of restless knights to remain calmly on their own side of the river."

"Have your father's wounds healed?"

"My father is made of iron, in flesh and in will. His leg began to heal the instant Lady Servanne set her hands to it."

"Mmmm . . . You have been gone from Amboise three months? I warrant it was not the laying on of milady's hands that wrought such miracles."

Eduard closed his eyes and pressed his head back into the rush-filled mattress. He could not argue with Gabrielle's theory; his father and stepmother were as much in love now as they had been when they had married fourteen summers ago. The slightest look or most innocent touch could still send them hurrying behind closed doors—where they had, in truth, spent most of the past seven days and nights.

Eduard himself had managed to resist such fleshly pursuits until today, until the sights and sounds and smells of a lusty autumn day had sent him wandering across the draw and down into the village of Amboise, to the tiny mud and wattle cottage where he knew he would be welcomed without any questions, without any demands of any kind.

Well, hardly any demands.

He drew as much air as his lungs could hold and tried to steady himself, tried to ignore the lapping, wet heat that was determined to show no mercy this day. He heard a muffled laugh and he cursed, knowing he had gone too long without a woman to count on any measure of control now.

The taste of success made Gabrielle's mouth bolder and the shock sent his hands down, sent his fingers curling into the black waves of her hair. Her zeal was genuine, her energy boundless. Gabrielle had been widowed three times in nine years by men who, it was generally agreed, had wasted away from sheer exhaustion—all with deliriously wide grins on their faces. She was four years older than Eduard, looked ten years younger, and made no secret of what she considered to be the fountain of youth.

It was well over an hour later when Eduard ducked beneath the low-slung lintel of the door and stepped out into a cool rush of shaded air. The sun had already dipped below the tops of the trees, casting long, slender shadows across the surface of the nearby river. The village, nestled securely in an elbow of the Loire, was all but completely swallowed by the silhouette of the castle that dominated the high ridge above. When viewed against a hazed, blood-red sunset, Amboise's ramparts, towers, and spires were magnificent and magical; seen emerging from the vaporous morning mists, it was a cold and menacing display of Norman military efficiency.

As Eduard walked up the steep and narrow approach to the enormous barbican towers that guarded the entry to the castle grounds, he grinned at the lingering weakness in his limbs. It was not the first time he had cursed the height of the earthworks surrounding the outer walls, nor the first time he paused at the drawbridge to catch his breath and glance back down at the thatched roof of the widow's cottage. In fairness, he should not have strayed today, not after leaving his men strict orders to work themselves and their horses through their paces. The past seven days and nights of inactivity had left him restless, and while the others had made good use of their wives and whores the first few days of their arrival home, Eduard had raised a sweat with sword and lance, practising from dawn until dusk.

As much as he had missed the peace and serenity of Amboise, lengthy periods of inactivity were a curse he found increasingly difficult to bear, especially when he knew the French were pressing hard to advance into the province of Touraine. In the past month alone, he had led two skirmishes that had driven Philip's army back across the Loire; he had won a resounding victory in a third when French knights had attempted an ill-planned assault on their encampment. Eduard and his father had returned to Amboise a sennight ago, neither in the keenest of spirits to do so, but Lord Randwulf had been sorely wounded in the ambush and it had taken all of his son's considerable powers of persuasion, plus his armed insistence, to convince the mighty Black Wolf of Amboise he would heal faster at home.

Home, Eduard mused, gazing up at the formidable battlements.

Amboise Castle was designed like most Norman strongholds, with the original inner keep being the central structure around which the other buildings and wards had been added and built up over the generations. The main keep rose sixty feet from its widened base, buttressed by earthworks and protected by a draw that had rarely been raised over the past century, but which could, if necessary, seal off all access to the massive stone tower. The surrounding moat no longer held water except in times of heavy rains, and clusters of buildings had sprung up around the earthworks to house the barracks, stables, armoury, psalteries, cook houses, smithy, and weavers cottages—all comprising a small community contained within the inner curtain wall, a block and mortar barrier fifteen feet high, guarded by double-leaf iron doors and flanked by tall, square watchtowers.

This was the heart of Amboise, and to reach the heart, one had to successfully breach a well-defended outer bailey, which contained among other things, the practice fields and tilting grounds, also the pens and stables that housed the livestock.

A second wall enclosed this outer bailey and was the castle's first defense. Built strong enough to withstand attack by catapult, battering ram, or trebuchet, the fortified battlements were forty feet high and eight feet thick, faced with rough-cut limestone blocks mortared around a core of rock rubble. Entrance was gained through the huge iron portcullis gate, which required the combined efforts of ten men on winches to raise and lower. The jagged iron teeth were suspended no higher than the measure of a man on horseback, the spikes held so tautly on their chains as to hum ominously in any breath of wind.

The flanking barbican towers were, in turn, built like small fortresses, the walls thick enough to house passageways for archers, and slotted with chutes for pouring boiling oil and pitch on the heads of would-be attackers. No one passing through the main gates was not well and truly aware of the strength of the garrison patrolling the crenellated battlements, or doubted that the other towers constructed at hundred-foot intervals along the span of the wall were equally prepared to discourage unwelcome visitors. Day and night the walls were

manned by sentries whose armour, swords, and helms reflected
jabbing needles of light to observers from the village below.
Each boldly displayed the black and gold device of Randwulf
de la Seyne Sur Mer, bearing the menacing depiction of a
prowling wolf, the head full-faced and snarling.

The Wolf's pennants had not always flown over Amboise.
The castle and its vast adjoining demesnes had been deeded
to La Seyne Sur Mer as a reward for his many years of faithful
service to Eleanor of Aquitaine. He had taken up residence
fourteen years ago, the same summer he had wed Lady
Servanne de Briscourt; the same summer he had fought a
Dragon and outwitted a future king.

Up until then, the Wolf had been content to roam the
tournament circuits of Europe as the dowager's champion,
known to all who dreaded his appearance in the lists as the
Scourge of Mirebeau. Under the black armour and black silk
mask that had been his trademark was another identity he had
preferred to put behind him for over a decade—that of Lucien
Wardieu, Baron de Gournay, rightful heir to rich estates in
Lincolnshire that had been won by his great-grandfather when
the Normans had first wrested England from the Saxons.

Lucien had had a brother, bastard-born and weaned on
jealousy and malice. As close alike as twins, Etienne had followed Lucien Wardieu on crusade to Palestine where, under
cover of a bloody battle for the Holy City, he had ambushed
the De Gournay heir and left him to die under the hot desert
sun. Returning to England in triumph, Etienne had then assumed the guise of his dead brother, and for the next thirteen
years had ruled Lincolnshire as Lucien Wardieu, Dragon Lord
of Bloodmoor Keep.

Unbeknownst to the Dragon, his brother had not died.
Through a dark mist of treachery and deceit, the Wolf had
survived, had worked to heal his ravaged mind and body, and,
by dint of loyal service to the dowager queen, transformed
himself into Randwulf de la Seyne Sur Mer, one of the most
feared and respected knights in all of Europe.

When Lord Randwulf, on a mission for the queen, had
returned to Bloodmoor Keep to reclaim his name and honour,

he had not known he would also be reclaiming a son, born a few scant months after he had left on crusade. The mother, a woman of incredible beauty and spine-chilling evil, had played mistress to both brothers and used the bastard child to further her own corrupt ambitions. Eduard's early years had been years of cruelty and abuse, loathed by a dam who thrived on giving pain, tormented by a man who saw everything that had been noble and valiant in his dead brother growing to manhood before his hate-filled eyes. It was a wonder Eduard had maintained a grip on his sanity. An even greater wonder he had maintained a grip on his life when the Dragon and the Wolf had clashed in their final bloody confrontation.

The death of Etienne Wardieu had set Eduard free. The Wolf had accepted his son proudly and without reservations, but, realizing it was only a matter of time before the prince regent avenged the death of his pet dragon, Lucien had brought his family home to Touraine. There, because he preferred to be known only as La Seyne Sur Mer, Eduard had also, eagerly, severed all ties with the Wardieu and De Gournay names.

The Wolf and his beautiful bride had done everything in their power to erase the effects of those lost and lonely years, and indeed, Eduard had matured into a powerful man, an undefeated champion in the lists, a master with sword and lance whose courage and fighting skills were a source of bowel-clenching terror to enemies who saw him sally forth onto a battlefield or tournament ground. Moreover, he was content, despite Lady Servanne's best efforts to turn him into a country noble, to continue serving his father to the utmost of his ability, to ride by his side and proudly bear the black and gold standard of La Seyne Sur Mer.

This uncompromising loyalty from the Wolf's son as well as from his vassals and liegemen was one of the main reasons why the long and sinister fingers of King John had never been able to reach this deeply into the Aquitaine. As prince regent, John had allied himself with the Dragon of Bloodmoor Keep, and had been humiliated at the Wolf's hand when forced to expose Etienne Wardieu as a usurper. Barely a month after the

Wolf's return to Touraine, John had declared the De Gournay estates in Lincolnshire forfeit due to unpaid scutage. On the Continent, however, he was forced to tolerate the Wolf's presence at Amboise, both because of the size of Lord Randwulf's private army, and because of his defensive proximity to the French border. Nevertheless, he rarely missed an opportunity to besmirch the Wolf's name or remind his numerous admirers that the Baron d'Amboise had slain his own brother and stolen the dead man's bride.

Another reason for John's reluctance to do more than verbally assault the renowned knight was that La Seyne Sur Mer was still in the queen's favour. It was Eleanor of Aquitaine who kept the Black Wolf leashed when he would have risen in support of Prince Arthur as successor to the Lionheart. Instead, it had been the black and gold pennants of Amboise that Arthur had encountered first upon his foolhardy attempt to lay siege to his grandmother's castle at Mirebeau. It had also been to a black and gold war pavillion that the hapless prince had been taken upon his capture, for despite the Wolf's disdain for King John and his genuine liking for the Duke of Brittany, he was first and foremost loyal to Queen Eleanor.

And so, by blood and sword, was Eduard FitzRandwulf d'Amboise. Though his heart had been with the young prince, he had ridden with his father to relieve the siege on Mirebeau, and, although the English king's power was being eroded in Normandy, Brittany, and the Aquitaine, as long as Eleanor commanded the Wolf's allegiance, the black and gold would continue to defend her borders.

Eduard was anxious to return to that defense. His temper was short and his patience lacking. He had practised with such zeal in the yards the previous day, there had been no unbruised or undaunted men lining up to challenge him this morning. After a few lackluster rounds of archery—again with no wagers placed against him—it was the surplus of raw, unfocussed energy that had sent him prowling through the bailey and down into the village.

And kept him there, he thought with chagrin, far longer than he had intended. The castle could have come under siege and he would not have known it. Pestilence and peril could have descended and he would not have noticed.

What he did notice now, as he crossed the outer bailey and headed toward the arched gates of the inner curtain wall, was a marked lack of activity in the yards. It was not so late that the quintains should have been put away and the knights all retired to their barracks.

"Sweet St. Cyril, rot my teeth!"

Eduard stopped, startled out of his musings.

"Nay, he should take my teeth, my toes, and all my fingers if I could but once lay a hand to the scruff of my lord Cockerel's neck at the first call to do so."

FitzRandwulf squinted upward, tracing the source of the familiar plea for dismemberment. Above, seated between the crenellated teeth of the flying arch, was the diminutive figure of the castle seneschal, Sparrow. Dwarflike in stature, with a round elfin face and a mouth puckered tight with self-importance, Sparrow had found a perch overlooking the main entry to the inner bailey and had settled there with the patience of Job, waiting for his quarry to come into sight. Seated beside him, obviously relieved to have won a reprieve from Sparrow's company, was Robert d'Amboise, firstborn son to the Wolf and Lady Servanne.

"Rest an eye on yon fine specimen of knighthood," Sparrow lectured sardonically. "Take heed, young Robin, of what can befall a man who heaves over to debauchery at the merest wink of a comely eye."

Eduard followed Sparrow's gaze down to where his shirt was rumpled and loosely caught about his waist; to his hose, haphazardly rebound to only half the required leather points and bagging sadly around the knees.

Seeing that the black eyes were dancing at the prospect of creating some mischief, Eduard feigned innocence and kept walking under the flying arch. "You have been looking for me?"

"Looking for you? *Looking for you?*" Sparrow gave an indignant squawk as he leaned too far forward on the wall and nearly lost his balance.

Eduard emerged from the shadow of the archway into the setting sunlight again and, as if by magic, Sparrow was there to greet him, his arms squared on his hips, his stubby legs planted firmly in the path.

"Look you to my heels, Groutnoll, and you will see them worn to the bone from hunting and searching. Your father has torn block from mortar with his bare hands this past hour waiting on your tardy appearance."

Eduard glanced sharply up at the main keep. "An hour? Why the devil did you not fetch me at once?"

Sparrow's eyebrows took a belligerent leap toward his hairline. "Both Robin and I have turned the castle grounds upside, hither, and yon! Why the devil were you not where you were supposed to be? After scouring the first hundred or so trysting nests, these old bones of mine began to aggrieve me."

"I should aggrieve you with the back of a broom," Eduard scowled, starting briskly toward the keep.

"Eduard! There you are!"

FitzRandwulf stopped again, too suddenly for Sparrow, who had taken up the chase with malicious intent. The wood sprite stumbled into the back of the knight's thighs with enough of an impact to send his cap slewing sideways over his ear.

"I see Sparrow found you," said Alaric FitzAthelstan. "Has he told you the news?"

"News?" Eduard frowned and glared down at the seneschal. "What news?"

"The Marshal of England is half a day's ride from Amboise," Alaric announced. "He has begged leave to rest here on his way back from his meetings with the French king."

Eduard was surprised. "I had heard that Lackland had sent him to negotiate terms of peace, but not that the earl marshal would be passing this way on his return to Rouen. For that matter, are we not a considerable distance south and east of where he wants to go?"

"Considerable," Alaric agreed. "And no doubt the news of his imminent arrival has caused a small flurry of excitement for the Wolf and his lady." He paused and gazed thoughtfully up at the keep. "I warrant the entire household will have been turned turvy by now and set to cleaning, scrubbing, airing, and cooking. We would be wise, perhaps, to tarry a while longer before we answer our summons lest we find buckets and brooms thrust into our hands."

"Father sent for you as well?"

Alaric was not only Randwulf de la Seyne Sur Mer's closest friend and ally, but he had been deeded adjoining lands. Tall and lean, deceptively mild-mannered and scholarly in appearance, Alaric was never far from the Wolf's side in any battle, and was, to Eduard's knowledge, the only man he had ever seen best his father with a sword. He had, admittedly, been jealous of their closeness in the beginning, but it was exceeding hard not to like Alaric FitzAthelstan; harder still not to like a man whose logic and levelheadedness could defuse many explosive situations before the skill of his sword arm was put to the test.

"Actually, the more urgent plea came from the Lady Servanne. She knows your father's temper when it comes to any dealings with King John, and I gather she does not trust him to keep from speaking his mind. Not that the Earl of Pembroke is any great believer in John's ability to keep the English banners flying over Normandy, but the earl has the advantage of his age and wisdom, and the respect owed him as advisor to three kings. As for this mission to see Philip . . ." Alaric shook his head in disgust. "It was a useless venture, designed to humiliate the earl and nothing more. Philip wants all of Normandy and both sides know John does not have the resources or the strength to fight for it."

"Do you think he will fight?"

Alaric opened his mouth to respond, but a raucous volley of shouts and jeers drew his frowning attention to a window high on the tower wall. "What in God's name . . . ?"

A flurry of waving arms accompanied the noise, all directed at a red-faced Robert d'Amboise, who was trying without much success to ignore them and to keep as solemn an expression as was warranted for a man newly promoted from page to squire.

Eduard turned and regarded him with an arched brow.

"I . . . I am sorry, my lord," Robert said, fidgeting. "They are still children and think I have nothing more important to do with my time than play at winks and binks with them."

Eduard nodded solemnly. "Have you seen to my armour?"

"Aye, my lord. I had the links repaired and the lot rolled in hot oiled sand until the iron gleamed like silver. I groomed Lucifer and fed him a double rasher of oats, then had your sword sharpened and the hilt of your lance repaired."

"You have been busy."

"Busier than most, I warrant," Sparrow muttered under his breath.

Eduard ignored the comment and dismissed Robert with a tilt of his head. "Go along then. Pull your brothers' noses for me and give each of your sisters a pinch."

"I will, my lord. Thank you, my lord."

The young squire scampered off at a run, shouting a warning that effectively ended the hooting and waving on squeals of mock alarm.

"Well," Sparrow harrumphed, clearly distempered, "I suppose you arrange for a teat for him to suck before he accompanies you onto a battlefield?"

"Robin is a fine squire, and Eduard a tyrant of a taskmaster," Alaric allowed. "No thanks to your own tutelage in their early years, Puck. In fact, one can only hope you do as well with Randwulf's other sons."

Sparrow frowned, torn between a boast to acknowledge the flattery and a desire to expound on the detriments of a weak master. He knew full well how strict Eduard was when it came to training or discipline on the field, but there was still a natural tendency to spare a younger brother the bite of a whip if he showed a lack of proper respect between master and squire—respect that was necessary to learn the ways of a noble young man rising through the ranks of service. While Sparrow loved all the Wolf's children with equal fervor, Robert—little Robin—had been just a tad more special than the others.

Charmed somehow. Destined for some great future his diminutive mentor did not intend to see squandered for want of common sense.

" 'Tis better to be harder on the boy than softer." Sparrow scowled at Alaric, not wanting the comments to pass *completely* unnoted. "Your own young William shows a sad lacking in discipline, mooning about the castle like a lovesick calf, weeping so hard in his pallet at night, we have taken to calling him Will-of-the-Scarlet-Eyes."

"William is only six years old and fostered into Lady Servanne's care less than two months," Eduard said defensively. "I vow you wept and mooned and calved aplenty when you were that age. You still do, for that matter, as well as carp and wheedle and complain and aggravate beyond endurance."

Sparrow spluttered and Alaric laughed, clapping a hand on Eduard's shoulder to steer him toward the main keep. "I can see this past week has been a long one for you."

"And growing longer each hour that passes."

"Aye, well, you should marry and see how much you miss these lengthy solitudes."

Eduard grinned. "No, thank you. I will never be in *that* much pain. How is Lady Gillian, or dare I ask?"

"Oh—" Alaric drew a deep breath and released it in a gust. "Cross at everyone. Complaining her belly is too big and gets in the way of her bowstring. Blaming me, of course."

"Of course. The babe is due this month, is it not?"

"Sooner, I pray, than later."

"Another lout with more brawn than brain," Sparrow griped. "If the men of this shire paid as much heed to sowing their fields as they do their wives, there would be enough crops to feed all of Christendom."

Alaric passed a wry glance over his shoulder. "Whereas, if a certain thimble-sized codpiece were loosened now and then, I have no doubt its owner would have less cause to see only doom and gloom lurking beneath a woman's kirtle. What *was* the name of that pug-nosed little vixen who had her eye on you the last time we were home? Bettina? Lettina?"

"Letticia," Eduard provided helpfully.

"Letticia!" Alaric snapped his fingers. "Aye, that was it. Round and pink-cheeked, and determined to steal a peek up his tunic each chance she came by."

Sparrow skidded to an indignant halt on the drawbridge. He gaped at the two men as if they had suddenly grown horns and breathed fire. "That troll-necked shrew? Sooner would I bed a foul-breathed sin-eater than let that drudge clamp a thigh around me. Saints assoil me! A walking mort, she is. Schooled by Old Blister herself."

"Ahh, yes. Mistress Bidwell." Alaric winked broadly as Eduard smothered another grin. "Now there is a well-kept secret if ever I heard one."

"Secret?" Sparrow gawped. "What secret?"

"Nay, nay. You need not act the innocent with us, Puck. 'Tis a well-known fact: the harder a man protests against the virtues of a fine woman, the better . . . and more *intimately* he knows her."

They had arrived at the stone pentice—the covered stairwell that gave access to the great keep's living quarters. Alaric bowed Eduard on ahead, the stairwell being comfortably wide enough for only one large man at a time, while pointedly ignoring Sparrow's outraged denials.

The stairs climbed in a gradual spiral to the second storey of the keep. Archers' *meurtriers* were carved into the wall every few paces and admitted air and filtered light, but at the top, the landing was shrouded in a thick gloom, relieved only dimly by the light emitted by the entrance to the great hall. From where they stood, they could see down into the cavernous interior of the keep's vast audience chamber. As Alaric had predicted, there were servants everywhere laying new rushes, spreading clean linens on the trestle tables that had been set up along both flanks of the room. The flames of a hundred candles twinkled through the haze of disturbed dust. The curling smoke from the torches blazing along the walls traced upward to the arched window embrasures, where the only outside light that gained entry was webbed and patterned by the huge crossbeams that supported the ceiling. The fires in the long cooking trench were shooting flames ten feet high in the air casting sparks in all directions as the cooks stirred the coals and prepared the hot beds for the spitted haunches of meat that stood waiting. Out of sight, behind the tall woven screens that concealed the entrance to the main kitchens and cook houses, there would be more frenzied activities as food was prepared and decorated, pastries baked and sweetened to the point of pain, soups, stews, sauces, and jellies boiled and set aside to complement each of the ten or more courses that would comprise the evening feast.

In the midst of all the confusion, a towering, broad-shouldered knight stood in his black velvet finery, his fists clutched around the necks of a pair of throttled, featherless capons.

Sensing the arrival of his son and his neighbour, the Wolf's piercing gray eyes cut through the gloom and found the entryway.

"By Christ's pricking thorns, it is high time the pair of you turned up!"

Randwulf de la Seyne Sur Mer's voice boomed out over the shouting of servants and the squabbling of dogs, momentarily distracting a few sweaty faces from their tasks. One other face, oval and lovely despite the harried frown, looked longer and harder than the rest before murmuring something to a varlet and dispatching him on an errand.

"I should have known," declared Servanne d'Amboise, chatelaine of the castle. "I should have guessed the two of you would remain out of sight until most of the work was done. Eduard—cease your grinning and get you down to the cellars to help choose the wine and ale. Alaric—where is Gil? Surely you have not allowed her to sit a horse in her condition!"

"I had to steal all of the animals out of my own pens to prevent her doing just so, but nay. She follows in a litter, an hour or so behind. I would have ridden with her, but with a dozen knights already at her beck and call, I did not think she would notice my absence. Besides," he added with a faint smile that encompassed the limp capons, "the message I received warned of dire consequences should I not put my feet on the road at once. When is the marshal expected? I was told half a day or thereabouts."

"That was half a day ago," Servanne declared curtly. "The Earl of Pembroke and his entourage have been inside the castle walls for several hours now. Thankfully, he was weary from a long sojourn in the saddle and begged leave to wash the dust from his feet and rest his eyes until we supped. Eduard! Why do you stand there still? Wine! Ale! The best tuns you can possibly find. Alaric—dearest Friar—can you not find it in your heart to take my husband and sit him somewhere with a tankard of mead? I have tripped over his feet so many times my toes are blue."

"I was only trying to help, my love," the Wolf said, thrusting the capons at a passing servant. "But if I am not needed—"

"You are *not* needed," she assured him, snatching the capons from the one churl and handing them to another who had been waiting to skewer them. At the sight of her husband's scowl, she sighed and smiled, and reached up a delicate white hand to press against his cheek. "*Wanted* . . . yea, a thousand times over, my lusty and handsome wolf's head, but at the moment, definitely not needed. *Sparrow*!" The chatelaine's sharp blue eyes flicked past the Wolf's shoulder as she caught sight of another movement in the shadows. "Sparrow, where have you been! Biddy has been scouring the rafters for you."

"Well, I am found now, am I not?" he groused sullenly. "And I should like to see the day Old Blister scours anything for anyone."

"*Is that so?*"

Sparrow felt, rather than saw, the knuckled fist swing out at him from the gloom of the landing.

"Forsooth, I should scour the ears from your head after I box them free, you rancid little puffin of a man!"

Biddy had crept up on him with the stealth of a cat, and if not for lightning reflexes and elfin speed, Sparrow might well have taken an unexpected flight headlong down the steep span of stairs. As it was, he ducked and pivoted on a heel, then took intentional flight upward with a hop and a skip, landing on a ledge carved halfway up the wall.

Biddy's grasping fist was mere inches behind, and, with an "*Aaawk*!" of genuine consternation, Sparrow leaped again, seeming to climb by finger and toeholds to an even safer sanctuary. Reaching a window embrasure, he plumped himself on the stone casement and glared down at his nemesis.

"Scour me now, Troll," he snorted, his arms folded in smug defiance over his chest. "Would you had not eaten half a harvest at noontide, you might have succeeded."

Biddy countered the insult with narrowed eyes. "Would that you *had* eaten half a harvest at noontide you would be able to remain on your perch through the smells of the coming feast. As it is, however, your belly will send you down long before I grow tired of waiting."

Everyone within earshot snickered. Rare was the day that passed when the two were not exchanging verbal or physical blows. Sparrow had been the Wolf's man for nearly three decades, while Biddy—well past her sixtieth year and still full of spit and vinegar—had been nurse and maid to Servanne's mother before becoming the fiercely protective guardian to the daughter. Over the years, Sparrow had managed to maintain the youthful appearance and agility of a wood sprite, but Biddy had grown as round and plump as a larded dumpling. What she had lost in speed, however, she had gained in perseverance, and their positions as stalked and stalker reversed on a regular basis.

This day, their minor drama was eclipsed by the arriving hail of tiny booted feet. Three dark-haired boys and two squealing girls raced full tilt out of the darkness of the upper landing and tumbled down the stairs into the great hall. They ran toward their parents, converging from five points of attack to grasp a leg or an arm or a folded pleat of skirting. Robert followed at a more sedate pace, the sixth and youngest bundle of energy squirming in his arms and wailing to be set free to join the general melee.

"Sweet Mother Mary," Servanne said with a helpless laugh. "Why do I even think I can run this household as a normal dwelling? I should simply throw the gates wide and invite Chaos to move in amongst us."

The Wolf glanced down at his beautiful wife and his look of adoration encompassed the seven handsome children she had given him. "Chaos is already here, my love, and in truth, I would not have had it any other way."

"Liar," she muttered, but tilted her mouth up to his for a kiss that left both their eyes shining.

The Wolf felt the clutch of a tiny fist on his sleeve and turned to answer the wail of his youngest babe, but a sudden stab of pain in his hip and thigh transformed the movement into a dizzying moment of instability.

"There," Servanne said smartly. "Did I not tell you you were trying to do too much too soon! Children—leave go of your father. Robin, give Rhiannon to Biddy and fetch your father's walking sticks."

"Robert—stand fast," the Wolf commanded. "I neither want nor need any blasted walking sticks. The wound is a nuisance, nothing more. And a good deal less than what I have endured in the past."

"In the past, you were a good deal younger," Servanne reminded him. "Robin, the sticks, if you please."

"Robert . . ." The warning in the Wolf's voice was as silkily deceptive as the faint tug of a smile that curved his lips. "You may indeed fetch the sticks. Fetch them directly into the fire."

Robert looked from his mother to his father. He handed the babe into Biddy's pendulous arms then picked up the two carved and polished oak staffs the castle carpenter had fashioned into crutches. One after the other, he tucked the sticks under the crooks of his father's arms, securing them with a look of icy blue challenge in his eyes.

"After so many similar battles," he said with a pragmatism far beyond his years, "do you still think you can win an argument with Mother?"

The Wolf stared at his son for a long moment—a moment poised between violence and grudging respect—and because he could not help but see his wife in the boy's eyes, he tilted his head back and broke the tension with a deep, husky laugh.

"By God, he must be a fitting handful for Eduard."

"He is a true wolf's cub," Alaric agreed lightly. "I see more of you growing in him each day."

"Whereas I see more of his mother." The gesture that accompanied another robust roll of laughter sent Lord Randwulf swaying off balance again and both Alaric and Robert reached out hastily to offer assistance. "Bah! Heave off, the pair of you; I am not ready to meet the floor just yet. Come with me while I hobble and limp my way into a corner where, *Deo volente,* we shall be left in peace with a tankard or two of good, strong ale. Where the devil is Eduard? Surely, by St. Anthony's longest whisker, he has not been away so long as to forget his way to the cellars?"

Chapter 4

✝**E**duard could have found his way to the huge cellars blindfolded. The descent into the bowels of the keep took him down a winding corkscrew staircase, the passage lit at intervals by torches propped in iron cressets bolted to the stone walls. Where there was a torch, there was usually a landing or passageway marking the entrances to the rooms used for storing grain and vegetables, bolts of precious cloth, oaken bins of recently harvested apples and turnips. In this vaulted underbelly of the castle there were also chambers originally designed for confining prisoners, and, in a salle one had to pass before reaching the deep, cool core where the casks of wine and ale were kept, there was a complete armoury that could be used in times of siege to repair and replace expended weaponry.

Neither the donjons nor the armoury had been used in recent years, although both were lit and cleaned regularly to discourage rats and other rodents from increasing their families. The armoury was also used to store the castle's private stock of weaponry, with racks of swords, lances, crossbows, and precious hoards of raw iron. Here, with its heady smell of well-oiled metal and leather, Eduard had often come to admire the Wolf's cache of deadly trophies won in tournaments and battles he had fought from one end of the Continent to the other. The walls of the great hall were hung with crossed swords and lances, decorated with the pennants and prizes won from his foes . . . hundreds of each, to be gazed upon with proud remembrances, each with its own story of victory, of meeting and overcoming impossible or improbable odds. But here, in the darkest heart of his castle, was where Lord Randwulf kept his private victories. Here were kept the stories he would not boast of before a roomful of boisterous knights.

There was the sword King Richard had given him on the redoubt outside Jerusalem—the same sword he had *not* used to obey the command to aid in the slaughter of a thousand unarmed prisoners Richard had had no further use for. There was the armour, black and gleaming, he had worn the day he had met his brother Etienne in mortal combat at Bloodmoor Keep . . . and never worn again. There was the sword—oddly shaped and fitted with iron sleeves that could add or decrease the weight and balance of the weapon—the Wolf had used this long ago to strengthen an arm so ravaged by hideous wounding the physician had predicted he would never use it again.

Eduard's footsteps slowed, as they often did when he passed the armoury. The door to the chamber was partially open and a light glowed from inside—nothing unusual in itself, and he might not have stopped, might not even have taken a second glance had the faint but unmistakable rasp of a sword leaving its sheath not set the fine hairs across the back of his neck prickling an alert.

FitzRandwulf's hand dropped instinctively to the hilt of his own sword and he stepped quickly to one side of the door, his back pressed to the wall and his body immersed in the darkness.

A shadow cut across the path of the light where it spilled out into the corridor and Eduard's gaze flicked to the wall on the far side of the chamber. A silhouette bloomed larger than life on the rough stone, thrown there by whoever was cutting and capering in front of the torch. It was the silhouette of a woman, identifiable by the unbroken sweep of her skirt. She was holding a sword, testing its weight and balance, and as she spun to parry the thrust from an imaginary opponent, the long, unbound waves of her hair lifted around her shoulders.

Eduard's hand relaxed from his sword and he let out his breath in a slow, steady stream. Whoever the girl was, she had a deal of gall to be in there touching things she had no business touching. He took an angry step toward the door, but was brought to a dead halt again as the intensity of light was broken a second time, not by a shadow, but by the flesh and blood outline of the guilty culprit herself.

The woman's shape was blurred by the loose-fitting tunic she wore; more so by the incredible abundance of fiery red hair that tumbled and swirled about her shoulders in a sleek, shining mass of curls. Her movements—twisting, dodging, pivotting on her heels—caused the gleaming red waves to dance like live flames in the torchlight, fanning out in a bright coppery swirl when she spun, and crushing to her shoulders in a froth of red and gold and amber when she stopped or suddenly changed directions.

"Hah! Foiled, Sir Knight," she muttered in smug triumph. "And such a pity to have to bleed all over your fine new tunic."

Intrigued, Eduard folded his arms over his chest and watched. The girl was not familiar to him, but then he had been absent three months and would have no way of knowing any new servants on sight. Although he should have known her. He should have been able to spy the unusual colour of her hair from across the widest part of the bailey.

Eduard's train of thought, along with his breath, was interrupted abruptly as the girl turned fully into the light and used an impatient hand to push the mist of curls away from her face. It was a face designed to turn a strong man's knees to water, for it was heart-shaped and presented on a slender, arching throat. Her skin was fair and flawless. Inordinately large, thickly lashed green eyes were set above an exquisitely delicate nose, complimented by a mouth as full and lush and perfectly shaped as any sent to torment a lusty man's dreams, and Eduard was forced to modify his original assumption that she was a common maid who worked in the castle. Nothing about her was common. Not the colour of her hair, not the colour of her eyes, or the tilt of her chin. Even the wool in her tunic was of the finest weave and the hose he had glimpsed molded around a trim ankle was of sheer, unblemished silk.

She was no stranger to the feel of a sword either. Her grip was firm, her wrist steady. Granted, the weapon she wielded with such gleeful bloodlust was a woman's shortsword, but it was maneuvered with a confidence and expertise gained only through much practice. Even as he watched, she carefully lifted the blade and sighted along the length of the steel, turning it slightly this way and that to gauge its character against the telling flare of the torchlight.

Midway through her inspection, something beyond

Eduard's line of sight caught her attention and she slowly lowered the sword again. She moved out of the light and Eduard heard the clink of metal as one weapon was set aside and exchanged for another. When she moved again into the centre of the room, she was holding a heavy longsword, the blade a full three feet long and fashioned from twice-tempered Toledo steel. Eduard recognized the sword. He was familiar with its weight and balance and his first thought was that she must possess an excellent eye to have picked it out from among so many others. His second thought was that the notion was preposterous. A woman knowing one blade from another? Doubtless he would have to step in soon to prevent her from slicing off her own foot.

In the meantime, the girl traced a fine, delicate hand along the edge of the sword, her fingertips skimming over the shallow blood gutter that ran the length of the blade. Using both hands, she lifted the weapon so that the light flared and skipped along the surface of the polished steel, then she swung it in a slow, graceful arc, moving her body side to side, setting her feet in an attack stance.

Her first lunge was executed without fault; her second ended in a clumsy attempt to counter the momentum of the sword after her legs had become entangled in the folds of her skirt.

Eduard, still shielded by the gloom of the outer corridor, allowed a grin to steal across his face, somehow managing to stifle the guffaw of laughter that teased his throat.

The girl frowned and set the blade to one side. She reached up beneath her chin and, after a brief tussle with laces, dropped the cumbersome weight of her overtunic onto the floor. Dressed only in a knee-length pelisson, she swept the Castilian sword like a scythe, attacking the discarded pile of wool and sending it whirling away into the shadows.

Oblivious to the eyes following her every move, she lunged and parried, smote and hacked at her enemy with a two-handed vengeance that lured Eduard closer and closer to the open doorway. He could feel a dampening of his skin between his shoulder blades just as he could see a similar fine sheen gleaming at the girl's temples and across her brow. His heart was thudding loud in his chest. So loud, he reasoned afterwards, it must have been the noise of it that caused the girl to stop mid-stroke and stare out into the passageway.

The sight of two glowing eyes set in a disembodied head caused her to gasp and sent the sword flying out of her hands. It clattered into a nearby rack, unseating a brace of other swords as well as various pieces of armour plating. The metal clanged and banged, the sound echoing off the damp stone walls and bouncing out into the corridor.

Eduard bent to catch a steel disc as it rolled unerringly through the gap in the door, and the movement startled another choked gasp from the girl's throat.

"Who are you?" she cried. "What are you doing out there? *How long have you been standing there spying on me?*"

Eduard had his attention momentarily distracted by the sight of the long, willowy legs clad in silk to the knees. The pelisson would normally have allowed a gap of only a few inches above the garters, but part of the hem had become caught up under her arm with the happy result that a portion of her thigh was bared from her waist to the tops of her hose. His gaze, understandably reluctant to abandon such a comely sight for the blazing fury of her eyes, took its time making the ascent, lingering on the trim little waist and the agitated rise and fall of firm, round breasts.

"I asked you a question, Churl! Come forward at once and offer your answer!"

Eduard straightened to his full height and met her hot stare.

"Forgive me, demoiselle," he murmured. "I should have made my presence known."

"Indeed, you most certainly should have," she retorted. "I ask you again: Who are you and how long have you been standing out there spying on me?"

Eduard laid the flat of his hand on the door and pushed it wider, letting the light from the torch attach his head to his shoulders and cast a partial glow over his features.

"It was not my intention to spy on you," he assured her.

"Or to frighten you. As it happens, I had to pass this room on the way to the wine stores and—"

"And you thought you might as well stop and amuse yourself at my expense?" The look she gave him was one of utter and complete contempt—a look usually reserved for a creature of low birth who would dare lift his gaze to the level of his betters. Eduard remembered then that he had dressed in worn clothing that morning, intending to spend a sweaty afternoon in the practice yards. His shirt was of the same coarse linen worn by tillers of the soil; his hose were wrinkled and dusty. Because of this, she thought him a common, ignorant lout and, despite being half-naked in an isolated room with a man easily twice her size and strength, showed not a shred of hesitation in challenging him.

"In truth, I was more curious than amused," he said. The smile he was having difficulty concealing tugged at his mouth as he strove not to look down at the enticingly exposed hip. "You hold a battle sword as if you were no stranger to it. An unusual accomplishment for someone of such youth and . . . *bearing.*"

The blaze of green eyes narrowed, reducing the intensity, but not the impact. "There is no mystery in knowing how to defend oneself. Most especially from lechers and voyeurs who have the look and manners of gawping apes about them."

Eduard's smile won out. "An ape? Surely you misjudge me."

The ravishing beauty took a long, hard look at the man who stood before her. His smile was pure insolence, his stance bespoke an easy arrogance that came to one unaccustomed to answering too many questions. He was imposing in a rough-hewn sort of way. Long-limbed, with a fine spread of shoulders, muscled heavily no doubt from lugging full casks of wine to and fro the cellars all day. His jaw was square and capable of framing any expression save for humility; his mouth was a stern slash of cynicism. His eyes were the colour of slate after a thorough soaking—dark, yet flecked with sparks of some other hue . . . blue, perhaps . . . that would need the harsher revelation of sunlight to identify. Handsome. Swaggering. Besotted with himself. King of the scullery wenches and milch-maids, she surmised, with a directness in his gaze that was far too bold for his own good. For anyone's good.

She was very much aware of the musky, animal scent about him, an incense that made her draw upon all her defenses in order to keep from imagining the heat and texture of the flesh so carelessly exposed through the loosened vee of his tunic. She was not altogether successful in smothering her curiosity, for she found herself wondering, for one irreverent and irrational moment, if she *were* but a humble maid, unconstrained by birthright or propriety, if she would be so outraged by the obvious gleam of interest in his eyes.

She moistened her lips with care. "Misjudge you, knave? I think not. More's the like you misjudge yourself and your effect on women of unimpaired senses and sensibilities."

Eduard's mouth curved up at the corner and his gaze slid with shocking deliberation to where the outline of her breasts betrayed just how unsensible an effect he was having on her. The weave of the cloth was fine enough to echo the nervous tremors that were racing through her flesh. Fine enough to leave no doubt as to the sensations flowing through her body, making her breasts hard and full and exquisitely defined.

Ariel de Clare did not have to follow his stare to know what had drawn his lewd attentions. Partly to cover her own embarrassment and partly to put an end to any further liberties he might endeavor to take, she stepped forward, swinging her hand upward with a swift savagery that would have left bleeding scratch marks on his face had Eduard's reflexes not been a hair quicker to react. He leaned slightly back and twisted to the side, exposing his entire face to the torchlight as he did so. The shock of seeing the gnarled weal of scarred flesh that had, until then, been camouflaged by shadow, caused Ariel a split second's worth of hesitation—more than enough time for Eduard to catch her wrist and twist it around into the small of her back.

The action brought her crushing against his chest, whereupon he snatched up her other wrist and pinned it with the first for good measure.

"A spirited little dabchick," he commented wryly, averting his face to avoid the sudden thrashing of wild red hair.

"Unhand me, you ugly, cowardly brute! Unhand me at once!"

"Tsk tsk tsk . . . two insults in as many minutes. I would have a man's tongue plucked out of his head for less."

"Brute! Churl! Lech! Let me go, I tell you! *Let me go*!"

"I might consider doing so, my lady vixen, if you would but pay a small price for my leniency."

"Pay a price?" Ariel stopped struggling and glared upward, the fury sparking in her eyes like flashes of green fire. "*Me*?"

Eduard glanced casually around the armoury. "I see no other trespassers here."

Ariel huffed her breath free—a difficult task with her arms pinned at her back and her breasts crushed against a solid wall of granite. "Ahh. And because we are alone, this price you would ask, I warrant, would be a kiss or two, freely given?"

Eduard's intentions had been more inclined toward a name, or an explanation of her presence in the armoury, but her suggestion was not without certain appeal. Up close, the light from the torch threaded her hair with gold and showed her mouth to favour the shape of a sulky, moist pout. Her squirmings were emphasizing just how long and lithe her limbs were, and, because he saw no reason not to, he let a hand slip down to caress her bottom, pulling her even closer.

"I might be persuaded to accept such an offering," he murmured.

Ariel's anger took her almost beyond speech. It certainly took her beyond rational thought as she looked deliberately at the molten mass of scar tissue and hissed her opinion through her teeth. "A maid would have to be blind, drunk, and addle-witted to offer to kiss such a beast as you, sirrah. Now, unhand me at once or my uncle will have your ballocks for trophies, your eyes for archery targets, and your hands for tavern signs."

The muscle in Eduard's jaw flexed. His grip turned to iron and there was no longer any mocking gentleness in the way he held her against his body. "I tremble with trepidation, my lady. Dare I inquire after the name of this bloodthirsty fellow that I might bolt my door at night and crouch beneath my bed in terror?"

"Well you should hide and crouch," she spat, "for when my uncle, the Earl of Pembroke, Marshal of England, Lion of the Lists, finishes flaying you alive, there will not be enough of you left for the crows to feed upon!"

Eduard's arms sprang open as if he had been burned, and he stepped back so suddenly Ariel's struggles sent her in a full spinning circle before she realized she was free. She stood swaying in the centre of the room, her lungs heaving for air, her fists clenched by her sides, her hair a froth of shiny curls around her shoulders.

"The Earl of Pembroke . . . is your uncle?" Eduard asked, horrified.

"My loving, adoring, *devoted* uncle," she boasted. "And he will lovingly tear your heart out with his *teeth* for *daring* to touch me!"

"My lady . . . I had no idea—"

"*With his teeth!*"

Ignoring his further, futile attempts at an apology, Ariel snatched her tunic off the floor and stormed out of the chamber without another word or glance back. Eduard could hear her brisk, angry steps tapping hollowly along the stone floor and clipping up the stairwell, and, because it would indeed be a miracle if the earl did not take personal offence at the insult to his flesh and blood, he debated chasing after her and forcing an apology upon her.

With the next breath, however, he cursed and strode out of the armoury, continuing on his way to the wine cellar. He had never, in all his life, apologized to a wench and he had no intentions of doing so now. He might be dead by nightfall if he did not, but at least he would have the dubious honour of being run through by the greatest knight and champion of all time.

Chapter 5

✝ **W**illiam the Marshal, despite the three score and six years he had already put behind him, was still a handsome man, immensely strong, with limbs as stout as the abutments of a bridge. He bore a full mane of long, thick hair, the black less evident than it once had been, the gray streaking down into the neatly trimmed, luxuriant beard. His voice could quiet a battlefield and his eyes, bright blue, sharp as daggers, could turn a man's courage to water on a single glance.

He had been knighted by the old king, Henry Secund, and had spent most of his younger years in fierce and loyal service to his liege. He had been devastated by his mentor's death and sickened by the way all three of the king's surviving sons had conspired to break their father's spirit and drive him into an early grave.

When Richard had succeeded to the throne, he had considered himself a champion in all things to do with battle and combat. He had harboured an intense dislike for William since the age of eighteen when he had been unhorsed by the seasoned veteran and publicly humiliated in a tournament. But the Lionheart also had a keen eye for valour and had not only retained William in his service upon being crowned, but had invested him as Marshal of England and rewarded the reluctant bachelor with a marriage to the wealthiest and most sought-after heiress in the kingdom: Isabella of Pembroke.

Eduard FitzRandwulf had good reason to fear the earl's umbrage. At last reckoning, William the Marshal had championed over five hundred tournaments and single-combat bouts —an impressive feat that most likely would never be surpassed. His closest rival for trophies and honours was Randwulf de la Seyne Sur Mer, who could count slightly more than half that number of victories in forfeited pennants and prizes. But Randwulf had also retired from the tournament circuits over a decade ago and had no intention of picking up a lance again for the sake of amusement.

The two men had become friends over the years—a respectful friendship between two old warriors, both of whom had been men of action and honesty all their lives and who found it hard to tolerate ineptness or deceit, especially from their king.

"Give me a sword and show me an enemy to fight," the Wolf remarked dryly, "and I would gladly do so seven days of the week rather than have to debate a point of law for a single hour."

The earl shook his head ruefully. "The king's right to manipulate marriages is not even a law; more of a habit the crown has assumed in order to suit political needs. I myself had no choice in my bride, but . . ."

"But yours was a reward, not a punishment?" the Wolf suggested gently.

"I loved Isabella the moment I saw her," the marshal admitted. "If she was a reward, I cannot think what I must have done to deserve her."

"Possibly saved Henry's life a time or two; surely saved the throne for Richard."

The marshal chuckled. "Then 'tis no wonder John dislikes me so. Yet I had thought my family to be relatively safe from his interferences, especially now, when his mind should be occupied with other, far more pressing matters. I should have known better. When he is in one of his fevered moods of accomplishment, he can think on ten different subjects at the one time, giving each an equal amount of importance in his mind."

William of Pembroke had come into the great hall just after sunset, refreshed by his bath and nap, his dusty travel garb changed for clean, richly embossed velvets and leathers. He had assured the Lady Servanne he was in no hurry to dine and would welcome a few moments of quiet conversation with her husband before he had to don the smiling face of a guest.

"I should also have known, or at least anticipated, that he would not pay off his valued mercenaries in gold—which he does not have—but in lands and titles and bribes of respectability. In this case, he is merely returning an unprofitable estate he had confiscated from the family during his time as prince regent."

"Shall we assume your niece objects to being traded off as a reward?"

"She made use of the swiftest ship and fastest horses to bring me her opinion of the king's meddling."

"She crossed the Channel on her own?" Randwulf asked, mildly amused.

"Not entirely," William said, casting an acerbic eye at the fourth man who was seated in the alcove with himself, Lord Randwulf, and Alaric FitzAthelstan. Henry de Clare reddened somewhat and fidgeted under his uncle's fixed stare. "My nephew is as neatly and completely wrapped around his sister's finger as a length of twine, although I have no doubt she would have found a boat and rowed it across herself if she had to. She is . . . a little headstrong. My own fault, I suppose, for coddling her the way I have all these years. I should have taken the flat of a sword to her rump a few times, as Isabella suggested, and perhaps she would have already been safely wed and out of the reach of an avaricious king."

"Do we dare ask the identity of the prospective groom?"

William seemed to hesitate a moment before answering— "Reginald de Braose"—and even longer before meeting the Wolf's eye.

Lord Randwulf and Alaric both reacted visibly to the name, leaving only Henry to glance from one rigid face to the next and wonder what ghastly secret he had not been privy to.

"Reginald de Braose," the Wolf said with a deathlike intensity. "I have not heard that name in a long while, although it should come as no surprise to hear he is still in the king's favour."

"More so the father than the son," William explained. "A routier who bears mine own name: William. He was in command of the king's garrison in Rouen, although he and his wife Maude have both been in England these past two months, gleefully settling back into their newly restored estates at Radnor."

"And planning the wedding of his son to the House of

Pembroke?" Alaric whistled softly. "The king gives generous rewards to those who lick his spittle."

"I warrant De Braose did a good deal more than that," William declared. "He is a misfit brute who shares Lackland's tastes for blood and pain. I am told he was put in charge of the knights who were captured along with Arthur at Mirebeau, and how he did make them suffer for their misguided loyalties!"

"Twenty-four of the bravest knights in Brittany," Lord Randwulf said, staring down into his wine goblet. "I knew most of them by sight and reputation; a few have been welcomed guests at Amboise. We heard they had been transported back to England to stand trial for treason. Had I known that to be their fate, I would never have handed them over to John's guard, but paroled them on their own honour. Have you had any news of them? Have they been released yet, or has the king decided to keep them on royal display a while longer?"

William looked shocked. "You have not heard? No. No, of course not, how could you? You have been guarding the king's back at Blois." He paused and gripped his own goblet tighter. "You had best brace yourself, old friend, for the knights you speak of are all dead."

"Dead?" the Wolf gasped. "How? When?"

There was no easy way to say it, and the words came out like small gritty pellets. "They were taken to Corfe in chains and rags, there to be thrown into cells and left to starve to death. And although they were given neither a morsel of food nor a dram of water, I am told some took upwards of sixteen days to die."

The Wolf's breath laboured harshly in and out of his chest. His eyes turned black as coal and began to burn with a fury that spread to the grinding hardness of his jaw.

"They were *nobles*," he hissed. "They were *knights!* Most of them were my neighbours and friends. Brave . . . brave men, to a one. Fighting for what they believed was right and just. Christ Almighty, had it not been by mine own command, my son might have been among them. *I* might have been among them, by God, had they struck in any other direction but Mirebeau. And now dead? All of them?"

"All," William nodded. "To England's shame."

The Wolf pushed out of his chair, unmindful of the wound in his thigh. He turned away from the three men and slammed the palms of his hands against the stone wall in frustration. He slammed them a second time, then a third, then leaned his weight on his arms and hung his head between his massive shoulders.

"Stupid, *stupid* boy! I had thought his grandmother would have raised him with more sense. If only he had not joined forces with Philip. If only he had bided his time . . ."

"Arthur came by his rashness honestly," William pointed out. "His father Geoffrey was never wont to conceal his dealings with the French king. And they have both paid the highest price for their lack of judgement."

Lord Randwulf stiffened and faced the earl again, but the chill in his spine answered his question before it was asked. "Have the rumours of Arthur's death been confirmed then?"

"He has not been seen alive since the king left Rouen for Cherbourg more than two months ago."

"He promised his queen mother he would let the boy live."

"John has as little love for his promises as he has for Eleanor, although I suspect something about the deed has left him with a taste of guilt. When I last saw our noble king, his neck was hung with so many holy relics, he could barely stand upright under the burden."

"Would that I had his neck under my boot this instant," the Wolf snarled, "I warrant he would never stand again."

Movement out of the corner of Randwulf's eye caused him to glance over the marshal's shoulder and to acknowledge Eduard's arrival in the alcove. Because his expression so closely mirrored his father's, it was obvious Eduard had overheard most of their conversation. It was also obvious, by the steadfast way the Wolf and his cub were staring at each other, they were reliving some private argument they had had at the outset of the young duke's ill-fated quest to claim the throne away from John.

"You did try to warn him," Randwulf said evenly. "You

warned Arthur he would risk losing everything if he attacked Mirebeau. I warned you of the same thing and can only thank God you heeded me."

Eduard drew a deep breath. "It did not . . . *does* not change my belief that the Duke of Brittany was the rightful heir to the throne of England. Or that our present king is nothing but a greedy usurper—now a murderer—who would stop at nothing to keep the crown seated firmly on his head."

The Wolf sighed and eased himself painfully back into his chair. He noted the marshal's concerned frown, for King John's spies were everywhere, but he offered a smile that contained no sign of apology. "You have, I believe, met my son Eduard? He tends to be a little . . . headstrong . . . himself, at times."

The earl stood, his barrel chest glittering with the blazon of the Pembroke device—a black shield with bars of green and a lion rampant, embossed in gold. He thrust out a hand the size of a large slab of beef, and clasped FitzRandwulf's arm warmly.

"Aye, we have met. But it has been five . . . six years at the least, has it not?"

"More like eight, my lord," Eduard replied stiffly. "You were present when I won my spurs, and it was as much an honour to be in your presence then as it is now."

"We shall share the honours, shall we? I have been hearing how your reputation grows as a champion in the lists. Another year or two of seasoning and mayhap I will have to take you on myself."

Eduard's grace was a little strained despite the immeasurable weight of the compliment. He had bathed and changed his clothes and come quickly to the great hall in the hopes of finding the earl and offering his deep-felt apologies along with what he hoped was an amusing explanation of the misunderstanding with his niece. Now he was being flattered and asked about his successes on the tourny circuits.

"My triumphs are nowhere near as outstanding as your own, sir, and extremely modest compared to my father's."

"Nevertheless, you buckled on your spurs when you were seventeen; an admirable achievement by any measure." The marshal paused and glanced beside him. "I do not believe you have made the acquaintance of my nephew, Henry de Clare. Henry . . . bare a hand to the only man I might be inclined to bet against you in a match."

Henry moved forward and extended a greeting, noting the steady eye that met his.

"FitzRandwulf," he murmured amiably. "I confess my uncle's reservation intrigues me. Perhaps when there is more time for such things, we could put his faith—or lack of it—to the test?"

Eduard smiled tightly. An uncle *and* a brother to appease. Lord Henry's hair was not the same fierce red as his sister's, it was more of a brassy gold, but there was a distinct resemblance in the general character of the face—most notably in the stubborn cut of the jaw. Shoulders almost as broad as his own bespoke a comfortable strength, as did the fighter's eye for instinctively gauging an opponent's potential at first glance. De Clare would be no easy conquest in the lists or in hand combat, nor did he appear any more likely than his famous uncle to see humour in a case of misdirected insults against his sister.

The two knights eased the intensity of their handclasp, but not their mutual wariness of each other.

A disturbance further along the hall ended any further speculations. Servanne d'Amboise had returned from seeing the children tucked safely abed and her arrival was the signal for the cooks and servers to begin the final preparations for laying on the banquet. She had donned a gown of blue baudekin, a cloth from faraway Syria which combined azure silk and gold thread so that the folds shimmered and glowed with each step as though the copper rays of the sun had been caught and imprisoned in it. A girdle sparkling with jewels encircled her waist, and around her neck, a chain studded with sapphires and diamonds. Her long blonde hair had been divided into two gleaming plaits and bound within a woven crespine, over which she wore a thin, plain circlet of hammered gold.

Walking by her side, their arms linked, was Alaric's wife, Lady Gillian FitzAthelstan, very obviously heavy with child

and descending the stairs with the slow, careful steps of a
woman unused to such imbalance. Her skin wore a healthy tan,
attesting to her preference for remaining out-of-doors in all
weathers. It also camouflaged the faintly visible initial that had
been branded into her cheek. The mark of a thief was so faded
by the years as to be hardly noticeable—indeed, Alaric,
Randwulf, and Servanne had grown so accustomed to seeing it,
they would not even have acknowledged it by description if
pressed. Nor, for that matter, would any of the knights or men-
at-arms in residence at Amboise. They had far too much respect for the beauty of Gil's bow arm, for most of them had
been trained to shoot both the longbow and the crossbow under her expert tutelage.

"Ahh," said William the Marshal. "And there walks the
bane of my life; the curse of my old age; the true test of mettle
the likes of which I was never forced to meet in battle."

His remarks, delivered with a heartfelt sigh, were directed
toward the young woman who followed closely behind Gil and
Servanne. At first glance she looked demure and complacent
enough to suit the exalted company. Her tunic was a muted
nutmeg brown, drawn tight at the neck and wrists with bands
of green braiding. Her hair, that glorious abundance of fire
tamed by little else, was confined within the folds of a modest
linen wimple, its colour only hinted at in the glint of thick
auburn lashes that framed her eyes.

Those eyes, as green as the emerald clasp she wore at her
throat, roved from one end of the great hall to the other, clearly
awed by the rich trappings and barely able to conceal her
excitement at being there.

The small party consisting of Lady Ariel, her brother,
Lord Sedrick, and Dafydd ap Iorwerth, had left Pembroke and
sailed on board one of her uncle's ships to the tiny port town of
Fecamp, on the coast of Normandy. They had ridden quickly
and without mishap directly to Rouen, only to find they had
missed the lord marshal by a fortnight. He had gone, at the
king's behest, to meet with King Philip in Paris, ostensibly to
negotiate terms for peace. But since the French king's only
term was the safe return of Arthur to France—which John

already knew could not be complied with—William's quest had been a useless waste of time and diplomacy.

Hoping to intercept him on his return (and not wanting to linger in Rouen where the king's spies might apprise him of their presence) the De Clares had set off in pursuit of the marshal's caravan.

Returning to his pavillion one night to find his niece and nephew appeared from nowhere . . . suffice it to say, it was one of the few times Ariel could recall her uncle threatening her with physical harm—and meaning it. Neither tears nor tempers nor pleas for understanding had any effect. He roared and shouted and went back two generations to draw upon a slack-witted ancestor who happened to have the same shade of red hair as Ariel, and whose adventures had seen her into an early grave at a similar age.

Henry had fared little better. He was railed from one end of the pavillion to the other for agreeing to bring Ariel to Normandy in the first place, then to setting out across the country without a proper, heavy escort. Moreover, when the earl heard of the pact they had made with the Welsh prince—to kidnap the king's messenger and hold him to ransom—William's wrath knew no bounds.

To Henry's credit, he had remained rigidly silent during most of the earl's tirade. The blame for everything could easily have been settled on Ariel's shoulders, as indeed it should have been, but he bore the weight of the plottings with Rhys ap Iorwerth himself, with only a stoney glare directed at his sister now and then to warn her of the huge debt she would owe when the ashes had settled.

The third one to bear the brunt of the marshal's anger was Sedrick of Grantham. He too let wrath descend unchecked, waiting until the earl had run dry of invectives and spittle. Then, to everyone's surprise, the gruff and normally reserved knight corroborated Henry's version of the events, assuring the earl they had not had the luxury of time or precedence to make any other decision. Enlisting the help of the Welshman in waylaying the courier seemed like a convenient means of buying a few weeks' time—long enough to apprise the lord mar-

shal of the situation so that he might take steps to act upon it
Bringing Lady Ariel to Normandy had, in all likelihood, fore
stalled her from doing something even more foolhardy (an
here he too had casually added his own reservations concern
ing Ariel's heritage) when there would have been no one
around with the strength or wit to stop her.

The marshal had found logic in what he said; difficult to
argue.

A final trump was played when the letter Lady Isabella
had written was presented. It confirmed the loathsome pros
pects of the king's proposed groom, the deplorable audacity o
a sovereign who would abuse their loyalty in such a callous
manner, and the unavoidable necessity of enlisting the service
of renegades to protect their home and family in his, the lor
marshal's, continuing absence. Whether or not it was thi
veiled accusation, laying at least some of the blame on his ow
broad shoulders, that finally blew the tempest out of the mar
shal's sails, none of the others could say for certain. Somewha
mollified, however, he had announced he would sleep on the
matter but for none of them to be surprised to waken and fin
themselves turned back on the road to Fecamp.

That ominous announcement had been made over a week
ago, and now here they all were, standing in the majestic grea
hall of Amboise Castle, with minstrels settling into the uppe
gallery and servants rushing to and fro. Lights glittered every
where, but on the dais, at the table reserved for the lord and
lady of the château and their guests of honour, the candle
were backed by circlets of silver so that the flames glowed lik
small sunbursts.

Ariel had heard a great deal about the famed Randwulf d
la Seyne Sur Mer, and was not disappointed in meeting the
living flesh. He was equally as tall as her uncle, with a darkl
savage handsomeness that had deservedly earned him the
name Black Wolf. To his right was Alaric FitzAthelstan, an
other legendary knight of brave deeds and keen intelligence
She admired and respected him instantly for the open, un
abashed love he had for his wife—a woman whose predilection

for manly skills would have turned most men away in disdain
. . . or jealousy.

Lady Ariel had heard the stories, many and widespread
throughout England, of how the Black Wolf had taken a select
troop of knights into the forests of Lincolnwoods disguised as
outlaws. Poets and troubadours in as remote a region as the
Welsh Marches sang *chansons de geste* boasting of the great tournament at Bloodmoor Keep where the Wolf had slain the
Dragon lord and rescued his beautiful demoiselle from certain
death. They sang of the feats of Gil Golden, the best archer in
all of Christendom (though none ever specified she was a
woman) and of Sparrow, the magical wood sprite who could
sprout wings and fly.

Here they all were, in the flesh and blood, as normal as
normal could be, greeting her, welcoming her as if she were
already an equal.

". . . and my son, Eduard," the Wolf was saying, extending the introductions to a figure who had been standing a
little behind and to the side of his father, keeping well cloaked
in shadows.

Ariel's smile froze.

It was him. It was the scarred beast from the cellars. In
place of the linsey-woolsey shirt and coarse hosen, he wore a
quilted surcoat of the finest black samite, banded in stripes of
velvet and studded at each junction with knots of heavy gold
thread. He had given his jaw a close shave, scraping off the
dark stubble that had blunted his features earlier, but the
clean, square lines only emphasized the extent of the damage
wrought to the flesh of his left cheek, and drew attention to the
arrogant jut of his chin. His hair, while still looking as unruly as
if he had just ravished a dozen maidens in a row, had been
washed free of dulling dust and glowed the same rich chestnut
as his father's . . . but there could be no mistake. It was him:
The lout. The brute. The voyeur. And he was stepping boldly
forward to take up her hand in a formal greeting.

"Lady Ariel," he murmured, bowing his head respect-
fully. "God grant you health, honour, and joy."

"Peace and good health to you as well, milord," she answered by rote, cracking her words like nuts. She had also heard the heartwarming tale of the Wolf's long-lost son rescued from the donjons of Bloodmoor; the troubadours had sung of his many subsequent feats in the lists and she had been admittedly curious to meet this icon of chivalrous deeds and derring-do.

Met him she had, and at his scurrilous best. Sneaking about like a thief, spying through peepholes, terrorizing helpless women . . . *forcing* himself upon them at his merest whim, swelled by his own self-importance. She supposed she should be thankful he had not pilloried her on the floor of the armoury that afternoon. Had she not had the shield of her uncle's name to bring to her defense, she might well have found herself used as a brief diversion by the bold, ugly brute.

On the other hand (and here she almost groaned aloud with the mortification), what a sight she must have made in her pelisson and hose, capering about the armoury engaged in mortal combat with an imaginary foe. How swiftly would the story spread throughout the castle and how comical would the embellishments grow with each retelling? Were there hands being raised even now to conceal the whispering and sniggering? Were heads and necks craning to have a closer look at the addle-witted niece of the Earl of Pembroke?

As if to confirm her suspicions and deepen her discomfort, the level of noise rose markedly in the great hall. Knights and castle retainers had begun to fill the seats along the trestle tables that stretched down either side of the chamber, and the savoury odours from the cooking braziers were causing a general restlessness.

"Come, my lord," Lady Servanne directed, patting her husband's arm lightly as he grappled with the cumbersome crutches. "Best we seat ourselves before the rabble begins to chew on the linens. My Lord Marshal, will you honour my husband's right? Eduard . . . you will partner the Lady Ariel, of course, and Lord Henry, you may take your sister's left, unless you would care to have the trouble of sitting next to Sparrow."

Henry weighed the dark look he saw on Ariel's face

against the brief introduction he'd had to Sparrow earlier, and chose the least damaging threat to his digestion.

"I am advised Sparrow has vast knowledge on many subjects."

"Advice which came from his own beak, no doubt," Alaric said dryly. He slipped his hand beneath the crook of Gil's elbow and started to lead her toward the dais. "Trust that you will rue the day you ask him to expound on any of it."

Laughter prompted the others to walk away from the alcove, leaving only Ariel and Eduard to share a terse silence.

After a long moment, he cleared his throat and offered his arm. "Shall we, my lady?"

She glared at his arm, then followed the black samite of his sleeve up to his shoulder, finally braving the cool slate gray of his eyes. The wry amusement she saw reflected there did nothing to temper her resentment, and she drew on the only defense she had—her anger.

"I am but a mere breath away from scarring the other side of your face, *my lord*. You would be wise not to challenge my patience . . . or my silence."

Eduard glanced around, then lowered his voice to match hers. "My own lips have been sealed fast these past few hours, but a challenge, alas, is a challenge, and we have here a good hundred pair of ears and eyes to judge who was in the right and who in the wrong."

Ariel's eyes sparkled a moment before darkening around her retort. "You are known as *Fitz*Randwulf d'Amboise, are you not?"

"I am," he admitted after a wary pause.

"Then I should think these hundred ears and eyes already know you to be the *bastard* you are. They require no further proof from me."

Her eyes swept his broad frame with a final look of derision before she turned and walked, unescorted, to the dais.

In spite of the earlier pandemonium that had ruled the great hall, a creditable feast was set out in honour of William the Marshal. A steady stream of varlets flowed from the kitch-

ens with cauldrons of soups and stews, platters mounded high
with roast mutton, boar, capon. There were chines of pork and
whole peacocks stuffed, roasted, and presented in fully restored plumage. Jellied eel and grilled trout came smothered
in garlic and leeks, lavished with spices, swimming in thick
sauces. Consumption of it all took several dedicated hours; a
challenge met with undisguised glee.

The men ate and belched to make the walls tremble. The
women chatted and laughed and tried to make themselves
heard over the rumble of countless conversations. Dogs
begged and rooted noisily for scraps tossed into the fresh-
strewn rushes. Minstrels strummed the lute, viol, and guitten
from the balustraded gallery that protruded overhead.

When the many courses of hot and hearty fare had given
way to frumenty custard and wafers, tumblers took to the floor
to display their talents, dancing and juggling and performing
feats of acrobatic skill. Two wrestlers, stripped to the waist and
oiled like carp, fought a heated match amidst howls of encouragement and heavy wagering.

Ariel was conscious of everything but able to concentrate
on nothing in particular. Her every sense was held hostage by
the broad-shouldered knight who sat so mockingly attentive
by her side. Since it was the custom for couples to share a
goblet and trencher at formal dinners, she had no choice but to
suffer his company. Despite the fact she suffered it with a
coldness that should have left ice crystals forming on the food,
he was the model of solicitousness. He wiped, with exaggerated care, the gold rim of the goblet each time he offered it
into her hands. He selected only the choicest tidbits of meat,
fish, fruit, and legumes to adorn her half of the trencher, and if
it seemed her appetite was waning, he called for sweeter,
richer, more elaborate delicacies with an air that was patroniz-
ing enough to draw the concern of the host and hostess if she
refused. If he spoke to her directly, which he often did purely
to irritate her, she experienced such a heated rush of conflict-
ing emotions, she more often than not returned his stare
blankly, forcing him to repeat his initial question slowly and
carefully, as if querying a dolt.

Fortunately for her patience, Alaric FitzAthelstan was seated on her right and proved to be an interesting conversationalist. In contrast to the startled responses she garnered in mixed company on the other side of the Channel, discussing politics or warfare at Amboise's table, with men and women sharing an equal voice, appeared to be the normal state of affairs. Doubtless it was due to the mettle of the women who occupied the prominent seats on the dais. Lady Servanne showed no hesitation in confronting her husband on a point of order, nor did he attempt to exclude her from any subject under discussion. Lady Gillian, despite being in the very delicate state of pregnancy, argued the most efficient use of siege weaponry as if she had just walked off a battlefield. More than once, Ariel thought she could envision her aunt Isabella's flustered, even shocked reactions to such talk coming over a course of poached salmon, and it was all she could do not to smile.

She forgot herself once and was rewarded by the sensation of a thousand tiny hairs across the nape of her neck standing on end.

"Do you always stare at your guests so intently?" she asked, turning slowly to confront the source of her discomfort.

Eduard FitzRandwulf grinned through an overbearingly white slash of unchipped teeth. "Only when I see something so totally out of keeping, it astonishes me."

"What, prithee, could have caused such an upheaval?"

The bold, smokey eyes descended languidly to rest on her mouth. "You smiled. And nothing cracked or broke when you did so."

Ariel's gaze narrowed. Why, the arrogant, self-serving beefwit. Was he about to try flattery now?

She was not to know, for her uncle chose that moment to thump his goblet on the table and call for silence from the gathered throng.

"A toast, my lords and ladies, to our gracious host and hostess. God grant I still have the strength in my legs to carry me off to my chambers after partaking of such a feast as has been set before us tonight. A king could expect no better fare at his table, nor better company at his side. *À l'Amboise!*"

Benches scraped and booted feet shuffled to attention.

"*À l'Amboise!*" echoed a chorus of voices.

Cups and tankards were raised, swords drawn and held high in a salute to the lord of the manor and his exalted guest. Many remained standing, including those on the dais, for the varlets had begun clearing away the remnants of the meal. Ariel kept to her feet as well, pointedly turning her slender back on Eduard FitzRandwulf. She had borne enough of his sarcasm and mockery, and had no intentions of lingering to watch the foolish games of strength and dexterity with which the knights would amuse themselves while they drank their way into a drunken stupour.

A pair of boasting combatants were taking to the centre of the floor even as she watched, their swords drawn, their challenges earning shouted wagers from the laughing onlookers.

"A pity women are not invited to participate," a voice murmured close to her ear. "With what fancy footwork as I witnessed this afternoon, a canny opportunist could make a handsome profit over the course of a bout or two."

Meant as a compliment to the skills she had displayed in the armoury, Eduard's words were, naturally, misconstrued as being anything but complimentary.

Ariel turned her head and found her gaze level with the top of his shoulder. He was standing infuriatingly close—enough for her to mark the individual stubbles of hair that grew on his chin and neck, and to see the pale line of white flesh where a second scar slashed through the arch of his eyebrow. Had that been the only mark on his face, she would have had to admit to a distinctly unnerving handsomeness. His body was certainly adequate. There were few, if any, knights who could have the term *lean* applied to their builds; fewer still who were not muscled like plowhorses simply from the weight of the armour they wore and the rigorous training they endured to become champions. Exchanging iron link mail and bullhide gambesons for studded and embossed velvet surcoats softened the effect somewhat, but there was no possibility of completely camouflaging massive shoulders, chests, and thighs. *Partially* camouflaging it was an art. Done with careless charm and sensual indolence, it was a breathtaking achievement.

Eduard FitzRandwulf d'Amboise *was* a breathtaking achievement in raw masculine power. He was a beast in his prime. His arrogance, scorn, and cynicism, however, reduced him to the level of a brawny oaf.

Eduard was easily able to translate each of the Lady Ariel's fomenting opinions of him in the hot green sparkle of her eyes, but in truth, he was enjoying the backwash effects of baiting her. Each highly charged emotion she communicated by word, glance, or flush met with a strange reaction in the way his blood flowed through his veins. He could not fathom why, for his dislike for women of high self-regard was thorough and unchangeable, and the Lady Ariel de Clare undoubtedly held herself in the highest regard possible. Perhaps it was the image burned into his mind's eye of her spinning and jousting half-naked in the torchlight of the armoury. The demure wimple could not erase the memory of flame-red hair swirling around her shoulders in a fiery cloud. Nor could the modest, almost drab tunic blunt the recollection of firm, upthrust breasts and coltishly long legs hidden beneath.

Eduard arched a brow and Ariel frowned.

The way he was looking at her . . . why . . . it was almost as if he could see clear through the brown cendon of her tunic, through the sheer linen of her blanchet to her bare flesh.

Their eyes met without warning and in the taut, vibrating silence that followed, a fresh welter of heat flushed through Ariel's veins, prickling pink and warm into her cheeks.

"You have a bold manner, sirrah," she said in a furious underbreath. "And a tongue that wants disciplining when in the company of your betters."

"My . . . betters?" The smokey gray eyes scanned the room and his grin widened. "You mean, of course, that I should be seated below the salt with the other bastards in the hall?"

"Such arrangements are not unheard of," she replied primly.

"Whereas the practice of seating petulant children on the dais . . . *is* a little unusual."

Ariel drew a deep breath. This was too much. He was pushing too far. Something—the loud snap of a bone clenched between the jaws of a nearby wolfhound—cracked the last shreds of her composure, but her hand had no sooner started on its upward intent to slash the grin off FitzRandwulf's face, when it was caught and held in an ironlike grip.

"You tried that once and failed miserably, my lady," he warned quietly. "I would not recommend you attempt it again . . . not unless you crave the thorough embarrassment of finding yourself flat on your backside."

Two bright, hot spots of colour appeared high on her cheeks. "Do you dare threaten to strike me? Have you no shame whatsoever?"

"Not when it comes to dealing with women who pout and taunt and repeatedly disdain sincere attempts to apologize," he said evenly. "A simple misunderstanding occurred this afternoon. You were found somewhere you should not have been, touching things you should not have touched. Even so, I made certain assumptions I should not have made and reacted in a manner which obviously caused offence. Thus, I would say we were both in error to some extent."

"And do you now expect *me* to apologize to *you?*"

Eduard's penetrating gaze held hers for several moments longer before sliding down to where his fingers were slowly relaxing from around her wrist. "Wringing an apology from you was not my intention, demoiselle. I regret you did not enjoy your meal or the company with whom you shared it. With luck, however, the experience will not have to be repeated . . . for either of us."

He offered a curt, mocking bow and walked away to join an animated conversation Lord Henry was having with Sparrow. The heat ebbed and flowed in Ariel's cheeks and she massaged her wrist with a hand that trembled visibly. Lout. Buffoon. *Bastard!* How dare he speak to her like that. How dare he *presume* to lecture her on the rules of polite behavior.

"Lady Ariel . . . ?"

She spun around, her face set for further battle. "What is it?"

Dafydd ap Iorwerth flinched an involuntary step back. He and Sedrick had been seated with the other knights, close to the dais as befitting their status, but too far to have joined any conversations. He had witnessed the hostilities between Ariel and FitzRandwulf, and had thought to offer himself as a diversion.

"F-forgive me for disturbing you, my lady. I only thought to inquire if you enjoyed your meal."

The deep green sparks in Ariel's eyes flared. "Enjoyed it? It is a wonder my belly has not soured beyond redemption. And the air . . . it is so stifling, I can barely breathe."

"If the air is close, my lady," he suggested eagerly, "perhaps you would care for a walk in the garden? I have been told of Lady Servanne's success with winter roses."

Just like a Welshman, she thought angrily. Or any man for that matter, thinking to placate her with a walk in the gardens, as if the workings of nature should be the most important thing on her mind. Ariel steadied herself to tell him precisely where he could put each and every thorn of those winter roses, but a gust of masculine laughter farther along the dais lured her eye to where FitzRandwulf and Henry were standing together. Henry was looking her way and nodding with one of his wretchedly indecipherable smiles; the Bastard was deliberately *not* looking her way, but she could tell he was watching her nonetheless.

Seething, she slipped her hand through the crook of Lord Dafydd's arm. "A walk among the roses would be just the thing, my lord," she said loudly. "I thank you for your concern."

Henry, his mouth still crinkled with amusement, watched the Welshman and his sister beg their leave of the lord and lady of the château before making their way toward the rear of the great hall.

"Odd," he mused. "I would not have wagered she knew the difference between a rose and a thistle."

Eduard glanced at the departing couple. "Whereas I would wager neither have as many prickles as her tongue."

Seeing Henry's slow frown, FitzRandwulf sighed and hastened to add, "I fear your sister did not enjoy my company overmuch this evening. We, ahh, happened to have met earlier in the afternoon when I found her in the castle armoury, and when I attempted to ascertain her reasons for being there, she apparently took umbrage at my manner."

Henry stared at Eduard for a long moment before allowing the corner of his mouth to relent and turn upward again. "Pay no heed. Ariel tends to take umbrage easily, especially when she is caught doing something she should not be doing. I wondered why she acted as if she had caught a mouthful of hornets when the introductions were made. Raiding your armoury, was she?"

"Inspecting it, more's the like. With a surprisingly keen eye, I might add."

"She has a surprisingly keen ability to go along with it," Henry advised.

"I will bear it in mind."

"Bear also that she *is* my sister, and I love her dearly despite her faults."

Eduard nodded slightly, acknowledging the sentiment and the warning.

Sparrow, who had thankfully been distracted during most of the exchange, received a nod from Lord Randwulf and looked up at both knights. "A finger has wiggled at us, inviting us to a private meeting with the lord marshal. Where is the Welshman gone?"

"To smell the roses," Eduard said dryly.

"Eh? Just as well, he was not invited anyway. Come, my bold blades. Touch your toes to my heels and bring yon tankards. What *I* am smelling bodes nothing sweet ahead."

Eduard spared a last glance at the far stairway, all but obscured behind the haze caused by the smoke and roisterous atmosphere raised by so large a gathering. Ariel and Dafydd had reached the top step and were a moment away from being swallowed into the heavier gloom of the outer landing. At the last possible instant, Ariel turned to look over her shoulder, but her face was nothing more than a pale blur and Eduard could not be absolutely certain she saw him, let alone his mock salute.

Chapter 6

†**E**duard declined to take a chair and stood with his back to the wall as his father and the marshal settled around a large oak table with Lord Henry, Alaric, and Sparrow. They had retreated to one of the private chambers partitioned off from the solid block walls of the hall. It was not much bigger than the alcove they had occupied before the meal, save it had a narrower entrance and let fewer sights and sounds escape. A further, casual nod from the marshal's leonine head was acknowledged by Sir Sedrick of Grantham, who took up a position close to the chamber to discourage any potential eavesdroppers.

"A sad day indeed," Lord Randwulf remarked, "when a man has to guard his tongue under his own roof."

"It would be sadder still to give the king a reason to asseise Amboise," the earl returned bitterly. "It will already require fancy word-work on my part to explain why we journeyed so many leagues out of our way to stop here, but . . ." He shrugged his big shoulders as if to express an opinion of the king's wit.

The Wolf held his thoughts until a large flagon of ale had been tipped to fill their tankards and the servant dismissed with a wave of his hand. His leg was aching abominably but he suspected, with the same acumen Sparrow displayed, his wound would be the least of his concerns before the hour was out.

When the men were alone, he put forth the question bluntly. "Why *did* you stop here, old friend?"

William ran a thumb around the rim of pewter and took a deep swallow of ale. "Before I answer—and God grant me your mercy that you do not take offence—I must have your pledge as knights and men of absolute honour, that not one word of what we discuss here tonight is breathed beyond this circle. Not to your wives, not to your lemans, not to a priest should he be incanting the last rites over your ascending souls."

The Wolf's steely gaze reflected the flame of the single, thick candle that sat in a puddle of its own translucent wax. Were it any other man demanding such an oath, swords would already have been drawn to answer the insult. That their weapons remained sheathed was not only a measure of the respect they had for the marshal, but an ominous indication that they all felt a strong degree of apprehension at his presence.

With a deliberate firmness, Lord Randwulf extended his hand and clasped it over Pembroke's.

"You have my most solemn oath," he pledged quietly.

Alaric leaned forward, as did Eduard and Henry, and finally Sparrow, who had to kneel upon the tabletop to reach his pudgy hand to the mound of others. Each gave his oath in turn, vowing to die by his own hands if necessary, to preserve the trust they were forming this night.

"I came," William began, after they had settled to their seats again, "because I fear Merlin's prophecy will soon come true: 'That the sword shall become divided from the sceptre, Normandy from England, in the reign of a dark-eyed king.' I came," he added, "because the French monarch had a grin on his face when he sent me on my way. And I came . . . because I know you to be a man of your word, a man I can trust with my life, and the lives of my family, if need be."

The Wolf remained motionless but for a brief glance at Alaric.

The earl laid his hands flat on the table, splaying the thick, blunt-tipped fingers. "I loved John's father, Henry Second. I rode by his side for nigh on two score years, and even though his sons conspired against him time and again, I grudgingly gave him my blood oath to stand by the throne and to defend the crown with my last breath.

"Richard was a blunderer. A magnificent blunderer, but a fool nonetheless. His God and his England were the sword, and so long as he could wield it in bloody combat, he considered himself a good king and defender of the faith. To England itself, while he amused himself slashing at the throats of the Saracens, he gave John—an open sore, worse than any fistula from any plague—and in the name of safekeeping the throne in Richard's absence, John stripped England to the bone and bled every last coin from those who could afford it least. He maimed and crippled her with cruelty, greed, and corruption. When Richard fell at Chalus, John—instead of spreading balm on any wounds he may have made during his vicious reign as regent—set about exacting his revenge on those who had dared to challenge his authority. You yourself lost lands and holdings of no small value."

"I did not suffer for the loss," Randwulf said warily.

"Nevertheless, the people have. Your people. Vassals and serfs who were given no choice, who had no say in who would own the land, and in turn, own their lives. They, like the rest of England's commonry, have come to accept, through trials of fire and sword, that cruelty, hunger, and poverty are forever to be their lot in life."

Randwulf shifted uncomfortably on his chair. "I had no idea you harboured such love of the common folk."

"And I had no idea you harboured such disdain. Nor would I ever have guessed it from the well-fed bellies we passed on the roads leading through Amboise."

"Are you suggesting I could save all mankind by re-claiming Bloodmoor Keep?"

The earl shook his head grimly. "No. Bloodmoor . . . nay, all of England is well beyond the redemption of a single man, I fear. And will be so long as this . . . this flatulent Softsword sits on the throne."

"We do hear he has become quite full of himself," Sparrow chuckled. "Painfully so at times."

Pembroke's blue eyes creased at the corners for a brief moment. "He has grown so sour now, the gasses pop and wheeze out of him almost continually. Not long ago, he bent over too quickly—to pick up a copper groat, the story goes—and such a clap of thunder was heard to break from his arse, the guards came to his chamber at a run. 'Twas not a clean clap either, for he had to hasten away to change into fresh braies."

The men's laughter was strained, but Sparrow ho-hoed with such belly-mirth, he tumbled backward off his bench.

"Aye, 'tis a sad and sorry state to laugh at your own king," the earl continued with a sigh. "A king who sits farting and counting his plundered coins while a French panderer steals the very lands that birthed our ancestors. Certes, he is the meanest king I have ever served. He has turned nearly every baron in England against him by misusing his power, misusing his position. He has put himself above the law, and, if he was indeed responsible for ordering Arthur's death, he has also put himself above God. Quite simply said: I hate the man. My fingers ache to squeeze around his throat whenever I am in his presence. I know he is my king and I have forsworn to serve him, but . . . ah, Jesu, Jesu . . . if I had half a measure more courage, I would gladly send him on his way to hell."

No one moved. No one drew a breath. Was the Marshal of England about to appeal to one of them to assassinate the king?

Pembroke noted the silence and his piercing blue eyes passed over each taut face in turn. "Rest easy, friends. I have not come to ask of you what I cannot do myself. But I have come to put forth this to you: we must begin to take measures to limit the throne's power. As you must already know, Poitou, Anjou, Maine, and Brittany are seething with revolt, burning and pillaging everything tainted by the king's corruption. The barons in England watch and wait. They meet by twos and threes and know wherein the blame for all of this dissent lays, yet short of calling for a civil war, none are in a strong enough position *on their own* to lead a campaign against John Plantagenet. Randwulf—you spoke more wisely than you knew when you cursed the impetuousness of Arthur of Brittany. Had he bided his time, had he not thrown his lot in with Philip of France, had he but *waited* and built up his strength and support among the barons who, in the days ahead, *might well have been willing to throw their lot behind an alternative to John's greed and treachery* . . . well . . ." He sighed and the huge, calloused hands came together, the fingers locking so as not to betray the tremors of anger and impotence that shook them.

"Were you not the one who said the barons of England would never favour a boy over a man? Were you not the one who said it was better to take the devil we knew than the princeling we knew not?"

William glared at Randwulf. "Walter de Coutances, our wise and vainglorious Archbishop of Rouen, predicted I would rue the day I threw the lot of England's nobility behind John's claim to the throne. He would also be crowing with delight to hear me decry that decision now."

"I am hardly crowing," the Wolf said. "But since the boy is more than likely dead, it does little good to talk of what might have been or could have been had Arthur lived."

"Where the interests of England are concerned, men will always talk," William advised solemnly. "Most especially when there is another possibility to talk about."

Alaric whistled softly under his breath, having already surmised where the discussion was leading. But it was Eduard who stiffened with a complete look of horror on his face.

"The Princess Eleanor? You would have Arthur's sister call England to a civil war?"

"Were apples apples and oranges oranges, Eleanor's claim does precede her uncle John's," William pointed out. "And although he beds his nubile young wife day in and day out, he is as yet without a legitimate heir of his own. If he were to die tomorrow of gout and flatulence, Eleanor would succeed him as queen of England."

"With or without his untimely demise," the Wolf asked, "are you suggesting the barons would hold with putting another woman on the throne of England? After the hell they went through with Matilda?"

"No. They most certainly would not trust her to rule alone. But if she were to marry *wisely*, and with a man the barons elected themselves, a man who could be trusted to place the welfare of England before all else . . . then some might see a benefit in making her queen. Let me put the question to you: Would Eleanor of Brittany be able to unite the barons of England?"

"She is Geoffrey's daughter, Henry Secund's granddaughter," Randwulf said with careful consideration. "She has the charm and wit of the one, the sense of justice of the other. Eduard—?"

"She is honest and God-fearing," said the darkly handsome knight. "Her beauty lights a room when she enters and leaves a terrible sense of loss when she departs. She is wise and brave, loyal beyond call—"

"And obviously possesses the knack of winning devotion," William interrupted with a smile.

"Have you any candidates in mind for her consort?" Alaric asked.

"There are several," William admitted, betraying the fact that the matter had been much discussed already. "Each with his own merits, each capable of gaining and holding the respect of the barons . . . and more importantly, their armies."

"Forgive my lack of wit this night," said Randwulf, "but it still does not explain why you have brought this meal to my table. I have no holdings to speak of, no vast army in England to draw upon, no influence there at all except with the royal executioner."

"Your modesty does you no justice. Moreover, England is not the crucible—Normandy is. If the pennants of the Black Wolf were not firmly planted on the banks of the Loire, how long do you think it would take Philip to bring his armies across? I know, after standing in the Frenchman's court and counting the number of familiar faces in the audience, the deals have already been cut with half the barony of Brittany, Maine, and Anjou. In exchange for retaining their lands and titles, none will lift a lance against Philip's forces when he attempts to make Normandy part of France. Only you and your absolute devotion to the dowager stand in his way. You are Aquitaine's champion. You carry her pennant above your own in battle. You have proven your loyalty time and time again; she and her granddaughter both trust you. More importantly, they would listen to you with an open mind."

Under different circumstances, the Wolf might have laughed out loud, for the cobwebs had finally been blown off his senses and he knew why the earl had come to Amboise.

The battles, verbal and physical, that Queen Eleanor and her
husband Henry II had engaged in were the stuff of legends.
Henry had even kept her under lock and key for seventeen
years fearing she would lead her sons in open revolt against
him. There had been no love lost between Eleanor and the
blustery William either, and upon Henry's death, she had
heaped double the scorn on Pembroke, going so far as to rail
her son Richard in public for making the old warrior Marshal of
England.

Yet the Wolf was not laughing. He was not even smiling.
He was, if anything, having difficulty controlling his fury.

"You would have me intercede on your behalf and convince the princess to play the cat's paw to your political
maneuverings, even though she has spent most of her life
being used and manipulated like a piece on a chessboard?"

"You would prefer to let John decide her fate?"

A second, frozen hush descended over the group and this
time it was Sparrow who broke the shocked silence.

"Softsword has not dared to lay a hand on our Little Pearl,
has he?"

The earl's eyes turned into chips of blue ice. "He dared to
take her prisoner with her brother at Mirebeau, and he has
dared to keep her confined in a tower room at Rouen all these
months. Now, if the eyes I have watching those tower rooms
are to be believed, he has dared to move her to Cherbourg, and
from there, to transport her by ship to England."

"To *England*!" Eduard surged forward, the scar on his face
turning a livid white with rage. "The bastard has moved her to
England?"

William nodded. "John himself is getting ready to bolt.
He has no men, no money, no army. He knew before he sent
me on this fool's errand to see Philip that the French would
never agree to a peaceful compromise, and he knows, once he
shows the barons of Brittany and the Aquitaine how little he is
prepared to risk in order to hold their loyalty, the fleur-de-lys
will fly from every battlement west of the Seine. Normandy
will be under French rule by the spring and there is nothing

anyone can do to prevent it once John removes himself across the Channel."

"And the Princess Eleanor?"

Pembroke was silent a moment. "Because of Arthur, because he once renounced his claim in supposed good faith only to reappear some months later at the head of an army . . . Eleanor could pledge her oath of fealty from the highest rampart in the land, she could shout it before the largest court assembled, and John would not be inclined to believe her. As long as she is alive, there is another whose claim to the throne precedes his own. And as long as she is alive, he knows there will be men gathering in dark rooms to speak of civil war."

"The king would not dare harm her," Eduard declared evenly. "Every knight in the realm would turn their backs on him. He would be spitting in the eye of chivalry itself, and no amount of guilty penance, no weight of holy relics strung about his scrawny neck, would redeem him."

"You place more faith in his concern over public opinion than I do," Pembroke remarked. "In any case, she is a danger to him and he would not contemplate returning to England without her. As his prisoner or his hostage—call it what you will—the Pearl of Brittany will never be allowed to walk free again, not so long as John sits upon the throne."

Eduard, standing in the silence and shadows, steeped in quiet fury. He raised a hand unselfconsciously and pressed it over his breast, feeling the bite of the tiny gold ring. Eleanor had given it to him the day he had won his spurs; the same day he had vowed, with drops of his own blood, to perform all deeds of bravery and honour in her name, and to serve and protect her unto the death as her champion.

He had not trusted John's motives from the outset and had wanted to go, by himself if necessary, to bring her away from Mirebeau. But his father and the dowager had both worked to cool his temper. Eleanor herself had assured him she was being treated well and was quite certain her uncle meant her no harm. At the time, she had also been quite certain Arthur would be set free again, and had even gone willingly to Rouen in the hope of being closer to him. As recently as a fortnight ago, she had held hope Arthur was somewhere in the castle donjons being kept in isolation and darkness until his Angevin stubbornness could be broken.

If John had given the order for Eleanor to be moved to England, she must be aware by now that the rumours of her brother's death were founded in truth. She would be frightened. Alone. She would know she could no longer trust her uncle's promises and assurances.

William the Marshal was watching Eduard's face closely. "I would hasten to add that if any overt force was brought to bear against the king to win her release, it would invite upon her the same fate her poor brother suffered. Nay, even the *threat* of force would turn John's hand against her."

Eduard met the marshal's eye. "Do you suggest we do nothing to correct this travesty?"

"I suggest we do the only thing we can do." William drew a breath through his teeth and looked at each man in turn. "I suggest we steal her back."

"Steal her back?" Alaric exclaimed.

"Aye. And the sooner the better. The farther from Brittany she is taken, the deeper into John's domain she travels, the less likelihood there will be of wresting her from the king's grasp."

"You have obviously ruled out appealing to the dowager for help," the Wolf assumed.

"For all of his faults, his past treacheries, and for all that he bestows upon her the affection of a moulting snake, Eleanor of Aquitaine has always favoured John among her sons. She would not knowingly intercede if it meant threatening his position on the throne. As much as she loved Arthur, she ordered a hail of arrows be delivered upon his head when he sought to take Mirebeau. As much as she loves her granddaughter, she would not condone any act that might lead to putting her on the throne in John's stead.

"Not," he stressed, "that it would be necessary, or even probable, for the barons of England to band together to do so. It might well be enough just to be able to *threaten* to do so in order to win some compromise of power from the throne—

compromises we *must* have to limit the power one man has over an entire kingdom."

"So you would use her," Eduard spat contemptuously. "You would free her from one form of captivity only to place her in another?"

"There would be no donjon walls and no gaolers to watch her every movement," William insisted earnestly. "She would be free to marry and have a family and look forward to having her children's children pulling at her skirts. With John, she will have none of those things. Not even the dreams."

Lord Randwulf pursed his lips thoughtfully. If the marshal was serious—and there was no reason to doubt he was not —he was placing the men of Amboise in an extremely awkward position. The dowager would not only resist any attempt to use her granddaughter to control her son's powers, she would never sanction her champion's involvement in any such plot. Conversely, Randwulf was aware of the friendship and affection that had developed between Princess Eleanor and his son over the years, and he knew Eduard well enough to be fairly certain no amount of threat or method of persuasion could convince him to leave this thing alone. Randwulf had practically had to declare open war on France himself in order to keep Eduard in the battle lines and away from Rouen.

"You say she has already been transported to England?" he asked.

"From Cherbourg, aye."

"And taken where?" Eduard demanded.

"I do not know for certain, but from past experience, the best guess would favour a landing at either Lyme or Purbeck. John has used both Bristol and Corfe Castle for his political prisoners in the past, as they represent the most difficult challenges for a rescue or an escape."

"There is also the White Tower, in London," Alaric reminded him. "No one has ever escaped from there."

"True enough," the marshal agreed. "I also considered London, but it might draw attention to her presence in England, and attention is what he will want to avoid at all cost."

"It is what we will want to avoid as well," the Wolf said

darkly, "for all that we are about to commit treason on a rather grand scale."

The marshal's eyes glittered in the candle flame. "Then you agree she must be taken out of his hands and delivered into safer keeping?"

Randwulf glanced over at his son. It was madness to agree. If the men involved were caught or even recognized, their lives would be forfeit. And if an attempt at rescue was made, but failed, not only their lives, but the life of the princess would be taken on the spot.

"Before you answer," the marshal interjected cautiously, "and because I come to you with more boldness than our friendship perhaps warrants, it must be said that the men entrusted with this bounden duty must not be known to the king or to any of his minions. Certes, not well enough for any of them to say to themselves: ahh, there is the Wolf's head we have been waiting so many years to thrust onto a spike. Or"— the piercing gaze shifted from Randwulf to Alaric—"there is the good Friar who would better serve a monastery in hell. Second, the leader must be a man well-enough known to the princess that she would not fear or hesitate to go with him if he should suddenly appear before her." The earl stopped and looked directly at Eduard. "It would be a mission fraught with danger and given slim chance of success."

Since the possibility of *not* aiding in the princess's rescue had never entered his mind, Eduard was able to return the marshal's stare with a creditably hard one of his own. "Allow me to select a few good men, and I will leave at first light."

"You may count me among them," Henry volunteered at once. "I am familiar with both Bristol and Corfe, having spent a drunken fortnight in the one and a miserable month of service in the other."

"Then your help and company will be most welcome," Eduard agreed.

"Aye, and what will the pair of you blundernoses do?" Sparrow asked with a snort. "Prance through the gates of Corfe and inquire if Her Highness is receiving rogues that particular day? You will need to draw a plan, fools. And the plan will have to be looked at this way and that, upside and down, with guts spilled and charted so as to leave nothing to chance. This is no game or gambit to be entered with a righteous toss of plumery and a silvered scarf tied to the lance. This is a few against many, an assault on fortified battlements, with our Little Pearl's delicate white throat poised on the edge of a blade! Leave at first light, will you?" he groused. "Paugh! Go then. And when you are caught circling the castles with your rumps sour with sweat, offer the king's men my fond regards before they put out your eyes and roast your livers over an open fire."

Lord Randwulf gave the chastisement a moment to echo around the small enclave before looking calmly to Alaric. "Friar? A balancing opinion, perhaps? Or a rebuttal against the marshal's assessment of our worth?"

Alaric steepled his hands together on the tabletop, placing the pad of each tapered finger carefully against its opposite. He spared the briefest of glances for the crutches leaning against the wall before he met the Wolf's eyes.

"I think . . . Eduard and Lord Henry have the advantage of speed, if it is needed, and the luxury of noble passion where it is most wanted. In other words, in the time it might take you or I to think of a way to breach a gate, they would be through it and out the other side." Alaric left his unblunted point to sink in and looked at Sparrow. "I also think the lord marshal has not quite finished laying all out before us. I suspect he would not have come to us without a plan, Puck, and for what it may be worth, we should hear it first before consigning anyone's gizzards to a fire pit."

Sparrow snorted again and glared belligerently at the earl.

"I have indeed given the matter much thought," William nodded. "But until recently could not settle on any scheme that did not offer more risks than rewards." He paused and addressed Eduard. "Firstly—is it true you have managed to exchange several communications with the princess in spite of the heavy guard placed around her at Mirebeau and Rouen?"

Eduard saw no reason to deny it. "We have passed a letter or two through the walls."

"Do you think you could pass another through thicker

walls if you were to come within striking distance? And would
she know beyond a doubt the message came from you and no
one else?"

Eduard's eyes narrowed. For over a decade he and Eleanor had communicated by coded letters—a youthful fanciful-
ness they had begun when she had been six and he thirteen
. . . but how had the earl known of this?

The lion-maned palatine smiled faintly. "The young maid
who attends the princess as her personal tiring woman and
companion . . . her name is Marienne, is it not?"

The muscle that tightened across Eduard's jaw was answer enough.

"Many years ago, her mother and I were . . . more than
just friends," the marshal confessed softly. "It seemed to be
the least I could do at the time to see her situated comfortably.
But content yourself; Marienne is a good and loving child. She
has betrayed your secret to no one else but me, and then only
because she has come to love the princess so dearly she is
desperate for some way to save her from a life of captivity and
deprivation. She gave me your name in the strictest confidence
and trust, and it will remain so, locked by the same vow we all
gave as we sat at this table."

"So," said the Wolf, "being unsure of how *I* might react to
your request, you came prepared to ask my son to take advantage of the trust and friendship he and Princess Eleanor have
developed over the years."

William weathered the sarcasm without apology. "I never
had any intention of asking you to risk yourself in this venture.
How could I? John has had a legion of spies watching your
every move for the past ten years. It was you the queen dispatched all those years ago to pay the ransom he demanded for
the princess's safe return the first time his greed and ambition
prompted him to take her hostage. He will assume any attempt
to rescue her now will originate here, at Amboise, and that you
would trust no other man but yourself to such a hazardous
undertaking."

"In this, Lackland shows remarkable insight and intelligence," the Wolf commented dryly.

"He has his moments."

"Even though I am a cripple and a doddering old fool?"

"No one is calling you either," William insisted. "Which is precisely why you must remain here, visible and accessible at all times. Thus, while he debates and ponders and concentrates all of his efforts watching you and waiting for you to come after the princess, he will not have much notice to spare on my niece."

A general stirring occurred around the table as each man wondered at the connection.

"Your niece?" Eduard asked. "What has your niece to do with any of this?"

"As I mentioned earlier, the king has thoughtfully arranged a betrothal between the Lady Ariel and the son of William de Braose. My niece, through terms of her own concocting, has managed to avoid receipt of the charter, but it is only a matter of time before we are required to acknowledge it."

"Ariel will never acknowledge it," Henry insisted. "She will take herself to a nunnery before she agrees to marry the son of a common routier."

Eduard, who was hearing of this proposed union for the first time, temporarily set aside his concerns for the princess and spared a muttered thought for the abbess. "I pity *anyone* who tries to teach her complacency and obedience."

William smiled, causing a faint ruddiness to rise in Eduard's throat as he demonstrated the excellence of his hearing. "I would be the first to agree she is in possession of a high spirit. Nevertheless, she is of my wife's blood and a De Clare, and I do not thank the king for interfering in my family matters."

"You will refuse his command?" Alaric asked.

"Outwardly, no. I intend, in fact, to send her back to England at once to comply with the king's writ . . . in the company of a heavily armed escort, if necessary."

"It will be necessary," Henry murmured bleakly.

"I am counting on it," William assured him.

Sparrow perked instantly. "For in this heavily armed escort . . . ?"

". . . Will be a few handpicked men who will break away at the proper time and . . ."

". . . Pluck our Little Pearl out from under Lack Jack's nose before he even sniffs a plot afoot!" Sparrow finished, puffing his chest with smug delight, pleased to have proved himself beyond worth yet again.

Not all of the conspirators were so smug or so pleased.

"How will you determine where to find the Pearl in order to pluck her?" Alaric asked with a frown, attacking the most obvious weakness.

"I . . . have my own sources of information among the king's equerries," William said carefully. "The right amount of gold in the right hands will buy what we need to know, and in plenty of time for Eduard to make his plans before he embarks from Normandy."

"You predict the destination will either be Corfe or Bristol?"

"Those would be my choices."

"They would be mine too," Alaric admitted honestly, glancing at the Wolf. "For neither are hospitable to strangers and neither open their gates readily to visitors."

"Aah, but they might . . . if they thought those visitors travelled by the king's command, escorting the bride of his choosing to the groom of his choice. Since both castles lie along the route to Radnor, it would not seem unusual for the bridal party to pass by."

"To pass by, aye," Sparrow said, his enthusiasm waning under a puckered frown. "But to breach the gates, pluck the Pearl out of her shell, and make haste away with all heads still attached to shoulders . . . ?" He paused and sucked a stubby finger, clucking his tongue with grave approbation.

"We have one other thing in our favour," the marshal said, leaning forward. "The man assigned to guard the princess is known to me. His name is Brevant and he has a fondness for gold that matches his dislike for the king."

"Neither reason warms my cockles," Sparrow declared.

"Nor can they be counted upon to bear the strain of too close a brush with danger. But even assuming our stout fellows keep their ears and eyes and entrails, where do they go afterwards? Every road pointed back to Normandy will be too hot to tread upon."

"And so thick with the king's men," William agreed calmly, "they will have few to spare on the roads heading north, into Wales."

"Wales?"

"Northern Wales, to be even more precise. Powys. Prince Gwynwynwyn has promised to give Her Highness sanctuary for as long as is necessary. This too fits neatly into the scheme of things, for the Braose lands are in Marcher country; Powys falls in a more or less direct line north and west of Radnor."

Henry clenched his teeth against a curse of exasperation. "I thought you had agreed against delivering Ariel to De Braose?"

"Just so. But the king will not know this until it is too late—hopefully—and she has been safely delivered to the real groom."

"The *real* groom?"

William nodded. "If the plan is agreed upon, I will have the contracts drawn, signed, and dispatched with all haste."

"Dispatched where?" Henry asked, bewildered.

The lord marshal took up the spluttering candle and tilted it so that a pendant of hot wax fell onto the tabletop. "Corfe Castle," he said, drawing an imaginary line beneath it to mark the English coastline. He dripped a second bead directly north and announced, "Bristol." The third drop was placed an equal distance north again, along another quickly sketched impression of the Severn River. "Radnor."

With all eyes following the candle, the next blot of wax splashed due west of Radnor, landing too far south of the region ruled by Gwynwynwyn.

"Snowdonia," the marshal said quietly. "The heart of Gwynedd."

Henry's eyes widened and he looked up at his uncle. "You are not serious."

"I am deadly serious . . . as your sister should have been when she rashly enlisted the rogue's help in the first place. Lord Rhys ap Iorwerth," William explained to those who were still befuddled. "His brother is Llywellyn ap Iorwerth, Prince of Gwynedd, and a staunch ally of King John. He is, in fact, betrothed to John's bastard daughter. And, lest anyone think I have arrived at this decision in haste—or madness—be assured it is not the first time I have considered it. Lord Rhys has impressive holdings in Gwynedd and has the ambition to replace his brother as leader of all the clans. He already rules Cardigan and Deheubarth with the airs of a dark prince and craves nothing better than to strike an alliance with the House of Pembroke through willing and mutually beneficial terms. His younger brother, Lord Dafydd, whom you have already met, has presented Lord Rhys's case most convincingly."

Henry sagged back in his chair. "Ariel may not be so easily convinced, nor am I certain she will see much benefit."

"Was this union not her own suggestion?"

Henry smiled wanly. "I do not think she planned it to go further than just that: a suggestion."

"Then I will *suggest* she look upon it as a choice—a *final* choice between a prince of Wales and a gaoler's son."

Sparrow, who gave less credence to a woman's right to choose a husband than he did a dog's right to choose a flea, tested his patience against more pressing concerns.

"Think you the king will not question the eager bride's timely appearance, or, when he discovers his prisoner has gone a-missing, that he will not add the one's appearance to the other's *dis*appearance and dismiss neither as being coincidence? For that matter, will he not know, by those same eyes and ears who watch my master's every nose-blow, that your niece is here in Normandy with you?"

William spread his hands flat on the table again. "Until the introductions were made shortly before dinner, no one has actually breathed the name De Clare or identified either my niece or nephew by name. Ariel arrived in my camp garbed as a squire and has remained thus until tonight. Therein lies another reason why I have brought her here to Amboise. My own personal guard, I trust with my life. They are loyal to a man and would burn in hell before betraying me or mine. When I leave here, however, I ride for Falaise, and then on to Cherbourg to join the king. I do not want Ariel with me. Waylaying the king's courier was one matter, waylaying the king himself would be another and I doubt very much, once he laid an eye upon her, or suspected she was in my entourage, he would be so easily persuaded to let her go her own way again. Moreover, he would see, by virtue of touching the smallest hair on her head, how he could twist mine own heart within my chest, and it might be he would not send her on to Radnor at all. At the very least, he would assign his own guard to escort her, if and when he thought he had tormented me enough.

"No," he continued determinedly. "She must not stay a moment longer in my company. She must be taken by an entirely different—and secretive—route to the coast, and from there across the Channel to England. Once across, I would again support the utmost secrecy with regards to her whereabouts until and if it becomes necessary to adopt the guise of a bridal cortege. At that time, if they are stopped for any reason, it will appear they are headed in the right direction, following the king's command. As to any coincidences the king may or may not suspect, unless something goes dreadfully awry—and I pray we speak only in terms of supposition now—unless the men involved are captured or killed, the king will have no real proof as to the identity of the thieves. He may suspect. He may *know*. He may even accuse . . . but without proof . . . ?" He shrugged and folded his hands together again. "Further to my hopes, by the time the castle guards finish scouring the niches and crannies of the castle, searching frantically for explanations that might keep them *their* heads, my niece will be well on her way into Wales."

"When she fails to arrive at Radnor?" Alaric asked. "What then?"

William smiled tightly. "The king will be incensed. He will be livid and foaming and threatening to drench the land in blood . . . but again, he will not be able to lift a hand against her—not without risking the dissolution of the treaty he en-

tered with Llywellyn ap Iorwerth. In truth, he will have no
means of knowing when Ariel left Pembroke, or if she had any
knowledge of the writ naming Reginald de Braose as the prospective groom. Since his envoy was waylaid by Lord Rhys, it
might even be argued that it was the Welsh prince alone who
knew of the king's charter and, because he and I were already
discussing terms for my niece's hand, he thought it a fine irony
—with the best romantic intentions, of course—to delay the
writ until he and Ariel were safely wed. This is the story I will
hold to. John will undoubtedly cry false and levy a large fine
for both mine and the Welshman's impudence, but he will do
nothing to risk losing Llywellyn as an ally and opening the
Marches to warfare again."

"Has the Lady Ariel been asked her opinion of any of
this?" Eduard wanted to know.

"I have every faith she will see her duty—and her salvation—and be only too willing to assist in any way she can."

Henry looked dubious and Eduard felt a ridge of tension
forming along his spine. "My lord, your motives are honourable, no question of that, but . . . to knowingly place your
niece in such peril . . . ?"

"My niece has put herself in peril, FitzRandwulf," the
earl declared, blistering the air with a moment of heat. "I am
only trying to find her a way out. If, at the same time, there is
an opportunity for something to be done for Eleanor of Brittany, then we must take the risk. I did not settle upon this plan
lightly. Nor will I be entrusting her into your capable care with
anything less than a blood oath that you will deliver her to
Wales unharmed, untouched, unblemished by so much as a
bruised fingertip. If you are unwilling or unable to promise me
this, then I shall find another who will. I did not say it was of
prime importance to have someone familiar to the princess in
command of this rescue, only that it would ease the way. I
have a score of knights in my own troop who would eagerly
take charge without a single question asked."

Eduard's jaw flexed, the scar again standing out white and
angry on his cheek, but it was the Wolf who responded coolly
and calmly to the earl's challenge.

"Neither my son's abilities nor his willingness is the question here. What worries him—and me—is the state of Lackland's mind and the lengths to which he might go for revenge. You seem confident this Lord Rhys will protect your niece, but who is to say he will not turn his coat and sell the princess back to John in lieu of paying any fine, and well before she can safely cross Gwynedd's lands into Powys? For that matter, there is Gwynwynwyn himself. How do you know you can trust *him*?"

"To answer the first part of your question, Lord Rhys ap Iorwerth will see that marrying my niece with my full knowledge and support will be of far more benefit to him than double-crossing me. And my niece, for her part, will not consent to the marriage until Eleanor is safely ensconced in Powys. To answer the second question, Gwynwynwyn hates John with a passion that has even chilled my blood on occasion. He will safeguard Eleanor if for no other reason than to know he has helped put the English fox's neck in a snare."

"Nor will he overlook the possibility of having one of his sons chosen as her consort," Alaric added wryly.

"I will not deny, he is one of the candidates," William admitted.

Eduard felt another ripple of tension. Eleanor would indeed have to marry, and marry well if she were to pose any kind of threat to her uncle. Gentle, sweet Eleanor. Sadder and more solemn than a princess of eighteen years should have been, she had already suffered immeasurably from her family's political maneuverings. In the past five years alone, she had been betrothed three times to three rulers in exchange for promises of future alliances. Each time she had been supplanted by a more favourable candidate. Here was a proposal for a fourth, and the promise this time was freedom—but freedom to what fate? Eleanor was sunlight and music; Wales was darkness and barbaric clan wars. Could he embark on this rescue only to see her banished to a bleaker prison?

As the Lady Ariel had so tactfully pointed out, he was bastard born and as such should not even dream of a marriage with noble blood, let alone royal. It did not stop him from loving Eleanor, however, or from caring deeply about her happiness—something he could not see her obtaining in the arms of a rutting Welsh bull.

Yet, even as the image took shape in FitzRandwulf's mind, it was not the helplessly pinioned body of the princess he saw being cruelly ravished; it was the flame-haired Lady Ariel de Clare who was crying out in rage and despair, desperately imploring him for help.

Chapter 7

✝ **A**riel could not sleep. She paced the narrow confines of her chamber, her robe gathered tightly around her shoulders, her sandaled feet making soft slapping sounds on the plank flooring. The room was small, located in a tower that abutted the main keep, and cool in spite of the iron brazier full of hot, glowing coals.

There was only one window in her chamber, the embrasure tall and thin in design. The opening was barely the width of a pair of slender shoulders, and so deeply recessed into the wall she had to sit on the stone ledge and crane her neck well forward to see even a portion of the sprawling grounds below. There were wooden shutters affixed to either side, and a woven arras hooked above the window which could be lowered in the winter months to keep out the winds, or in the long days of the summer to keep out the heat and stench from the moat. Tonight the room had been muffled against the threat of an approaching storm, but even though the shutters were a snug fit, the arras moved like a woolen lung, alternately swelling and sucking inward as the wind buffeted the outer walls.

The furnishings offered no relief for her restlessness. A bed, built in the style of the French court, sat on a raised platform and was enclosed in a thick swath of curtains which rose in an elegant twist above the top of the frame. There was a writing table and two chairs, a leather coffer for storing clothes, and a small pallet tucked beneath the bed where a page or maid—neither of whom Ariel had with her at present —could sleep.

A crucifix was hung prominently on one wall, but Ariel had already said her evening prayers and could see no benefit in overtaxing her knees. On another wall, someone had painted a gay profusion of tulips and roses over the whitewashed blocks, but after a while they seemed more of an irritant than a comfort, assuming the shapes of twisted, deformed faces that leered at her on each walk past. A tall, mul-

tibranched candelabra stood by the table, the five thick candle-
sticks blazing lustily in the errant drafts. Someone had sprin-
kled fennel leaves over the coals in an hospitable attempt to
give the chamber a mellow, sweet smell, but Ariel found it
cloying in a room already burdened with the odour of tallow
and cramped tidiness.

She had accompanied Dafydd ap Iorwerth into the gardens after supper, the residue of her anger keeping her warm
as they wandered the well-tended paths of flowers. Most of the
more delicate plants had succumbed to recent days of frost and
cold, but sheltered against the wall, there were indeed several
rosebushes determined to give flowers and buds.

There had been no moonlight to speak of, only hints of
light here and there through the thickening banks of cloud.
The promise of a storm had grown stronger on every gust of
wind that swirled over the top of the stone walls. Dried leaves
rushed across the cobbled path at every footstep; the air tasted
metallic with the threat of thunder and rain.

Normally she loved stormy weather. It suited her temperament somehow to watch all that power and fury unleashed in
a limitless sky. Once, as a child, she had been caught out-of-
doors during an especially violent display of God's wrath, but
far from being terrified by the experience, the brilliance and
ominous beauty exhilarated her to the point where she still
stood before an open window during a storm, hoping to recap-
ture the excitement.

Dafydd ap Iorwerth had not been so enthralled by the
elements. He kept glancing upward, as if he expected demons
and dragons to appear in the sky above him. Ariel, as hard as
she tried not to, was growing almost fond of the young Welshman. He was well mannered (in comparison to most other
Welsh barbarians) and quiet. He was shy to the point where
Ariel had amused herself by seeing how many times she could
raise a blush on his face. He spoke enthusiastically of Wales,
leading Ariel to believe he was more comfortable in his dark
forests and misty mountains than he was in the bustle of a
civilized town or city. He spoke eloquently of his homeland
and ancestors and agreed, with no reservations whatsoever,

that the Welsh were a violent race—but with good reason. Generations had been raised on blood and warfare, fighting for their freedom against the Saxons first, and then with the arrogant Normans, with whom they still battled to keep their identity. He recounted stories of villages and crofts where the forests were known to stir and rumble at night as the ghost of their great king, Arthur Pendragon, gathered a new army around him, anticipating the day when England would falter to its knees and be ripe for conquest. And, with the lords of Gwynedd being direct descendants of Pendragon, it stood to reason they should always be prepared to take up the call to arms.

Ariel had listened to most of this with a gently arched brow, but the young prince was so earnest and so intense, it was difficult to mock him openly. It was not so difficult to assume a wary guise when he spoke of his brother Rhys, for she sensed there was more he did not tell her than what he did. She fully expected to hear he was the bravest, boldest, most feared knight in all of Wales, but at the same time, she could not help wondering why young Dafydd's eyes could not hold hers for any measurable length of time while he extolled these endless virtues, or why his voice seemed flat and lacking any real conviction.

Conversely, with the scent of winter roses swirling on the currents of a rising storm, the Welsh prince could barely contain his enthusiasm for the bold knights who dwelled in Château d'Amboise.

"Did you know, my lady, the Wolf fought a real dragon, one with glowing red eyes and a forked tongue that spat fire?"

"His brother, was it not? Did you never think your own kin had serpentine qualities when you were young?"

"Your pardon, my lady?"

"Never mind," she sighed. " 'Twas only a jest."

"Only a jest?" he repeated in some awe. "To be in the presence of such men? I was not fully convinced they were even *real* much less that your uncle would bring us here to meet them."

Ariel's polite smile had launched him into another tale he

had thought was a figment of some bard's imagination, but she
was only half-listening. Her uncle had ridden a day and a night
out of his way to seek the ear of Lord Randwulf de la Seyne
Sur Mer and Ariel's curiosity had been kept at a peak to know
why. Henry, normally as malleable as clay in her hands, had
been displaying an unusual ability to avoid answering her
questions, and, since being advised of the earl's decision to
visit Amboise, had taken care not to be caught alone with her.

It could be nothing, or it could be something. But if the
something had anything to do with her, she wanted to know.
She had a right to know, did she not? Especially if any of these
secrets and meetings involved her or her future.

Returned to her room, sequestered with her thoughts and
her privacy, no amount of pacing seemed to provide any logical
answers. The closeness of the walls and the staleness of the air
seemed also to hamper her ability to breathe, and after a futile
struggle with the heavy arras, she snatched her mantle off the
edge of the bed and climbed the spiral stone staircase to the
rooftop. She had to wrestle a moment with the unfamiliar latch
of the trap-door, but with the aid of a timely gust of wind, she
was able to fling it open and step out into the rush of bitingly
fresh air.

Her hair, unfettered by braid or wimple, blew forward, a
mass of tumbled waves that blinded her for as long as it took to
sweep back the escaped curls and tuck them more securely
beneath her hood. The air was cold and sharp, tainted with the
slightly earthy tang of dampness and stone. Clouds were racing
across the sky, their underbellies blue-white and roiling. The
light was weak and murky, doing little to alleviate the ghostly
shadows thrown by the ramparts.

No sentries were posted on this section of the roof; none
were necessary. Ariel's tower adjoined the section of the keep
that faced out over a sheer drop of jagged rocks that spilled
over the banks of the river Loire below. There were no windows on this side of the keep, no handholds, no toeholds, not
even a postern gate at the base of the mighty stone walls. Only
a fool or a goat would attempt an assault from the river, and
then, because there were a dozen other towers and barbicans

affording a breathtakingly clear view of all the surrounding lands in the valley, the warning would be given long before an enemy could begin to conquer the turbulent currents of the river.

The Wolf had displayed a keen eye for defense and privacy when he had chosen Amboise as his reward for serving the dowager queen. The village, hugging the shadow of the castle's fortifications, would have no cause to worry after the safety of its inhabitants. Once locked inside these walls, a warlord and all of his retainers could withstand a siege lasting many months and mete out more damage than they would sustain.

Ariel bundled her woolen mantle tighter around her shoulders and followed the ramparts around and down onto the broad, flat roof of the keep. As she passed each square-toothed crenel of stone, the wind sheared through the gap, tearing more strands of her hair free from the hood. The moon appeared briefly, and if she had not been distracted by a rough cobble underfoot, she might have noticed the second figure sharing the blustery solitude of the rooftops. She might have seen him make an abrupt halt in his own circuit of the ramparts and melt into the blackness of the parapet in the hopes of avoiding notice altogether.

Eduard recognized the cloaked and hooded figure at once. The long streamers of fiery red hair had been bleached by the eerie light to a dull coppery sheen, but there could be no further chance of mistaking Lady Ariel de Clare for a common serving wench.

Eduard watched her haphazard approach, noting the way she paused here and there to peer out over the stone parapet, or the way she turned against the force of the wind to give chase to the escaping tendrils of her hair. Once the wind caused her mantle to bell out behind her and he was given a filmy white view of the linen blanchet she wore beneath.

He leaned against the stone blocks and wondered again at the wisdom of using her as a shield for their activities. He wondered even more at Lord Henry's obvious discomfort with the situation—a discomfort that was not, he suspected, caused entirely out of fear for her actual safety, but more for her temper, obstinance, and single-mindedness.

Sparrow had been the least reluctant to point out that, if caught in any compromising positions, most women were wont to reveal far more information than any casual questions warranted. In fact, they tended to chatter on and on like magpies until the head ached and the fingers longed to throttle. Both Henry and the lord marshal had come to Lady Ariel's defense on the charges of chattering and revealing, but they seemed generally and uncomfortably to agree that she had a mind of her own and would not hesitate to plague them with arguments, suggestions, even conditions against her participation in any adventure, regardless of the possible perils.

Not exactly an encouraging testament from either brother or uncle.

As for Eduard's opinion of women . . . ? With very few exceptions, he considered them to be cold-hearted, lightheaded, and ruthlessly conniving when it came to furthering their own ambitions. Wealth, influence, and power were what put smiles on their faces; greed and a shrewd sense of survival were the prerequisites that put them in the beds of men they might otherwise shun like lepers . . . or bastards.

Most tended to share Lady Ariel's opinion of bastards and rarely saw any advantage in marrying one, regardless of whose by-blow he might be. Eduard, in no particularly frenzied haste to bind himself to a wife and breed fine "respectable" sons to succeed him, saw no reason to expend any untoward effort in changing their minds. He was not averse to finding himself in the bed of some noble beauty—he was usually given a flurry of invitations to do so after each display of his talents on a jousting field. It amused him to display his talents elsewhere, and to leave those same beauties decrying the lack in their own husband's skills. For the most part, however, he preferred to keep his distance from the nobility. It suited him to have women like Gabrielle, who made no demands on his time or affections. Most of all, it suited him to have emotional ties to none but his family . . . and Eleanor.

Eleanor of Brittany was a beauty among beauties, chaste in body and spirit. A fragile heart who could not find it in her soul to think evil of anyone. Not her mother Constance, who had urged Arthur to form the ill-fated alliance with France; not Philip, who had betrothed her to his son, the Dauphin, only to renege when it seemed likely Arthur's quest for the throne would fail. She had not even seen the madness in Arthur's plan to attack Mirebeau, or the insanity of accompanying him, knowing . . . *knowing* that failure—and it was inevitable he would fail—would mean imprisonment and possibly death.

Standing in the Wolf's war pavillion, with the torchlights flickering over the proud features of the last true Plantagenet prince and princess, Lord Randwulf had tried speaking to her like the father she did not have. He had advised her to come away with him and wait to see how the king's mood would swing. For Arthur, there had been no such option, but for Eleanor, there had been a chance to get away, protected by the might and sword of Amboise. Randwulf had left Eduard to talk to her, to try to convince her of the folly of remaining a brave front by her brother's side, but she had only smiled and pressed herself into the comforting arms of his friendship, and assured him she was not afraid. It was her duty and her honour to remain with Arthur, to give him what strength she could to see him through the humiliation of renouncing his claim forever.

Eduard's hands had been tied. He had watched Eleanor and Arthur led away and he had been unable to help either one of them. Now, however, with proof her uncle was breaking his word by taking her back to England to remain his prisoner indefinitely, with or without the marshal's sanction, Eduard would have gone after her. Without or without the cooperation of the marshal's niece, he was going to free Eleanor and, Lord Gwynwynwyn of Powys be damned, he was going to bring her back home to Brittany.

The wind gusted and Ariel's footsteps slowed again. She turned her head slightly and stood as still as a statue, so close to Eduard FitzRandwulf that a long stride would have put her within arm's reach. The same husky, masculine scent that had swamped her senses throughout the evening meal came to her now; the scent of woodsmoke and leather and crisp wintery sunshine.

Startled to discover she was not alone on the rooftop, and increasingly certain of the identity of the interloper, Ariel fought a sudden urge to turn and flee back to the safety of her cramped bedchamber. She fought it and conquered it, forcing herself to stand calmly in the whirling breezes, her eyes searching the midnight shadows until she located a shape that was not a part of the wall.

"Is it always your custom, sirrah, to spy from crevices and darkened hallways?"

Lightning flashed overhead, giving brief substance to the niche where Eduard stood. His shoulder was against the wall, one of his booted feet was raised and propped on a wooden joist that protruded from the mortar. He returned her stare impassively, looking anything but chagrined or embarrassed.

"Is it always *your* custom to wander where you are not invited?"

Ariel bristled at the wry retort. She was doing nothing wrong, breaching no protocol. Surely she needed no one's permission to seek a breath of fresh air. "Are the rooftops private, then? If so, the doors should have been barred and a guard placed at the exit."

"I somehow doubt that would have held you," he murmured.

Ariel could not see him clearly through the gloom, but she caught the dull glint of the sword he wore at his hip, and of the buckles and studs that ornamented his surcoat. His hair was curled forward over his cheeks and throat like strokes of black ink; he looked dark and dangerous and none too concerned to find her alone on a stormy rooftop.

He shifted forward suddenly, straightening from the wall, and Ariel was startled into taking a step back, a reaction that brought forth a weary sigh from the shadows.

"My lady . . . is it possible we started out on the wrong

footing this afternoon? Can you have imagined me to be more of an enemy than I am?"

It was possible, Ariel conceded. But not probable. He had mocked her and made her the brunt of his amusement. He had grabbed her and laid his lecherous hands on her, begging her pardon only upon learning her identity. He was obviously accustomed to having his attentions returned eagerly by every wench who took his fancy, tumbling them at will or want.

On the other hand . . .

On the other hand, had they met for the first time in the great hall, would she have been so hasty to read insolence and sarcasm behind each glance or action? Would she have baited him at every turn of phrase? Or deliberately provoked him into returning her every barb and insult in kind?

Had she first met this brooding, dark-haired knight in the bustling atmosphere of the great hall, with his pewter gray eyes and heart-ravaging smile, would she not have taken his solicitousness at the meal table as flattery?

Ariel chewed thoughtfully on her lip. "You are right, Sir Knight. Perhaps I was somewhat rude this evening—with good cause, though, you will admit. 'Tis not often I am groped and fondled by a complete stranger."

He bowed slightly. "I assure you, Lady Ariel, 'tis not normally my habit to grope *or* fondle without invitation."

"Well . . . I suppose I *should* apologize for being in the armoury. I . . . took a wrong turn and simply followed the light."

"An understandable error."

"And since I was there, I did not think there would be any harm in looking."

"None whatsoever," he agreed. "In truth, those were my very sentiments. I might not have even intruded had you not tried to slice off my leg with a targe."

"It was an accident."

"So it was, and no harm done."

Ariel regarded him narrowly. Was he mocking her again? He was certainly waiting for whatever gem might fall next from her lips and she looked up at the sky, over the ramparts towards the river, anywhere but up into his face.

"I . . . could not sleep and thought a walk might tire me. I suppose, with the rain feeling so close, I should return now."

Without waiting for his reply she started to retrace her steps and was startled again to hear his long strides drawing him abreast.

"I confess I was surprised to see anyone else venturing forth in this weather, and at such a late hour. Is your room not to your liking?"

"The room is fine," she said quickly. "As to the weather, I enjoy stormy skies. Tonight especially, it . . . suits my mood."

"Ahh. Yes. Your uncle did mention you were a little out of sorts with the entire world these days."

She stopped so suddenly the hem of her mantle creamed around her ankles, and Eduard carried forward several more steps before noticing he walked alone.

"So. He discussed me, did he?"

FitzRandwulf bought an awkward moment of respite by walking back to her side. "He . . . mentioned why you were here, in Normandy. That you were not pleased with the king's writ."

Ariel planted her hands on her waist. "He discussed my *marriage* with you?"

"Only in passing. And only by way of explaining why you are here, defying the king's decree."

"I am not defying him. I am refusing him."

"You are not pleased with his choice of husbands?"

"Not pleased? *Not pleased*?" She held her temper in check with a visible effort. "Why, I am delirious with joy. Why should I not be? Marriage to a gaoler's son—a rough-handed, large-nosed, bull-legged churl with the manners and odour of a wild boar—" She smiled sweetly. "How could I be anything but *blissfully* delighted with my sovereign's keen interest in my future happiness?"

Eduard hid his own smile even though he doubted she could see it. "I gather you have met the happy groom?"

"I certainly have not," she snapped. "Nor have I any intentions of doing so."

"Not even if the king commands it?"

"Not even if the king takes me by the heels and drags me to an audience!"

"Are you not worried your refusal might put your uncle in a worrisome position?"

Ariel whirled around and glared over the parapet, her hands small and white where they gripped the stone casement. "My uncle is the Marshal of England. He is accustomed to being in worrisome positions. I cannot believe *for one instant* he would take the king's defense over mine."

"He may not have a choice in the matter," Eduard offered gently.

"My uncle has never lacked for choices. Nor has he ever backed away from John Softsword in fear. Did you know"— she turned and confronted Eduard with a sparkle of pride in her eyes—"the king once dared to question my uncle's loyalty before the court. *My uncle*! The man who made him king! And when my lord marshal demanded the Plantagenet usurper settle the matter by sword . . . not one of John's so-called *champions* dared to pick up the gauntlet. Nay, they all turned their faces and lowered their eyes, and their knees made such a knocking sound in the audience chamber, the king had to shout his recantation to have it heard above the din."

Ariel lifted her chin and presented her shoulder to Eduard again. "When I marry, it will not be to some bung-nosed, sin-born gaoler's son. It will be to an earl, at the very least! A landed baron, a palatine of equal or greater rank than my uncle."

Eduard chose not to remind her of his own sin-born heritage, but he could not resist mentioning, "A Welsh prince, perhaps?"

"Saints sieze me!" she cried, whirling on him once more. "Was there nothing about me that went undiscussed?"

Eduard hesitated, knowing it was neither his place nor his desire to reveal her uncle's intentions. "I am certain the earl mentioned it only because he thought you found the prince a more deserving match than the son of a . . . a common routier.''

Ariel watched his mouth form the words. He was out of the shadows now and she could see his features much more clearly. It was a fascinating mouth, full in shape and rather more sensual sculpted by the stormy half-light. Further tricks of the uncertain sky drew her eye to the vertical cleft that divided the strong chin, and to the absurdly long lashes any woman would have drawn teeth to possess. Indeed, it was a shame about the scar. Without it . . . or even with it . . .

She looked abruptly away and swallowed hard. "Anything would be preferable to a gaoler's son, but yes, I did suggest to my uncle that Lord Rhys ap Iorwerth would be more acceptable. He was''—she curled the fleshy pad of her lip between her teeth and made a hasty correction—"he *is* certainly my first choice amongst the many suitors my aunt and uncle have proposed. He is handsome. Charming. A prince, for mercy's sake.''

"The husband of every maiden's dreams," he concluded wryly.

Ariel's jaw snapped shut. "The thought amuses you, does it?''

"My lady?''

"The notion of my marrying a prince," she said tautly, glaring up at him. "You find it laughable?''

"I am not laughing.''

"But you do have an opinion.''

"My opinion, my lady"—he paused and watched a lick of shiny red hair blow across the lush pout of her lips—"is that I have no opinions whatsoever when it comes to marriage. Only that I would be content unto death to remain well out of it.''

"You have no lady love?''

"No.''

"Never craved one?''

"The very notion of craving a wife—''

"I did not say wife, I said lady love. Have you never been in love?''

"Craving . . . and loving . . . are two entirely different

matters," he said, wondering how the devil he had become trapped in this conversation. "Neither of which, I am happy to recount, have plagued me to the point of sleeplessness."

His answer was sharp and perfunctory, meant to discourage any further probings. Naturally, it had the opposite effect on Ariel and she had to stop herself from openly speculating on what kind of woman would earn the affections of this scarred, enigmatic knight. He was a bastard, true enough, but there were many households where five and six daughters needed husbands, where the youngest and least dowered would look only too readily on a union with the D'Amboise name. Had his aim been too high, perhaps? Was it the reverse of her own situation, where she, being of noble blood, would not be expected to marry below the salt, regardless if the groom was selected by the king or by the pope himself?

She sighed, the importance of Eduard's situation, real or imagined, being supplanted by the desperation of her own.

"I suppose I am partly to blame for what has happened," she said miserably. "I should have heeded my aunt's advice and paid more serious attention to the parade of suitors who have called at Pembroke. There have been so many," she added sardonically, " 'tis a certainty more than a few would have passing acquaintance with the king. Perhaps . . . I should have made myself so horribly unappealing, no man would have taken an interest in me. No man would have touched me, through craving *or* loving."

As if on cue, a long, silky strand of her hair escaped her hood and slithered past his cheek. It was very shiny and very metallic, also the only thing about her that retained any colour other than blue or black. As he reached up to disentangle it from his shoulder and sleeve, he remembered all too vividly how it had looked that afternoon—a crushing abundance of pure flame, red and gold. Unlike anything he had ever seen before.

Unlike anything he imagined he would see again.

Thus distracted, he was taking so long to offer the expected and chivalrous reassurances that nothing she could do short of boiling her face in oil and studding it with iron spikes could render a man anything less than speechless with her beauty, she was forced to glare up at him again.

"Unless, of course," she said in a brittle voice, "I am already so ugly I should *expect* nothing better than a gaoler's son?"

Eduard met the dark sparkle of her eyes. "I hardly think you need fear that, my lady."

"Do you not? Was that why you thought to steal a kiss from me earlier today . . . because you thought me to be so *beautiful*?"

Beautiful, Eduard mused. Half-naked. Delectably defiant. A grin pulled at his mouth as he considered all of these reasons. "In truth, I might have thought to steal more than one had you not put me in my proper place."

Now she *knew* he was mocking her, and Ariel felt the heat rise in her blood. "Just because you have been put in your place . . . does this mean you no longer find me desirable?"

Eduard's gaze roved over the shape of her face, lingering on the full, pouting lips before sliding lower. The swirling wind grasped at the opportunity for mischief and swept the hood of her mantle off her head and sent the fluttering wings of wool ballooning out behind her. The blanchet she wore beneath was pale and shapeless, but the wind molded it to her body like water, and the linen glowed almost silver in the glowering light. A second gust filled the air with long, rippling drifts of her hair. It clouded her face and shoulders; sleek, curling ribbons of it were flung across the gap between them, the strands clinging to his shoulders, tangling with his own dark mane.

Despite his opinion of her being a spoiled, sharp-tongued brat who deserved to be bound to a dung collector to learn humility, Eduard could not in all honesty deny the response she aroused in his body. She *was* a beauty, and he was no monk. His blood began to flow slowly and sluggishly, just as it did in the still moments before a battle. There was a heaviness in the pit of his belly, an expanding and swelling that not only took him by surprise, but prompted him to step forward, not back, and to meet the bright challenge in her eyes.

• He lifted his hands and caught two slippery fistfuls of her hair, gathering them back out of the wind, trapping them at the nape of her neck.

"Would you *like* me to find you desirable?" he inquired softly.

Ariel's mouth dropped open. An odd, giddy rush of hot blood flooded her limbs as she found herself staring up into eyes as dark and turbulent as the sky overhead.

"I . . . want nothing from you, sirrah," she managed to whisper.

Thunder cracked overhead and Eduard used the brief distraction to rake his hands deeper into the glory of those copper curls, twining them around his fists so that she was forced to arch her neck back and to press her body closer to his.

Ariel was startled by the contact, stunned by the bold intimation of his hands and body. She tried to turn her head, to wrest it out of his grip, but he held firm. He crowded her even closer to the battlements, his torso an immense, overpowering wall of muscle, his mouth a cruel torment that offered no compromise.

"You want nothing at all?" he murmured. "Not even a reason to prove me more of a bastard than I am?"

Ariel gasped but his head was already bending forward. His mouth, surprisingly warm and supple, brushed over hers, taunting her with the promise of further outrages to come. She gasped again, intending to rail him for his audacity, but before a word or breath could be uttered, her lips were no longer being merely brushed, no longer being taunted. They were being devoured, possessed, ravished by a mouth that was suddenly as ruthless and arrogant as the man himself.

There was a moment—a brief moment, she reflected afterwards—when she could, conceivably, have stopped him. It came halfway between a cry and a disbelieving whimper, when he lifted his head and stared down at her, fully expecting some violent display of indignation. In truth, her eyes were stretched wide with that very sentiment and her lips trembled with wordless condemnation . . . but it was her hands, freed from entrapment against his chest that forfeited any thought of reprieve. They climbed higher onto his shoulders and instead of raking bloody tracks into his face and throat, laced together at the back of his neck and invited his mouth to descend again, this time to slant with even more ferocity over hers.

Ever gallant, Eduard obliged. His arms tightened around her and his tongue thrust demandingly into the moist, silken recesses of her mouth. He thrust again, deeper and more determinedly, and he could feel her knees buckling with the shock of such lusty intrusions.

Ariel was no stranger to the act of kissing; kisses of peace were exchanged frequently in greeting her uncle's vassals and liegemen. But they were polite, chaste gestures, rarely given on the lips, and never openmouthed and devouring. Up until now, a kiss had held little more import than the touching of hands. It had never commanded the focus of her entire body. It had never caused her skin to constrict in the most alarming ways and places, never set her breasts tingling and her stomach churning, or spread such a welter of liquid heat *everywhere*.

A scalding wave of it coursed through her limbs causing her to clutch at the folds of his mantle. His tongue was lashing hers with slow, evocative strokes. Her hair had scattered in the wind and was wrapping them both in a sleek, slippery cocoon. Another ragged groan greeted the pressure of his hands as he cradled her hips and pulled them suggestively against his own, introducing her to yet another shocking aspect of his boldness. He was all heat and hard, virile muscles, and she wondered if this was what her aunt had meant when she said a man could sometimes do things to a woman that would render her senseless and without a will of her own.

She *was* without will. She *was* without senses and he could have taken shameless advantage of her helplessness and she would not have known how to stop him.

Reluctantly, grudgingly, Eduard stopped himself.

How, by Christ's blood, he did not know. He had not expected to be left palsied with the tremors of an eager youthling. He had not anticipated she would taste so sweet and hot and needful, or that his flesh would ache with lust for a woman he had scorned only moments before.

He moved her to arm's length and struggled to see past the thundering rush of blood in his temples. Her lips, swollen and wet from his assault, quivered slightly as she took quick, shallow breaths to steady her own pounding confusion, and he wondered if she was going to be foolish enough to ask him again if he found her desirable.

Drops of rain, fat as pendants, began to splatter the walls and turrets around them. Cold splashes of reality broke the spell and Ariel stumbled back another step . . . and another.

"If you have no more questions to ask of me, my lady, I would suggest you return to your chambers."

Ariel blinked away a heavy splash of rain and stared as a jagged fork of lightning sheared across the sky, fleeting and bright, throwing the terrible chiselled beauty of his scarred face into sharp relief. His hair lay dark against his throat, his eyes glittered with an unholy brilliance that seemed to draw the very breath from her body. Towering before her he looked like a demon. He *was* a demon, black to the soul, cunning and sly. Devious to the heart, mocking her with words and deeds.

"I cannot imagine myself asking another solitary thing of you," she gasped, her lips throbbing so badly she could barely form the words. "Except perhaps that you never make it necessary for me to have to look upon your face again!"

"Would that I could oblige you, my lady, for I would do so with the greatest pleasure. I fear it will be quite impossible, however, for your uncle has asked me to personally escort your party back to England and deliver you safely into the hands of your betrothed."

Ariel reacted as if she had been struck. "You lie! He has done no such thing!"

"You will doubtless hear it from his own lips in the morning."

Ariel shook her head. "You lie. *You lie!*"

A bolt of lightning cracked the sky wide open. The rain began to come down in solid sheets, blurring Ariel's form as she turned and fled along the ramparts. Eduard could only stand and watch. His body was coiled as tightly as a spring; a step would shatter the tension and release the pressure like a quarrel shot from a crossbow.

He turned his face up into the full force of the rain, hoping the icy needles would cool the heat of his blood. It had been a stupid, mindless mistake to touch her, for no other reason than she belonged to someone else. To her Welsh prince. A man with noble bloodlines, untainted by the sins of the past.

A sudden thought startled a laugh out of him and Eduard opened his eyes.

He had told her he was delivering her to her groom, but he had not identified the groom by name. No doubt she was thinking her uncle had chosen to bow to the king's command and was dispatching her, under heavy escort, to Radnor and Reginald de Braose.

No doubt as well she would assume the omission had been deliberate on his part. It would set her temper on fire all over again and she would feel twice the need to seek revenge. And perhaps that would be a good thing for both of them. Perhaps it was for the best, for he had the distinct feeling he would be safer dealing with her anger than with soft green eyes and a lush, pouting mouth.

Chapter 8

✝ **A**riel launched herself through the trap-door and flew down the stairwell, unmindful of her hair and cloak snagging on the rough stone walls. She passed through her chamber in a furious blur and swept on down the main spiral of tower stairs, her damp footsteps slapping each riser in angry haste. Her uncle's chamber was on the floor below hers and she barged through the outer door, startling a page into leaping out of his sleeping-cot as she blew past. The crash of the inner oak door sent her uncle's ancient squire scrambling for his sword; the dramatic flinging aside of the closed bed curtains brought the marshal bolt upright and groping for weapons that were not there.

Ariel stood at the side of the bed, her arms spread wide beneath the folds of her mantle, her fists clutching the panels of curtain. Raindrops sparkled in her hair causing it to glitter like a halo in the light of the single candle left burning at the bedside. The candle was meant to foil evil spirits and keep the devil away, but as Lord William knuckled the sleep out of his eyes and stared at the bat-winged spectre hovering over him, his first wild thought was that the charm had somehow failed.

"I have come to give you fair warning, Uncle," Ariel declared, her breasts heaving, her cheeks flushed from running. "I will not marry the lout. I will not even return to England if that is to be my fate, and if you try to force me, I will climb to the highest turret of this accursed castle and throw myself from the peak!"

"Ariel? Plague take me, girl . . . what is the hour?"

"It is late," she snapped. "Far too late to offer apologies or excuses. I *trusted* you. I came to you because I loved and trusted you as I have always loved and trusted you!"

William, whose habit was to sleep naked, drew the blankets up over his belly. His chest was a mass of knotted muscles and swarming gray hairs, the latter frothing like a covering of fresh snow in the candlelight.

"Sit you down, girl . . . no! Fetch a stoup of wine first; my mouth tastes like a farrier's bib."

Ariel thought his eyelids looked polished and heavy enough from drink, and she told him so under her breath as she walked over to the bedside table and poured a measure of wine from the standing ewer. She could hear him grumbling as he pulled on his bliaut and braies, and ordering his man— Tinker, who was almost as old as the marshal and far from being in the blush of his squiring days—to fetch a mantle for warmth.

Ariel drained the goblet of wine she had poured, bracing herself for the fiery thrill as it coursed down her throat. The strength of it brought a sting to her eyes and caused her to reach out and grasp the tabletop for support, but she weathered the dizzying rush and hastened to pour her uncle another goblet full before he emerged from behind the bed curtains.

He scowled at the fire in passing as if to confirm, by its life and brilliance, that he had not had his head to the pillow long. The men had spent several hours debating strategies and schemes, seeking weaknesses and trying to anticipate problems in the plan to rescue the princess. When the candles had melted into puddles and several flagons of ale had been emptied, they had decided to adjourn and meet again on the morrow with clear heads and fresh thoughts . . . which would hopefully have been encouraged by a few hours' sleep.

"Could you not have waited until morning to give poor Tinker cause to think his heart had stopped?"

"No," she said adamantly. "I could not."

William grunted and eased his big body into a chair. He waved for her to bring him the wine and indulged in several deep swallows as he peered at her over the rim. She looked like a wild woman, one of the Welsh Furies who were said to roam the barren, rocky coastline in search of souls to steal. Her hair fell in damp spirals over her shoulders, and her face . . . something was odd about her face.

"Where have you been this late of an hour and who have you been talking to with such fine results?"

"I have been on the roof, seeking air, and I have been talking to the Bastard, FitzRandwulf."

"FitzRandwulf? What has he said to twist your nose into such a knot?"

"He said"—she plumped her hands on her hips and glared down at him like an avenging angel—"you have charged him with the task of delivering me back to England, *back into the arms of my betrothed.*"

William took another mouthful of wine. "And so I have. He looks a capable enough fellow. Together with your brother, they should manage not to lose you."

"Lose me? *Lose me?*"

William winced. "Must you shout, Niece? My head aches enough as it is."

Ariel whirled, paced to the far wall, then paced back. "Aye, it appears I *must* shout if I am to make myself heard. Uncle! How can you send me back knowing what waits in store?"

"What waits in store if I do not? Setting aside the fact that the king does not take kindly to blatant acts of rebellion, you are eighteen years old—almost nineteen! You should have been wed half a dozen years ago. Would have been, by Christ, had I only listened to your aunt. You have rejected too many offers to recount, for too many reasons too flimsy to support the weight of a feather. No, you are long overdue for a husband, whether he be of your choosing, the king's, or *mine.*"

"You support this match?" she asked in disbelief.

"It may not be one I would have actively sought had I the luxury of your time and fastidiousness, but it is a good one. The man has lands and wealth and ambition enough to support you in a comfortable fashion. Nor will he suffer for his brother being in the king's favour. Lord Rhys will make you a fine husband and breed on you fine, handsome children. Now, be a good niece and fetch more wine."

Ariel moved by reflex and was almost to the opposite side of the room before the name of the prospective groom cut through the barrage of arguments fomenting on her tongue.

She stopped cold and stared at her uncle. "Did you say
. . . Lord Rhys?"

"Rhys ap Iorwerth. Is he not the scoundrel with whom
you made your devil's pact?"

"Well . . . yes . . . but . . ."

"Is he not, as a prince in the house of Gwynedd, a suitable
enough match for your noble tastes and temperaments?"

"Yes, but—"

William sighed. "And did you yourself not promise the
man consideration in exchange for his assistance in waylaying
the king's messenger? Did you not, in fact, *suggest* it?"

"I . . . offered to lay the matter before you, but—"

"But what, Niece?" William's blue eyes reflected the
flames burning in the hearth. "Are you in the habit of making
willy-nilly offers to powerful men in exchange for treasonous
favours? Or can it be you have changed your mind again and
would prefer to warm the bed of this . . . Reginald de
Braose?"

"*No*! No, I have not changed my mind. It is just that I
thought . . . I mean, when FitzRandwulf told me you were
sending me back to England . . ."

"Yes?"

Ariel curled her lip between her teeth and bit down hard.
The wine was making her head swim. The sudden, close heat
in the chamber was causing her cloak to steam and taint the air
with the smell of damp wool.

"He neglected to mention the name of the intended
groom," she said in a quietly ominous voice.

"Did he now," William grunted. "Perhaps it slipped his
mind."

Ariel flushed and continued to the bedside table. Reaching for the ewer, her grip tightened around the pewter neck
until her knuckles glowed white. Oh, the arrogance and treachery of the man! The smug, insufferable gall of the lout to enjoy
such a grandiose jest at her expense! *Slipped his mind*? Not for a
moment. And not for a moment would she believe it was not
another deliberate attempt to humiliate her!

She muttered an oath of contempt and raised her hand,

scrubbing the back of it across her mouth as if she could wipe away the memory of his lips. He had probably been laughing all the while he was kissing her. All the while he was kissing her *and* laying his lecherous hands on her body!

"What else did FitzRandwulf tell you?" William asked mildly.

"What?"

The earl was taken aback by her sharpness. "FitzRandwulf . . . was that all he told you of our discussions tonight? That he and your brother were escorting you back to Wales?"

"What else was he supposed to tell me?" she demanded irritably. "That he would be acting as groomsman to Lord Rhys? Or as a witness in our bridal chamber? Or perhaps that he has a bride of his own waiting for him in Wales—more's the pity to her, poor thing."

William uttered a word of thanks as she refilled his goblet, but made no immediate move to lift it to his lips. Instead, he cosseted the vessel in his hands and stared down at the reflective surface of the blood red wine, his thoughts tumbling faster than a jongleur at a fair.

Why not? Why not leave Ariel in ignorance of their true purpose until and unless it became absolutely necessary to enlighten her? He had supposed he would have to tell her if only to convince her to return peaceably to England. But if she was accepting this Welsh prince readily enough—and it appeared she was—there was no pressing need to tell her anything about the princess or the danger or the risks to them all if a word should slip by accident into the wrong ear.

There was no question in his mind but that she would keep a secret unto the death if it was asked of her—especially one of this magnitude—but if she was blissfully unaware of any secrets that needed keeping . . . would she not act more normal on the journey? There would be enough spice to satisfy her quest for adventure if she believed she was outmaneuvering the king by having Snowdonia as her final destination and not Radnor.

"Uncle . . . ?"

He looked up and realized he must have been staring at

his wine for some time without hearing what she was saying. Before he could bring his thoughts back in proper focus again, they took another unsettling leap—to Pembroke this time. To the face of another whose safety was being placed in jeopardy without her knowledge or consent.

Sweet Isabella. Ariel had inherited her aunt's delicate features and lithe, coltish body. If not for the flame red hair and dragon green eyes of a De Clare throwback, it might have been his dear wife dropping to her knees in front of him. Verily, it might have been Isabella moistening her lips and gazing up at him with a wistful smile that said, *give me but a moment to explain the foolishness of the world and you will see that my way is the only way*.

William held his own smile in check but braced himself anyway.

"Uncle . . . I know I have been a great deal of trouble to you over the years." She halted in anticipation of a denial, and when one was not forthcoming, she frowned and continued as if it had. "You must also know that none of it was due to a need to be *truly* willful or troublesome. If I have not picked a husband before now, it is because none of them have measured by half the fine example you have set before me. You call it being contrary and fastidious; I call it unfair that I should have to settle for someone not as strong, as bold, as kind, as loving, as honourable as my own Uncle Will."

He could feel himself starting to curl around her little finger and took refuge in another draught of wine.

"Indeed," she continued, "you have always treated Henry and me as if we had sprung from your own seed."

"I am glad to hear it. I would not want to think I had been so mean and overbearing as to rouse feelings of vindictiveness in either of you."

"We would do nothing . . . *nothing* to hurt you or Lady Isabella!" Ariel cried sincerely. "Surely you know this?"

William's eyes narrowed. "Just as you must know I would not force you to do anything your heart was set against. If you harbour strong objections to this Welsh prince—if his nose is too large, or his legs too spindly—then by all means, voice

them now and I will place myself and my sword between you
and the king's choler, regardless of the consequences."

Ariel gazed steadily up into the penetrating blue eyes and
knew, despite the wry twist behind his words, he was making
both their positions quite clear. She was the one who had
chosen to defy the king's orders; she did not have a choice now
and neither did he.

"Lord Rhys has a fine nose," she said softly. "And his legs
are as straight as pillars."

"Your aunt did mention, now that I recall, he was a handsome rogue."

Ariel lowered her head and rested her cheek on William's
knee. She tried hard to conjure an image of Rhys ap Iorwerth
in her mind, but the best she could manage was a picture of a
man who was dark and bearded, powerful in stature . . . with
a slain fawn slung over the crupper of his saddle.

"Will you be happier with him than with the gaoler's
son?" William asked quietly, smoothing a gnarled hand over
the shiny crown of her head.

"I will be content," she said.

"Have no fear—he will know, by the terms of the agreement and by the dower estates I contract into his keeping, that
I place an extremely high value on your safety and continuing
happiness."

She tilted her chin up and smiled. "Mayhap it will temper
his need to lift so many of your cattle."

"Aye. We can always hope."

They shared a few moments of comfortable silence before
Ariel ventured to speak again.

"Uncle . . . I will be *more* than content with Lord Rhys
for a husband, but . . . must I endure the company of the
Bastard d'Amboise for an escort? Henry and Sedrick managed
well enough on their own to find their way here; surely you
trust them well enough to follow their noses home again."

"It is not a question of trust, child, it is a matter of necessity. In the short time you have been in Normandy, armies
have moved, towns and cities have been besieged—most by
men who either know FitzRandwulf on sight or by reputation.

For all that he rubs your fur the wrong way, little kitten, he is also known as a friend to their cause and would not attract the same hostilities as our own Pembroke lion might."

"A friend to their cause? He would see Normandy split from England? He would throw his lot with King Philip of France?"

"It is not so much a case of throwing his lot *with* Philip, as it is a case of *not* throwing his lot with King John."

"In other words, he cannot make up his mind? He has not the courage of his convictions to make one clear choice over another? You would trust a man like this with our defense?"

"FitzRandwulf's courage has never been questioned. He has fought long and hard with his conscience, as have we all. He supported Arthur's claim to the throne, yet for honour's sake, not only had to help bring the young prince to his knees at Mirebeau, but he then had to stand aside and watch the duke be led away to his doom. To have done otherwise would have broken faith with his father—another man of immeasurably tormented loyalties, bounden by blood oath unto the dowager, yet more than eager to see John crushed by his own corrupted powers."

"The dowager is very old, is she not?"

"She has seen eight decades pass by."

In a time when most people rarely lived to see half that many years, Ariel could not begin to comprehend Eleanor of Aquitaine's longevity. "Surely she will have to die some day. What will happen then?"

"The heavy chains that hold both the Wolf and his Cub will snap and methinks our good and brave King John will feel the reverberations from whatever hole he finds to crawl into."

"La Seyne Sur Mer has this much power?"

"He has the power to strike fear into men's hearts, aye, and such power cannot be taken lightly, even though he does so himself."

"You have just as much power, do you not?"

William saw where her questions were leading and he sighed, feeling suddenly far too old and weary to deal with the pride he saw in his niece's eyes.

" 'Tis true, I wield enough to give the odd man cause to squeeze a clod of dung into his braies now and then. 'Tis also true I could give Henry and Sedrick writs of safe passage across Normandy and across the Channel into England. It is *not* true, sadly, that I could guarantee these writs would be honoured by the lords who seek to sharpen the blade that rests across John's neck. I am still the king's man in their eyes. Taking my niece and nephew hostage could put quite a feather in the caps of those who would use such leverage against me."

"They would not dare!" she gasped.

"If they would dare open rebellion against their king, they would indeed dare to use an impulsive pair of truants against the king's marshal. Especially if those truants were themselves defying the king's orders."

The seriousness of her uncle's words sent her heart plummeting into her belly like a rock thrown into a pond. "I did not know," she whispered in horror. "I did not even think! Supposing someone does capture us? Supposing someone does recognize us . . . ?"

"Precautions will be taken to guard against that happening. When you leave here, you must travel in absolute anonymity, keeping to the crooked, less frequented roads, and in as nondescript a manner as possible. Henry has suggested, since you made such a fine squire on the way *to* Normandy, you might make an equally good one on the way back. Above all, you must obey FitzRandwulf's orders to the letter, for if anyone can see you safely through, he can."

Ariel chewed her lip until she drew blood. "We *were* foolish for coming here, were we not?"

William laid his hand on her cheek. "Would that I could tell you otherwise, but you followed your heart and who can say that it is always such a foolish thing to do?"

"It was not my heart so much as my pride."

"Ah, well. There you have the downfall of us all. But take cheer, all is not lost yet. Nor will it be, praise God, if FitzRandwulf can see his mission safely through."

Ariel studied the crags and creases of her uncle's face, noticing for the first time the deeply etched lines of fatigue and worry. He was staring into the fire and his hand was trembling as it moved against her cheek, and she had the strangest feeling, all of a sudden, that he was not talking about *her* impending journey to Wales.

"Uncle?"

His eyes lingered on the flames a moment and he was careful to arrange a smile on his face before he looked down at her. "Niece?"

"I do love you, you know. With all my heart."

"And I you, little kitten. I take comfort in knowing Cardigan is but a day's ride north of Pembroke. You will not be entirely out of my grasp."

She returned his smile—not quite so cheerfully—and rested her cheek on his knee again.

"In the meantime, however, you will try to stay out of trouble, will you not? You will try not to give FitzRandwulf and Henry cause to tear their hair out by the roots?"

Ariel sighed. "I always *try* to stay out of trouble, Uncle. Sometimes, though, it just manages to find me."

Chapter 9

William the Marshal departed Amboise the following day and Ariel was tempted, even to the last moment before his guard vanished along the forest road, to change her mind and go with him. She was filled with a sudden, inexplicable sense of foreboding that had no reason or cause other than her own uncertainty as to whether she had agreed too quickly to the union with the Welsh prince; if she had been too hasty, too proud, too stubborn . . . too weak in accepting her uncle's ultimatum, despite the fact that it had been of her own devising.

What other choice did she have, however? Her uncle had displayed remarkable tolerance and patience where another would simply have had her whipped and sent to De Braose gyved hand and foot in heavy chains. If she had balked, or refused Iorwerth after all the trouble she had caused and all of the trouble this planned foiling of the king's command *would* cause . . . ? How could she have refused? How could she have done anything less than agree to put herself into Fitz-Randwulf's hands, however abhorrent the thought might be?

And so, well before the grim, ash-colored light of a second dawn rose above Amboise's battlements, an equally grim, cold group of travellers assembled in the inner court of the bailey. Horses stamped and snorted white funnels of mist into air already laden with frosted crystals; the groomsmen who held the reins shivered through chattering teeth and checked cinches and buckles continuously, if only to keep moving and keep warm. The occasional swirl of wind rippled saddlecloths and caused the scarlet leaves of the ivy that climbed partway up the walls of the keep to shift in blood-red waves. Those with the poorest grip on the vines were torn free and slapped wetly on the cobbles. Others merely shook and spattered dew on the heads of the men who gathered outside the covered entry.

The four knights—FitzRandwulf, Lord Henry, Sedrick of

Grantham, and Daffyd ap Iorwerth moved to and fro like large gray moths in the uncertain light. At a casual glance, they might be mistaken for pilgrims returning from the Holy Land, for they carried no pennants or shields emblazoned with armorial bearings. Over soft linen shirts and woolen tunics they wore sturdy leather gambesons—sleeved vests made of two thicknesses of cowhide stuffed with fleece and quilted in broad squares. Atop this they wore full suits of chain mail. Their hauberks were sleeved to the wrist and hooded for added protection, their chausses covered their legs from thigh to booted foot. Gypons were dull gray and shaped like a tube, belted at the waist, slitted front and back for riding, and here was the only splash of colour each wore: the red Crusader's cross was stitched boldly on the gypon, front and back.

Ariel, in her guise as a squire, wore an abbreviated mail byrnie, not much longer than a slitted shirt, over a coarse undertunic padded more for bulk than protection, and certainly not for comfort. Her shirt and hose were of the roughest weave, scratchy and cumbersome. Her shoes were neither leather nor felt, but made of hard wooden soles and cloth cross-straps that had to be wound, like bandages, almost to the knees. A slouched felt hat sat like a flattened pillow on her head, covering and containing all but a few shiny red threads of hair that balked at such an ignoble confinement.

She had her suspicions FitzRandwulf had deliberately ordered the drabbest, bulkiest garments that could be found. She looked and felt the part of a red-nosed dullard, and there were areas of her body that already itched so abominably she dared not let herself wonder from whose lice-infested wardrobe he had commandeered the rags.

In another way she welcomed the misery for it would be a constant reminder of his warped sense of self-importance and would make it that much easier to ignore him whenever he was in her presence—the latter not a difficult challenge, since it seemed he had made the same resolve. Her best efforts at frosty disdain were wasted on the broad expanse of his back.

The sixth member of their group had caused the most debate. Were Robert d'Amboise any other than Eduard's own half brother and La Seyne Sur Mer's legitimate heir, a second thought would not have been given to a squire accompanying his lord. But he *was* Eduard's brother, and he *was* the Wolf's heir, the child conceived in the magical waters of the Silent Pool, and the one Sparrow claimed was destined for great things in the future. The Wolf himself had paled somewhat when Eduard had quietly alerted him to the dilemma. To leave him behind would show a lack of confidence that would humiliate him to the core. To take him along could put *any* future at dire risk—a risk FitzRandwulf was not altogether certain he was willing to take.

Robert's strongest ally, oddly enough, had been his mother, Lady Servanne, who had reminded them all, with her heart in her throat, that a battlefield was no less dangerous than a trek through England and Wales, and that neither her husband nor Eduard had objected to Robert's presence at Blois. Moreover, the blood of the two most courageous men Robert knew flowed through his veins and he looked upon the plight of Ariel de Clare as a chivalric adventure of the highest order. Safeguarding her from the king's clutches, delivering her to her one true love—a royal prince of Wales, forsooth—was a quest clad in shining armour and he would not be deterred by anything less than sheer brute force.

Thus, Robert d'Amboise stood in the cold and dampness of the morning light, his shoulders padded under layers of wool and leather, his throat muffled by a scarf woven by Biddy and bound to him with a tearful vengeance, laced with many warnings, emphasized with an emotional vigor that had come close to bruising him.

Lastly, there was Sparrow. His lithe, wood sprite's body was clad in forest colours of green and brown, his only armour a modified vest made of stitched plates of stiffened bullhide. He stalked around and between the horses' legs, poking here, adjusting there, muttering to himself at each turn, and in louder tones whenever anyone was foolish enough to lend an ear. The young Welshman was targeted twice; once when he was supervising the loading of a small mahogany writing box onto the back of the packhorse—a waste of space they could ill afford, Sparrow declared—and again when he had declined to bow his head for the priest's blessing—an act that surely identified him as a Celtic devil-worshiper, drinker of blood, purveyor of doom . . .

"Sparrow," Eduard interrupted with a sigh, "is all in readiness?"

The little man planted his booted feet wide apart and glared up. "The boysters are loaded, the firmacula are firm. Freebooters are well on the roads by now, laying in their ambuscades waiting for purses to filch and throats to cut. If we delay much longer, we might as well announce our departure with trumpets and tumblers."

Eduard turned to his father. "If God and luck be with us, we should be well beyond Tours by noon."

"I would feel better if a troop guarded your back at least as far as the border of our lands."

"At the first sight of black and gold on the road west, the rumours would start to fly. Ten men would be reported as a hundred, then a thousand."

"Aye," Sparrow snorted. "And from there the buzzing would grow and swell until it foretold an army on the move, striking blood and thunder in its path. The king would change his hose at every toll of the bells; each town and port would be put on its guard and our fine, noble cockerel would be clapped in irons the instant he shewed his pretty face anywhere near St. Malo."

"It was only a suggestion," the Wolf said dryly. "But you are probably right. The spies are as thick as flies on a carcass and what they see today has the uncanny ability to reach the king's ear on the morrow. Still, it . . . does not sit well with me to stand idly by and do nothing while two of my sons set out on such a bold adventure. The very idea of it galls me and leaves me feeling more of a cripple than these damned sticks. Yet, at the same time"—he paused and his voice thickened with emotion—"I would have you know, I have never been prouder in all my life."

Eduard held his father's gaze a moment longer then went down on one knee before him.

"It goes without saying that you have my blessing," Lord Randwulf said. He laid his hand on Eduard's head and led the small group in a prayer for safe passage. Before it was finished, his steel gray eyes settled on Robert and he felt a wrenching tightness in his chest for the boy was no older than Eduard had been when they had stood together on a windswept cliff, the boy demanding to be recognized as a man.

Cool, slender fingers joined the Wolf's where they still rested on Eduard's bowed head, and he glanced down. He saw the love and pride shining on his wife's face and some of the tightness eased. Enough, at least, to allow him to send his sons on their way in a loud, steady voice.

"God bless and God speed," he said, his fingers twining with Servanne's behind his back as Eduard rose. "You will send word from St. Malo when you arrive?"

"The very moment."

"And . . . from Wales, if all goes well?"

Eduard smiled. "I will bring word myself, I swear it."

When William the Marshal had ridden away from Amboise it had been his intention to head directly north to Le Mans, then on through to Falaise where he would rejoin the slower-moving body of the cavalcade that had accompanied him to Paris. With his stamina and strength of purpose, he estimated it would take him three days. Eduard's group, because it would wind west around Tours and Angers, then north to the coastal port of St. Malo, would take upwards of a week or more to complete this first leg of their journey—time enough, it was hoped, for the marshal to confirm where Eleanor of Brittany had been imprisoned and to send a coded message to Fitz-Randwulf at either Rennes or St. Malo.

Eduard established a steady pace, neither too slow, nor seeming to rush too fast. They were, after all, supposed to be knights returning from a pilgrimage to the Holy Land. Since their shields were covered in gray bunting and they travelled under a black banner to signify mourning, to be seen galloping across the countryside at full tilt would have sent heads twisting after them in askance.

Another factor that determined their speed was their choice of horses. Because of the nature of their journey, the decision had been made to forgo the encumbrance of too many extra animals. The knights rode their destriers—brave beasts, but not known for their enthusiasm for plodding miles on end with no bloody battles or tests of derring-do to show for their trouble. To add insult, their saddlecloths were of the plainest, dullest weave, frayed into sad neglect. The snaffle bits were unadorned iron, the saddlebags were coarse canvas without any fringes or armorial bearings. Ariel and Robert rode palfreys, with each leading by means of ropes strung through loops on their saddles, two extra rouncies laden with equipment, spare weapons, and supplies.

The roads FitzRandwulf chose were not much more than trampled dirt tracts leading from one stand of silent forest to the next. Twice they skirted around clearings large enough to hold a huddle of mud and thatch cottages, but although there were men tilling the fields and tending the smoke huts, they were not challenged. They were, if anything, deliberately ignored, for it was not healthy to show too much curiosity to knights who might take a fancy to a particularly plump chicken, or an especially ripe daughter. FitzRandwulf was neither offended nor in a mood to reassure them. It suited him well to avoid any contact, even with the lowliest crofter, at least until they were far enough away from Amboise for a man bearing a scar over half his face not to be readily identified.

That decision also meant they would not be seeking shelter for the night, but would make their own camp in the woods. Reminding herself she would sooner carve out her tongue as complain, Ariel met the news with barely more than a scowl. She helped Robert unpack bedrolls and build the fire. She even helped prepare the evening meal—bread, cheese, and a brace of fat hares roasted over the open flames. When it came time to serve, she offered to carry FitzRandwulf his portion, a gesture that put a queer frown on Henry's brow until he saw the extra handful of salt and spices she rubbed into his meat.

They rode, rested, ate, and slept in the uncompromising

bulk of chain mail and coarse wool. The men seemed quite accustomed to it, snoring and farting in their bedrolls with equal ease. Ariel, wrapped in layers of blankets, lay wide awake, shivering and uncomfortable, wary of every snapping branch and rustling leaf beyond the lighted circle of their camp fire. FitzRandwulf was the only one who shared her sleeplessness, for he sat up most of the night, his face glowing demonic red in the firelight, his hands occasionally moving to stir the embers with a long, gnarled stick.

As tired as she was, Ariel found it difficult not to watch him from beneath the muffling cocoon of her blankets. Robert had thought it his bounden duty to keep her occupied with conversation throughout the day, and one of the whispered topics had been the scar on his brother's cheek. It had come as a result of a single-combat match, one Eduard had won with such clear ease his challenger had not been able to bear the insult. He had struck with a cat's eye when Eduard's back had been turned, and it was only by God's grace the metal spikes had not torn out an eye and ear.

"What happened to the other fellow?" Ariel had asked, only half-interested.

"Well, Eduard was sorely injured, as you may well understand, but in enough of a rage to have killed the lout then and there—as would have been his right by tournament law. But Prince John . . . now the king . . . had been one of the ajudicators, and he declared a fine to be sufficient—a meagre sum that was more of an insult than the unchivalrous attack. So you can see why he is not altogether unhappy about taking you to Wales instead of Radnor."

"Mmm. Yes. I do see. Vengeance against the king."

"No, my lady. Vengeance against Reginald de Braose. He was the cowardly lout who struck when my lord's back was turned. Tricking him out of his bride is a small matter by comparison, but one that Eduard will relish nonetheless."

Ariel had been struck dumb by the revelation. FitzRandwulf had said nothing to her to indicate he had even recognized the name of her prospective groom, let alone that they shared a history. The Bastard's ability to keep such a thing to

himself had haunted her for the rest of the day. Not even
presenting him with the hellishly oversalted meat had improved her mood, nor had seeing him drain cup after cup of
water in an effort to quench his thirst.

Ariel finally did manage to drift off to sleep, but it could
not have been more than a few minutes later that she felt
Robert's hand brushing gently over her shoulder to waken her.
At first she did not budge, for it was still as black as pitch in the
forest and cold enough outside her cocoon to send stabs of
chilling shivers down her neck and spine. Robert—Robin, as
he had insisted she call him—persisted, however, bringing a
horn-sided lantern close enough to her face to cause a minor
explosion of yellow starbursts behind her eyelids.

"I thought you might want a moment of privacy down by
the river, my lady," he whispered. "Before the others take to
the bushes?"

Ariel thanked him grudgingly. She pulled her blanket up
over her shoulders and took the lantern, following Robin's
pointed finger along the path toward the river.

As bright as it had seemed when thrust in her face, the
lantern light was dull gray by the time it reached the ground,
and illuminated an area no larger than a broad pace. It made for
weird and grotesque shadows crouching behind every copse of
bramble and brier; combined with sleepy eyes and a thin veil
of mist, it also made for more than a few missteps over half-
buried roots.

One such stumble, recovered with the aid of a muttered
oath, announced her arrival at the riverbank and she was forced
to draw to an abrupt halt as a slash of cold steel came out of the
gloom and stopped an inch from her throat. Eduard FitzRandwulf was at the other end of the blade, startling her a second
time with a far more graphic oath than anything she might
have coined. He was also bare from the waist up, his face,
neck, shoulders, and chest glittering above the ferns as if belonging to some gilded satyr.

"Have you no better sense than to sneak up on a man in
the dark?"

Ariel was aware of the blush rising in her cheeks and was

hopeful he could not see it. She wished, just as heartily, she had not interrupted his morning ablutions, for it was difficult not to notice the magnificent bulk of muscles ranging across his upper torso; harder still to resist a quick glance down the hard, flat plane of his belly and waist.

"I . . . have a light," she said, clearing her throat of hesitation. "So I was hardly sneaking. I should think it was more the poor condition of your eyes and ears that deserves the blame."

His eyes narrowed. He resheathed his sword with a gesture of disgust and threw the weapon back onto the ground.

"I was washing. Do you mind?"

"Not at all. Shall I stand guard?"

His mouth curved down but he did not rise to the bait. Instead, he returned to the river's edge and resumed splashing handfuls of water over his face and shoulders.

Ariel, cold through all the heavy layers of her clothing and a blanket besides, watched him with gently arched brows. Raised in a household with five male cousins and an energetic brother, she was more than passingly familiar with a man's unclothed body. More than once, she had caught Henry naked and grappling in the arms of some buxom wench, so she was not even maidenly ignorant of how a man and woman fit together. For all their muscle and bravado though, most men were white as milk from the neck down, seldom struck by the desire to expose any skin to sunlight, or, for that matter, soap and water.

FitzRandwulf's body was certainly a match for any she had seen as far as width and breadth and sheer mass of plated muscle. But he was also as bronzed as weathered oak, his skin smooth and hard-surfaced, gleaming like fine camlet in the glow of the lantern. Dark hairs formed a natural gorget over his chest, narrowing to a cable's width where it trailed down onto his belly. His forearms bore a light covering of those same smooth hairs, as would, she imagined, the long sinewy legs. He carried no excess flesh anywhere that she could see, and where she could not, did not bear supposition.

The threat of a second discomforting flush prompted her

to turn away, but not before a glimpse of something that was not flesh or fur lured her gaze back to his chest. Hanging there, threaded onto a leather thong, was a small gold ring. It swung back and forth with the action of his arms, but Ariel could see it was a woman's ring, ornately filigreed to decorate and flatter a slender finger.

Her brows inched delicately higher.

A woman's ring worn about the neck signified deep affection. Moreover, a gold ring, wrought with such exquisite craftsmanship would not have come from the finger of a common trull. It was a token worth far more than a simple silk scarf or a bit of tinseled ribbon usually bestowed upon a knight by his lady of choice. Worn beneath the tunic, borne next to the heart, this particular talisman could be nothing other than a pledge of undying devotion to and from a secret love.

Secret . . . because she was a noblewoman of high birth?

Ariel's eyes darkened with the possibility of an intrigue, for had he not denied the existence of any lady love? Had he not denied it *most emphatically*?

Her reflections went no further as Eduard stood and shook the water from his hands, scattering a bright spray of silvered droplets into the mist.

Not wanting to be caught staring, Ariel glanced away. The darkness was lifting and the sky to the east was beginning to glow with a ruddy luminosity, as if some unearthly giant were approaching, carrying a flaring torch before him. A layer of soupy fog hovered over the surface of the river—steam off a witch's brew. There must have been a village somewhere nearby, for the current was interrupted by a series of wattled enclosures built to dam the water and trap fish.

When she looked at FitzRandwulf again, he had donned his shirt and tunic and was shaking the loose bits of twig and soil off his gambeson, preparing to buckle it in place over his shoulders. The ring, she noted, was once again safely concealed from view.

"I would ask that you do not dally too long, my lady. We want an early start."

"Naturally," she mused. "Now that *you* have bathed and freshened yourself."

He surprised her by misting the air with a soft, husky laugh. "If you would care to bathe, my lady, I have no objections. Neither will they, I warrant."

She traced the faint tilt of his head to where two men were watching them from the far side of the river. They were peasants, probably come to check their weirs for fish. The drabness of their clothing made them blend into the earthy tones of the riverbank and she might have missed seeing them altogether had one not been careless enough to peer around the trunk of a tree at the exact moment she looked.

"What should we do?" she whispered, moving instinctively closer to Eduard.

"Certainly nothing to rouse their curiosity any further," he recommended wryly, drawing her attention to how close she was standing. "A knight and his squire, embracing in the woods, would make for interesting gossip even among these simple runklings."

Ariel stepped hastily away. She watched him bend over to collect his hauberk and sword belt, and give a last, seemingly casual glance over his shoulder before he started back along the path.

"Where are you going?" she asked, startled.

"Back to camp."

"You are just leaving me here . . . *alone?*"

"Oh . . ." His eyes flickered to the opposite shore. "I doubt you need worry about them. One glimpse of your hair and they would suppose you to be a harpy out in search of souls to steal."

Ariel's jaw sagged. Before she could think of a suitable retort, he started walking again, his legs slicing through the ferns, his body displacing the fog in tiny swirling dervishes.

The morning passed without further incident; midday brought the first appearance of the sun, a welcome change from the constant cloud and threat of rain that had followed them from Amboise. The wind, which had remained at their

backs most of the time, shifted to cut from the east, painting
the ground they rode over with a constant tumble of orange-
and rust-coloured leaves. It carried the occasional hint of wood
smoke to indicate a village or hamlet in the vicinity, but although they travelled across fields of recently harvested corn
and wheat, they saw no one. It was to their advantage to pass
anonymously through the countryside, but by late afternoon of
the third full day of travel, the thought of another bland meal
of bread, cheese, ale, and whatever the knights managed to
skewer from the river or stop with an arrow, sent at least four
sets of nostrils flaring in the direction of a sweetly acrid scent.

"Venison," Sedrick announced, boasting the largest nostrils and therefore the most accurate perception. "Roasting
slow and sure over a bed of . . . ash, be ma guess."

Since his size and appetite gave no one reason to doubt his
expertise, the next question concerned the identity of someone bold enough to cook royal game so openly. There were no
châteaus in easy distance. The section of forest they traversed
was too dense and hilly to attract any inhabitants but the four-
legged kind, the river too wide and swift-moving to be hospitable to man-made traps.

"A witless poacher, be my guess," Henry said. "One with
intentions of falling asleep tonight with a full belly."

Sedrick's stomach rumbled so loudly at the notion, it
caused Robin and Lord Dafydd to exchange a smile.

"What manner of lax lord allows poachers and foresters to
run amok in their wardens?" Sedrick protested. "As knights,
sworn of an oath to protect the realm from such thievery,
would it not be our duty to investigate, nay, even to confiscate
such ill-gotten gains?"

"We have a ready meal in our pouch," Eduard reminded
him.

"Aye, but can ye deny a bellyful of hot roast venison
would suit better for the long, cold night we have ahead of
us?"

Eduard shrugged. "You had best take care they *are* poachers before you act out your knightly vows, else you come away
with a bellyful of arrowheads for your trouble."

Sedrick grinned and searched the treetops a moment. "Where is that poxy elf when ye need him? He would be better able to tell us the whos and wherefores."

As if by magic, a whoop of glee brought Sparrow swinging down off a tree branch, his arms and legs splayed wide to catch the air in the pockets formed by his clothes. He was the only one of the group who had disdained the need for a horse of his own, declaring he was slight enough to share a saddle when he grew weary of his own company, or to curl up in a contented bundle amidst the nest of supplies carried on the rouncies when he craved sleep. Several times, when the woods thinned and gave way to long stretches of meadow, he had swooped down without warning to land on the nearest horse's rump, surprising the animal and rider with devilish glee. To everyone else's relief, that rider was more often than not Sir Sedrick of Grantham, who seemed to have taken Biddy's place as the favoured object of torment.

He flailed his arms and cursed as Sparrow splatted into him like a large bat.

"Did I hear you calling me, Sir Borkel?" he asked, standing on the destrier's rump and peering forward over Sedrick's shoulder. "Do I deduce you require more than your nose to point the way to a tasty dinner? Hah! I have already anticipated the roar in your gullet and can tell you there are four varlets dozing by a fire five, mayhap six of your paltry bowshots"—a finger cut across the front of Sedrick's nose—"that-a-way. Robustious common stock," he added, answering the question before Eduard could ask it. "Bumpkins by the look of it, for they are fast asleep. They should not argue overlong at the need to forfeit a portion of their victuals."

Sedrick swelled his chest and drew his sword. "Bah! And here's me thinking I've not had a good argument for days. Are ye with me, Henry?"

Henry drew his blade and looked in turn to Dafydd ap Iorwerth. "My lord? You, above all, must be missing the sweet taste of venison."

The Welshman grinned. "No doubt 'tis sweeter taken

from King John's warden, but aye, the tongue does squirt for a taste of royal fare."

FitzRandwulf declined, with thanks, leaving only Ariel and Robin unasked, the latter clearly aching to ease the boredom of the last three days.

"Come along, lad," Sedrick shouted, wheeling his steed in the direction of Sparrow's stalwart finger. "Ye can help choose the fattest haunch."

"May I, my lord?" Robin asked eagerly.

"Go ahead," Eduard agreed, reaching for the rope that led to Robin's packhorse. "Tell the others to catch us up by the river."

Ariel watched them ride away and scratched savagely at a faint burrowing sensation on the side of her neck. She had managed to pass the last day and a half without wasting a single word on the arrogant beast, nor had she allowed herself to be caught alone with him again. This begged for comment, however, and a look of utter disdain.

"If you are so worried about drawing attention to ourselves, should we not press on instead of stopping for such tomfoolery?"

"We have covered a fair distance today, under the circumstances. Perhaps the men, like the horses, need to burn off some of their excess energy."

Narrowed green eyes sparkled out from beneath the brim of the drooping felt hat. "Are you insinuating you could have travelled farther and faster without the *circumstance* of my company to hinder you?"

Eduard acknowledged her scowl with one of his maddeningly insincere half-smiles. "Actually, I was referring to the poor conditions of the road, but if *you* think we travel too slowly . . . ?"

Ariel's glare turned brittle. In keeping with the tawdry raiments, she had been assigned a low-bred, knock-kneed, sway-backed palfrey that walked like a ship wallowing in heavy seas. Travel too slowly indeed. Had she the luxury of a Pembroke steed and her own riding clothes, she could have passed this clanking booby and left him splattered in mud all the way to St. Malo!

Regretting she had even ventured to open the conversation, she gave the brim of her hat a shove to push it off her forehead and followed him in icy silence, her eyes boring into the back of his neck. Her resentment ebbed and flowed in her cheeks with each new vision of torment she wished upon him: Hot irons crimped to his flesh. A bed of sharpened spikes with rocks heaped upon his belly one at a time. Lashmarks, oozing blood, enough to cover him head to toe . . .

A twig snagged the brim of her hat, dragging it off to one side of her head before she could free a hand to snatch it back. Recovering her balance, she spurred her palfrey forward and noticed they had veered off the main road and were cutting along the basin of a shallow gully. Rising on either side were gentle slopes covered in a thick carpet of fallen leaves. Ahead was the sound of the river, and above, the stripped lattice of tree branches allowed wide, clear patches of sky to shine through. The wind was stilled to a whisper and the air was almost liquid with bluing shadows. It was quiet, peaceful, secluded. And Ariel found herself glancing over her shoulder, wondering how long it took to convince a band of poachers to share their ill-gotten gains.

FitzRandwulf halted Lucifer beside the river. After a few moments of contemplating the lushness of the setting, he dismounted and stretched his arms and back, angling his torso this way and that to ease the tightness in his muscles. Despite what he had said to Ariel, he was pleased with the time they had made and the distance they had covered. They were perhaps a day's ride from Rennes, a city large enough and crowded enough to afford them the luxury of spending the night in an inn. While he was well aware of Lady Ariel's stubbornness and her determination not to complain or betray any sign of weakness, he was also aware of her soft groans at night each time she shifted on the hard ground.

He glanced over at her now and saw that she had not yet dismounted. It took a further moment for Eduard to discard the ridiculous hat and ill-fitting byrnie and remember there was a woman beneath the disguise—a high-born woman who still deserved the courtesies that were her due, regardless of the pouting lower lip.

Without inquiring if she needed or wanted his assistance, he approached the palfrey and placed his big hands around her waist, lifting her down with an easy swing of his heavily muscled shoulders. The palfrey moved a skittish step to the side and Ariel had to grasp the folds of Eduard's gypon for additional support. The gesture brought her more in contact with his body than she would have wanted, but luckily, he was distracted by the hooted exchanges of a pair of owls and did not take advantage. At the same time, he presented her with an unimpaired view of the scarred cheek—something he self-consciously avoided doing, especially in the unforgiving harshness of daylight.

It effectively dampened her own urge to maim. The wound, she surmised, must have been very painful in the earning, for the flesh had been torn from the base of his jaw to the indent of his temple. It was not so much the ugly, mottled, festered tapestry of misshapen gore she had aggrandized in her mind's eye, but a pale, ragged weal of raised scar tissue that was thickest in the hollow of his cheek and might easily have been camouflaged, or at least blunted, by growing a full beard over it.

Not that he impressed her as a man dictated by vanity. He wore the scar as comfortably as he wore his masculinity, giving little credence to those who might judge him by either.

"Most women find it repulsive," he said quietly, letting her know he was aware of her close scrutiny. He gazed directly down into her eyes and she could see that he expected some comment—an apology, perhaps? Or a stammered excuse for staring that he could slough off as easily as he sloughed off the reasons that made her stare? He was smiling, baiting her with a worthless little gesture that was scarcely more than a slight thinning of the lips, and she felt a chill that had nothing to do with the weather or the sudden, stark silence suspended between them.

"I doubt the reaction is caused so much by the wound as it

is by the man who bears it," she said with a breathless attempt to undermine the power of those eyes.

"Strong words . . . for someone who so recently sought my opinion of her own desirability."

"I sought no such thing!"

"No? Does that mean you *always* have to ask a man to kiss you?"

"I do not . . . *did* not ask you to kiss me!"

"Nor did you enjoy it, I suppose."

"Certainly not!"

He leaned closer and the air went out of her in a gust. A moist, heated shudder rippled deep within her, a reaction to his closeness, she supposed, and one she was uncomfortably unable to control . . . just as she was unable to control the slow, measured steps that forced her against the flanks of his enormous rampager. He was going to kiss her again. He was going to kiss her and there was nothing she could do to stop him.

"When I tell you to," he murmured casually, "I want you to take the horses and move back behind those trees."

Ariel blinked in surprise. "Wh-what?"

"Lucifer might try to fight you—he has less patience with women than I do—but you will have to try to hold him. Do you think you can manage?"

Ariel started to gasp another protest, but he was no longer looking at her. He was staring instead at something over the top of her head, and when she attempted to turn and determine what it was, she caught only a glimpse of forest shadow and mottled sunlight before a calloused thumb and forefinger were pinching her chin, forcing her to look up at him again.

"What is it? What is wrong?"

"Owls usually sleep in the daytime," he said calmly, "yet we seem to have attracted a few lively fellows around us."

Ariel tried to look again, and again was manhandled forward.

"Will you just do as I ask? Get behind those trees and keep your head down."

"I am not completely witless, you know. I can use a sword and a bow to good effect. I can *help*."

With one hand, Eduard lifted and fastened the protective flap of the linked iron camail that covered the lower half of his face and throat. While he did so, Ariel suffered the full, unleashed power of his eyes.

"If I find I need your help, my lady, I will call upon it. Until then, just do as I say, by Christ, and with no more of your arguing, or—"

The threat was never completed. A low, whining rush of air passed over their heads and a split second later, a solid *whonk* left the pair staring at the short, iron-tipped crossbow bolt quivering in the tree trunk behind them.

Chapter 10

✝ **W**ithout standing on ceremony, Eduard pushed Ariel toward the trees and smacked the rumps of the horses, startling them into bolting for the river. He snatched his bow and quiver from the sling on Lucifer's saddle, then stepped behind a clump of bushes—a sight met with a distant, muffled guffaw of laughter.

"Aye, run and hide, Graycloak. You would fare far better just to pay us a toll and pass along the road without further ado."

Eduard cursed and clamped the shaft of an arrow between his teeth while he leaned his weight into the strong arch of yew to tighten the slack of his bowstring. Common outlaws. Deserters . . . or men paid by the French to disrupt the flow of traffic through Normandy. They travelled in small packs like dogs, robbing, killing, plundering . . . taking hostages to ransom.

Three, perhaps four more voices echoed the sarcasm of the first, their jibes accompanied by a brief hail of stubby crossbow quarrels. Only one came anywhere near the first; most of them plunked harmlessly into the soft earth, well short of their targets. The villains were either extremely poor shots or they were in too much of a hurry to show strength over caution. One foolhardy fellow even danced a small jig, hooting and hollering when his bolt came close enough to shave a strip of bark off the tree Eduard stood behind.

Almost contemptuously, Eduard stepped out into the open. He raised the graceful sweep of his longbow and nocked the arrow to the string. With the string and feather fletching drawn back to the curve of his jawbone, he straightened his fingers and snapped the arrow free, sending it into the distant greenwood with the impact of a thunderbolt. The dancer was lifted back and thrown off his feet, the steel-tipped arrow piercing clean through his chest and protruding half its length out the back. A second outlaw, farther along the gully, jumped up to gape in horror at his fallen comrade and, too late, heard the soft *hiss-s-s* of a second ashwood arrow streaking toward him. This time the lethal tip passed through the width of the man's neck and struck a tree some twenty yards behind, still carrying enough speed and power to become embedded deep in the wood.

Yet another fool stood to rearm his crossbow, a costly necessity in the handling of the clumsy weapon. Placing the stirrup of the bow on the ground, he slipped his foot through the metal ring and, with a heave and a grunt of air, pulled back on the resined gut until it fit tautly over the metal hook of the trigger. He died where he stood, his face showing more surprise than pain.

Eduard pulled two more arrows from his quiver, his eyes glinting coldly as they scanned the slope of both hills for the next target. He ducked, and missed by inches, the barbed tip of another bolt that was fired from the cover of a large pine tree. His verbal response was muffled by the iron link camail, but there was nothing to mute the hard blaze of anger in his eyes as he fired both arrows into the dense growth of boughs. A cry of pain sent two more outlaws scrambling for thicker cover, one of them doubled over and clutching a skewered arm.

Any thought of celebrating was quashed as a shout parted a curtain of evergreens and two more men came hurtling down the slope, their swords raised and sparking in a flare of sunlight. Eduard tossed his bow aside and unsheathed his own blade, bracing himself as the first man slashed for his head and met the broad side of cold steel instead. The villain was not nearly as tall as FitzRandwulf, but he had the power of a bulldog in his arms. He wielded the sword in both hands, windmilling it close enough to be a threat, far enough to avoid Eduard's blade while his companion sought to maneuver himself into a position to strike at the knight's back. The outlaws hacked at knees, thighs, belly, and shoulder . . . anything that looked vulnerable, testing Eduard's instincts and his skill at sending their blades scraping at steel and empty air. They did not find him lacking.

The sound of clashing swords echoed through the trees

and along the gully, drawing the attention of the two bowmen Eduard had flushed from behind the pines. The one with the arrow jutting from his arm showed no interest in turning back to join the fray, but the second one, armed with a crossbow, stopped, grinned, and started running back toward the river.

Ariel, observing from behind a tree, saw the villain stop to rearm his weapon. He was well within the crossbow's ideal range. Close enough, in fact, to pierce through the mail links of FitzRandwulf's armour. The swordsmen were aware of this and kept Eduard's back to the gully; he, on the other hand, probably was not even aware the danger existed.

Eduard's bow was lying in the leaves where he had thrown it, the quiver alongside. Not stopping to think of the danger to herself, she ran out from behind the shield of trees, retrieving both, then dashing for the protection of a large oak. The longbow was enormous, larger and heavier than any she had used at Pembroke, but she was not unfamiliar with the weapon itself, having practised with the Welsh style of bow more often than the shorter, lighter type favoured by the English.

She nocked an arrow and sighted along the shaft, drawing the string to her chin with an effort that almost peeled the flesh from her fingers. She let loose at the crossbowman, who had seen her as the easier target and had aimed and fired his bow in the same length of time. While her arrow carried more speed, it also carried well over his head and was lost somewhere in the greenwood behind him. His bolt, meanwhile, thudded into the trunk of the oak with a distinctive enough bite to send bits of bark flying in Ariel's face.

Her teeth set in a grimace, she pulled another arrow and slotted it to the string. Eduard saw her, saw what she was doing, and was shocked enough to do what the pair of attackers had been unable to manage thus far—he turned his back on one of their swords. Ariel heard Eduard's shout and fired her arrow just as the swordsman started to lunge with his blade. The steel tip of her arrow caught him just under the hook of his nose, splitting the cartilage and bone, and plowing upward into his skull.

Eduard whirled, then whirled again, his sword flashing in a deadly arc that cut through his remaining attacker's wrist, parting flesh and bone, then sliced through the exposed stretch of his throat, severing all but a narrow flap of sinew at the nape. Head and shoulder split apart in a fount of blood, and as the body fell, it sprayed the leaves with a crimson fan.

Eduard ran over to where Ariel was standing. The bow was still raised to shoulder height, the string was still humming in the sudden, dead silence. Eduard followed her gaze and saw where her third arrow had taken the crossbowman high in the chest, the tip punching through the bullhide armour like a knife through cheese.

She looked up at FitzRandwulf, her eyes shining, her cheeks flushed. She had lost her hat somewhere in the excitement and her hair lay uncoiled over her shoulder in a thick, sleek braid.

With her heart pounding in her throat, she watched him reach up and unhook the scaled pennyplate camail. His breath had caused spickets of moisture to become trapped in the hammered links and as he lowered the flap, it glittered in folds of burnished silver beneath his jaw. The iced gray coldness of his eyes combined with the harsh, uncompromising lines of his mouth sent the blood rushing through her veins with enough force to bring on a moment of dizziness.

"The next time I give you an order and you do not obey it," he snarled, "I will strip a six-foot willow lash and flay such a pattern on your arse, you will be unable to sit for a month."

Two stormy spots of colour darkened Ariel's cheeks. "You are very welcome, my lord. And the next time I see you in ambush, I will indeed sit by and take pleasure in seeing you laid to ground."

His eyes narrowed but his retort was lost under the thundering beat of horses' hooves churning through the woods. Henry and Robin were the first to arrive in the gully. They brought their beasts to a skidding, rearing halt when they saw Ariel and FitzRandwulf standing unhurt by the river, then drew abreast at a slower pace, their swords in their hands, their heads swivelling as they appraised the carnage on the forest floor.

"Well," said Henry, "it seems we did not have to hurry back after all."

"The four Sparrow counted were dead," Robin explained breathlessly. "And not too long."

"Aye," Henry nodded grimly. "We must have surprised these curs before they could finish their grisly work. Christ's blood, how many—?"

While he took a silent count, moving lips and gauntleted fingers, Sedrick and Lord Dafydd came riding around the bend in the gully, herding the injured forester in front of them.

He was young for an outlaw, not more than sixteen or seventeen years of age. Long and lanky, his legs accounted for nigh on most of his seven feet of height. Sparrow stalked in his shadow, taking four steps to every one of his, in danger of putting a crimp in his neck from trying to see above the bony shoulders. There was not much to see. The makings of a sparse beard were sprouting over the lower half of his face; the upper was dominated by a pair of deep-set eyes as dark a blue as the midnight sky. His clothes were threadbare, not improved by a vest of matted hare's fur that stank as badly as it was stitched together.

The shaft of Eduard's arrow was stuck through his arm, splintered near the fletching where he must have fallen in his efforts to evade the two pursuing knights.

Eduard went to each body in turn, checking for signs of life and salvaging the valuable steel arrowheads. At the first body, because the shaft had met no resistance from bullhide or armour, he nudged the corpse onto its side and used his boot to snap the protruding arrowhead free. The next two men were as dead as the first, the eyes wide and staring, offering no protest as Eduard twisted and pried his arrows from their bodies. Robin had already ridden down the gully to retrieve the arrow intact from the trunk of a tree, leaving only Ariel's last kill for inspection. The arrow was too deeply wedged in flesh and gristle to pull free, and while Eduard debated digging for it, Sedrick and Dafydd arrived by his side.

Their prisoner had stopped as well, his face grim through the layers of filth, his mouth curled in a sneer as he looked down at his slain comrade.

"Greedy bastards," he spat. "I warned them no good would come from ambushing men who wore the Holy Cross. Show me a pilgrim with two coins to rub together, I said, and I'll show you a monk with ten wives. But no. They were not satisfied with the four fat routiers who were addled enough to build a cook fire in these woods. They wanted more, and so they got it."

Eduard was frowning at the gangly youth. The lad had muttered to himself in Saxon English, not a common occurrence in the forests of Normandy. "Where are you from, boy?"

"England," was the dry response.

"Where in England?"

The midnight blue eyes screwed into wary slits, for Fitz-Randwulf had addressed him in his own language. "Nowhere a fine Norman pricker like yourself might be acquainted with. 'Tis a small village, though, if it should please you to know. Small and poor and worked by men who are kept half-starved to pay for the king's follies."

"Is that why you have come to Normandy? To make an honest, decent living for yourself?"

"I was not brought here willingly," the boy hissed. "I was forced to come, forced to leave my family, with my father a cripple and my mother coughing blood, so the king of soft swords could claim a loyal army behind him. As for wages—" He stopped and snorted disgustedly. "We were paid with strokes of the lash and with such frequent generosity you can be assured we praised our valiant king's bountifulness nightly."

Proud and defiant, he was showing no inclination to guard his tongue, no fear of having it slit from his mouth for uttering treasonous words. He must have assumed he was already a dead man in the eyes of these Norman knights, with nothing to be gained or lost by holding his silence or his contempt.

"What is your name, boy, and how did you come to be

here in the forest, robbing honest pilgrims?" Eduard asked evenly.

The lad drew himself straight and matched FitzRandwulf's uncompromising tone. "My name, if it holds such importance to you, is Alan, son of Tom, yeoman of the Dale of Sherwood in Nottingham, and if it will please you to know, I came by way of breaking a guard's head. Split it in two, I did, for him thinking he could use me like a whore. When he came for me, I butted him, all right, with the top of my head against the top of his. Doubtless the sodomizing bastards would have called it murder, so I cut for the forest—a place I thought I knew well enough." He paused and gazed about him with a gravely disparaging look on his face. " 'Tis not like an English forest, though. The trees here are thin and unfriendly, the ground too hard for a good night's sleep. As for finding fit companionship—" He gave the corpses another black look. "Faugh! I've only been with them a day and a night and look where they have brought me. All I wanted was someone to show me the way home."

"Ye didn't know they were thieves and freebooters?" Sedrick scoffed. "Ye thought they would show ye the way home on the blunt of an arrow?"

"Aye, well, they might have called themselves bowmen, but there was not one of them who could bung the side of a cart at more than ten paces."

Eduard smiled faintly. "Should I presume, then, it was your skill that nearly carried away my ear?"

The boy hawked and spat. "If I'd wanted your ear, my lord, or the nail on your little finger, I could have had it. Even with a great bloody piece of lumber and iron like that," he added, indicating the crossbow clutched in the dead man's hands.

He was not bragging but making a simple statement of fact, and while Eduard debated whether to be amused or annoyed, Ariel de Clare came up behind them. Having overheard the latter part of the exchange, and understanding enough of the Saxon tongue to follow the gist of the insult, she cast about her with a heavy sigh.

"Would that your own aim had been better, FitzRandwulf, then we would not have the need to waste valuable time
explaining these rogues to the local warden."

Sedrick and Dafydd, still on horseback, turned their heads
toward her in unison, their helms creaking ominously with the
movement. Sparrow sucked in enough air to give a fair impression of a beetle about to explode, while Eduard directed the
far less kindly force of his unvisored eyes on her, skewering
her as neatly as his arrow had skewered the outlaw's arm. She
realized her blunder at once, of course, letting a name slip
when so many precautions had been taken to guard against
easy identification. Of secondary import, but equally remiss on
her part, was the fact that she had not retrieved her hat or
made any attempt to conceal the shocking red proof that she
was a woman in squire's clothing.

"Since you seem to be so concerned with waste," Eduard
said evenly, "perhaps you could busy yourself by retrieving my
arrowhead."

Ariel glanced down at the body. From the depth of the
shaft, she judged the tip to be lodged between the knuckles of
the villain's spine. Freeing it would probably require some
digging and cutting . . . a job worthy of making the strongest
of stomachs turn in revulsion. She looked up at Henry, but saw
no mercy in his frown. Sedrick, who could usually be counted
on for a soft heart, merely shook his head and muttered something unintelligible under his breath. There was no appealing
to Sparrow, who would have emblazoned the scene on a tapestry had he been in possession of needle and thread. Robin was
off chasing down the rouncies and Dafydd's protest was
choked back on a cold glance from FitzRandwulf's steely gray
eyes.

She drew a calming breath and stared down at the body
again. If the Bastard was hoping to humiliate her by seeing her
weep or run from the task with her stomach spilling into her
hands, he was sorely ignorant of the De Clare bloodlines.
Squaring her shoulders, she dropped down onto one knee and
gave the shaft of the arrow a halfhearted tug, feeling her gorge

lurch into her throat as the steel tip grated on two discs of bone.

Eduard observed for a moment, then turned back to their prisoner.

"Well, Alan, son of Tom, yeoman of the Dale of Sherwood, think you you could find your way back to England without joining company with any more unlucky villains?"

The youth looked over suspiciously.

"Moreover, if we felt inclined to let you keep your eyes and tongue as well as your life, could you give your word not to make me regret denying the carrions another corpse to feed upon?"

"You would let me go free?"

"I see no benefit in keeping you. Nor, as has been so sagely pointed out to me, have we the time or energy to waste in finding the local justicar and making endless explanations."

"Would it not be easier just to shoot him?" Sparrow asked.

"Aye, Puck, it would. And we will if he feels we cannot trust his word . . . and his silence."

If the young giant read more into FitzRandwulf's generous offer than was intended, or if he began to suspect these knights and their "squire" were reluctant to draw any more attention to themselves, he wisely kept silent.

"Well? Do we have your word?"

"Aye. If you will take it, then you shall have it."

"Go then. I give you your life . . . and whatever coin you can trade for a fine, twice-tempered arrowhead. It should be more than enough to buy you your way home."

The lad glanced down at the arrow stuck in his arm. The fletching dangled by a splinter, which he snapped off and flung aside. With the faintest grunt to mark its passage through, he grasped the barbed arrowhead and pulled the shortened length of ashwood out the back of his arm, gripping it tight for a moment while a shudder of pain passed through him.

"The one debt will be enough to repay," he said, placing the bloodied shaft with its valuable steel tip in Eduard's hand. "And repay it I will, my lord. You have my word on that as well."

The erstwhile outlaw touched his hand to a greasy forelock before turning and ambling off down the gully. Although his arm must have been screaming with pain, a thin and merrily whistled tune drifted back through the trees as he made his way into deeper shadows.

"You are just letting him walk away?"

Eduard took a firmer grip on his patience before he responded to the disbelieving accusation. Ariel had worked the arrowhead free and was standing behind FitzRandwulf with the dripping trophy clutched in her hand.

"I thought we had made enough corpses for one day."

"But . . . he knows who you are."

"So he does. Not, however, because of anything *I* have said or done."

"He is a murderer; he admitted as much. And a thief. *And* a traitor to the king."

Eduard folded his arms across his chest. "A traitor, is he? For speaking ill of his sovereign? For choosing to boast openly of his contempt for our good king's methods of winning loyalty. What of the others who have chosen not to obey the king's will—indeed, *who have gone to extraordinary lengths to defy him outright?* Are you suggesting there should be one set of laws for those who wear peasant's rags and another for those who wear ermine? If so, my lady—" He reached up and took Dafydd's longbow out of his hands and thrust it into hers. "By all means, exact your justice. See, he is still well within range. If you so strongly disagree with my decision, feel free to remedy it yourself."

With a parting look of disgust, Eduard started walking back toward the river. He had gone no more than ten broad paces when he heard Henry's warning shout, followed almost instantly by the distinct twanging of a bowstring. He leaped to one side a split second before a lick of hot air shot past him and *thonk*-ed into a tree.

For an inordinately long, throbbing minute, no one moved. Eduard gaped at the tall, slender woman who still stood with her feet braced apart and her body at right angles to the humming longbow.

"There are many things I may indeed be tempted to remedy, sirrah," she said through her teeth, "beginning with your manners. A mistake was made; I will be the first to admit it. It was made the moment I trusted myself into your care."

Ariel cast the bow aside and stormed past the dumbstruck knight, unmindful of the dirt and leaves she kicked up in her anger. Eduard stared intently after her, his face ruddy, his eyebrows drawn together in a single, unbroken line. A small vein in his temple was beating furiously. His fists curled and uncurled, and there was a distinctly menacing gleam in his eyes.

Lord Henry leaned forward and draped his forearm over the front of his saddle. "In case I neglected to mention it, my sister tends to react poorly to anyone who treats her as if her head is filled with nothing but twattle and birdsong. It makes for an unfortunate lesson for any man who tries to tame her."

"Be assured I have no wish to tame her," Eduard replied tautly. "Only to severely hamper her abilities to walk and talk. As for warnings, you would do well to issue one to her, for the next time she dares to raise a weapon to me . . . it will be the last."

Chapter 11

When the sun set that evening it pulled a heavy layer of cloud across the skies behind it, blotting out the sunset, shrouding the forest in a chilling mist. FitzRandwulf had decided, with so many dead bodies littering the road behind them, it would be best to keep riding well into the darkness, but when the mist became a fog and the fog a heavy downpour too solid to see past a horse's nose, they followed the sound of a droning monastery bell and begged shelter under the roof of the almonry.

Sedrick had refused to leave the perfectly good and fully cooked haunch of venison behind, and it was partly due to the savoury aroma accompanying them that they were readily admitted so late after dark. The monks accepted their explanation of having come across poachers in the woods, and were in solemn agreement that it would have been a waste to leave such a fine roast to rot.

It was deemed best to keep Ariel's gender hidden from the monks, thereby relieving the good fathers of any responsibility they might feel to mention there had been a woman travelling in the company of the knights. Since it would have seemed odd to request a separate sleeping cubicle for a mere squire, Ariel found herself sequestered in the same large pilgrim's hall offered as shelter for the men.

The hall was long and narrow, the stone walls holding in a dampness that was unrelieved by the two tallow candles supplied by the spartan monks. A double row of low pallets lined each side of the chamber; over their heads, the arched beams of the roof glowed like the yellowed ribs of some decaying skeleton. There were only two windows, neither more than slits in the wall, and a single vaulted doorway, the height of which would have made Sparrow seem tall.

Sparrow, by his own choice, elected to remain in the forest for the night, preferring the company of owls, he claimed, to pointy-faced doomsayers who spent their days toiling on their knees and their nights counting sins.

At least the pilgrim's hall was dry, and, when Sedrick scrounged wood to build a fire, it would be warm. In the meantime, the air was rank with the smell of sodden wool and wet armour. Ariel stood shivering off to one side and watched in forlorn silence as the men divested themselves of their hauberks and chausses, then shrugged their heavy gambesons blissfully aside. She was just as wet and dank-smelling as the others. In their three full days of travel, she had not had an opportunity to undress completely or to steal a decent wash. Her skin flamed with rashes in a dozen places, some of them too private to earn even the briefest reprieve from a good scratching.

Not once since leaving Château d'Amboise had anyone deigned to inquire after her comfort. Henry had undoubtedly assumed she *would* complain if she had cause. Sedrick and Dafydd had already seen her travel from Pembroke to Normandy with ease and would not suppose this travail would pose any greater hardships. It would not occur to them that she had chosen her own clothes on the initial journey, or that none of them had been coarse or confining, none encrusted with filth or infested with lice. She had worn soft chamois leggings and fine linen camlet next to her skin. She had not been strapped and buckled into garments designed to make the simple task of tending to body functions an exercise in frustration. The hose alone were a nightmare. A maid had initially helped bind her into the innumerable leather points that held the hose snug to the tops of her thighs, seemingly with an easy twist of the fingers. But the art of unfastening and tying them properly again had eluded Ariel, and her handiwork had begun to sag more obviously and more comically each passing day. And the byrnie . . . ! Buckles that were double-looped and twice bound? They were impossible contraptions, invented by the French and fostered on the Normans in the true spirit of vindictiveness.

"Do you require assistance, my lady?" Robin asked, pausing beside her. He had helped Eduard with his heavy suit of

mail and was sucking avidly on a finger torn open on a rough
link.

"No. Thank you. I can manage," she said, pushing back
on the brim of her hat. It was heavier than normal with the rain
it had absorbed and persisted in sending drops steadily down
her nose.

"I have a spare tunic and an extra pair of hose—both very
clean," he assured her. "They would be a good deal drier and
warmer if you would care to take lend of them."

"N-no," she said, giving her hat another shove. "I would
not want to put you to any trouble."

"It would be no trouble," he insisted.

"Go and fetch them, Robin," Eduard said, coming up
behind them. "I will help Lady Ariel with her buckles."

She waited until Robin was gone before she turned and
scowled up at FitzRandwulf. "If I needed—or wanted—your
help, I would ask for it."

She had blurted out words very like his own and she saw
the memory of them register as a dark flicker in his eyes. At the
same time, and for the first time in their brief and stormy
acquaintance, she thought she saw a trace of genuine admiration soften the stern shape of his mouth.

"Lift your arms," he ordered quietly.

Ariel's gaze flicked past his shoulder, but Henry had gone
with one of the monks to see to the provisioning of their
horses; Sedrick and Dafydd were preoccupied with lighting
the fire. Watching the small frown form across her brow,
Eduard countered with an exasperated sigh.

"Do you feel you have to prove yourself the equal of *every*
man you meet, or is it just me you have chosen to plague to
death?"

Ariel was taken aback. "I have not chosen to do any such
thing."

"No? You just decided to use my head for target practice
this afternoon?"

"You were . . . being uncommonly rude and beastly to
me."

"You were uncommonly deserving. Had you truly been

my squire, you would be shy a few layers of skin on your backside for disobeying me. And for flinging the arrow . . . ?" He shook his head and clucked his tongue softly. "Now, unless you prefer to have the buckles on your armour rust permanently closed, I would suggest you lift your arms and allow me to loosen them."

Ariel chewed on her lip and raised her arms slowly above her head. The movement caused the flattened bulk of her hat to slide forward over her brow again, leaving only one clear green eye free to glare up at him as he began working on the row of swollen leather straps.

"I do *not* deliberately set forth to prove myself the equal of every man," she insisted sullenly.

"No," he agreed. "I warrant you already know you are better than most."

The single green eye narrowed. "What is that supposed to mean?"

"It means . . . I have seen you wield a sword and would not be too hasty to place a wager against you. As for your bow arm, I have only seen one other woman with a steadier hand."

Ariel glanced sidelong at him, expecting to see a mouth curved with mockery, trembling with mirth, but neither was evident, and she was perplexed into acknowledging a tiny shudder of pleasure at the compliments. Not that she *wanted* compliments from this beast. A compliment might require a friendly word in turn.

"How can you be certain it was not sheer luck that guided my arrows this afternoon?"

"I cannot speak for Lord Dafydd's bow, but I made mine myself, and if luck was the only thing guiding your hand, you most likely would have taken off all your fingers and shot your own foot in the process of drawing it."

Another welter of heat flooded her belly and trickled down into her limbs. When she found the strength to look up at him again, the smokey gray eyes were waiting.

"Unfortunately," he mused, "the same cannot be said about your skill in the cooking and spicing of meat."

Ariel lowered her lashes quickly. She was wise enough to

hold her tongue and not attempt to deny the charge of tampering, although she found she was a disconcerting flush away from returning his grin.

"You have a knack of pricking my temper, my lord," she said finally.

"I would hazard to say we seem determined to prick each other's," he amended.

Ariel drew a very slow, very cautious breath, aware that his hands had paused in their duties and were resting against the side of her breast. It was ridiculous to regard it as a deliberate liberty, what with the outer shell of chain mail, the inner vest of cuir-bouilli, and the rough woolen shirt standing as barriers between her flesh and his. Yet it did not stop her skin from constricting and pulling tight across her chest as if she suddenly wore two bright circles of fire.

Compliments, smiles, intimacy . . . what next? she wondered. And why was it affecting her so? Why, for instance, was she having difficulty keeping her eyes from straying to the loosely opened vee of his shirt? And why, each time they did, was she having *no* difficulty remembering how each bulge and slab of satiny muscle had looked sheathed in river water and gleaming under the soft flare of lantern light?

His hands started to move again and her lashes fluttered slightly with the relief. When the last buckle was unclasped, he straightened and studied her profile a moment before giving way to the urge to pluck the sorry felt hat off her head. The long rope of her hair uncoiled like a snake down her back, the colour muted by the dampness and shadows but still an unsettling enough contrast to the drab browns and grays of their surroundings to hold Eduard's attention longer than was comfortable for either of them.

As it happened, *he* was having no difficulty remembering the wild, silken tangle of it gilded in moonlight, cloaking her shoulders in a mass of fire and silk.

Eduard cleared his throat and grasped the lower edge of the byrnie. Ariel aided him in maneuvering the parted flaps over her head, and, when rid of the burden, was rid of a pent-up sigh as well. He helped her remove the thickly padded vest of boiled bullhide next, granting a respite that prompted her to roll her neck this way and that, to stretch her spine and curl her shoulders forward and back in glorious freedom.

Eduard could hardly be blamed for taking advantage of her closed eyes and innocently sensual movements. Having become accustomed to seeing her muffled in bullhide and chain mail, he had almost forgotten the ethereal beauty of the woman he had met on the ramparts of Amboise. The recalled vision of her hair had stirred other memories, although now it was not the wind molding her clothes to the shape of her body, but the dampness making them cling to the round thrust of her breasts. The shirt, rough as it was, could not conceal the smallness of her waist or the whiteness of the skin revealed by the deeply slitted neckline. Even a monk, sworn to resist any and all such temptations, would have felt a distinct desire to peel away the wet cloth and explore what lay beneath.

Eduard lifted a hand and touched it to the side of her neck. Ariel froze at the contact and the fiery brightness that had begun to fade from her breasts returned with a vengeance, spreading upward to where the backs of his fingers gently eased aside the edge of her shirt and held it away from the red, angry rash on her shoulder.

"Why did you not tell someone the clothing was too coarse against your skin?" he asked with a small frown.

"Should I also have told them the horse was too clumsy, the weather too cold, the ground too wet and lumpy?"

"Requesting to have the skin saved from being chafed from the bone is hardly an admission of weakness."

Ariel held his gaze for a long moment, then shrugged away his concern with a slight roll of her shoulder. "Would that we were all like you, sirrah: open and honest with your admissions at all times."

Eduard met the sarcasm with another frown. "In what way have I been *dis*honest?"

"Oh . . . in the way you think of me, for one thing."

"My lady . . . I think of you in the manner which I am bound by oath and honour to think of you—as Lady Ariel de

Clare, niece to the Earl of Pembroke, intended bride to Prince Rhys ap Iorwerth of Gwynedd."

"How very proper of you," she murmured.

"To think of you in any other way would be . . . rather *im*proper of me, would it not?"

"There would be nothing improper in treating me as if I had a brain in my head and a spine in my back. Pushing me behind trees to hide and speaking of nothing more sinister than the weather when I am in your company does more to prick my temper than any ten challenges to prove myself equal."

"Henry did warn me you had no love for bird songs," he mused.

"Nor do I have a love for riddles," she said flatly. "Or *secrets.*"

"Secrets, my lady?"

"Secrets. Whispered confidences. Conversations that cease abruptly when I come near. Sketched pictures in the dirt that a boot discreetly scrubs away before I look too closely." For a moment, just a moment, she thought she had caught FitzRandwulf off guard with the charges and her unexpected success emboldened her. "You see? I am neither blind nor stupid, and if you are plotting something that involves me in any way, I have a right to know."

"My lady . . ." He spoke slowly to give himself time to adapt to her quickness. "The only plotting that involves you has to do with the oath we gave your uncle to see you into the happy arms of your groom unhurt, unblemished, untouched. If we whisper among ourselves, it is because we discuss the ways and means of doing so without causing you undue concern. If we draw lines in the dirt and erase them, it is from force of habit, nothing more. With spies lurking behind every tree and beneath every rock, it has become necessary to keep a private thought private."

"So now you accuse me of being a spy?"

"No. No, of course I do not think you are a spy . . ."

"Yet you do not trust me?"

The steely eyes widened guilelessly. "Demoiselle, you

wound me. I had thought there was a possibility we could become fast friends."

"Friends?" she scoffed. "You dream, my lord."

"And you imagine conspiracies where there are none."

"Are there not?" She allowed her smirk to tell him she believed him as much as she believed pigs could fly. "Why did you not tell me you were acquainted with my intended groom?"

"Iorwerth? I have no knowledge of the man other than what his brother lets slip."

"Not *that* groom," she said irritably. "The other one . . . Reginald de Braose."

Ariel had struck a second, unexpected blow to his composure, undermining it enough to put a sudden tautness in his jaw and bring to life a fine blue vein that throbbed in his temple.

"Where the devil did you hear about De Braose?" he asked harshly.

"Does it matter? The point is, I did not hear it from you, which I find odd in the extreme, considering how *earnest* you pretended to be that night on the ramparts . . . how very apologetic you were for the misunderstanding in the armoury . . . how very forgiving you were even after I called you a bastard in front of your peers."

"I *am* a bastard, my lady," he said, bowing sardonically.

"You are also adept at changing subjects when you do not wish to discuss them."

Eduard smiled faintly and turned his head enough for the light to glint gold on his lashes and to trace over the puckered flesh of the scarred cheek. "You are absolutely correct, my lady: I have no wish to discuss Reginald de Braose with you."

"Why? Because of what he did to your face? Or because he is somehow a part of the other reason why you are going back to England?"

"*Other* reason?" he asked carefully.

"My uncle tried to tell me your presence on this journey was crucial because of your familiarity with the land and your friendship with the rebel lords of Brittany. As such, it was a reasonable explanation, yet lacking several merits."

Eduard crossed his arms over his chest and found himself almost as intrigued with the way her mouth formed the words as with the words themselves.

"Go on," he urged. "You have won my complete attention."

"The first incongruity," she said evenly, "is that you have not, by your own admission, been back to England in thirteen years. Not since your father rescued you from the donjons of Bloodmoor Keep."

Eduard's gaze made the slow climb from her mouth to her eyes. "Robin," he mused. "I am glad he has been keeping you entertained with our family history."

"Some of it I knew already, but he is justifiably proud of his father and half brother, although it would be difficult for him to feel otherwise, I would venture to say, even if only half of the accomplishments he credits you are true."

"You are too kind," he murmured dryly. "And is that your dilemma? Do you find these stories hard to believe?"

"Not at all. I believe every one of them. If anything, I find it difficult to believe you would ever want to set foot in England again—for any reason. And please, do not patronize me by quoting any more oaths of honour. An oath to see me safely to the coast at St. Malo would have been sufficient. An oath from Henry and Sedrick to see me the rest of the way across the Channel and into England would have been equally sufficient."

"A fair point to argue," he admitted, "but hardly enough proof to condemn us as plotters and conspirators."

"I have more."

"I am, dear lady, breathless with anticipation."

"Breathe a little longer, my lord," she pleaded sweetly, "and I will tell you what I see before me. I see a man who has no love of England or its king . . . truth or falsehood?"

"Truth," he admitted after a moment.

She copied his stance, folding her arms over her chest and squaring her shoulders. "I also see a man who has—also by his own admission—no vast knowledge of England's roads and by-ways."

"North is north in any country," he reminded her. "What is more, your brother has been scratching out such faithful maps these past few nights, I feel I could find my way to Gwynedd . . . or Radnor . . . with my helm on backwards."

Ariel dismissed his sarcasm with an airy wave of her hand. "I also see a man who has only the prospect of being enter-tained in one of the king's prisons as his reward for being recognized or caught on the other side of the Channel. I see all of this and I am forced to wonder why you would do it. I am driven to wonder what other reason is taking you so far from a home and a battlefield where your vaunted talents could be put to better use. I had thought revenge to be part of the motive when I first heard of the connection—dare I say coinci-dence—with De Braose. But no. Somehow it seems too petty an impulse, too lacking in the glory befitting such a noble champion."

Only Eduard's jaw flexed in response to her sarcasm and he wondered how someone could change from being an object of lust one moment to an object sorely in want of a good shaking the next. His hand did shoot out, but not to strike or throttle. He had caught sight of Robin returning to the pil-grim's hall and wanted to halt the boy before he came close enough to interrupt.

He need not have worried. Robin, catching one look at the expression on his brother's face, did an abrupt turnabout, veer-ing over to where Sedrick and Lord Dafydd were finally cele-brating some success with the smouldering pile of kindling and pine knots.

Eduard, meanwhile, continued to regard Ariel de Clare with a calmness that belied the very fine thread his patience was stretched upon. He was not a man to suffer too many questions where either his motives or his honour was con-cerned. Nor was he wont to offer endless explanations where one should have sufficed, especially to a green-eyed minx who was proving to be far too clever for her own good.

He had not deliberately kept De Braose's name to himself; he simply had not thought it important enough to mention to her, not when there was so little likelihood of either of them coming face to face with their mutual nemesis. Nor had he been particularly enamoured of the earl's notion to keep his niece in the dark as to their real intentions. He believed a man —or woman—walking into danger should not do so blindly, and using Ariel de Clare to shield their attempt to rescue Princess Eleanor from the king's prison was about as dangerous a situation as he could envision. She would have to be told eventually, of course. Even the Welshman would have to know eventually, but because it had been the earl's express wish to delay the telling until it was absolutely necessary, Eduard was, in turn, bound to maintain the charade as long as possible. Even at the expense of his patience.

"Has it not occurred to you, Lady Ariel, that I may indeed have very good reasons for returning to England; that those reasons may not have anything whatsoever to do with you or your overabundance of grooms; that those reasons might be *private* and *personal*?"

"Where a man is concerned, anything private or personal usually has to do with a woman. Is that what you want me to believe?" she scoffed. "That you are going to England because of a woman?"

Flung from her lips as a casual mockery, Ariel was surprised to see a distinct tightness alter the shape of FitzRandwulf's jaw. Already iron-hard, it tensed even further so that each sinew was ominously well defined and the mottling of scar tissue stood out white and rigid. His eyes took on a glow not unlike the embers of a fire, burning away the thin veneer of politeness, and leaving only the cold gray ash of contempt in its wake.

Ariel, puffed with her own smug assurances, felt the strength of them leak out of her, deflating her composure as surely as if a knife had been thrust into a bubble of dough.

He *was* going to England because of a woman!

She was not quite certain why the idea should have shocked her, she only knew it did. Shocked . . . or unsettled . . . in truth she knew not which, but she found her gaze falling instinctively to the broad, muscled wall of his chest. The ring was not visible through the dark mat of hair that filled the open vee of his shirt, but she could sense it hanging there, ornate and delicate, warmed by the animal heat of his flesh.

"Is it so outlandish a thought, my lady?"

"N-no, of course not."

"Or do you find it beyond belief that you might not be the prime consideration in *everyone's* mind?"

She met the accusation with a hot flush of mortification, for he was smiling. Grinning, actually, even as he mocked her vanity and arrogance.

"Was there anything else you wanted to know?" he asked solicitously.

Ariel took refuge behind the rapid lowering of her lashes, and clasped her hands tightly together. "No. No, there is nothing else."

Eduard beckoned for Robin to join them. "Hold a blanket for Lady Ariel while she strips out of these wet clothes. When she is dry, fetch some of Biddy's unguent out of my saddle pack and see that she applies it thickly over any rashes." He paused in his instructions and glanced at Ariel. "Unless of course you would prefer me to oversee the application myself. I would, naturally, be most happy to render my full and undivided attention."

Heat flared in Ariel's cheeks again as the wolfish smile broadened. Part of her knew enough to be outraged by the suggestion; another part of her shivered through a sudden image of those big, powerful hands slicked with oil, skimming over her flesh.

She blinked. "I am sure I can manage on my own. Thank you."

He offered an exaggerated bow and strode away to rejoin the others in front of the budding fire. Ariel waited until he was too far to hear the words she mouthed under her breath, then turned and plumped herself down on a low, three-legged stool.

Robin had heard quite clearly and stood staring, a bundle

of clothing in one hand and a goblet of mulled wine in the other.

"Have . . . you and Eduard argued?"

The *again* was unspoken, but loudly implied.

"Your brother does not argue," she snapped. "He prefers to exchange insults."

"My lord brother has never been a man to say twenty words where one is sufficient, and so he sometimes seems more . . . brusque than he really intends to be. He does have a great deal on his mind."

"We all have a great deal on our minds," she countered. "But we do not all walk around acting saddle-galled, as if parts of our bodies were held in a constant crush."

Robin's mouth trembled as he tried unsuccessfuly to contain a grin. "If he appears impatient at times, it usually means he is impatient with himself."

Ariel accepted the wine goblet he offered and sipped at the spicy-sweet contents while she glared at the three shadowy figures in front of the fire. FitzRandwulf's silhouette was unmistakable with his long legs braced wide apart and his shoulders blotting out a fair portion of the view.

"At any rate, it is better than the black moods he used to suffer."

Ariel dragged her eyes away from the fire. "Black moods?"

"Oh aye, my lady. He used to have dreadful nightmares. Horrible ones that left him white and shaking in the mornings. Even now, you will notice, he does not sleep overmuch. An hour or two at a time, rarely any longer. It . . . had to do with what happened to him when he was younger. When he lived in England with the man he *thought* was his father, and where he was beaten and tortured. Why . . . he bears a scar this long"
—Robin held his hands a foot apart—"where the Dragon thrust a knife into Eduard's thigh and tried to make him betray our real father. And his mother . . . !" Robin shook his head like someone who has never known anything but absolute love and respect. "Biddy told me she was the most malefic woman who ever lived. She bathed in blood and used to torture people for the sheer fun of it. She *laughed* while the Dragon cut into

Eduard's flesh. She laughed and entreated him to stab again, and again. Biddy saw it all. She was there. And so was my mother, Lady Servanne, and Lady Gillian, and Sparrow, and Friar . . ."

He stopped, for he could see his credibility was beginning to drain away along with the wine in Lady Ariel's goblet.

"It is true," he insisted quietly. "You could ask Eduard himself, except that he tends to blacken eyes and break heads at the very mention of the name Nicolaa de la Haye."

Ariel lowered the goblet slowly from her lips. Even in as remote a place as Milford Haven, the name of Nicolaa de la Haye was synonymous with death and evil. Mothers invoked her spirit to frighten their children into obedience. Bards cast her as the witch or the sorceress or the bride of the anti-Christ when they retold tales spawned in the dark mists of Lincolnshire. Ariel had not thought someone so hellish had actually existed.

"Nicolaa de la Haye was Lord Eduard's mother?" she asked in a fascinated whisper.

Robin glanced over his shoulder and showed the first signs of reluctance, as if he might have said too much already. "Aye, my lady. He bears the scars of her motherly affection to prove it. You . . . will not tell him I told you? You will not say anything . . . ?"

"No. No, of course not, Robin. Ease yourself. I will say nothing."

"Thank you, my lady," he murmured, not sounding the least convinced.

"Robin . . ." She waited until he looked over at her. "I swear it on our friendship: I will say nothing. In fact . . ." She straightened and set the goblet aside. "I have forgotten it already. What *were* we talking about? Oh yes, I have it now. Blankets. You were going to fetch blankets so I could change out of these wet clothes before I freeze to death."

Robin smiled gratefully. "Yes, my lady. I shall fetch them right away."

While Robin was kneeling over one of the saddle packs, Ariel's eyes strayed back to the fireside. A man born of a sorceress who had mated with a wolf and a dragon: this was the man her uncle had entrusted her safety to. A man who suffered black moods and nightmares.

It would be sheer luck if *she* did not have nightmares this night, for although she had promised Robin she would speak no more of it, it would be almost impossible not to think about it.

As quiet as the forest had been, with only the sound of the wind sifting through the trees, the abbey was like a tomb. Ariel lay in her straw-filled pallet with her eyes wide open, the very pores of her skin wide open as well, steeped in the silence of holy reverence. Sedrick had stoked the fire high before retiring to his own pallet, but the logs had been too damp to sustain a blaze for long and, apart from the odd crackle and hiss, it smouldered disconsolately in the grate.

Ariel had consumed rather a large quantity of wine after her confrontation with FitzRandwulf. Combined with the subsequent revelations by Robin, she filled her cup several times and eventually tottered to her bed with the room canting on a distinct angle downward.

Contrary to her earlier fears, she had been enjoying the best night's sleep she'd had since leaving Château d'Amboise, when she was wakened—not by visions of demonic witches and ritual sacrifices, but by an uncomfortable fullness in her bladder. Twice before retiring she had ventured out into the night air and picked her way along the well-worn path to the lean-to that sheltered the privy holes. The fact that she needed to venture out a third time was threatening to keep her wide awake until something was done about it.

If I were a man, she thought miserably, I could simply piss in the corner pot and be done with it. But there was only one pot and it was a tall, long-necked thing she would probably knock over in her attempts to straddle it.

Apparently monks did not allow for pilgrims to have more pressing needs during the night.

Ariel lifted her head and searched the gloom, but there was not much to see. She pushed herself cautiously upright

and swung her legs over the side of the cot. The dull red glow
from the fire gave the bound staves at the ends of the pallets
the slightest hint of shape and substance, and allowed her to
steer her way across the chamber without tripping over packs,
saddles, armour, and furniture.

Like most doors in a monastery, the hinges were well
oiled to prevent the devil from knowing there were souls wandering about. Ariel slipped through the arched portal of the
pilgrim's hall and hurried along the stone corridor that divided
the hall from the almonry. Exit through another silently swinging door let her out into the clammy dampness of the evening
air. The rain had stopped but the mist was thick and pervasive,
wetting her skin almost instantly and clinging in tiny droplets
to the blanket she had draped around her shoulders.

Hemming in the fog, the pale walls of the abbey were her
only link with reality. Here and there, the branches of a low
bush plucked at the dragging ends of her blanket, and twice
she managed to shrivel her own skin with lurid images of
crouched, stalking grotesques with bony fingers and grasping
claws.

At first she thought it must be nearer daylight than she
had supposed, for the fact that she could see the walls at all
suggested a general easing into daylight. But then she quickly
realized there was a source of light somewhere up ahead, a
concentrated source that bore the acrid tang of a pitch torch.

The stable where the horses were kept was directly behind the pilgrim's hall, and it was from there the torchlight
bloomed, yellowed and hazed by the mist. Ariel guessed it was
a monk going early about his chores, and she remembered to
pull the blanket up over her head to conceal the length and
colour of her hair.

Her footsteps slowed, however, as the sound of voices
came toward her. They were familiar voices, one of them as
readily identifiable as her own.

"If you are worried about the state of the road between
here and Rennes," Henry was saying, "surely there is a way to
bypass the town entirely."

"There is," Eduard agreed, "but one of us will still have

to ride into the city to see if the lord marshal managed to dispatch a messenger there. He mentioned Rennes or St. Malo as being places where a courier would be sent to meet us; both towns are big enough to show little interest in pilgrims passing through."

"And if you are wrong? How will we know to stand fast?"

"I will have Sparrow with me. If there is any reason why you should not come near the city, one or both of us will double back to warn you. In truth, though, I do not anticipate any trouble. The leader of the rebelling forces is Hugh of Luisgnan—doubly vexed with the king for divorcing his first wife and taking Hugh's betrothed as his new queen. He is a good man, not known for wanton pillage and murder. If his armies have occupied Rennes, he will be more concerned with restoring the peace than prolonging open hostilities. He wants all of Normandy to unite against the usurper; he cannot do that if he rouses sympathy for the English king."

The light shifted and the fog swirled, retreating before the heat of the torch as three men emerged from the stables. Ariel, not wanting to be caught on the path spying on them, slipped behind the bulky shadow of an ancient fig tree a step before Henry, Sedrick, and FitzRandwulf materialized out of the fog. FitzRandwulf was leading Lucifer behind him. The enormous rampager was fully geared and as Eduard spoke he adjusted the corner of the saw-toothed saddle cloth.

"Leave here as close after dawn as possible and keep to the main road. If neither Sparrow nor myself rejoin you before midday, assume the way is clear and push on to Rennes."

"Will you find us, or will we find you?" Henry asked.

"If I am not there to meet you at the town gates, go directly to an inn called the Two Fighting Cocks. The hostler is a friend and will provide all your needs. Whisper the words *à outrance* in his ear and he will know you come from Amboise."

"The Two Fighting Cocks. *À outrance.*" Henry nodded. "And if you are still not with us when we are ready to leave again?"

Eduard smiled grimly. "Then I am undoubtedly dead and your sister will have realized her fondest desire."

FitzRandwulf led Lucifer forward again, seemingly toward the solid wall that enclosed the monastery grounds. But as the torchlight burned away the fog, a postern gate took shape amongst the withered ivy and overhanging tree branches. It was just tall enough and wide enough to allow Eduard to lead the destrier through, and once on the other side, he swung himself up into the saddle and was swallowed into the darker mist without so much as a fare-thee-well.

Henry and Sedrick stood at the postern until the sound of Lucifer's heavy hoofbeats had faded into the woods.

"He's a hard fellow to like," Sedrick commented. "Cocky as well."

"Cocky," Henry agreed, "but tolerable for another fort-night or so. In truth, I have never had a great love for these provincial barons—nor their bastard cubs—but this one seems to know what he is about."

Sedrick chuckled gruffly. "The Lady Ariel might find cause to argue his worth."

Henry glanced back at the ghostly silhouette of the abbey. "In this, Ariel will do as I say. She already has the means, with the Welsh princeling eager to climb into her bed, to win back the estates and titles rightfully belonging to the De Clare name. Once we have the Pearl in our possession, we will have the means to ensure those lands and titles remain ours for a very long time."

Sedrick's frown, as slow to form as some of the thoughts in his head, regarded the young lord speculatively. "Ye would fain help steal the Pearl to use as barter? But ye swore—we all three swore an oath *on our lives*, that once stolen, the Pearl would be placed in safekeeping, far out of reach of the king."

"So we did. And I have no intentions of breaking that oath, nor do you. But keeping the Pearl out of the king's hands, and well within our own, are two different matters."

Sedrick's scowl turned dubious. "I would not want to let FitzRandwulf hear ye say such things. He's prickly enough as it is planning one theft without having to worry about planning another."

Henry sighed as if greatly put upon to explain the obvious.

"We do not have to steal the Pearl a second time in order to keep the king on tenterhooks. It is enough to *know* . . . and to have *him* know . . ."

"That *we* know where the Pearl is," Sedrick concluded brightly.

"Thy wit is unsurpassed," Henry said, laughing dryly. "Now come, man, these are heavy thoughts to burden so tender a brain at such an hour and place as this. God's truth," he added, shivering as they started walking back along the path, "I will be happy to be quit of this place. I swear the shadows move and the fog has eyes."

Sedrick crossed himself hastily, his hand falling to the hilt of his sword as the gnarled trunk of a fig tree took shape beside them. He too could have sworn he saw movement, but there was nothing there, only the moving, swirling banks of opaque mist.

Chapter 12

✝ **A**riel had dashed back to the pilgrim's hall and made it into her pallet a scant few seconds before she heard the faint rasp of the door and the sound of stealthy feet seeking out their beds in the gloom. Her heart had pounded in her throat and her lips had curled between her teeth in an effort to counter the pain of a stubbed toe, and for the next hour she had lain there wide awake, her bladder throbbing while she replayed a bewildering array of thoughts, most of them centring around the exchange she had overheard between Henry and Sedrick.

What was this talk of a jewel—a pearl valuable enough to use as barter? Barter with whom? For what purpose? It had to be *extremely* valuable if the king possessed it . . . doubly, trebly so if it was worth the risk of all their lives to steal it.

And the thought of FitzRandwulf as a common thief, willing to travel so far to steal a pearl? It made no sense whatsoever. Not for any of them.

Henry, with his own modest successes on the tournament circuits, was neither so penniless nor so witless as to resort to such desperate measures as stealing from the crown. Wealth, in any form, had never been of prime consideration in any of Sedrick's plans either. He was the marshal's loyal liegeman and as long as he had ale to drink, food to fill his belly, a wench to bed, and heads to break, he was content.

FitzRandwulf's capacity for avarice was unknown to her, but from what Ariel knew of his personal worth—admittedly not much more than what she had gleaned from Robin's stories over the past few days—he was not suffering from a cringing poverty. He had estates in Touraine and the Aquitaine, possibly more in Lincolnshire that would have come to him through his mother. Would he kill for a pearl? Would he travel to England and risk all for the sake of stealing a polished bit of stone?

Moreover, had he not already admitted he was going to

England because of a woman? Had he admitted it . . . or had
he simply not disagreed with Ariel's supposition? And if it *was*
a woman luring him out of his lair in Normandy, was it a
woman in possession of this mysterious pearl?

Ariel had barely sifted her way through these convoluted
deductions when she heard Henry's call to rise. Determined
not to betray any knowledge of their conversation—and here,
she at least had the satisfaction of knowing she had not imagined the whisperings and intrigues—she made her prayers and
greeted their meal of ale and bread with her usual morning
scowl. Knowing it would be expected of her, she made a point
of inquiring where their choleric guide had taken himself, and
of expressing her heartfelt opinion that they could do just as
well without him.

They left the abbey when the sun was still a pale blot on
the horizon. They took infrequent stops along the way and by
noon had left the thickest tracts of forest well behind them.
Fields began to look well tended, hemmed with stone fences
and hedgerows. Haystacks were built up around the trunks of
trees, so high only the topmost branches showed. Flocks of
sheep dotted the hills and once a black and white dog ran
along the road beside them, loudly protesting their trespass.

There were increasing signs of pedestrian traffic as well.
Fresh cart tracks and footprints had been set in the mud by
farmers hoping to find eager buyers in the city. Several times
they passed men on foot who glared at them with wary eyes
and closed mouths, but there were no overt signs of an army on
the move, or of the burning and pillaging King John had al-
leged was running rampant through Brittany and Normandy.

There was no sign of FitzRandwulf or Sparrow either.
Henry and Sedrick held a huddled discussion when they broke
for the noon meal, including the Welshman out of respect for
his princely state, no doubt, but leaving Ariel and Robin to
pack away the remains of their food and utensils. She at least
knew where FitzRandwulf was, having been privy to their
strategies last night. But Robin, his face mostly concealed beneath the hood he had taken to wearing against the cold, was
not so much concerned over his brother's absence as he was

hurt over being left behind. He was, after all, Eduard's squire. He, not Sparrow, should have accompanied his lord into Rennes, regardless of any threat of peril.

All told, it was not a happy group of three knights and two squires who approached the gates of Rennes. The city itself was indistinguishable from most others that had grown up around a Norman stronghold. The first sighting was of towers and needle-thin spires rising above the crest of a hill. Boundary stones placed beside the highroad marked the beginnings of the town's land and divided the arable strips of meadow where the residents grew their crops and grazed sheep. Running alongside the city were the brawling, turbulent waters of the river Vilaine, a tumbling rush of wicked currents into which a man crossing the draw could fall and be swept a dozen leagues downstream before popping up to catch a breath. Entry into the walled city was through a stone archway and vast wooden gates that were kept closed and guarded from sundown to sunrise. A fat wart of a porter with a bulbous red nose and runny eyes collected a toll from the five travellers, allowing them to pass only after they and their packhorses had been thoroughly inspected.

Here too were the first signs of open defiance against the English king. The pennons of Brittany and France flew prominently over the main gate; the leopards of England were conspicuously absent.

Glancing past the shadowy arch of the tollgate, the new arrivals had no difficulty envisioning a bullhide-clad sentry lowering his crossbow upon the gatekeeper's signal. There were more sentries boldly placed on top of the walls and in the watchtowers, all of them wearing the blazons of Hugh of Luisgnan.

Inside the walls, the narrow, winding streets that formed a labyrinth of districts and guilds around the heart of the inner city were crowded, bustling with vendors and peddlers hawking their wares. Ariel strove to keep her head down and her face shielded under the brim of her hat, but there was too much to look at, too many sights that offered a change from the damp isolation of the past few days. Shop windows were open and goods displayed on hooks and tall, heaped shelves. Wooden booths were crammed into every nook and corner, selling everything from soap, garlic, and coal, to grindstones, shovels, and honey. The din was fierce and only grew in measure as they rode deeper into the city. Everyone shouted to be heard over their neighbour; church bells tolled unceasingly, babes screamed and dogs yapped. There were people and horses everywhere, knights with glinting bits of armour pushing through slower-moving groups of churchmen or ruffians. Once, Henry had to signal the others to move aside for a pair of hand-carried litters bearing two noble young ladies in a laughing, pointing hurry to spend their rich husbands' money.

Most of the buildings were built from timber, three and four storeys high, with a tendency to sag with age. With streets rarely more than seven or eight feet wide, the upper levels of the buildings hung over the alleyways, creating a tunnel-like effect with scant space between for daylight to shine through. Painted signs swung and creaked over doorways, some low enough to whack an indolent horseman to attention. With three and four families living over each shop, the stench of so many closely packed bodies was nearly as overwhelming as the din. Household refuse and ordure were heaved out of the windows with little warning, scavenged by pigs and kites that contributed their own slimy offerings to the general ambience.

For convenience and protection, most bakers and cook shops were located in one warren, goldsmiths in another, linen makers, tanners, fish merchants all in their own. A blind man could find most by smell alone, following the sweet and heady scents of the bakers to the acrid mix of tannin and mashed brains for the leather makers. Worst was the butchers' row, where the gutters and cobbles ran red with blood. Here the beggars and those of lowly descent fought with the dogs and gulls over dripping strings of entrails tossed into steaming heaps and deemed worthless even for the making of soap or casings.

In the centre of the town were the fine stone houses of the richer citizens, the guildhall with its belfry tower, the market-place where ladies and their tiring women congregated to in-spect the newest velvets imported by the Venetian merchants. Linens from Flanders were sold here, almonds and spices were offered in fragrant handfuls by swarthy-skinned Greeks. At the very heart was the town square with its raised dais and tall wooden cross where the town crier stood to make all public pronouncements.

As in most cities, there were nearly as many churches as houses, built to play on the guilty consciences of the masses of sinners. There was a monastery for training acolytes and a nunnery for the welfare and safekeeping of beautiful or rebellious young daughters. In almost as great a number were the taverns, inns, and wine shops located where merchants could eat, sleep and drink with other merchants, Jews with Jews, sellers of iron and bronze with the brawny men who fashioned weapons and suits of fine chain mail. These, like all other establishments, bore no written names on their signposts, for only the very rich and privileged could cipher lettering. They were identified with graven pictures carved and painted brightly—a snarling boar to depict the Boar's Head Inn, or a sprig of yellow weeds to harken patrons to the Golden Thistle.

The inn where Henry finally called a halt boasted a swinging wooden sign painted with two strutting red cocks. At first, Ariel could scarcely believe it had been FitzRandwulf's choice, for it was surely the most squalid, drunken tilt of warped boards and half-rotted thatching they had encountered. After an intense few minutes spent contemplating their surroundings, her brother was of the same shocked opinion.

"I am not keen on the look of this place," he said unnecessarily.

"Aye," Sedrick mused. "He might have chosen a place less extravagant nearer the butchers' mart."

"Are you certain this is where Lord Eduard instructed us to meet him?" Dafydd asked in an awed whisper, his eyes rounded and fixed upon a man and woman strolling past, the latter scantily clad and screeching with laughter as the man thrust his hand under her bodice and gave her breasts a hearty fondle.

Henry peered up at the sign to doubly verify it in his own

mind. "Robin . . . perhaps you and Ariel should remain out here with the horses until we have had a look inside."

Ariel, already dismounted and standing on the cobbled street with the others, laid a hand on the hilt of her shortsword and shook her head. "I go where you go, brother dearest, and in this case, I prefer to have a look myself, thank you."

Henry frowned, but he was not in any mood to argue now, not with the daylight waning and the gloom becoming less wholesome by the minute. He hailed a burly looking scoundrel from a doorway nearby and held up a silver coin.

"This is yours, fellow, if you will stand with the horses and guard against any curious hands straying too near."

The man nodded and grinned through a blackened grate of broken teeth. "Not so much as a finger, my fine lord, or you will have it on your plate come morning."

"My companions and I will fetch *your* fingers, along with your heart and eyes if you make the mistake of being too curious yourself."

The lout glanced at Sedrick, who looked big enough and powerful enough to do the fetching himself, without aid of a knife or sword, and he nodded again.

Henry girded himself and led the way.

Inside, the cramped taproom was gloomy from lack of light. There were no windows and the only dim illumination came from a meagre supply of tallow candles smoking on the tabletops. The stench was like nothing Ariel had ever choked on before and she lifted her hand to cover her nose and mouth, preferring the leather smell of her gloves.

When her eyes adjusted to the amber-toned shadows, she could see crudely built trestles and benches lining three of the walls. Along the fourth was a counter consisting of a warped board propped between two oak casks. A blowsy, amazingly buxom barmaid stood behind it exchanging ribald comments with a patron who was evidently haggling over the price of something more than ale. There were other, dark, surly look-ing characters seated at the tables. Their voices, likened to a low droning of bees, fell silent the moment the three knights came through the door. Ariel felt the chill of a dozen pairs of watery eyes questioning their presence in this swineherds' paradise. Some of them, she guessed, had never ventured more than a stone's throw from these walls and could not begin to understand why anyone beyond their fetid little community would venture in.

Others might have chosen this place deliberately as being a low enough and sordid enough stew to bypass any close inspection. These were men who would slit a throat for a penny and not care if the throat was noble or common.

The wench behind the counter was not so impartial. Seeing Henry start to walk toward her, she gave the already loosened laces across her bodice an enthusiastic tug and swatted away the hands of the dullard who had been pestering her.

"*Oui, monsieur?* And what might your pleasure be on such a fine, lusty evening as this?"

"A tankard of ale to wash the dust from our throats," Henry said, his words slowing noticeably as the truly awesome size of her bosoms came into the light. Fully as large as two ripe melons, they earned as hard a stare as the large, fat cockroach that lay belly-up on the counter. "And a word with the innkeeper, if you please."

"Monsieur Valois is not here," the wench laughed. "He has spent the last few nights fettered in iron bracelets for smashing a bottle over the head of one of the justicar's lackeys." She leaned farther over the counter, crushing the hapless roach under the smothering weight of her breasts. "My name is Lizabelle. Is there nothing *I* can help you with?"

"There . . . might be," Henry agreed cautiously.

"Speak, monsieur, and it is yours."

"Have you any rooms to let for the night?"

Lizabelle grinned. "For the *whole* night, monsieur?"

"If it is not too much trouble."

"It is never any trouble, m'sieur. In fact, it would be my very great pleasure to accommodate you"—she took a deep enough breath to send a brown, puckered nipple popping over the neck of her bodice—"so long as you have the coin to pay."

"I have the password," Henry assured her, lowering his

voice. "À `outrance`. I was told it would provide us with all our needs."

"Password, m'sieur?" she asked guardedly. "No coin?"

"I have coin, which I will not grudge parting with for fair value."

"I am relieved to hear it, m'sieur, but just in case—"

In a wink, her grin disappeared and her hand came up from beneath the counter, the sharp glint of a dagger flashing in her fist. Henry jerked back, but not fast enough to completely avoid the needle-like point. It slashed a thin red line along the side of his jaw and came back for a second stroke, but by then he had moved out of her reach . . . into the grasping clutches of the two burly men who had obviously been waiting for a signal to close in behind him.

Each grabbed an arm, preventing him from drawing sword or knife. A wild glance over his shoulder found Sedrick in similar straits, swarmed by half a dozen stout men at least, all of them straining mightily to bring the roaring giant to his knees.

Ariel, standing a little to the side and behind, had seen the men shifting stealthily into position, but before she could shout a warning, a thick, sour-tasting hand had clamped itself over her mouth and an arm had circled her waist, lifting her and dragging her back into the corner. Kicking and flailing, she watched as Henry was disarmed of his weapons and flung so hard against the wall, his brow cracked against the solid planking. Dazed, he wavered on his feet and staggered a half-turn before stumbling into one of the trestle tables. Tankards, ewers, and chunks of stale bread were scattered across the floor as one of his attackers started beating him with a wooden truncheon. Hampered by the weight of his armour, and with his brain still spinning from the contact with the wall, Henry floundered under the rain of heavy blows, barely aware of a second man searching his clothes for a purse or money belt.

Sedrick lunged like a mastiff, carrying the shouting wave of assailants with him. He managed to wrestle an arm free and sent one of his attackers flying over the wooden counter to land squarely in the upflung arms of the shrieking Lizabelle.

The impact sent them both caroming backwards into a rack of crocks and tankards. One of the swarm broke away and took up an oak bench, swinging it at Sedrick's head, but a shout brought Dafydd ap Iorwerth plunging out of the shadows, his sword drawn and wrested away from the men who had not been quick enough to bring him to ground. The villain saw the blade coming and blocked it with the bench. The steel bit deep into the wood, lodging there solidly enough that he was able to twist it out of Dafydd's grip. Two more villains leaped on him from behind while the lout with the bench swung it again, slamming it over Dafydd's outstretched arm with a re-sounding *craaaak!*

Robin, meanwhile, had sailed to Ariel's aid, but managed only a bloodcurdling promise of chivalrous revenge before a pewter tankard knocked the words and the sense out of his head. While he reeled blindly toward the door, Ariel kicked and clawed and gouged for her captor's eyes and ears. She twisted and turned like a slippery eel, using the wooden soles of her shoes to good advantage, barking his shins time and time again until a curse made him loosen his grip. The respite was brief. Something solid slammed into the side of her face—a fist or a cudgel, it had the same effect—and her world exploded in a burst of white light. It struck again, carrying her hat away with it, and she could not be certain if it was the redness of her hair spilling over her face, or the red of her own blood.

Discovering it was a woman he held, the man paused a moment in confusion and surprise—a moment too long and a surprise so absorbing he failed to see the door of the tavern smash open and a tall, mail-clad arbiter enter the arena.

Dispensing judgement and justice on every thrust of his sword, he sent two men screaming into the shadows, clutching at severed clothing and spurts of gushing blood. A third for-feited the ability to scream at all as the blade slivered through his throat. He spun in a spray of blood and scattered the men clinging steadfastly to Sedrick. They saw the sword and the steely-eyed demon knight who wielded it, and they aban-doned their attack to bolt for the door.

The sword flashed several more times, striking flesh with

the impact of a hatchet biting into wood. Ariel felt the pressure around her waist spring free and she folded into a small heap on the floor. Her vision dimmed behind a wall of pain. A warm, wet liquid was running between her fingers and down her hand, and she feared to let go of her head lest it fall off and be trampled underfoot.

The door swung wide a second time and the flare of light revealed a scene from Bedlam. There was blood splattered everywhere. Bodies of the slain and wounded men lay twitching on the floor; broken crockery and dark puddles of ale littered the area, heaviest around the groaning bulk of Lizabelle and her unconscious accomplice. The light also touched briefly on Eduard FitzRandwulf's visored helm, showing a brief glimpse of eyes that were neither gray nor blue, but washed of colour by the heat of battle.

Caught in the light, a second newcomer was silhouetted in the doorway. His diminutive form was brushed aside by a pair of fleeing villains, and Sparrow spared but a fleeting breath on a graphic oath before he unslung his harp-shaped arblaster from his shoulder and let fly a speedily armed quarrel after the departing culprits. The tip of the arrow punched into a well-rounded buttock and, with a squawk of glee, the wood sprite fit another short, stubby bolt to the bow and set off in further pursuit.

The door swung shut behind him but Eduard had stared at the opening long enough to lose concentration. An assailant came up behind him, a dagger driving for the opened slit under the sleeve of mail. It was Iorwerth's shout that brought Eduard spinning around, his sword cutting cleanly through the villain's bony elbow. The forearm split away and cartwheeled into the shadows in a burst of blood, the hand still clutched around the hilt of the knife.

The man screamed. His eyes bulged and his remaining hand reached quickly to clutch the stump of his arm as he lurched for the door and ran out into the street. He made one full turn, spraying the cobbles with blood, before he stumbled off down one of the laneways, scattering the onlookers who had been drawn by the sights and sounds.

Eduard remained tense, his body poised to meet the next threat, but there were none. All who could run had done so. Those who could not dragged themselves, groaning, into the darkest, blackest shadows.

Eduard saw Robin leaning against the wall and reached him in a single stride.

"Are you all right? Are you hurt?"

Robin shook his head and cursed his own ineptness. "Lady Ariel . . . ?"

Sedrick was slouched over one of the tables, groaning and swearing with equal aplomb. Lord Henry was in the process of trying to find his balance and swayed on his feet like an Infidel drunk on Christian blood. The Welshman sat in a dazed crumple against the wall, his face as pale as ash behind the beard, a bloodied arm cradled against his chest.

And Ariel . . .

Eduard whirled around, his eyes probing the shadows, identifying the bodies. Lady Ariel de Clare was nowhere to be seen in the haze of disturbed dust but before Eduard could broaden his search, Sparrow came crashing through the door with enough self-importance to send FitzRandwulf into a wary crouch again.

"Poxy scullions," he announced disgustedly. "One ran this way, one ran that." A pudgy hand waved side to side to supplement the telling with a visual description. "Both were heavier with iron for their trouble, however," he added, chuckling as he patted his arblaster, "and neither too likely to walk so upright or so fast in the days to come. Well then what is this? Maledictions, but we leave you on your own for half a day and see what trouble you find yourselves!"

Sedrick glanced over and snarled, "Where the devil did ye come from?"

"From the bowels of your conscience, it seems," Sparrow answered blithely. "Not a moment too soon, I warrant. Three hulking great oafs and . . ." He looked around and grew noticeably still. "Has someone gone a-missing?"

Eduard had already detected movement behind him and was stalking toward the back of the tavern.

"Lady Ariel?"

There was no answer. He sheathed his sword and crouched down on one knee, the dull light from a candle reflecting off his chain mail. He had to bend his head to peer under the table, and there he followed the curled end of a shiny red braid until he found himself staring into a pair of accusingly dark emerald eyes.

"It is quite safe to come out now, my lady," he said, extending his hand. "The excitement is all over."

She muttered something that sounded suspiciously like a slur on his heritage and Eduard arched his brow. "I am glad to see your spirits have not been sent into hiding. Now take my hand and let me bring you out of there before the rats take to liking your company."

"Go to the devil," she said and batted his hand away.

He sighed and reached forward with both hands, grasping her by the shoulders and lifting her up and onto a seat on the edge of the table. He was about to comment on her sense of gratitude when he saw the blood streaking down her temple and cheek.

The shock delayed him a moment and he found himself needing to take a strong breath before he angled her head gently into the candlelight. He stripped off his gauntlets and carefully pushed aside the hair that had been glued flat with all the blood, and, after a few tentative probings of the area with his fingertips, was assured the wound was not life-threatening.

" 'Tis only a small cut," he announced. "Not half so bad as the amount of blood might suggest."

Ariel saw no reason to rejoice. The pain was excruciating. Her stomach had already taken several violent turns and was threatening to rise up her gorge if the room did not stop spinning.

"Are you hurt anywhere else?"

"False concern . . . does not become you," she whispered tautly. "We might all have been killed."

"If you had been killed, my lady, it would have been because your brother could not distinguish the difference between fighting cocks and red hens."

Ariel attempted to glare up at him, but closed her eyes when he split in two and began slewing sideways. "Nonetheless, two ambushes in as many days . . . it does not bespeak high praise for your abilities to protect anyone."

Eduard suffered her sarcasm, but only because she was bleeding already. "Are you able to walk?"

"Away from you? Gladly."

"Away from here will have to suffice for the time being," he countered smoothly, "unless you would prefer to remain and address your complaints to the local justicar?"

Ariel opened her mouth to respond, but the sickening stabs of pain she had been fighting sent a sudden, hot bubble of vomit up her throat. She swallowed it on a sour gasp and reached out a hand for support, clutching at a fistful of Eduard's gypon.

"My lady . . . ?"

She managed to tilt her head up toward the dark, frowning visage and fought the spinning mass of bright pinwheels for as long as she could before her pride crumpled.

"It . . . hurts," she sobbed raggedly. "It . . . hurts too much to bear."

She heard FitzRandwulf murmur something, but the words were too far away to hear. Closer and more importantly, she found herself suddenly cradled against a body that wore a hard casing of armour and leather—neither of which should have been soothing or comforting, but were both. She knew he lifted her into his arms because there was no longer any need to fight for her balance or steady herself against the swimming motion of the walls and floor. All she had to do was curl her arms around the strong column of his neck and burrow into the safety of his embrace.

Dimly, she was aware of the deep vibration of his voice as he called to Sedrick and Henry to help Dafydd out of the tavern. Henry's face loomed in front of her for a moment, but it was an easy enough thing to do to transfer the blame to his shoulders, and she turned her face away, refusing to acknowledge his concern or his offer to carry her out to the horses. She heard Robin's voice and Sparrow's squawks of distress, and then they were out in the street in the midst of another minor storm of noise and shouting.

FitzRandwulf's voice conquered them all. He was still a formidable threat, even with his arms full of fainting woman, and the crowd parted, giving them access to their horses.

Ariel was not sure how far they rode or in what direction. She was not even sure how FitzRandwulf managed to swing himself up onto Lucifer's back without once loosening his grip or tipping her over on her head. If anything, she felt molded to his body, as if he had taken her as a part of himself, absorbing any movements that would cause her pain or discomfort. She must have drifted out of consciousness for a while, for when she woke again, there was no light at all in the sky and she feared the blows on her head had blinded her. A cry sent her fingers across her brow, and in so doing, she pushed aside the heavy curtain of her hair that had blown over her face. Still later, she stirred when she realized she was being carried again, this time into a blur of brightly flickering tapers. She had a vague impression of a clean, well-lit room with whitewashed walls and a large, roaring fire in the hearth, more voices, none of them familiar, making her press herself closer to Eduard's body, unmindful of the sharp edges of mail that imprinted on her skin.

Carrying her as if she weighed nothing, he mounted a narrow flight of stairs two at a time, shouting at someone behind him to bring water and bandages. Ariel groaned softly and tried to bury her head deeper into the crook of his neck, but although he had removed his helm and loosened his mail hood, there were too many rough edges and the dark mane of his hair seemed too impossibly high to reach. The underside of his chin was not, however, and she found her lips touching his flesh, tasting the salt and heat and bold, heady maleness of him. When he shouted again, she recoiled with a shiver that took the heat away from her lips.

"What is it?" he asked. "Are you in pain?"

"Too loud," she gasped.

"Too *loud?*"

"Your voice. When you shout, it is so loud . . . it makes my *feet* ache."

Eduard was taken aback. "Forgive me, my lady. I was more concerned for your head than your feet."

"My head is broken," she moaned pitifully. "There is no hope for it."

"There is always hope for something so hard," he assured her with a wry smile.

He cradled her a moment longer before leaning over the side of a bed and settling her down as carefully as he could. She was deathly pale except for the growing blue patch on her forehead . . . and the blood. There was a wide, smeared streak of it running from the cracked egg on her scalp to the collar of her tunic. It was matted in her hair and staining her hands; a small red rosette of it blotched the front of his gypon, just above the Crusader's cross stitched on the gray wool.

Her skin was so white, her eyes so green and deep . . . capable of drowning a man's best intentions. Eduard reached up to unlace her hands from around his neck, but she resisted, and her fingers were so cold, he took them no further than the caressing warmth of his lips.

"You . . . will not abandon us again?" she implored.

He cupped her hands in his and kissed the soft hollow of each palm. "No, my lady, I will not abandon you again."

"I . . . would have your most solemn oath on that, sir-rah," she whispered, her gaze fastened on his mouth.

In the sudden stillness, Eduard was acutely aware of the beating of his heart and of the soft, shallow breaths that parted her lips. He knew she was half in a daze and not fully responsi-ble for what she said or did, but somewhere between a sigh and a whisper, he bowed his head closer to hers.

"You have my most solemn oath," he murmured. "I will not abandon you."

"Seal it," she said on a rush.

"My lady . . . ?"

She untangled her hands from his and laced them around his neck again, drawing his mouth down to within a warm breath of hers.

"Seal it, damn you, before I—"

Eduard's mouth came down lightly, obligingly over hers, smothering her words, changing them into soft, throaty sighs. That was all he intended it to be—a means of silencing her—and all it would have been if a second sigh had not parted her lips beneath his, and if his own had not betrayed him by giving her what she wanted, taking what he himself wanted.

It was madness. He knew it was madness, yet he could not stop once the taste of her flooded his senses. Ever since she had challenged him to kiss her on the ramparts, the memory had haunted him. It had taunted him in the mists by the riverbank and it had intruded again in the abbey last night. He had not set out alone in the chill and fog because of a need to scout the road ahead; he had set out alone because he was not altogether certain it was only the heat of his temper being aroused by Ariel de Clare. He feared a heat of a different, dangerous kind was beginning to disrupt his instincts, erode his judgement, but if he had been hoping to prove himself wrong, he had failed miserably in his quest. All through the day he had caught himself thinking about her. Wondering. Worrying. Then in the tavern, when he had seen the blood, and felt her reach out to him . . .

Eduard ignored instinct and judgement now as his lips became almost bruising in their need to atone. Ariel shivered once, violently, and he broke abruptly away, fearing he had hurt her, but her eyes were wide and dark and trusting, and he kissed her again, groaning as he shared the exquisite, shuddering crests of pleasure that quivered through her body.

Ariel's hands went slack around his neck and the breath fluttered from her lungs on a long, blissful sigh. Her lashes fought a moment longer before they drifted closed and Eduard caught her hands, holding them a few seconds more than was necessary, releasing them only when he heard the squeak of a floorboard behind him.

Thinking it was the matron arrived with water and bandages, Eduard was startled when he turned and found Henry de Clare's hazel eyes waiting for him.

Eduard had not heard the knight follow him up the stairs,

nor had he any idea how long De Clare had been standing in the doorway, although, to judge by the warmth of his complexion, it was safe to assume he had not just arrived.

Henry looked as if he had just come from a battlefield, not a tavern brawl. His jaw bore a long gash that had bled profusely down the front of his tunic; his face was bruised, his lip cut and swollen. His eyes were bloodshot and red-rimmed, but they stared at FitzRandwulf with a hard, cold clarity of purpose.

"I trust she is not hurt too badly?" he asked evenly.

"She will be fine," Eduard said, rising up off his bended knee. "The cut is clean and not too deep."

"I am glad to hear it. The Welsh are a primitive breed, and I rather doubt Rhys ap Iorwerth would take too kindly to having his bride delivered in less than pristine condition."

Eduard's jaw clenched and he started across the room. He did not get fully past Lord De Clare when a hand reached out and grasped his arm.

He stared into the narrowed hazel eyes for a moment, then glared down at the restraining hand.

Henry relaxed his grip and smiled tightly. "Consider it a friendly warning . . . this time."

His face set, Eduard walked past him and had to step neatly around the plump, red-faced matron as she panted up the last two steps, her arms filled with cloths, a collection of various medicinals and herbs for poultice-making, as well as a large, sloshing basin of water. She huffed a greeting and managed a polite bow before hurrying past Eduard and Henry to see to her patient.

Eduard watched a moment, then turned and walked sharply down the steps. As he descended, he unfastened one of the buckles that kept his hauberk strapped snugly over his shoulders. The flap of heavy mail fell forward over his gypon, straining the seams of the garment almost as much as his temper was strained at the sight of the motley group gathered in the taproom.

Sedrick was sitting on a bench by the hearth, his hands poking and prodding at bruised muscles. He had sustained several stout blows to the head and shoulders, but his armour,

like Henry's, had protected him from the worst of it, though
his neck bled from a gridwork of cut marks left by the iron
links.

Robin was seated alongside, occasionally giving his head a
shake as if to uncross his eyes.

By far the worst off was Dafydd ap Iorwerth. Eduard's
shouts upon their arrival had brought the innkeeper and his
wife bustling out of the back rooms to take immediate charge
of the young Welshman. They had managed to divest him of
his gypon and armour before the pain had rendered him unconscious—an easier path to take, all things considered, than
to remain awake and aware of the injured arm being jostled
free of the rest of the clothing. The break was midway between the wrist and elbow, and the master of the inn, M'sieur
Gabinet, was in the process of pulling and fitting the grating
ends of bone back together again.

The blood that had soaked the young lord's sleeve and
tunic came not from the shattered edges of bone tearing
through the flesh, as Eduard had feared, but from a large sliver
of wood that had been driven into the arm when the bench had
smashed. Fully the length of a man's hand, the splinter had
already been removed and lay red and glistening on the table
as M'sieur Gabinet worked on the arm.

"Comment va-t-il? How is he?" Eduard asked.

"Bah! He is young and strong," said M'sieur Gabinet
"The break is clean, the wound ugly but . . . *pftph!* . . . it
will earn him much sympathy from the women, no? He will be
uncomfortable, but he will not die from it."

Eduard nodded his thanks and the innkeeper carried on,
packing the wound with cobwebs before wrapping it tightly in
strips of lyngel. A young boy, his son to judge by the similarity
of face and shape, was issued brisk orders to cut strips of wood
to use as splints, then to see to hot food and drink for their
guests.

Eduard requested a small change to the order of priorities,
and two brimming flagons of ale arrived at the table the same
time as Henry returned from his sister's room. He joined the

others, barely glancing in Eduard's direction as he helped himself to a tankard of ale.

"I suppose you expect me to take the blame for this," he said, wiping a foam moustache from his upper lip. "But how was I expected to know there were two accursed taverns in this hellhole with cocks hanging over the door? You might have at least mentioned the one had crossed swords as well."

"It was an oversight we remedied just in time, it seems. I assumed you knew the difference between fighting cocks and a pair of prancing fowls. Did you honestly think I would dispatch you to such a pestilent hole?"

Henry pushed back his mail hood and raked his fingers through the flattened, sweat-dampened locks of tawny hair, discovering a lump the size of a toadstool cap behind his ear.

"In truth," he muttered, "I was of the opinion you were possessed of an odd sense of humour, therefore it was more than possible you would send us to a brothel. I must say, however, this is far more to my liking."

The taproom was large, well lit, furnished with sturdy tables that looked scrubbed clean daily. Fresh rushes covered the floor. A fire crackled in the hearth, warming the air as well as whatever savoury concoction bubbled and burped in an enormous black cauldron suspended over the flames. They were the only occupants; a thick wooden bar had been dropped across the door after their arrival to ensure against unwanted interruptions.

As Henry's gaze roved around the room, it settled on Sparrow's belligerent features. The elfin seneschal was perched on the lip of a table, his legs swinging over the side, quite content to see two prime specimens of Norman knighthood lick and suck at their wounds.

"Lucky for you we came along when we did, my Bold Blades," he chuckled. "Other else, you might have found your arses swived on the end of some lumpkin's pike."

"Our thanks for your sympathies." Henry grimaced. "How *did* you happen along when you did?"

"*Happens* we were waiting and watching, to-ing and fro-ing when our gracious host"—Sparrow paused and flourished a hand in M'sieur Gabinet's direction, who in turn paused in his bandaging and took a small bow of acknowledgement—"made mention of another scurrilous inn on the ot side of town where a man could have his brains addled for the price of a sop of ale. It seemed an odd place to go a-looking for lost souls, but a-looking we went, and hey-ho, there you go. Fists flying, tables crashing . . . and nary a sword unsheathed. Aye," he added with a much-put-upon sigh, "lucky we came along when we did."

Sedrick scowled and in no uncertain terms advised Sparrow where he could thrust his luck, with or without the aid of a lumpkin's pike.

"Tsk tsk, Sir Borkel. Save such hasty wishings for another time. Where we are going, we will need all the luck we can gather about us."

Henry glanced quickly over at Eduard. "You have had word from my uncle?"

Eduard shook his head. "No, but M'sieur Gabinet has his own sources. Hopefully the marshal will be able to confirm it by the time we reach St. Malo, but for the moment, our destination appears to be . . . Purbeck."

Henry suffered a twist in his gut that had nothing to do with the beating he had sustained. He had prayed sincerely to hear the princess was being held at Bristol . . . or even the London tower . . . if only for the added physical comforts that were available for a prisoner of such noble delicacy. But Purbeck . . . It was on the Dorset coast and, looming over it like a satyr's eye, was Corfe Castle, a bleak and hellish place, seeming always to stand gray and ugly under a wind-blown, evil sky. Many prisoners disappeared inside the walls of Corfe Castle. Few were ever seen or heard from again. None, to Henry's knowledge, had ever escaped.

"Well then," he said. It was all he said, all he could think to say before he turned away and took several more deep swallows of ale.

Sparrow looked from one solemn face to another and supposed it was up to him to suggest a word or two in their favour. Unfortunately for his good intentions, one of the logs in the fire chose that same moment to send a shower of sparks bursting out over the hearth. When he glanced at the grate to see what had caused the minor eruption, he saw that the small body of a bird had fallen out of the chimney and lay outlined against the glowing bed of embers. It was a sparrow and it was only there for a blink or two before the heat curled the wings and the tiny body caught on fire.

Sparrow felt an uncomfortable scratching at the base of his spine and he looked up to see if anyone else had noticed.

No one had, and when he looked back, the body of the bird was gone, leaving only the acrid scent of death behind.

Chapter 13

✝ **W**illiam the Marshal's confirmation came by way of a monk, who carried the message consisting of a single word —Purbeck—from the earl's temporary lodgings at Falaise Castle. FitzRandwulf's party had already been in St. Malo a full day and had met with the captain of a small ship that same evening to arrange passage across the Channel.

It had taken two days to travel from Rennes to St. Malo, days of riding with aches and bruises, with broken bones and dark moods. Robin and Ariel were kept busy watching Dafydd ap Iorwerth, for he was not as much of a floppy puppy as his appearance had suggested. He had been fully prepared to leave Rennes the morning after their ignoble arrival, broken arm or not, and left little doubt he intended to keep to his saddle if he had to tie himself on.

Ariel had wakened with a blistering headache and no clear memory of anything that had happened after being clouted on the head. She might have remained blithely ignorant had she not had an early visit from her brother.

He had strided into her chamber unannounced, his one cheek and eye a massive purpling bruise, his nose swollen and decidedly to the left of straight.

"You should not cast stones before you see yourself in a glass," he had remarked.

"I have no need to see myself. I can *feel* it ugly enough."

Henry had spared a glance for the blue and yellow goose egg she wore on her forehead, then helped himself to a chunk of cheese off the tray Robin had brought her earlier.

"You have heard, I gather, that the Cub has decided to rest here the day."

"Because of Lord Dafydd's arm?"

"Among other reasons," Henry agreed.

"I hope *I* was not one of those 'other' reasons. It was my head that was cracked not my rump—I am perfectly able to sit a horse."

"He predicted you might say that," Henry mused. "But alas, he was more concerned with the horses than he was with your head."

"The horses?"

"The packhorses, to be precise. He must needs replace them. It seems the threat of plucking out eyes and hearts carries little weight in Rennes. The destriers would have been too difficult to conceal or dispose of, but the rouncies must have been stripped down and sold to harness before the tavern door swung fully shut."

"They were stolen? With all of our supplies?"

"We were hardly expecting to walk into a nest of vipers."

"Or the wrong nest, for that matter."

"An easy mistake. Anyone could have made it."

"But it was not anyone, dear brother, it was you. You who pride yourself on your cunning and quick wit. You who claim to be able to travel from one end of the realm to the other with only your shield and merciless eye for protection."

His scowl returned. "I could have carved the lot to shreds easily—"

"Had you not been distracted. Indeed, your merciless eye was lodged so far down the wench's bosom, it was a wonder it was not torn from the socket when you were attacked."

Henry leaned over. "If you would care to exchange insults, sweet Ariel, harken back to where you were when the truncheons flew and the blood spattered. Under a table? In a corner? The darkest you could find? Here, I would have expected to see you in the thick of the fray, for all your practising and boasting."

Ariel started to return his scowl, but the effort faltered. "In truth, I can remember very little of what happened inside the tavern . . . and nothing at all of this place," she added, indicating the clean, tidy room.

"Nothing at all?" he repeated skeptically.

"Fragments only. Robin had to tell me most of what occurred at the first tavern, else I would have thought we came here by magic."

"Magic," he murmured. "I suppose some damosels would

regard such a bold rescue as being magical—enough so to bind themselves in the rogue's arms for a romantic ride to safety."

"I would hardly call a wild dash through the streets romantic," she said dryly. "Nor was I *bound* in his arms. I was in a faint."

"And so you sought the strength of his lips to hold you up?" He saw her gather herself for a denial and wagged a finger. "Before you splutter needlessly, be advised I was standing right there"—he pointed—"in the doorway. I warrant it may be just as well I was, for neither one of you looked in too much of a hurry to take leave of the other."

Ariel's mouth dropped open. "I . . . was obviously not in my proper senses."

"You will hear no argument from me. You will hear a warning, however. He is fire, Ariel, and if you dally with him, you will be burned."

"Dally with him!" she exclaimed. "I have no intentions of dallying with him!"

"I am glad to hear it, for I would remind you the bloodlines of the De Clares are purer than some who would aspire to be kings and queens. FitzRandwulf may wear the black and gold of La Seyne Sur Mer, but he is a bastard and as such would only breed more bastards on whoever he takes to his bed."

Ariel was dumfounded. Almost speechless. "How . . . *dare* you even take it upon yourself to say such a thing!"

"I dare because we only have each other to watch out for, Ariel. I dare because I am the head of the De Clare family and, frankly, I would dare a great deal more to see our pennon flying over the ramparts of Cardigan Castle again."

"Do you doubt I want the same thing? Have I not agreed to marry the very man who has the power to restore our family name to its proper place?"

"Indeed you have," Henry agreed with quiet intensity. "And indeed you will, even if I have to gird you in an iron belt and tie you to my side every step of the way."

Ariel's response had been to heave the entire tray and its contents at his head, forcing him to duck back out the door.

And while Henry had not exactly girded her or tied her to his side, he had all but transformed himself into a hawk for the close and predatory watch he kept on her after that. He took precautions never to leave her alone with FitzRandwulf. He even limited the time she spent in Robin's company lest the lad boast of too many more of the Bastard's accomplishments.

If Ariel objected to this new attentiveness on her brother's part, she did not put voice to any complaints. She had been given more than just a knock on the head to think about and she was not altogether certain she trusted herself around Fitz-Randwulf.

Not that she would have known, by anything he said or did, that whatever intimacy they may or may not have shared had left a lasting impression. He was his usual cool, brusque self, preoccupied with finding horses and supplies to replace what they had lost, and then with speeding them on their way to St. Malo with no further delays or mishaps. Only at night, during the still, dark hours when the only sound was the beating of her own heart, was she aware of the slate gray eyes watching her across the fire. Then, if she still had reason to doubt the validity of what Henry had told her, she needed only to feel the warm wash of sensations sliding through her belly to know his concerns were real.

St. Malo was a crowded and busy port city. The smell of fish and salt water, canvas and wood rot, permeated everything.

It was also a secretive city, filled to the eaves with men who made their livings carrying other men back and forth to England who preferred to keep their travel arrangements to themselves. Fully a third of John's meagre army had returned to England without the permission or knowledge of their captains. Another third waited in dirty taverns, rolling dice and hoping to win the price of a berth on board the next ship heading home. Voices in the shadows railed King John as a usurper, a liar, a foul murderer. There were brawls in the taverns and throats slit every night. Fevers ran high in favour of the rebel forces seeking to oust the Norman king from Brittany, and even humble pilgrims were not immune from the effects of widespread dissent, twice fielding sprays of rotten vegetables thrown by invisible hands.

FitzRandwulf's party sought lodging at another inn that opened its doors wider to the words *à outrance*, and though the owners were neither as portly nor as amiable as the Gabinets, the rooms were clean, the food hearty, the ale strong and plentiful. Henry and Eduard wasted no time making arrangements for their crossing. Passage for the men and their horses was won at an exhorbitant price, paid in silver to guarantee the captain would not sell their berths to others as eager to remove themselves from Brittany.

When the men returned to the inn for the evening meal, they behaved as if at least a portion of the weight on their shoulders had been lifted. It showed in the amount of ale they consumed with their food and in the lighthearted banter that flew across the platters of mutton, quail, fish, and legumes. Henry was so relaxed, his eye kept wandering to the shapely figure of the innkeeper's daughter, who all but ignored him as she filled their tankards and carried the meal to and from the large dining table. His wandering eye became a general restlessness and, after Ariel declared her intentions to retire for the night, he confided he might partake of a walk to another tavern where the patrons were less solemn and the wenches less prone to keeping their thighs clamped together. It was their last night in Normandy, after all, and there was naught left to do but find their way to the docks before midnight the following eve.

Sedrick, heaving a sigh of vast indulgence, said he might as well accompany the randy young lord to save him from having his brains rattled again. Sparrow, declaring the pair of them needed watching, sharpened his eyes for mischief and followed after them. Neither Robin nor Dafydd ap Iorwerth expressed any further craving for adventure. The Welshman's arm was healing, but painful, and he bid a weary good night to all and did not protest when Robin tucked himself under his arm and supported his weight up the stairs. They left Eduard brooding in front of the fire . . . where he was still to be found an hour or so later when Ariel descended from her room in search of a cup of honeyed milk.

At first, she did not see him, for his dark clothing blended perfectly with the shadows. Nor did he make any overt move to draw attention to himself, letting only his eyes follow her progress across the room.

She had indulged in a bath earlier that afternoon, scrubbing a week's worth of sweat and pine sap out of her hair. Weary of braids and pins and pillowed felt hats, she had left it loose to dry and had caught the bulk of it at the nape of her neck with a scrap of linen. There were unruly sprays drifting around her temples and throat, a soft nimbus of bright red curls that glowed like a halo in the firelight. The bruise on her scalp was still visible although the angriest blue had started to fade. She wore a loose-fitting tunic made of fine camlet cloth—a deliberately feminine concession to the leggings and coarse linsey-woolsey she had worn all week. A modest enough fabric in daylight, it was rendered pale and luminous by the firelight, playing teasing tricks with shapes and shadows so that Eduard could feel his mouth going dry even without looking at anything lower than her collarbone.

An earthenware jug of mead stood on the table, left over from dinner. Ariel pondered it a moment before deciding it would be just as likely to help her sleep as warmed milk. It was while she was helping herself to a measure that she became aware of the silent figure seated in the shadows. She was quite proud of her ability to finish pouring the mead without spilling a drop. She was even able to set the jug aside and stare directly into the watching eyes as if she had known he was there all along.

FitzRandwulf did not call her bluff, nor did he question her presence or apologize for his own. He merely rose and selected another log to add to the fire.

He was out of armour, dressed comfortably in a long belted tunic and hose. His hair curled thick and glossy across the back of his neck, drawing attention to the breadth of his shoulders and to the way his gladiator's muscles bulged and rippled with the motion of his arms.

Ariel took a sip of mead and waited.

He set the fresh log and took an iron rod to the embers, stirring and rearranging them so that sparks fountained in all directions and a cloud of smoke heaved out the wide opening. The log was dry and caught at once, with hungry red snakes of flame exploring the ridges and hollows, curling under the bark and hissing triumphantly over the discovery of some small burrowing creatures.

FitzRandwulf poked and stirred. When he realized she was probably not going to go away until he acknowledged her, the teal gray of his eyes turned and took a deliberately slow perusal of the fire-bleached tunic.

He had managed, since leaving Rennes, to keep his thoughts pure and his mind clear of any lingering images. There were moments, however, like this one. Moments that came out of nowhere and struck without warning. Moments when it would have been far safer for both of them if her hair had remained braided and her body armoured in filthy squire's rags. Moments when *she* should have known when to look away and when it was safe to fill those sea-green eyes with challenges.

"Your brother would not be pleased to come in and find you here alone with me," he said quietly.

"My brother is not my keeper."

"He is concerned for your welfare."

"Are you so dangerous a man, my lord?"

"Some might think so."

A warm, swimming sensation that had nothing to do with the fire or the mead coursed through her, catching at her breath, making the timbre of his voice seem to resonate to the tips of her toes. Power, and the ability to draw upon it at a moment's notice, was apparent in every line of his body—more so as he straightened to his full height and stood towering over her in all his savage splendor, the amber glow of the fire beside him, a black void of shadow behind him.

"Should *I* think of you as a dangerous man?"

"That would depend, my lady."

"On what?"

"On your definition of danger. For instance, I have had several cups of ale and am in no mood for exchanging gauntlets, yet you stand before me with the devil in your eye and, if I am not mistaken, a question scorching your tongue that will not give you any peace until it is asked and answered. If you ask it and you do not like my answer, then yes, it could be very dangerous . . . for both of us."

"How do you know I have a *specific* question in mind?"

"Oh . . . a wild guess, I suppose. That and the fact you have been acting most decidedly *saddle galled* since we left Rennes."

Ariel could not stop the flush from rising in her cheeks. She supposed she should have known Robin would share confidences with him, this despite the solemn promise he had exacted from her not to betray his revelation about FitzRandwulf's dam.

Ariel set her goblet on the table, hard enough to splash some of the contents over the rim. She turned on her heels, fully intending to make it another two days before she deigned to speak to him again, but instead, she stood in a glowing cloud of camlet and curled her hands into tense little fists.

"Why did you kiss me at the inn in Rennes?"

It was the question he had been expecting and he answered it so politely and with such smugness she wished she had the means to scar the other half of his face. "I was merely complying with a request, my lady."

"A request? From who?"

"There were only the two of us in the room at the time," he said evenly.

Ariel whirled around and gaped. "Are you suggesting . . . implying . . . I *wanted* you to kiss me?"

Eduard furled a brow. "I may behave like a rogue and a black-hearted bastard at times, but I am not in the habit of forcing myself on helpless women. On the other hand, if the request is thrust upon me, chivalry dictates I can hardly refuse."

"Even if the woman making the request is *not in her proper senses?*"

Eduard shrugged and seemed to move closer though she could swear his feet had not. "I am hardly a qualified physic to know when a woman is in her proper senses or not—especially a woman who has made such a request before."

Ariel suffered through another ruddy wave of heat. He was standing too close. His formidable upper torso was like a wall of muscle before her, making her feel small and insignificant, and distinctly at a disadvantage.

"Do you know Henry saw us?" she asked.

"He and I have already exchanged a word on the subject."

"He exchanged more than that with me. He seems to be under the impression I may be developing certain . . . ill-advised urges . . . toward you."

"I trust you corrected his impression."

"I assured him—as I assure you now—he was mistaken. I have no urges. Not toward you . . . or any other man, for that matter."

Eduard's gaze took another long, slow slide downward, making her uncomfortably aware that *he* was aware of the sudden new shape her nipples had taken beneath the camlet.

"Are you absolutely certain of that?" he mused.

"Absolutely. Why, I could kiss you now and feel nothing whatsoever."

His eyes rose to the challenge, and Ariel realized her mistake, too late to withdraw it. She did not want to look at him for fear he could see the confusion beginning to crowd her senses. She did not want to look away either, for his fine gray eyes were subtly telling her how beautiful she was, how he did not believe for the merest instant she was not feeling *something*.

"Such confidence could easily be put to the test," he murmured. "At the same time, it would help me prove to myself that I was only offering my comfort and sympathy."

"You . . . require such proof?" she asked on a half-breath.

"I require something to keep my thoughts pure and mine eyes elsewhere."

This time she saw him move a step closer and she matched it with a step back. He lifted a hand and Ariel felt a gentle tugging at the nape of her neck, but reacted too slowly to stop him from tossing aside the scrap of linen that bound her hair. Her hands were cold, her feet hot. Spans of flesh everywhere on her body felt tight, stretched to the limit, as if the slightest touch would send her bursting out of her skin.

He had been drinking a fair amount of ale, she could smell it on each heated exhalation of air. It was not the ale speaking, however. It may have emboldened him to speak, but it was not the ale speaking.

"I . . . do not think it would be wise to try to prove anything right now," she stammered, conscious of his fingers combing through her hair, spreading it across her shoulders. "It might be best if I just return to my room . . . and . . . and we forget the whole thing."

Eduard smiled faintly. He coiled a shiny red ribbon of her hair around his fingers. The silky heat of it slithered over his skin and sent a surge of hot blood pulsating into flesh that was already growing thick and heavy in response to the dark green sparkle in her eyes. His body was responding to a woman's challenge, but it was the plea of a child—a spoiled child accustomed to getting her way in all things—who suggested they could just walk away and forget.

"Go then," he said quietly, dropping the strand of hair. "And do not fling any more of your righteous airs of presumption in my face, for I could make of you, here and now, a woman of very strong urges indeed."

He started turning away and something made Ariel reach out to stop him. His face was unreadable in the guttering firelight, his thoughts untouchable, and Ariel imagined she saw a shiver of a warning in the small muscle that flexed his jaw.

Very deliberately, she laid both hands flat on his chest. Keeping her eyes locked on his, she spread her fingers wide and skimmed them steadfastly up to his shoulders. Using the heat of his own muscles to bolster her nerve, she pulled herself up on tiptoes and pressed her lips over his, holding them there for a count of several pounding heartbeats. She broke away just as slowly, just as deliberately, and wilted lightly back onto her heels again.

"Pleasant," was her analysis, given with only the barest tremor undermining her voice. "But rather too soured by ale for my liking. Perhaps another time, when there is nothing clouding *your* senses . . . ?"

He raised a hand, startling her smugness into a faltering silence as he brushed the backs of his fingers along her cheek. The pad of his thumb stroked across the fullness of her lower lip, resting there while his fingers curved under her chin and started to tilt her face upward. His mouth began its descent and Ariel tried to pull back, but the heat of his hand shifted lower onto her neck, skimming around until it was pushing into the curling mass of her hair. She could not move in any direction but that of his choosing, and he chose to hold her steady a scant inch from his mouth.

The blush in her cheeks grew hotter and to her utter mortification she began to tremble. Her eyes began to shimmer with a film of silvery tears and her lips quivered apart as the tremors of shock shivered through her limbs, her breasts, her belly. She stood transfixed, doubting she could have moved even if he had set her free, and she realized the best she could hope for was to emerge with some shred of pride intact.

If he allowed it.

Ariel gasped as his mouth closed the gap between them, his lips slanting hard and full over hers. It was not so much a kiss as it was a claim, a warning not unlike the one her brother had given her about playing with fire. FitzRandwulf *was* fire. He was heat and flame and slow, hot breaths that scorched her cheeks and flooded her body with liquid incandescence.

She groaned as his lips forced hers wider apart and his tongue thrust past the barrier of her teeth. The bitter tang of ale gave way to the sinfully bold taste and feel of a man whose power she had already acknowledged to be formidable and uncompromising. Her body betrayed her, weakening with each deep, wet thrust so that her hands closed around fistfuls of his shirt and her breasts pressed shamelessly into a heated wall of muscle.

He *was* fire and she was flaming gloriously under his searing assault.

Streaks of sensations brought on by his hands, his lips, his tongue started to sweep through her, hot and icy, sharp and sweet, fierce and tender all at the same time. Her entire body seemed to be shivering, shuddering under a deluge of bright, burning sparks and she began to kiss him back, welcoming each bold stroke of his tongue, feeling the raw, primitive rhythm repeat itself in the staggeringly explicit ache that throbbed to life in her loins. His hands slid down from the tangle of her hair and pressed into the small of her back, coaxing her even closer, inviting her to share even more shocking intimacies.

Eduard kissed her until her mouth was chafed and swollen, then sent his lips chasing down the strained arch of her throat. Her skin was smooth and warm, the flesh so white against the tanned darkness of his own, it looked like cream. Like a big, hungry cat he lapped at the fluttering pulsebeat in the crook of her neck, then sent his tongue swirling into the pink shell of her ear. He could feel the deep, wracking shudders of pleasure that shook her with each nuzzling caress, and he was aware of the dangers of continuing . . . but she was all heat and soft, gasping wonderment, and he was as hungry to feel her lushness crushing against him as she was to feel the lushness spread and shimmer throughout her whole body. Her arousal was like an intoxicant in his blood, far more potent than any amount of ale he could have consumed and he wanted to drink his fill of her before the sobering effects of reality intruded.

Reality tried to intrude when his lips encountered the laces joining the edges of her bodice. The camlet was thin and airy and molded easily to her breasts as he stroked his hands around their fullness. The pebble-hard buds of her nipples strained against the cloth, shadows beneath the whiteness, and it would have taken a far stronger man than he to ignore their pleas to be set free. It took only a few swift tugs of his fingers to unfasten the laces and push the offending wings of camlet aside. He caught at his breath and ran his hand over the smooth surface of her skin, circling his palm around the cool heaviness of her breast before he lifted the puckered crown to his mouth.

His tongue traced silky, wet patterns over her skin and Ariel nearly crumpled to her knees under the stunning torrent of heat that poured into her belly and loins. His lips closed around her nipple and her body spasmed with the shock, with the pleasure. His tongue and lips suckled more of her, all of her that he could hold into the well of his mouth and she cried out, arching her head back in a violent, shiny whiplash of colour. He sank down onto his knees and she did not think to stop him. She thought only to press her body closer as he lavished her breasts with warm, ravaging caresses, and she became like quicksilver in his hands, hot and eager, eager and willing, willing and wanting . . .

For the first time, Eduard made a sound. It was muffled, distorted by the pliant sweetness of her flesh and by the taut edges of camlet that intruded on his senses again. He had not expected to lose his own grasp on reality. He had intended to kiss her just long enough and purposefully enough to frighten her into understanding this was no game they were playing. He had not expected it to go beyond a stern lesson against challenging him to any more tests. He most definitely had not expected to end up on his knees before her, his body fevered with needs.

But he was on his knees, drowning in the clean, womanly scent of her flesh. There were no more laces to unfasten, but the temptation was there, just below the gentle curve of her belly—another shadow beneath the pale cloth, outlining the triangle of fiery red down that cushioned his lips and teased his senses with images of delicate pink folds and sleek, mother-of-pearl surfaces.

Eduard pressed another groan into the juncture of her thighs and felt his noble intentions shudder away beneath his lips. He could feel the tension in her limbs and in the trembling tips of her fingers as they pushed into his hair, too shocked to know what he was doing, but telling him she did not want him to stop.

A curse sent his hands stroking down to the hem of her tunic, lifting it as he dragged his palms up the lithe, supple length of her calves and thighs. He lightly feathered the velvety flesh of her inner thighs, still expecting—hoping?—she would jerk away in alarm or maidenly decency, but he had taught the lesson too well and she had not the strength or the will to defy him.

Ariel's hand clutched at his shoulders. Waves of shame, hot and fierce, swept through her only to be chastened by the hotter, wilder urges he had promised, and she moved with the sliding pressure of his fingertips; she strained into their deft, sure explorations and she melted around the slow, deep incursions that brought her shivering, trembling down onto the hearth beside him. She clung to his shoulders, his mouth. She panted against his husky, whispered assurances that in no way prepared her for the rush of brilliant, searing ecstasy that flared through her body.

Eduard knew, and it was both his torment and his pleasure to watch her, to hold her as her body stiffened and writhed in his arms. He kissed her almost breathless, covering her mouth with his and swallowing her cries. He kept his fingers buried deep inside her, his strokes slowing only when her tremors started to fade and the drenching heat of her threatened to strip him of the last shreds of control. He had no choice then but to withdraw everything—his hands, his lips, his body. Especially his body, for it could not be trusted with any further contact, not unless that contact was full and complete in every way.

He stood, lifting her with him, but when she would have leaned forward into his embrace, he backed away, steeling himself against the wide, dark incomprehension in her eyes. Dazed by what she had just experienced, Ariel started to take an unsteady step after him, but he held out a hand to stop her —a hand that shook visibly with the effort it was taking to deny her.

"Eduard—?"

She had never called him by his Christian name before and the sound of it only made the fist clench tighter in his

groin. Making matters worse, her tunic gaped open from throat
to waist, revealing flesh as pale as moonlight save for the two
pinkened buds of her breasts. Her hair was tumbled and wild,
framing the beauty of a face that would probably haunt him
now until he drew his last breath.

"Eduard . . . what is it? Is it something I have done?"

"No," he rasped. "No, it is nothing you have done."

"Then what—?"

"Cover yourself," he pleaded in a whisper, turning his
face into the safety of the shadows. "For the love of God, cover
yourself."

Ariel's body still burned, still throbbed with a tense, tight
feeling she did not understand. She did not understand his
anger either, for had she not reacted just the way he had said
she would react? Had he not discovered and unleashed more
womanly urges than she had even known she possessed? The
slick proof of them was on the hand he still held out to keep
her at arm's length. It was in the wetness that streaked her
thighs and in the shifting, slithering ribbons of heat that continued to curl through her flesh as if he was still there, pleasur-
ing her. As if she wanted even more of him there, thick and
thrusting and hard.

Colour flamed in her cheeks as she looked down and saw
how brazenly she stood before him. She had wanted to come
away with some of her pride intact, but she had shivered it all
away in the cradle of his arms.

"Jesu," she whispered. "Sweet Jesu, what have I done?"

"You have done nothing," he said bluntly. "And *will* do
nothing, by the mercy of that same sweet God, so long as you
do not put us to any more tests of willpower. You are still a
virgin, still in possession of your groom's honour."

In a flush of mortification, Ariel hastened to lace the front
of her tunic. Her fingers were trembling so badly she could not
manage the task and at one point she thought she saw Eduard
relent and step forward to offer assistance. The look of utter
and complete horror on her face stopped him, and he retreated
to the far side of the hearth, then into the heavier shadows
beyond the glowing circle of firelight.

"Forgive me, Lady Ariel," he said hoarsely. "This . . . should not have happened."

She bowed her head over her laces again, twisting them with more prejudice than they deserved. "It was not all your fault," she said tersely. "I could have stopped you."

"No," he said succinctly. "You could not have stopped me. I was determined to prove as much, was I not?"

Ariel pressed her lips together, tasting him. "You would not have been so determined to do so if I had not goaded you."

"Again," he muttered.

"Again," she admitted.

After struggling a few more seconds with laces that refused to untangle, she gave them an exasperated tug and flung her arms down by her sides. This time, when Eduard emerged from the shadows, she did not stop him. She did not even look up at him.

It was just as bad, keeping her eyes cast downward, for she was given no choice but to watch the long, blunt-tipped fingers try to resolve the knotted thongs. It was worse knowing that at least one of those very capable hands was the cause of all the damp stirrings she felt inside, and she blinked too late to stop the single fat tear from escaping her lashes. It splashed squarely on his hand, bringing an abrupt halt to what he was doing, and for a long, suspended moment, neither of them moved. They barely breathed.

The smallest hint of a tremor took the purpose out of Eduard's hands and they went limp around the crumpled laces. Ariel felt another tear slide down her cheek and she heard the slow release of the breath he had been holding. Whether it was because he could sense what she was wishing for, or because he just needed the same thing, he opened his arms and wrapped them around her, drawing her gently into his embrace, holding her closer than she had ever been held before.

"Ariel," he whispered. "Ariel, you must believe I did not intend any of this to happen."

"It w-was not all y-your fault," she insisted softly, burying her face in the warm curve of his shoulder. Her arms circled his

waist and her hands were spread flat on the broad slabs of
muscle that armoured his back; she shamelessly drew on his
heat and strength, rejoicing in the loud hammering of his heart
within the chamber of his chest. She closed her eyes to savour
the moment, wondering if one so exquisite would ever come
upon her again.

The moment and the closeness had to end, of course, but
it was accomplished with less abruptness than their previous
parting . . . and still with the nuisance of her laces to deal
with. This time, however, she was less reluctant to look up into
his face while he worked, and it was to her advantage that she
could study all the planes and angles from a strangely new
perspective.

The inflexible line of his mouth and jaw was suddenly
revealed to be very flexible indeed, his mouth generously
shaped, fuller on the bottom than on top, and textured with
finely etched lines that flattened when he smiled and deep-
ened when he scowled. It was a mouth that knew how to give a
woman pleasure, knew tenderness and seduction, knew how to
offer more than barbs and jests.

The fire cast a reddish glow on the strong column of his
neck and on the straight, almost patrician nose. It was a very
noble nose, she decided, augmented by eyebrows that were
thick and dark enough to join in a single line when he frowned.
Intimidating, she thought, unless those creases and furrows
were caused by uncertainty and indecision.

The scar was still an unavoidable detriment to his laying
waste to a score of women's hearts. She suspected he did not
weep for the loss, but used their aversion to his own advantage,
keeping everyone at a safe distance who might otherwise want
to know too many of the secrets he kept locked inside.

His eyes were by far his most unnerving feature as well as
his most formidable weapon. They could reduce a woman's
pity to ashes on a single glance, or freeze her warmest intentions without ever giving her a reason why. Long-lashed and
deep-set, they held more secrets than she would ever know,
more loneliness than he would ever reveal. A trait they appeared to share, Ariel concluded, since she had never felt more

lonely or abandoned as she did when his hands finished their task and dropped away.

"Have you not had your fill of questions answered?" he mused, aware of how closely she had been studying him.

"I only have one more," she said quietly. "Why *did* you stop?"

"You wanted more?" he asked, attempting a wry smile. "Rather greedy of you, I must say."

"You assure me I am still a virgin. Did you deny yourself the pleasure of taking my maidenhead because you wished to prove yourself so much more able to resist earthly urges than I . . . or because you deemed it to be of so little value to anyone other than a Welsh brigand?"

He stared at her until her knees threatened to buckle beneath her and Ariel thought: definitely ashes. Ashes and ice, because he does not know whether he should hate me . . . or pity me.

"Your uncle places a very high value on more than just your virginity," he said flatly.

"Ahh yes, the oath he made you swear . . . to deliver me to my groom unhurt, unblemished, untouched . . ." She paused and moistened her lips with the tip of her tongue. "But it would seem, since I have been hurt—with the result that I do bear a blemish—and I have been somewhat touched . . . would not all three parts of your oath appear to have already been broken?"

"They may have been bent slightly, but not broken. Not entirely."

"Such a noble distinction."

"Nonetheless, a distinction worth maintaining. A man's sworn oath is the foundation of his honour. How much would you trust me if I paid so little heed to the difference between the *bending* and the *breaking* of vows?"

"No less than I trust you now," she said simply. "With my life."

She had startled him. She could see it in the silvery depths of his eyes and in the absolute stillness of the powerful body. She also thought she could see, as suddenly and as clearly as if

someone had blown a film of dust off her eyes, that it was not
the vow to her uncle he was intent upon preserving so much as
it was the vow he had made to another.

"It is because of her, isn't it?" she asked slowly. "Because
of the vow you made to *her.*"

Eduard frowned and the intensity of his gaze faltered under a wave of genuine confusion. "Who . . . ?"

"*Her.* The woman who is luring you back to England! Are
her charms so much more desirable than mine, or is it just her
jewelry that attracts you?" She did not wait for an answer, but
paced to the hearth and stood trembling in front of the bright
flames, unaware that in doing so, her tunic became all but
transparent. "You did not seem to be a man governed by
wealth or greed, but I suppose I must be proven wrong in this
aspect of your character too."

Eduard's eyes narrowed. His flesh was still thick and hot
and pulsing with hunger for this woman, yet his hands were
aching to reach out and shake her. It was not the first time the
two desires had overlapped, and not the least of the reasons
why he considered the thinking processes of most women to
be far beyond his mortal comprehension.

"Might I know the reason why my character has so suddenly fallen into decline?"

"You lied to me about not having a lady love. And lest you
try to shrug me off again, I will tell you I have seen the ring
you wear next to your heart. I saw it the first morning, by the
river."

A reflexive reaction sent Eduard's hand toward his breast;
the look on Ariel's face halted it midway there.

"Is the pearl you are going to steal for her?" she asked
quietly, "Or is it just something you planned to pick up along
the way?"

Eduard began to understand—at least he hoped he did—
and he might have smiled if Ariel had not been trying to look
so hard as if his answers did not matter.

"So now I am a thief as well?" he asked gently. "God's
truth, I have tumbled from grace, have I not?"

"Do you deny you have been plotting with my brother

and Sedrick to steal a valuable jewel the king now has in his possession? A *pearl* to be precise. And again, it would not be worth the waste of breath to say nay, for I heard the three of you whispering about it one night. About *stealing the pearl out from under the king's nose.* Those were the very words I heard."

"Were you never taught the evils of eavesdropping?"

"Were you not concerned the evils of theft and skullduggery might tend to strain your vaunted code of honour?"

"My honour would be strained more if I were to stand by and do nothing," he said evenly.

"You are speaking in riddles again, sir," she accused.

"And you are speaking in ignorance. Ignorance," he said on a gust, "that has gone on long enough, methinks. If you will bring yourself away from the fire and sit with me a moment, I will tell you everything you should have known before we ever embarked from Amboise."

"Including her name?"

Eduard's gaze followed Ariel's to the deep vee of his tunic where a wink of gold peeped through the mat of coarse chest hairs.

"Her name is Eleanor. As it happens, she is also the self-same lady who is known to many as the Pearl of Brittany."

"The Pearl of—" Ariel's eyes widened. "Surely you do not mean—"

"The Princess Eleanor of Brittany, my lady. The only Pearl we would, any of us, be willing to go to such measures to steal from the king's clutches."

Chapter 14

"Princess Eleanor is in England?" Ariel gasped. "But I thought . . . I mean, we had heard she was being held in the Citadel in Rouen, with her brother Arthur."

"Indeed, she was until a few weeks ago."

At Eduard's insistence, they had moved a bench closer to the fire, but even with her cup of mead cradled in her hands and the heat from the roaring flames curling her toes, she felt chilled to the bone as she listened to his explanations of the events that had brought them to St. Malo. He told her everything—her uncle's involvement; the plans to rescue Eleanor and remove her to a safe haven in Wales; the reasons for their secrecy and their need for stealth.

"The king knows he is losing his grip on Normandy. You have seen yourself, he has very little support left among the local barons of Touraine, Maine, Poitou, and Brittany. John must also have realized that to leave Eleanor in Normandy would give the rebelling forces a rallying point. If Hugh de Luisgnan overran Rouen and freed her, he would have a legitimate claimant to the throne to lead them in a civil war that could extend across the Channel into England."

"Then the rumours about Arthur's death . . . ?"

"Can only be true, my lady. He must be dead or the king would have used him to stop Hugh's campaign long before now."

"I see. And is this what you want? Civil war?"

"No. No, it is not what I want. Nor is it what your uncle wants. Our prime concern is Eleanor's safety; of secondary, *political* consideration is her value, once she is beyond reach of the king's control, to limit the power he wields from the throne."

"Forgive me for asking so bluntly, but . . . why would the king have had Arthur killed, yet leave Eleanor alive? It would seem to me it accomplished nothing to remove the threat of one heir, knowing full well there was another waiting to challenge him. And why take her to England? What does he plan to do with her there?"

"It would be my guess he plans to keep her locked away in a prison cell for the rest of her life," Eduard said bitterly. "He has no other choice."

"But one," she pointed out gently.

Eduard snatched up the iron rod and thrust it into the bed of embers. He stabbed at them as if it was a sword he held, and as if the hot coals were the bleeding corpse of an enemy.

"It is your uncle's feeling—and mine—that Arthur's death was quite possibly an accident. The marshal was himself present on at least two occasions when the prince was offered his freedom in exchange for permanent exile and a public declaration of his uncle's right to succession. John threatened execution on more than just those two occasions, going so far at times to have his hangman present. But the public hue and cry were such that he was forced to try to reason with the boy. The last thing he wanted to create was a martyr. What finally happened is only speculation, but knowing the Plantagenet temper and John's bouts of insane jealousy, it would not surprise me to learn there is heavy truth to the story he 'arranged' an 'accident.' "

"His own nephew?"

"The rightful king of England," Eduard reminded her. "John spent too many years in Richard's shadow coveting the crown, playing regent, and ruling England as if it was his own by foregone conclusion. Do you honestly think he would hand the crown over to another simply because of blood precedence? Do you not forget, he hated Richard. He offered daily prayers for a Saracen's sword to cut him in half, and when the Austrian king took Richard prisoner and demanded John pay a ransom to free him, he delayed almost nine months and then paid only a small portion of the amount hoping Leopold would take the Lionheart's life by way of example. If he were not so inept and if he did not have grave misgivings on how God would look upon regicide, John would undoubtedly have slain Richard himself long before the arrow at Chalus did the business for him."

Eduard paused, set the iron rod aside, and shrugged as if he was arguing with himself. "Conversely, he may have out-grown those reservations and had Arthur executed despite any heavenly repercussions. He could have legitimized it in his mind—and in the eyes of the law, for that matter. Richard *did* declare John his successor and the barons of England did sup-port the nomination. Arthur had sworn homage to him two years earlier, the first time he had tried and failed to establish his claim to the throne. As John's vassal, then, attempting to lead a second uprising against the king was likened unto put-ting his own neck across the block. John had every right to put him to trial and execute him as a traitor. He did *not* have any such right where Eleanor was concerned, however, and to have executed her, then or now, would have caused every baron, knight, and commoner in the realm to rise against him. To kill a rebellious vassal is something the barons could justify; to kill beauty and innocence is something no man could condone."

Ariel glanced sidelong at FitzRandwulf, noting the ten-sion in his jaw, the hard narrowing of his eyes as he stared into the fire. She had never seen the Breton princess, but she had heard her uncle speak in awe of Eleanor's incomparable beauty. Hair as bright as polished silver, eyes as blue as pieces of the sky, skin so fair and white the weight of a feather might bruise it.

Was it any wonder this scarred, enigmatic knight who had been birthed into pain and ugliness would have fallen so deeply in love with her? It was just as easy to understand how a woman who had spent most of her life shuffled between the courts of an aging dowager and a French effete would fall under the spell of a handsome, brooding beast like Eduard FitzRandwulf d'Amboise. Nor was it any wonder he kept the ring hidden beneath his tunic instead of flaunting it for the world to see. Even a hint of an amorous liaison between the royal house of Brittany and a knight errant born on the wrong side of the blanket would mean the utter ruin of one and the agonizing death of the other.

Ariel stared down at her hands and saw they were trem-bling again.

"I do not understand why you simply did not explain all of this to me at the outset," she said quietly, meaning more than just the intended rescue of Eleanor. "It could have saved so much time and trouble."

"Your uncle thought it best this way. He was, I suppose, only trying to shield you, to spare you needless anxiety."

Ariel raised her head and actually managed a smile. "To keep me from interfering or getting in the way, you mean."

"To keep you safe," Eduard insisted, turning to her. That was a mistake, for her eyes were soft and lustrous in the firelight, reflecting the glow like polished gemstones. Her hair floated around her face like a tarnished cloud, all red and gold and copper sparks. There were blotches on the whiteness of her throat where the stubble of his beard had chafed her, and a swollen tenderness about the mouth, the cause of which a man would have to be blind not to recognize. She looked half ravished and more desirable than it was safe to appear to a man who had already come perilously close to consigning his honour to the fires of hell.

"Keeping you safe," he continued softly, "is even more important now, and will necessitate a change in our plans."

Ariel looked startled. "A change? Why?"

"To use you and the guise of a wedding cortege to gain access to Corfe Castle? No." He gave his head an adamant shake. "No. I did not like the scheme when it was first put forth and I like it even less now."

"Even if it is the only way to gain entry?"

"It is not the only way. It was just the most convenient way at the time this whole charade came into being. In fact, I am more than half convinced to dispatch you to Wales on the first ship leaving port."

"No!" she cried, sitting straighter. "I mean . . . no. No, you cannot jeopardize my uncle's position. By your own words, you said he might be charged with treason, and I . . . I would sooner marry Reginald de Braose than see any such thing come about. You say you have letters proving you are escorting me north to the Marches; it would seem then, and at least until we reach the Marches, my uncle's plan is the safest and soundest.

No one in all of Britain would dare challenge the seal of the
Marshal of England."

"Despite what I may have said, I have strong doubts the
king would charge your uncle with treason for attempting to
make a better marriage for his niece. He would exact a heavy
fine, no doubt—"

"Or he would take my uncle's five daughters away from
Pembroke and hold them hostage in castles of his own choosing until such time as he could find the lowest, most vile
grooms in the kingdom! Perhaps you could live with that, sir,
but I could not. And yes, before you say it: I should have
thought of them before now, but I was too busy thinking of
myself. I have already admitted and will admit again to anyone
who might care to hear it, that it was a foolish, childish, dangerous, thoughtless thing I have done, and if the plans for my own
future happiness go awry, it will be no one's fault but my own.
My uncle's future, however, and the future happiness of my
aunt and my cousins . . . sweet Jesu and all the martyrs! You
cannot be so cruel as to expect me to bear that upon my
shoulders too? You cannot!"

"What would you have me do?" he asked carefully, as
wary of her temper as he was of a naked blade. "Take you with
us when we storm the castle? Have you stand with bow and
arrow in hand, guarding our backs while we scale the walls?"

"It would not be the first time you have trusted my hand
or my eye," she reminded him.

Eduard smiled faintly and felt such an overwhelming
need to kiss her, that he did so. Lightly. Affectionately. And
very deliberately on the smooth expanse of her brow.

"This past sennight was child's play compared to what
will happen if we are successful in stealing Eleanor away from
the king's prison . . . assuming we are even successful
enough to get close to her. Here, in Normandy, John's Brabançons are too busy guarding their backs against the French and
the Bretons, but in England, they will have nothing more important to do than to hunt us down. There will not be an inn or
castle open to us for refuge, and even the deepest wilds of the
forests may hold as many enemies as friends—men who hold

only scorn for a knight travelling in any guise, be it pilgrim or Crusader."

"Yet you would carry the Princess Eleanor through these same dangers?" Ariel demanded. "Would the risks not be as great for her as for me—greater, even, since she would make a far more valuable hostage? Do you think her to be any better able to endure such hardships, or have you even given a thought as to *how* she would endure them? She *is* a princess, after all. You will not be able to simply toss her into squire's clothing and sit her on a sway-backed nag. For that matter, she has probably never had to dress herself or tend herself in any way. Do you plan to take the place of her tiring women yourself? Or do you plan to entrust her to Sparrow or Sedrick or Henry to bathe and dress her?"

Eduard's hand was still resting in a crush of copper curls, but she seemed not to have noticed the hand or the kiss. Her gaze was locked on his, steady and unwavering, and he could feel the effects rousing his flesh again, making his fingers tingle with the memory of where they had been, what they had discovered. A man could get lost in those eyes, he mused. He could be swallowed whole and never know, until it was too late, that there was as much steel as silk in their depths.

As to what he had discovered . . . it was odd, just as she was admitting she was spoiled and thoughtless, he was uncovering a part of her that was painfully innocent and uncertain. A part that wanted to hold and be held, to share something of herself instead of hoarding it all away until she became a creature like him, guarded and mistrustful, afraid of letting anyone know his nightmares.

"We will find a woman to tend her," he said slowly.

"You have one now."

"No."

"You would rather hire some village slut with black teeth and lice? To tend the future queen of England? You must love her very much indeed."

He was not prepared for her sarcasm. Being too unnerved by the emotions she had already stirred in his blood, he had no defense other than his anger to use against her.

"I have pledged my life to saving hers."

"You have pledged your honour to safeguarding mine. Moreover, you gave me your most solemn oath not to abandon me again. I find it exceedingly curious how you can put so much store in one oath, but play so loose with another."

"I am hardly playing loose with you," he said savagely, almost beneath his breath. "If I were, you would still be on the floor, with your skirts above your head and your body cleaved to mine."

Ariel's breath stopped in her throat but she managed to start it again before turning too many shades of red. Yet she did not wither or recoil from his crudeness. She kept her gaze steady and her chin held high. "Once again you remind me of the noble distinction between bending an oath and breaking it. Have you used the same distinctions in the past . . . with Eleanor?"

It was Eduard's turn to redden and he did so magnificently, glowing from throat to hairline, and even to the lobes of his ears. His hand fell from her shoulder and gripped her wrist, so tightly she feared the bones would snap in two.

Strangely enough, Ariel felt only envy. It was foolish and reckless to feel anything at all, but it was there, still hot between her thighs, still pounding against her rib cage. She should have known something like this would happen. She had been too free with her airs, scorning one suitor after another on the skimpiest of excuses, finding fault with all who were less than perfect in her eyes.

Here was a man . . . scarred, flawed, of anything but noble bloodlines, far from her wildest interpretation of perfect . . . and she could not even entice him to *want* her, much less *take* her.

"You must love her very much indeed," she repeated, softly this time, the statement muted by dispassion, prompted by despair.

The terrible burning anger in his eyes dissipated, and the bite of his fingers eased around her flesh. There would, she suspected, be another visible blemish on her flesh come morning, but she did not care to point this out to him. She did not care about anything other than salvaging what was left of her dignity.

"It seems," she whispered, "we were better suited as adversaries."

Eduard released her wrist completely and found himself alone on the bench, staring up at the proud, beautiful face of Ariel de Clare.

"You have not won the argument to keep me away from Corfe, however," she added. "You *will* need me, Fitz-Randwulf, and you will not find me so easy to slough aside."

Having nothing more to say, and naught but a few threads of courage holding herself together, Ariel dropped a faintly mocking curtsy and bid him a polite good night. Eduard stood and watched her climb the stairs to the chambers above. When she was gone, he moved stiffly around to the side of the table and reached for his tankard, but at the last instant, swept it and the flagon onto the floor in a spray of flying ale and clattering pewter. Ariel's cup would have followed if his eye and then his hand had not strayed to something lying on the floor by his foot. It was the scrap of linen he had torn from her hair, and, as he bent to retrieve it, the firelight glinted off several long, shiny strands trapped in the cloth.

He ran the fiery filaments through his fingers and glanced again at the top of the stairs.

She was stubborn, proud, haughty, courageous . . . and she had called him on his own bluff. Was a vow made to one person worth more than a vow made to another? Was a promise made against the spell of a supple pair of lips worth less than a promise given in youthful fervor?

Were his obligations to Eleanor worth more than the responsibility he felt for Ariel de Clare?

Ariel had asked him if he loved Eleanor . . . how could any man not? She was sweet, gentle, kind, loving. She was pure and noble, innocent and compassionate, loyal to her last drop of blood. He had watched her grow from a pretty unspoiled child to a ravishingly beautiful woman possessing none of the traits or pretensions of someone who could put their own reflection to shame.

Had Ariel asked him if he *lusted* after Eleanor of Brittany, his answer might have surprised her, for Eleanor was like a sister to him and their love was a result of the purest kind of friendship. When the Wolf had rescued them both from Bloodmoor Keep all those years ago, Eleanor had been the one to sit by Eduard's side and hold his hand through the feverish days and nights spent recovering from the wounds he had earned at the Dragon's hands. Physically, his thigh had been slashed open from hip to knee and crudely cauterized on a torturer's rack; mentally, he had endured thirteen years of hell at the beck and call of a man who hated him and a dam—Nicolaa de la Haye—whose tongue could be sharper and more painful than any knife or lash. Eleanor had heard his worst nightmares and had wept with him while he shuddered and sweated through the aftermath. She had not betrayed him by word or deed to anyone, not even his father or his stepmother, who were so proud of the boldness and courage he displayed in the daylight, but who had remained ignorant to this day of the weeping, terrified coward he became at night.

Eleanor's childhood had been only slightly less of an ordeal. Her father had died when she was two and her mother had regarded her as a nuisance getting in the way of her succession of lovers and her royal ambitions for Arthur. Constantly passed between her grandmother's castle at Mirebeau and the French court in Paris, Eleanor had been raised in two worlds but belonged in neither. When she came of age to be of interest to her mother's lust for power, she was put out on display like a sad little doll, pawed and bid upon by potentates, princelings, and fat Flemish dukes. Three times she had been betrothed and three times discarded for a better political prospect. Each time she had wept her fears and frustrations out in Eduard's arms . . . along with her relief.

There were only two people in Eleanor's world who knew her first and only love had always been for the Church. Eduard was one, her brother Arthur had been the other. Her mother, even her beloved grandmother, would have scoffed at the mere idea of an Angevin princess becoming a Bride of Christ;

they became brides of political alliances and profitable unions instead.

Arthur had promised when he became king he would free Eleanor to follow her heart's desire. With her brother's death, Eduard was alone in knowing Eleanor of Brittany was no threat to the throne of England. She would not seek it, nor would she ever accept it if the crown and sceptre were handed to her at Westminster. Certainly not at the cost of a bloody civil war.

Eduard had held his silence at Amboise because he saw no point in giving William the Marshal any reason *not* to free her. He had agreed to using the marshal's niece as a shield because at the time, he could have cared less whom he had to use or whose life he had to place at risk in order to win Eleanor's freedom.

Now, suddenly, it was not so easy. Now he found himself caring very much what happened to Ariel de Clare. It did not change anything between them. It could not, for she was still betrothed to a prince of Wales and he was still bound by his honour to deliver her to her groom. But it did mean he could not afford to make any more mistakes. He had made a large one here tonight, allowing his lust to override his logic.

It was a mistake that could not be repeated.

It could not . . . for all their sakes.

Corfe Castle, Purbeck

Chapter 15

If there was a bleaker, more sinister castle in all of King John's realm, a mortal man could not have envisioned it. Viewed from outside the sheer escarpment walls, the castle seemed always to be in darkness, for there were no windows, no lights in any chambers of any towers that rose above the height of the battlements. It sat in a solid, dark mass on the skyline above the village of Corfe—itself a small and sulky compilation of cottages that clung to either side of the single roadway as if they were poised for a hasty retreat.

There was a church in the village, and an inn. There was no fairground, however, and naught but a brief widening in the road to call the main square. Fierce winds constantly buffeted the steep hill on which the castle stood and the resultant low howl, which grew louder at nightfall, sent most of the village inhabitants scurrying off the street before dusk and kept them huddled by their fires until dawn.

Nighttime at Corfe was a time for whispers and clanking chains. It was the time for bloodied, shuffling feet and wagon wheels stumbling over cobbles, creaking for lack of grease and nerve. Few brave souls crept to their windows to see who the king's ire had put into chains. It was healthier not to know, or to see the faces and perhaps be haunted by the lingering images of wide, vacant eyes.

One such foolhardy lout had been wakened out of a fitful sleep on an early autumn night, and had counted on the stubs of his fingers three rattling cartloads of prisoners. The fourth had won enough of his curiosity to send him crabbing to the door and to open it a crack for spying. He had been in time to see the fifth loaded cart teeter past with its cargo of half-starved, filthy knights, bound in chains, garbed in the rags and shredded remnants of their former Breton finery.

Whispers the next day told him the poor sullens he had seen were the twenty-four knights captured at Mirebeau with the brave, if misguided, Prince Arthur. They had been sent to

Corfe Castle wearing the same chains that had been bolted onto them at their capture, there to await the king's pleasure. Over the course of the next fortnight it became obvious, by the shrouded, emaciated bodies carried down to the churchyard for burial, it had been his pleasure to starve them to death. Not one bite of food had they been given. Not one drop of water. The eve the last one perished, the winds swept up from hell, moaning and swirling around the towers the whole night long, the evil spirits so loud and so gorged on rotted flesh, a guard was driven mad by the sound and flung himself off the castle ramparts.

Madness was no strange occurrence to the residents of Corfe. The garrison was stocked with the dregs of the king's army—misfits and brutes who sucked suet and ale all day long, who kept whores naked and crouched between their thighs from dusk till dawn, who thought nothing of heaving their filthy, sweaty bodies over the screams of the women prisoners —and there were many—whenever the mood or the itch took them. Men and women alike screamed from the confines of their small, dank cells.

It was Bedlam and it was hell.

It was where King John had sent his niece, Eleanor, the Pearl of Brittany, to await his pleasure.

Marienne FitzWilliam crept on silent feet into the tower room, wary of disturbing the solemn figure who knelt over her evening prayers, her golden head bowed, her fingers smoothing comfortingly over the worn beads of a rosary. The candle burning in the prayer niche added its soot to the tall black stains already marking the stones from the countless candles that had burned there before. Marienne glanced at the tray of food she had brought into the room over an hour ago, knowing she would see only a crumb or two missing. Her poor princess barely ate enough to keep a bird alive. In the long months of her captivity, she had become thin and fragile, seeming to waste away before Marienne's eyes. Her skin had lost its pearl-like lustre, even her hair—a gossamer cascade of silvery blonde sunlight—was dulled to a flat yellow. So much of it came away each morning in the bristles of the horsehair brush, it was a wonder there was enough to braid and twine at Eleanor's nape.

Crossing the Channel had nearly accomplished what months of deprivation, heartbreak, and fear could not. The sea had been rough and the weather brutally cold. Marienne had suffered her own stomach to visit her throat several times during the voyage, and between bouts, had cradled Eleanor's fevered head in her lap.

In Corfe, Eleanor had recovered some of her strength, but she was still so thin! Tears welled in Marienne's eyes each time she saw her lovely mistress, head bowed, hands clasped in prayer, lips moving silently over pleas for forgiveness and understanding for those who would do their utmost to harm her.

Marienne would gladly have taken a dagger and plunged it into King John's heart with a dearth of forgiveness and understanding. She would have plunged and plunged and plunged and taken the greatest pleasure in seeing the blood spurt from the gaping holes she would make in his chest! He had laughed. He had laughed, shrilly and maniacally when he had told Eleanor of her exile to Corfe, and Marienne had been the one to hold her and weep with her and comfort her as best she could. She was only fourteen, but felt one hundred and fourteen, forced too young to witness so much pain, deceit, and treachery. Forced to hurt so badly each time she saw a tremulous, brave smile cross her dear mistress's face.

Eleanor offered one now as she detected Marienne's presence behind her. She did not interrupt her prayers or stop her fingers from smoothing over the ebony beads. She was in the last prayer of the last station and Marienne waited patiently until the small gold cross was raised and pressed reverently to her lips to seal the final amen.

She hastened over and offered her assistance as the princess rose stiffly from her knees and moved to the bed.

"If you are going to scold me again, do not trouble yourself," Eleanor said with a sigh. "I ate one whole round of bread and most of the poached fish. Any more and I would be belching like a wag."

Marienne could have pointed out the bread was the size of

a coin and the fish barely dented, but she held her tongue. It was more than her mistress had eaten the previous evening . . . and tomorrow was Wednesday. Wednesdays the cook mixed up a special treat of quenelles, one of the few things that seemed to tempt Eleanor's appetite.

When Marienne told her this, hoping to rouse a little interest, the princess looked surprised. "Another sennight has passed already? It feels as though only yesterday we feasted on capons and dumplings."

"Captain Brevant has promised to try to send us a flagon of real wine as well, not the soured vinegar they serve to the other . . . guests."

Eleanor's smile faltered somewhat and she reached out to stroke pale, slender fingers down Marienne's unruly mop of crisp brown curls. "My poor Mouse. How dreadful this must all be for you. Forced to serve me in this . . . this dark and gloomy pesthole."

"I am not forced, my lady," Marienne protested, clutching the princess's hand and holding it to her lips. "I am come willingly, of my own choice, and I stay willingly, knowing that one day soon we will both be able to walk out in the sunlight again."

"Sunlight," Eleanor whispered ruefully. "I have almost forgotten what it feels like on my face."

There were no windows in the tower room, only candles to provide light. The air was close and smelled so strongly of damp mortar not even a blazing fire could relieve the stench. Not that they ever had enough wood to build a fire that did more than smoke and hiss and spit off the odd red cinder.

The bedding was always musty, the curtains that hung from the bed were rotted through in places and rarely failed to offer up the droppings of some small inhabitant when they were let down for the night. The king had promised to keep her in comfort. He had promised their stay at Corfe would be a short one, but they had heard nothing from Normandy since their departure and Marienne could only wonder if by "short" he meant "not long of this world." He had evidently not instructed any special favours be accorded his niece. Day and night were the same, marked only by the arrival of fresh tallow candles each morning—two per day, to be used sparingly—and the emptying of the cracked slops jar each night. She was given a basin of water three times a week for washing, and once each week, for an hour, she was permitted to walk the ramparts between her tower and the next.

Almost since their arrival in Corfe, however, the weather had been bleak and rainy, the wind too fearsome on the rooftops for Eleanor to bear more than a few minutes' exposure even though it was her only chance for a clean breath. Her one solace was in prayer; her only pleasure was gained through communion with God. And because not even a king could deprive a soul from seeking salvation, each morning at Prime and each evening before Vespers, Eleanor was allowed to descend the long, twisting spiral staircase and share her prayers with Father Wilfred, a ritual closely supervised by at least two of the castle guards and more often than not, their captain, Jean de Brevant. The captain was a tall, gruff man with a face like hewn rock and a voice that sounded like a mountain avalanche. The top of Marienne's head barely reached his armpit and her entire body could have fit into one leg of his chausses —with room to spare—but now and then there was a sad look in his eye; a look only she, perforce, could see. And now and then, when the priest and the armoured roaches had slouched away, and the princess had begun the long, laborious climb back up into her tower, Marienne would linger behind a moment and share a word or two with the formidable Captain Brevant.

On this particular morning, the captain had whispered something in her ear that had kept Marienne staring down the long, vaulted corridor long after he had ambled away. He had told her, so casually she had almost not paid heed, of a party of knights returning from pilgrimage who were staying in the village of Corfe. One of them had required the services of an herb woman to tend an injury to his arm, other else they might have kept travelling. And since Brevant made it his business to always know when there were strangers in the area, he had been told of their arrival almost before the dust had been shaken from their clothes.

One of them, he also mentioned offhandedly, bore a scar on his cheek.

Marienne had all but forgotten to breathe. She could not remember climbing the stairs afterward, nor could she recall choking down the stale crust of bread and wedge of moldy cheese that broke their fast. She had debated telling her mistress . . . but what would she tell her? A knight with a scar on his face had taken temporary lodgings in the village? There were a thousand knights with scars on their faces; it did not follow it had to be *him*. Nor would it accomplish anything to raise her poor princess's hopes if it were just another wounded soldier returning home.

Brevant had promised to try to find out more, if he could, and to bring her word the following morning. Until then, she would have to hold her tongue and try not to betray her excitement to Eleanor of Brittany.

Eduard FitzRandwulf d'Amboise rubbed his eyes, feeling the grit of a thousand sleepless nights scratching beneath the lids. He rubbed and looked again, but the view remained the same as it had for the past few hours he had spent staring at Corfe Castle, save that the gloomy gray sky had given way to a wind-tossed black one. He had watched lights wink on in the village, but the castle walls remained dark and oppressive. No sign of torchlight or candlelight showed along the walls, and only the faintest hint of a dull glow rising above the baileys suggested there was any life at all within.

It had not been a day of blessings thus far. Why should he have expected Corfe to be anything less than an unassailable stronghold? Henry de Clare had warned him. He had, in the past two days since their arrival in England, sketched pictures in the sand, built replicas with stones and twigs, given a detailed accounting of the number of times *armies* had tried and failed to breach the castle walls. Armies, he had said, equipped with mangonels and battering rams, and catapults capable of throwing huge stones into and over the walls. King John had not chosen this castle by whim or fancy to house the prisoners he wanted least to escape. He had chosen it because no one ever *had* escaped. The guards were handpicked and had no use for bribes. The townspeople were too terrified of shadows in the windows at night to even speak to strangers who were just passing through.

Eduard had studied the land and the castle. He had observed the battlements from every conceivable angle and approach, and he had watched for traffic at the main gates, hoping to learn who was admitted and how frequently.

No one had crossed the draw all day.

The towers, walls, and baileys formed a roughly triangular configuration on the dome of a bald hill that overlooked the sea. The main entrance was through two sets of gates, each with their own drawbridges and flanking barbican towers. A man could possibly make it uninvited through the first set of outer gates, only to be trapped between the outer and inner portcullises. It was the sole entrance wide enough to admit horse-drawn wagons or carts and Eduard could envision the process of checks and double checks, watched all the while by crossbowmen and guards standing on sentry walks above.

Another tower guarded the north and west corner of the inner bailey and was protected by a portcullis and forebuilding. Here was where any foot traffic passed between the inner and outer walls, but of that too, there was very little. To judge by the speed at which the door opened and the departing visitor was ejected, and the slowness by which anyone was admitted, the castle guard was under a strict rule of no unecessary admissions.

No surprise, since their walls imprisoned the only person who could threaten the king's possession of the crown.

There had to be other ways in and out of the castle, of course. Eduard just hadn't found them. He judged it possible to raise a ladder to a section of the wall and clamber over it between patrols of the guards on sentry, but a sixty-foot ladder took time to build and would be difficult to conceal when there was not a tree or bush within a mile radius of the barren dome on which the castle stood.

A rope and hook could afford a man an alternative means of gaining the top of the wall, but again, there was sixty feet of height at the lowest point and he had not met an arm yet with enough accuracy to toss a grapple over a stone lip on the first throw. More than one attempt, ringing off the stone, would be sure to attract attention and again, there was nowhere to hide.

He had once heard of a man loading himself on a catapult and, in desperation, hurling himself up and over the walls of an impregnable castle. It was when Eduard also remembered the man had had his brains crushed to berry juice when he impacted on a stone cistern that he left the perch he had been occupying for the hours he had sat staring at the solid dark mass on the horizon.

The road to the village ran straight through the market square and climbed toward the main gates. The village church faced the outer war towers as if it had been deliberately placed there to ward off evil. The solitary inn was at the eastern corner of the square and even though it was still relatively early—only an hour or two past Vespers—the streets were deserted, and most windows were shuttered against the dread mysteries of the night. There was no sound to be heard anywhere save for the dull crunch of his own bootheels over the hard-packed earth.

Eduard slowed and tilted his head slightly to one side. His hand went to the hilt of his sword and his eyes searched the shadows on either side of him. He heard it again, a breath like a mountain might make the instant before all air is expelled from its catacombs.

"Put your hand away from your sword and stand fast."

Eduard was a split second too slow in reacting and before he could pull his blade more than an inch from its sheath, he felt a cold sliver of steel slide up beneath his chin. An arm the size of a haunch of venison circled his chest and pulled him back against something solid and armoured. His head was forced back at a critical angle, by a knife that nicked the skin, sending a warm trickle of blood down to his collar.

"*Away* from the sword," the voice hissed in his ear, "or our conversation ends here."

"Brevant?"

The knife sliced deeper. "Godstrewth! You do not know me and I do not know you, yet one of us stands bellowing a name for all the world of sin-eaters to hear!"

Since the "bellow" had comprised of little more than a pained gasp of breath, Eduard held his tongue between his teeth and waited for the knife to be taken away.

It lingered for effect then was removed on a grunted curse. Eduard relaxed the arch in his neck and ran a hand across the stinging cut as he turned to face his attacker.

The man *was* a mountain. Taller than Eduard by half a head and twice as broad from neck to waist to calf. The armour Eduard had felt had been the man's chest. He wore the leather buckler of a captain and the cloak of a man who did not want to be readily identified . . . although how there could be two of similar size and bulk was a question Eduard did not want answered.

"You are come from the Old Lion?" Brevant asked huskily.

"You will think I am come from hell if you lift a knife to me again."

Brevant grinned, baring two crooked teeth, like fangs, to the gloomy light. "Look about you, whelp. We are in hell already. Do I get an answer to my question?"

"Do I get an answer to mine?"

The mountain shifted in a general glint of buckles, studs, and metal clasps that adorned his surcoat. "I am Brevant, and because you could learn that much from any villager with eyes come morning, I give away no secrets."

"I am told you do not *give* away much of anything."

"The price of knowledge is not cheap," he agreed on a deep rumble of mirth. "And since I am not the one expected to pay, I do not want to know your name, or who you are, or where you are from. If you are come from the Old Lion, that is dangerous enough to know."

"The Old Lion recommended me to you," Eduard acknowledged. "But how did you know I was here?"

"I know when a dog strays into this village; I know where

it pisses, what it eats, how many fleas it has on its body. I know because it is my business to know and because it is healthier not to be taken by surprise."

Eduard felt the blood oozing down his neck and saw no argument. "Do you also know why I am here?"

"I know full bloody well why you are here," Brevant growled. "And after I tell you what you are up against, mayhap you will tuck your tail between your legs like all the others and scurry off back to where you have come from."

"There have been others?"

"There have been *others* since the Devil took the throne of England and began to use this place as a means of removing faces he never wanted to see again. They have all come—the fathers, the brothers, the valiant friends, even the wives, and they have all paced the hills and walked the shores. They have hunched for hours on the Eagle's Chair, just as you have undoubtedly done, and they have stared at the walls as if their eyes could put them through the mortar. They stay a sennight, sometimes two, then leave again, no better off than when they came, no closer to seeing who they came to see than they were when they arrived all full of fire and righteous brimstone. You would do best to take my advice—and this I give free of cost—and leave now before you find yourself with hymns being sung over your head and dirt being thrown over your feet."

"Are you saying you cannot help me get into the castle?"

Brevant looked astonished, and more than a little horrified. "Help you get in? Was that what the Lion thought I would do? *Help you get in*? A louse needs help to get in; a man would need aid from God. My skin is no safer than any others because there happens to be more of it. My actions are governed by Old Swill, and he answers only to the king. If he takes a notion in his head to question me on this or that, I am as good as dead—and not pleasantly so. No, no, my good man. My intention was not to spread my gizzards on the rack for this. If that was what you thought, keep your money and your ideas to yourself; I'll have no more to do with you."

Eduard reached out and caught his sleeve as Brevant

started to walk away. "Can you at least carry a message for me?"

"A message?" The shadowed visage peered around, this way and that. "If I hear words and am expected to repeat them, I could be asked at the point of a red hot pincer to repeat them again, and would be forced to do so. If I carry these words on a piece of paper, I could be searched and the paper found and the words read, and the pincers heated again. Do you see my problem, friend?"

"Do you see *this*, friend?" Eduard asked, holding up a small leather pouch. He shook it once to let the sound of coins silence the heaving catacombs, then loosed the string and spilled the contents in his palm to let the black eyes catch sight of the gold.

With his other hand he tugged at the cord around his neck and snapped it free, then fished the ring up over the thickness of his clothes.

"I will put these coins into your hand tonight and an equal sum tomorrow night when you bring me proof this ring was delivered into the right hands."

"A ring?" Brevant frowned. "By all the saints—"

"It is a small and insignificant thing. You could hide it in your cheek if you had to and simply spit it on the floor where a keen eye might find it. If it is found, an equally simple exchange would occur the next time you passed that spot. For your trouble, I will make you a very rich man."

Brevant looked at the ring, then at the coins. "What manner of proof will I be expected to carry out?"

"Be assured, the danger is no greater to you than this."

The captain snarled deep in his throat. Quicker than Eduard expected a man of his size to move, the ring, the coins, and the mountainous bulk disappeared along the deep crevice of shadow formed between two cottages.

He cast a sharp eye around him, wary of any sounds or movements that might indicate they had been observed or the captain followed. There was nothing. His heart was beating hard in his chest and there was still a smarting line of abraded

flesh where the ring had dragged summarily through hair and
skin in his haste to remove it. But it was done. Contact had
been initiated. It only remained to tickle the giant's greed long
enough to come up with a plan to rescue Eleanor.

Chapter 16

"The donjons, if I recall correctly, are located in the north end of the bailey," said Henry de Clare. "The fact that Brevant specifically mentioned a tower cell means the princess is likely being confined above ground, and for that much, at least, we can be thankful. The main donjons are beneath the Constable's Tower, in a labyrinth of tunnels and cells carved into the solid rock. Getting someone out of there would be like . . . like coaxing Sedrick backways through a mouse hole."

Henry looked at each solemn face gathered around the table, pausing over the two he had least expected to see there when the journey had begun. When FitzRandwulf had told him about Ariel's wild accusations to do with jewel thefts, he had agreed Eduard had been left with no choice but to tell her the truth. He was not as convinced she should have accompanied them to Corfe, but what other choice did they have? They would not have been able to rest any easier with her out of their sight once she knew what they were about. Short of staking her down hand and foot, he doubted they could have kept her away.

He had agreed, no less reluctantly, on the need to include Dafydd ap Iorwerth and Robin in their confidence. The former had listened and accepted their intentions with little more than a curse and a hard glare at his own broken arm; the latter had been almost too excited to keep a dry eye.

"I knew it!" Robin had cried, looking at his brother with pride bristling from every pore. "I knew you would come after her! I knew you could not, in the name of chivalry and honour, abandon our princess to her fate."

Eduard had smiled dryly and avoided making contact with Ariel's eyes. Sparrow had snorted something about reading too much poetry and becoming addled by too many faery stories, which had set the pair of them, squire and seneschal, arguing over the principles of knighthood.

"These towers," Eduard asked, fresh from his encounter with Jean de Brevant, "they have only one way in and one way out, I suppose?"

Henry shrugged. "Unless you are a bird and can fly up to the windows, aye. Only the one entryway."

"When I was a child," Robin said wryly, "I used to believe Sparrow could fly."

"With vines between my toes and the wind at my back, I can indeed fly almost anywhere," Sparrow agreed belligerently. "But these walls are bare and smooth, and the only wind is the devil's breath. Not even I, Young Staunch, could live up to such expectations."

"There are passageways connecting each tower," Henry added, leaning over the table and sketching an invisible diagram with his finger. "Access tunnels for the guards and porters."

"Porters?"

"Food carriers, dung collectors, the whores who move back and forth from one barracks to the next. Each tower has its own forebuilding and guardroom—" He sketched both roughly. "The postings change—while I was there, at any rate —thrice per deum, with most of those who come off duty going only so far as the nearest gaming table or barrel of ale. If there is any weakness at all, it is during this changing of guards, when one is perhaps arguing with another over a toss of the dice, or a man has had a particularly good whore beneath him and grudges the need to hurry away." He cocked an eyebrow in Ariel's direction and smiled tightly. "My pardons for my bluntness, sister dear, but you did insist we not curb our tongues on your account."

"I must suppose it is only the voice of experience speaking," she allowed, returning his smirk with equal aplomb.

Sedrick sighed. "Aye, well, experience or no, all of this will be for naught if Brevant brings a troop of guards with him the next time ye meet. How do ye know ye can trust him? How do ye know he is not, even as we speak, spilling his guts to the governor and setting a pretty trap for us all? He sounded none too happy to be dealing with ye."

"How he sounded and how he looked at the gold were two different matters," Eduard remarked. "A man honest in his greed will usually be honest in his dealings until the purse runs dry. Moreover, the marshal seemed confident we could keep him on our side, and that should be reason enough."

"Brevant," Ariel murmured, glancing at Henry. "Why does the name sound familiar?"

"Because we have been using it freely this past hour?" her brother suggested wanly.

Ariel frowned. Something was there, nagging at the edge of her memory, but Sedrick was speaking again and it slipped out of reach.

"On our side or not, eager for our gold or not, if he has balked over such a trifling thing as carrying a trinket inside his cheek, how do ye plan to convince him to carry us?"

"Mayhap he will not have to carry us at all," Sparrow said. "Merely stand aside as we pass. We still have the marshal's letters, do we not, or were they lost in Rennes with the nags?"

"We still have them," Eduard admitted grimly.

"Well then? Why were they written if not to be read?"

"What letters?" Dafydd asked, bewildered.

"My uncle anticipated we might encounter some difficulties along the way," Henry explained. "He wrote letters to state we travelled under his seal of protection. They also state we are en route to Radnor Castle, there to unite my suitably demured sister with her intended groom, Reginald de Braose."

"*Braose?*"

Sparrow dismissed the Welshman's exclamation with a flick of his wrist. "Keep your tongue in your mouth, Cyril. The letters were meant to be shown only in an emergency, and only if the king's men took to putting their noses too close to our business. Radnor lies in the path of our true destination and would lead any suspicious minds into believing we were following the king's writ. Besides, is your brother not supposed to be meeting us at a rendezvous well to the good of the road that would carry us to Radnor?"

Dafydd nodded. "He was instructed by the earl marshal to be waiting for us at Gloucester."

"Do you have doubts he will be unable to follow his instructions?" Sparrow demanded.

"He will be there," Dafydd said grimly.

"With his men?"

"With his men, aye."

"Well then?"

"Well then," Ariel interrupted impatiently, not wanting to dwell on the merits of Rhys ap Iorwerth's reliability or eagerness. "These letters—do you think they would get us through the gates of Corfe?"

Sparrow, who had for the most part managed to avoid, in all their days of travel, asking or answering a direct question of Ariel de Clare, scratched furiously at his mop of short black curls and screwed his face into a frown. He had his own reasons for disapproving of the marshal's niece being included in their discussions, but since it appeared as if she might have to play a crucial role, he would have to wait for a more prudent time to vent them.

"Aye," he grumbled, chewing back his reluctance. "They might. This hovel is not exactly of princely standards and the castellan might be convinced of the benefits of inviting one of the king's wards to bide a night or two under his protection."

"You do not have to agree to it," Eduard cut in, his voice as sharp as a knife. "In fact, you would be showing the greater amount of common sense to refuse. The risks are immeasurable and there is no means to vouchsafe we will be let out again, even supposing we are let in."

Ariel was well aware of the reason for the resentful mood around the table. She was here against their better judgement, proving to be pivotal to their plans, and there did not seem to be a damned thing any of them could do about it.

Her cool, steady gaze touched on each face in turn before settling on FitzRandwulf's. "Did any of *you* consult your common sense before setting forth on this venture? To my mind, there is no greater risk one can take in life than the one that proves you to be a coward."

Henry chuckled wryly. "Spoken like a true De Clare."

"Did you think I would refuse?"

"On the contrary, Puss. I somehow expected you to be the first one through the gates. I, for one, will be right on your heels. After all"—he cast a wink in Robin's direction—"we have a damosel in distress to rescue, do we not?"

Robin grinned and Sedrick scowled. "When do ye expect to hear from this rogue, Brevant, again?"

It was a moment before Eduard could drag his eyes away from Ariel, and when he did, he shook his head. "No mention was made of a time or place, but I imagine he will find me the same way he found me tonight."

"If so, you will have no gullet left by week's end," Sparrow snorted, eyeing the bloodied cut.

"A chance I will have to take."

"Less so if there is another pair of eyes watching your back at all times."

"Aye, and yer purse," Sedrick added, not convinced a bribe ensured loyalty.

"I have no objections to having a friendly shadow behind me," Eduard agreed. "So long as the shadow remains well out of sight."

"When have you ever seen me when I have not wanted to be seen?" Sparrow demanded. "To judge by the description you gave, I could crouch in the shadow of the knave's knees and he would not be able to see me from such heights."

Ariel's hand thumped the table with such vigor it sent the wood sprite jumping in his skin.

" 'His name was Jean Brevant,' " she quoted, " 'but since he was taller and broader than most trees, the men just called him Littlejohn. As big as thunder, he was, able to take ten men down with a single swing of his arm, yet helpless to do aught but weep like a babe when he found his wife dead from a birthing fever. Just a tiny thing she was too. Lively as a may-bug, all curly brown hair and laughing eyes. *He* never laughed after that and was sent to do service in some godforsaken castle in Purbeck.' "

Ariel leaned back in her chair and smiled triumphantly. "I *knew* I had heard the name before. Do you not remember, Henry? Uncle Will and Lady Isabella were sitting in front of the hearth one night and he was recounting stories of this brave man and that; stories he knew would bring a tear to Aunt's eyes and make her forgive him his long absences."

"I confess the memory escapes me," Henry said slowly. "But the description would seem to fit: a man as big as thunder . . ."

". . . sent to a godforsaken castle in Purbeck. It *must* be the same man. How else would Uncle Will know he would help us?"

"He has not helped us yet," Henry pointed out. "And may not, just because he mourns a dead wife."

"Saints aggrieve me," Sparrow muttered and peered hard at Ariel. "Did you quoth the earl marshal as saying the wife was possessed of a lively eye and curly brown hair?"

"As best as I can recall it, yes, but—"

Sparrow was already glaring intently at Eduard. "Think you: what does the little maid, Marienne, look like? Is she not here, in Corfe, loyal unto the death to our valiant Pearl? Did the marshal also not say she would be of some value to us in this venture?"

Robin gave a small gasp and felt the blood drain out of his face. "Marienne is here? In Corfe?"

"Who is Marienne?" Dafydd asked, floundering in the dark for the second time.

"The princess's personal maid," Eduard answered. "And possibly the very thing we need to help us gentle a giant."

Marienne bowed her head to receive Father Wilfred's droned benediction and a corkscrew of gleaming brown hair fell forward over her shoulder. She was kneeling behind her mistress and it was nearly driving her mad to know the burly captain was standing behind them both, less than a pace away. Her belly quaked with nervous anticipation and her skin felt sheathed in ice. She had risked only a single glance in his direction when she and Eleanor had first descended the tower steps, but his expression had betrayed nothing. His stance was casual, almost bored. Yet she sensed he had something of grave import to tell her; she knew it by the way her knees knocked and her chin refused to stop quivering.

"Dieu vous benisse," said the priest, making the sign of the cross over Eleanor's bowed head. Marienne hastened forward to help her off her knees, earning a gentle smile of thanks in return. The two guardsmen—one of whom had scratched at his crotch and the other his nose throughout the entire proceedings—waited for the princess to begin the steep climb back up to her cell, then fell into step behind the priest, scratching and picking their way along the dimly lit corridor.

Marienne delayed as long as she dared before putting her foot to the bottom step. She had begun to think her intuition had been wrong when she felt Brevant brush past her, too close for it to be entirely accidental. She went off balance and would have fallen if not for the huge, hairy paw that caught her. When she straightened, she was holding something small and hard in her closed palm.

"From the Scarred One," he murmured. "He says he wants proof I gave it to you."

Marienne opened her fist but the ring was not familiar to her. It was sized for a woman's finger, intricate enough in design to belong to royalty.

"What manner of proof does he want?"

"He says he will know it when he sees it."

Marienne's eyes danced with excitement as she looked up at him. "May I give you this proof tonight, after I have spoken with my lady?"

Brevant nodded and was rewarded with the sight of a brighter, wider smile than had been seen inside these glum walls in more years than he could remember. He stood for a long time after the hem of her tunic had flashed out of sight in the gloom of the stairwell, and, for as long as the image remained burning on his mind, he almost smiled back.

Marienne caught up to the princess halfway between landings, and nowhere near a source of light. Too eager to wait for either, she called out in an urgent whisper, "Your Highness, wait. Take this"—she pressed the ring into Eleanor's hand—"and tell me if you know it."

Eleanor frowned and ran her fingers around the surface of the gold circlet. "No. No, I—" She stopped and held the ring higher. She rubbed it harder and traced the distinctive filigree with the pad of her thumb before she gasped and slipped it over the smallest finger of her right hand. It was a perfect fit.

She reached out across the darkness and gripped Marienne's shoulders. "Where did you get it? Where did it come from? Dear God . . . *Eduard!* Where is he? Have you seen him? Have you spoken to him?"

"No, I have not seen or spoken to him myself, my lady, but the captain has. He told me yesterday—*whisht!*" She stopped and bit her lip, glancing back down into the darkness. "The walls may have ears, my lady. We should say no more until we are behind our own door."

Eleanor's grip tightened briefly, but she could see the reason for caution and practically dragged her young maid up the winding stairs behind her. Safe in the isolation of the tower room, they closed the heavy door and took the further precaution of sitting in the farthest corner of the solar, near the prayer nave.

"Tell me," Eleanor commanded. "Tell me everything."

"There is not much to tell, for 'twas only a chance remark yesterday that first caught my ear."

"What did he say? *What exactly did he say?*"

"He said . . . exactly . . . that a group of graycloaks were passing through the village and had decided to lodge at the inn while one of their party was tended by an herb woman."

"One of them is injured?" Eleanor gasped.

"Or possibly using it as a ruse."

"And? Was that all he said?"

"Not all, my lady. He also said . . . one of the knights bore a scar on his cheek."

Eleanor squeezed Marienne's hands so tightly, the maid thought her fingers might pop apart at the joints. The princess turned toward the crucifix that hung in the nave and made soft, choking sounds, as if she did not know whether to laugh or to cry.

"He has come. Dear, sweet Eduard . . . he has come. Oh but . . . Jesu, Jesu . . ." She whirled back around and gripped Marienne's hands more ferociously. *"Why* has he come? What does he think he can do? If the king's men discover who he is, or . . . or if they even suspect . . . !"

"Do not distress yourself, my lady," Marienne said. "Lord FitzRandwulf is no pudding-head. He is the bravest, boldest knight in all of Christendom—he will not have come without a clever plan to rescue you!"

"Rescue me?" Eleanor cried aghast. "Surely not! Surely he cannot be thinking . . . ! He would not try . . . ! *He has not come to take me back to Brittany!*"

Marienne looked puzzled. "Surely that is exactly why he has come, my lady. Brittany is your home. He has come . . . to take you home."

"Dear Mother Mary," Eleanor whispered, so weakened by the thought that she slipped down onto her knees. Her hands shook visibly as she ran them down the front of her gown, from breasts to belly, and when she raised them again, the tiny silver cross of her rosary beads was caught around her fingers. "I cannot go back to Brittany," she gasped. "Not like this. My uncle sought to shame me, and he has succeeded. I cannot go back to Brittany! I cannot let Eduard see me like this! It would . . . kill him."

"If he kills anyone, it will be the king," Marienne declared savagely. "And good riddance to him! As for the people of Brittany, they love you. They will never stop loving you, nor can they blame you for the king's perversions. They will be thankful enough you are still alive and not . . . not . . ."

"Not lying in a watery grave like my poor Arthur? Sometimes . . . I think I would have been better off beside him. At least then he would not have been alone, and I . . . I would not have had to bear the shame of Angevin lust and greed."

"Your Highness, you must not speak this way. Lord Eduard has come to rescue you, to save you from this place, and from the king's madness."

"Then he has wasted his time, for there is no rescue possi-

ble for me, only sanctuary, and this the king has already provided for me."

"Here? In Corfe? You would be content to remain the rest
of your days here?"

"The king has promised me I will not. Corfe is but a
temporary accommodation while I . . . while I adjust to my
condition," she finished in a whisper.

"You would still believe him? After all he has done to you
. . . the degradation he has forced upon you?"

"He did it to ensure I could never be a threat to his crown.
In that he has succeeded, for I could never be queen now,
never"—the words caught in her throat and took all of her
strength to sob free—"be looked upon with anything but pity
and derision."

"Lord FitzRandwulf will only look upon you with love,"
Marienne insisted. "Just as I do."

"No!" Eleanor said fiercely. "No, he must never look
upon me at all! He must be persuaded to go away from here
and leave me to my own fate. He must be convinced this is
what I want."

"But . . . how, my lady? He will not believe the word of
a gaoler, regardless of what proof Brevant gives him. He will
not believe this is what you have said or what you want unless
he hears it from your own lips."

"You must find a way. You *must* convince him I am better
left forgotten, for I could not bear to even imagine the look on
his face if he should see me like this."

Eleanor bowed her head and turned her body into the
nave. She clasped her hands around her beads and pressed
them to her lips, praying fervently between soft, muffled sobs.
Watching her, Marienne thought her heart would surely break
under this new burden of sorrow.

It was not fair. It simply was not fair that someone so
proud, so lovely, so virtuous should have to spend the rest of
her days with her head bent in shame.

Hoping to find a measure of the courage her princess possessed, Marienne took to her knees alongside her and appealed to the Blessed Virgin for guidance. She prayed all day as

she went about her chores and later that evening, when she again bumped into Captain Brevant and felt for the warmth of his large hand, she whispered her message, knowing full well it would take more than just a humble miracle to turn Eduard FitzRandwulf away from Corfe Castle.

"What do you mean she wants nothing more to do with me?" Eduard demanded, his anger rising swift and sharp to the surface.

"I am not the one to know what she means," Brevant snarled by way of an answer. "I only know she gave me this"—he shoved something round and heavy into Eduard's hand and withdrew his own as if the object had been glowing red hot and he was glad to be rid of it—"and sent a plea that you leave her to the fate God has chosen for her. Those were *her* words according to the Little One, and God curse my tongue for agreeing to carry them at all. Take my advice and do as she asks. The king is expected to sail from Cherbourg before the week's end. He will be stopping here before he makes for Portsmouth and you would be smart to have moved your ugly faces a hundred miles from here by then."

Eduard curled his fist around the ring Brevant had given him. He had no need to look at it, for he knew it was his own, wrought of gold and crested with the La Seyne Sur Mer device of a snarling wolf. News of the king's imminent arrival came as a surprise. If it was true—and he had no reason to believe it was not—they had no more time to waste weighing the risks. They would have to take a few.

"I want you to inform your governor we are here."

"Eh? Inform him you are here?" Brevant was stunned. "Are you mad?"

"We are all a little mad, my friend, some more than others is all. You have told us it is impossible to get inside the castle walls by stealth or force. It remains, therefore, the only other way is by invitation."

"Invitation? You expect him to *invite* you into the castle as his guests?"

"I would expect him, as the king's representative, to extend the offer of hospitable lodgings to Lady Ariel de Clare and her brother, Lord Henry de Clare, niece and nephew to William of Pembroke, Earl Marshal of England.''

The giant's jaw sagged open and his eyes bulged. "You want me to carry him a tale like that?"

"He must already know there are strangers in the village; it can only do you credit to go to him with the lord and lady's identity and inform him they are in possession of letters, signed by the earl himself, granting her safe conduct and all due courtesies on her journey north to be united with her groom, the king's own loyal vassal, Sir Reginald de Braose.''

Brevant grasped the hilt of his sword in a hand that could have crushed it. "You *are* mad, my bold fellow. Old Swill has no sense of humour and if he thinks, for one instant, the letters are a ruse and the lady is none other than Mistress Waycock from Strumpet Row—''

"The letters are genuine," Eduard said evenly. "As will be Lord Henry's wrath if he hears you have called his sister, the earl's niece, a whore.''

Brevant expelled all the air from his lungs, sending a wave of heat blasting past Eduard's face. "Perhaps you have no knowledge of the man who governs Corfe Castle. I do not call him Old Swill out of fondness, but because of the quantities of ale and wine he consumes each day in order to sleep through the screams of his prisoners at night. He was once one of John's champions, you see, who gained some prominence in the lists as a man who rarely carried a blunted sword into matches and who had no qualms about striking a man when his back was turned if it was the easy way to victory. He also managed to expand his holdings in Nottinghamshire through several *favours* he did for the then prince regent—a few quiet assassinations for parcels of land here and there—and set his ambitions toward becoming sheriff.

"When Prince John became King John, our bold but foolish Sir Guy of Gisbourne jokingly made reference to some of these past favours he had done, fully expecting his services would be rewarded by his appointment to the king's judiciary court. He was appointed here instead, with the promise of

Nottingham's seat if he could prove both his deservedness and his ability to keep his mouth firmly shut." Brevant paused and drew another deep breath as if to cleanse his lungs of some unknown foulness. "Gisbourne has been governor here at Corfe for two years, and has been striving to win his way back into the king's good graces ever since. He is especially vindictive and especially creative if he thinks he has a victim in his claws whose screams of agony would put a smile on the king's face."

Eduard's pulse was hammering in his throat. "This Gisbourne . . . he has not been near the guest in the tower cell, has he?"

"No. Not because he does not think the king would grin ear to ear, but because . . . he is not so foolish as to think he would sleep long without a knife cutting across his throat if he did dare to go near her."

Eduard felt a mild flush of encouragement. It was not much, but it *was* an indication that there was a vulnerable chink in Brevant's armour. If he could widen that chink, expose more of that vulnerability, maybe . . . just maybe there was a way to help Eleanor.

"Will you do it? Will you present our letters to Gisbourne?"

Brevant looked away and snarled. "If I did . . . *if*, mind . . . just how long would you be planning to play fancy with Gisbourne's hospitality?"

"If the king is expected in four days' time, we will be gone in three."

Brevant rumbled again and turned, pacing several ground-shaking steps into the shadows before stopping and pacing back. "Once inside . . . what then? What do you plan to do?"

"The maid—Marienne—she is not a prisoner, is she? Can she move freely about the castle?"

"Aye," Brevant nodded warily. "What of it?"

"I would see her then, and speak to her face to face. If I am convinced the one she serves is genuinely content with her fate, I will say or do nothing more."

It was on the tip of Brevant's tongue to tell the rogue

knight exactly why the lady would probably prefer to stay where she was, but it was not his place to reveal such things. Moreover he suspected even if he did tell the rogue of the lady's plight, he would only tear a hole in the walls block by block to get at her to see the truth for himself. Let him come into Corfe, Brevant decided. Let him come and see for himself, if that was what he wanted . . . if he dared.

"Be ready by noon tomorrow," he advised. "If Gisbourne takes the bait, I will come for you then. If noon passes and you have only your cap in your hand, I want your word you will put it on your head and ride out of Corfe without looking back."

Eduard was loathe to be bound by any more oaths, but the giant was adamant.

"Your word, my lord," Brevant demanded quietly. "Or this goes no further."

"You have my word. We will quit the inn one way or another by midday tomorrow."

Chapter 17

†**A**riel stretched, from the tips of her fingers to the ends of her toes, feeling every muscle pull and tauten, every knuckle of her spine straighten and nudge its neighbour awake. It was still gloomy in the room; the sky outside the tiny casement window was tardy in relinquishing the night.

Ariel turned her head slowly, wary of the sounds of the other sleepers around her. The inn only had the one room and one large bed that could have slept six head to toe if they were friendly. For the second night in a row, Ariel had been given the whole thing to herself, while the men had claimed various sections of the floor.

She had heard rain spattering the horn panes of the window during the night, and she could smell the dampness in the thatch overhead. It was even damper, she supposed, because the window was open a crack, but she was not of a mind to tell the man standing there to close the shutters and keep the chill to himself.

The last glimpse she had had of FitzRandwulf, he had been standing in the same position. He must have moved some time during the night, for his quilted leather gambeson had been removed and replaced with a rust-coloured jerkin. His profile was the same: hard and angular. The hand that rested on the shutter caught what light was blooming through the cracks, giving the veins and fine bones a raised pattern of shadows and planes, causing the signet ring he now wore on his thumb to glow blood red.

Ariel squeezed her eyes closed, but it was no use. The image of his hands, the memory of those hands boldly stroking over her body, would not be chased away. If anything, the memory caused little shivers to spread through her body, rippling across the surface of her skin, bringing on changes, disturbances everywhere. There was gooseflesh on her arms, but she was not cold. There was a shimmering weakness in her limbs, but she was not standing. Ribbons of heat, as unsettling as the pinprick shivers started to flutter in the valley between her thighs—a queer sensation, smooth and sharp at the same time, and it made her want to press her thighs together to keep the ribbons from uncoiling.

How could she have let him do such a thing to her? Surely it was a sin to allow a man such freedoms? And an even greater sin to enjoy them? He had certainly known just what to touch and how to touch it, and it made her wonder . . . if he had not stopped himself . . . what other skills he would have shared.

This time she did shake the thoughts away. Quietly, carefully so as not to disturb the others, she gathered the folds of the blanket around her shoulders and sat on the edge of the bed. FitzRandwulf's head had turned slightly to indicate he had detected the movement, but he did not look in her direction or move so much as a muscle anywhere else on his body.

Ariel glanced around the room. Sedrick and Henry were stretched along the floor on either side of the door, their faces to the wall, their arms folded over their chests as they slept. Robin was in a youthful sprawl, his mouth open, his hood folded forward almost to his nose, shading the upper half of his face. Sparrow was curled beside him, his hat crushed beneath his head as a pillow, his arblaster hugged against his body for comfort. The Welshman was partially hidden by the corner of the bed; all she could see were his feet, clad in their fine gray doeskin boots.

She stood, drawing the blanket higher around her chin. They had all slept fully clothed save for the bulkiest layers of armour, and she was careful how she put her boots to the floor, not wanting to waken anyone with a clumsy misstep. Apart from the tails of the blanket, which whispered softly where they dragged over the floorboards, she came up beside Fitz-Randwulf without a sound.

"What Robin told me must be true," she said on a hushed breath. "He said you never sleep."

The pewter-coloured eyes lingered on the scene outside the window, and she wondered if perhaps he hadn't even heard her. But he had. It just took him a moment to steel himself to look down at her—something he was hoping he could do without giving himself away.

There were soft pink creases on her cheek where she had lain on a fold of the blanket. Her eyes were heavy-lidded and her hair— Damn all the saints who strove to torment what few hours he did manage to sleep with thoughts of all that copper fire spread beneath a pale white body. Now it lay in a loosely plaited rope over her shoulder, with sprays and errant curls flying every which way around her face, making his fingers itch with the need to reach out and tuck it back behind her ears.

He turned to look back out the window again, judging it to be safer.

"I sleep when I need to, for as long as I need to. I had no idea my habits warranted discussion."

Whether it was because he was not a man accustomed to whispering, or because she had somehow touched an open nerve, his answer came out harsher than she expected and the ribbons in her belly shrivelled into a tight knot.

"We were not discussing, we were only . . . talking, and . . . oh . . . never mind. Talking is another thing I am well aware you do not do with any great fondness. Forgive me if I disturbed you."

She did not even gain a step when she felt his hand on her arm, stopping her. His hand remained through an awkward silence before easing away and falling to his side again.

"You were not disturbing me," he assured her quietly.

Go or stay, it was a difficult choice to make, but she re-traced the step she had taken and even added another that she might crane her neck and see out the small, boxlike window. There was not much to view apart from the tall, looming silhouette of Corfe Castle crouched on the hill. The sky was gray and dirty, promising more rain before cock's crow. Smoke and fog combined in viscous layers, opaque and undulant, like rivers of slow-moving cream that sought to fill the hollows where the village sat. It was eerie and ominous, but not worth staring at for hours on end. Especially not if someone was plagued by nightmares of another tall, bleak castle and the horrors it contained.

She wished she had the nerve to ask him about it, about his years at Bloodmoor Keep and his dam, Nicolaa de la Haye. There were so many dark secrets cloaked behind the brooding gray eyes, so many painful memories he must fight with, every day, just to survive to see another.

A lesser creature, battling these demons within, might have thrown up his hands when confronted with the formidable walls of Corfe. A far nobler coward might have cut his losses, assumed his duty done, and slinked away, striking back across the Channel before any hint of an alarm was raised.

Not Eduard FitzRandwulf d'Amboise. Not the son of the Black Wolf. Not even the very real possibility of being caught and stretched out on another torturer's table would turn him away. Not when the woman he loved was held prisoner inside those walls.

Ariel bowed her head and studied her hands.

"Do you suppose Brevant will have convinced the governor to admit us?"

Eduard offered a casual shrug. "He seems a persuasive sort, if the mood is upon him."

Ariel closed her eyes, aware of how close he stood, how sensual the vibration of his voice against her neck. She wished she could lean back and feel his arms wrapping around her. She wished he would hold her again, just once more, so she would know what it was like to feel safe and warm and protected.

"There is still time for you to change your mind if you are having second thoughts," he said softly. "No one will think any the less of you."

"I have not changed my mind. And *I* would think less of me, even if no one else did."

She did not look at him but she knew his eyes had not left her face. She knew also that if she did look up, she would doubtless make a fool of herself again, for he could read her thoughts with such ease, he could probably see her confusion, see the havoc he had wrought on her senses, on her perceptions. Words, oaths, resolutions, promises . . . noble blood, bastard blood . . . what did any of it mean beside a man who kissed like fire and brought ecstasy with a touch of his hand?

Behind them, someone moved, breaking the spell. Ariel stayed at the window but Eduard turned away at once, his boots striding deliberately through the silence, winning the desired chorus of groans, yawns, and shifting bodies.

Henry rolled himself upright and rubbed his fists into his eyes. "God love me, it cannot be morning already. I vow I barely closed my eyes an hour ago."

"Aye, well, mine eyes as well as mine nostrils have opened and shut like a fishmonger's mouth the whole night long," Sparrow grumbled. He slanted a meaningful glance at Sedrick, who proceeded to break wind with a satisfying grunt of pleasure. "Hark! The Toothless Wonder speaks again. A moment yet and we will all swear something died in yon breeks."

"Bah! 'Tis better than a belch for cleaning the pipes," Sedrick declared, blowing again for emphasis.

Sparrow screwed his eyes down to slits and hefted his arblaster. "If it be thine pipes that need cleaning, messire, I have a keener way to drill them through."

Henry, caught between the pair of antagonists, eyed the quiver of bolts Sparrow was reaching for and moved prudently out of the way. He saw Ariel standing by the window and joined her, hesitating half a moment before he ran his hand through his hair and ventured to speak.

"You know, no one will think any the less of you if you—"

"—find I have come to my senses during the night and changed my mind?" she finished with a wry smile. "Will you also act sensibly and remain behind with me?"

Henry frowned and scratched thoughtfully at his scalp. "I believe I had a sensible day . . . once. It is not entirely out of the realm of the possible to think I might be inspired to have another some day."

"Be sure to come and find me when you do. I will want to bear witness."

"Aye, Cardigan is only a day's ride from Pembroke; at least I will not have to look far to find you."

Her smile slipped a little at the corners, but she took his

hand and gave it a squeeze. "You are far more sensible than you will ever admit. That is why I had no fear in going to Normandy with you, and why I have no fear riding into Corfe with you now. Between you and"—she almost said FitzRandwulf, but caught her tongue at the last possible instant—"and the others, I know we will be riding out again . . . probably with more haste than what we ride in with, but intact all the same."

He tucked a finger under her chin and tilted her face up. "Good God, I believe you really mean it."

"I do, buffoon. And your doubting me does you little credit. You know I love you and trust you and value your opinion above all others. It may not always appear so," she added softly. "Nor do I always welcome your advice with grace and gratitude, but I always listen to it and trust it comes from the heart. As you say, we only have each other to watch out for."

A retort that normally would have been glib and dismissive was stalled in Henry's throat. She was being sincere and honest with her emotions, something that occurred all too infrequently, and he could not help but wonder at the cause. He was neither blind nor deaf, and he had been the one to scrape a boot on the floor and interrupt the conversation between his sister and Eduard FitzRandwulf . . . something that was beginning to occur all too frequently. He preferred to see Ariel's eyes hot green and flaring with contempt when she spoke with the Wolf's cub, not soft and questioning and afraid to make contact.

He would have to redouble his efforts to keep them apart, although, in light of where they were going and what they would be doing, he could not, in all honesty, wish a better man to be watching his sister's back.

Jean de Brevant and a small escort of men-at-arms rode out of the main gates of Corfe a little before noon. Having never seen the man in daylight before, Eduard was as surprised as the others by the captain's appearance. The mountainous silhouette of ominous shadows became a barrel-

chested pillar of brawn and muscle with a face that put a
carved grotesque to shame. He was younger than the harshness of his voice had suggested—twenty-two or -three, perhaps—and wore his authority with as much assurance as he
wore his impressive hauberk of jazerant work. Glittering rows
of round steel plates were attached to an underlying suit of
canvas, with each plate overlapping slightly like the scales of a
fish. Even more daunting to the eyes of the beholder was the
weapon he carried—no ordinary sword, this, but a glaive, long-
handled and curved like a scimitar, boasting a sharply barbed
hook on the concave edge. He made an impressive and intimidating sight riding down the street toward the inn. Villagers
stopped what they were doing to stare. Even the dogs and
kites that usually chased after horses' heels, yapping their imitation of Bedlam, cringed mutely by the roadside.

Sedrick of Grantham, who was accustomed to owning the
advantage of size in most company was clearly lacking in this
instance. And Eduard, who rarely felt slight by comparison to
any man, allowed a moment for his ingrained fighter's instincts
to reflect back over his years of training and combat and wonder what tactics would be effective against such a foe . . . if,
indeed, there were any.

Hopefully he would have no reason to draw upon them.

Brevant's mount, a behemoth of horseflesh in its own
right, drew to a halt outside the inn. Lord Henry de Clare,
assuming the guise of leader, walked out under the leaden sky
to offer greetings.

"My lord Gisbourne finds himself at a loss how to apologize for this oversight," Brevant announced without preamble.
"When he was informed there were members of the Pembroke
household"—his wary black eyes slid to the marshal's device,
now boldly displayed on the front of Henry's surcoat—"staying within sight of the castle, he immediately bade me—Captain Jean de Brevant—extend an invitation to you and your
party to share more suitable lodgings."

"My thanks to you, Captain Brevant," Henry responded.
"We would naturally be pleased and honoured to accept."

Brevant smirked and glanced at the inn. "I am also in-

formed there is a wounded man in your group? Does he require a litter?"

"An unfortunate accident," Henry allowed. "Serious
enough to waylay us a few days while he attempts to recover
his strength. A litter is unnecessary, but would be most appre-
ciated, I am sure."

While Brevant signalled two of his men forward with a
chair, Henry turned and raised his hand. The door to the inn
opened at once and Lord Dafydd ap Iorwerth, supported on
one side by Sedrick and on the other by Eduard, was helped
out into the street and lifted onto the chair. He groaned audi-
bly as his arm took a small jolt before the sling was adjusted,
whereupon he slumped forward in the seat as if he was only
able to maintain his balance with the utmost effort. Two more
of Brevant's men stepped out of line and joined their comrades
as they prepared to lift the carrying poles. Eduard, who was
trying to remain as unobtrusive as possible, met the captain's
eye over the top of the litter as it was hoisted, and acknowledged him with a slight nod of his head before taking up a
position beside Lucifer.

Ariel and Robin were the last to emerge, and the only ones
who wrought a noticeable change to the blank expression on
Brevant's face. Ariel wore a deep green velvet tunic she had
carried folded in her saddle pouch. The cuffs and hem were
banded with gold braid, the collar of miniver fur was turned
down in a deep vee to display the pure white delicacy of her
throat. Her hair had been parted in the middle and plaited into
two thick coils behind each ear, held in place by jeweled barbettes. Over all she wore a hooded cloak in a matching green
velvet, lined with fur and trimmed with bands of embroidery.
Her face was as pale as her breath as she said a few words to
Robin, who instantly darted forward as if to obey a command
from his mistress.

Oddly enough, it was Robin whose further actions were
followed by the jet black eyes, followed and frowned upon
with a look of distinct unease. The reason for this was made
clear when Henry was mounted alongside Brevant and the
latter was able to whisper a low warning.

"You might want to keep your squire close by your side and not leave him alone in Gisbourne's company. The governor has a fondness for pretty boys and has not seen one quite so comely in some time. Unless, of course," he added consideringly, "the boy has no objections himself. It would be the one sure way to keep Gisbourne's attentions occupied elsewhere."

Henry glanced over, startled. "I can promise you the lad would not be inclined to bend over for anyone, for any reason. Nor would it behoove you to suggest it in a voice loud enough for his *brother* to overhear."

The emphasis on *brother* was supplemented by a pointed nod in Eduard's direction.

"Godstrewth!" Brevant scoffed. "Brothers, sisters . . . happens did you bring a granny or two along to tuck you to bed at night?"

"Nay, friend," Henry answered blithely. "But we do have a faery dwarf who serves just as well."

"Eh? A *dwarf?*"

"Aye, a poxy little gnome who probably has your nose aligned along the shaft of one of his arrows as we speak. He has chosen *not* to accept the governor's invitation, preferring to remain here and keep a firm eye on who goes and comes from the castle once we are inside. He is the vindictive sort too; an eye for an eye, a tooth for a tooth. With the patience of Job when it comes to avenging himself on someone foolish enough to double-cross his master."

Brevant merely snorted aside the implied threat and turned his steed, calling to the others to follow his lead up the steep incline toward the castle. The porters lifted the chair and the men-at-arms fell into step behind the captain, the lady, and the three mounted knights.

Despite having had the walls and towers of Corfe Castle under constant scrutiny for the past two days, and despite having studied it from every angle and view conceivable, nothing quite prepared them for the effect of the king's stronghold once they had ridden close enough for the walls to grow and blot out the sky. The block and mortar showed the wear of heavy weather and sea air. With no moat to carry away the ordure and refuse dumped from the high battlements, there was a stench that lingered about the walls, as thick as the mists that dampened them. A blanket of lichen grew up from the base, greenest and richest where the dung heaps were mounded. There was another shallow gully, naturally carved in the land, where the rotting carcasses and entrails of animals won the screaming attention of gulls and other carrion.

From a distance, Corfe seemed bleak and forbidding. Up close, the walls were higher, darker, more unwholesome than any Ariel had ever seen. Knowledge of the cruelty and terror that awaited most visitors inside prompted a deeper chill than the weather, and, had either FitzRandwulf or Henry repeated the offer they had made earlier that morning, she would gladly have swung her palfrey around and bolted for cleaner air.

But even before the creaking portcullis was lowered behind them and the enormous inner gates were closed and barred, she knew there could be no turning back. She could not begin to imagine anyone—noble or common—being condemned to imprisonment in a place such as this. From the filthy, leering faces of the guards who sullenly watched them pass, to the steaming grates cut into the cobbles where air was vented from the maze of donjons carved below ground, the sights and smells of Corfe sickened her. If she could help to remove even one desperate soul from this place of insidious evil, she would not turn away now.

Brevant drew to a halt outside the largest tower—the King's Tower, he informed them, rising fully a hundred feet into the murky sky. The keep was surrounded by a dry moat, crossed by means of a footbridge wide enough to walk but three or four abreast. Long, mucky streaks of offal spilled from the bottom of dung sluices and clung to the mortar like slimy icicles. Ariel had not thought the stench could get any worse, but here it made her eyes water and caused a lump to rise up the back of her throat.

A balding toad of a man shuffled out onto the footbridge to greet them. A hunchback, he grinned over teeth as slimy as the walls and bade them welcome. A flurry of stable boys appeared to hold the reins of the horses and the toad assured Lord Henry they would be well fed and groomed for the duration of their stay. Lord Dafydd was helped out of the litter, groaning in genuine agony over the stench of the seneschal's breath as he was offered more assurances of expert medical attention.

Gallworm, as the seneschal was addressed by Brevant, was ordered to escort their honoured guests to the great hall, where the governor was waiting to greet them. The hunchback bobbed and nodded, crabbing backward with a shuffling gait, beckoning the others to follow.

Henry took Ariel's arm and gave it a squeeze for courage, then followed Brevant's lead across the footbridge, careful to place their steps where the captain's weight proved the warped and pitted boards could best bear the strain. Entrance to the tower itself was gained through climbing a steep flight of covered stairs. The paved platform at the top was perhaps ten paces square and fell directly under the eyes of a dozen sentries posed on catwalks above. Three doors opened off this platform, the one on the left led to the adjoining towers and barracks, the one on the right to the cookhouse and laundry. The middle was the largest and opened ónto a second stone platform that overlooked the great hall.

Half—nay, a third the size of either Amboise or Pembroke, the audience chamber was smoke-filled and poorly lit, stinking of mouldy rushes and unwashed bodies. Descending onto the floor was like walking down the ridges of a spine into a whale's belly, with the arched beams closing like ribs overhead and a narrow, rectangular shape that made the walls seem to crowd in on both sides.

At the far end was a raised dais, and on it, a single high-backed chair, large enough and ornate enough in carvings and design to resemble a throne. Seated there, clad in his capacious black robes of authority, was the governor of Corfe Castle, Guy of Gisbourne. Thin and ferretlike in appearance, he sat perfectly still as his guests approached; only his eyes flicked from one face to the next, from one cut of tunic to the next, satisfied to see his own finery would not suffer by comparison. His hands, with every one of his ten fingers bejeweled with rings, rested on the broad arms of the chair. One foot was stretched slightly forward of the other, the sharply pointed, exquisitely tooled leather of his shoe extending from beneath the hem of his robe. He wore a plaited sallet on his head, black with gold fancywork, crowning hair that was long and smooth and ended in a perfect curl just above the collar. His face was as narrow and pointed as his shoes, with a long hooked nose and eyes that were so slitted against the effects of the smoke and gloom, they could have been any colour from brown to black to palest blue.

"Ah. Lord Henry and Lady Ariel de Clare, I presume? What a pleasant and unexpected surprise to learn you were in the vicinity. But why did you not come instantly to the castle instead of taking up lodgings in that squalid little inn? I confess, I am somewhat puzzled . . . and offended . . . that you did not."

"The slight was not deliberate, I assure you," said Henry. "In truth, we had expected to spend no more than a single night in the village, as haste is our most pressing concern. But then our man was taken by a fever and—" He shrugged and smiled dismissively. "Such go the way of all good intentions, I suppose."

The hooded eyes slid past Henry's shoulder to where Lord Dafydd stood between Sedrick and Eduard. "We have an excellent physician here at Corfe. If your men would care to follow Captain Brevant, I am sure his wounds can be tended at once."

"My thanks," Henry said. "The fever has broken and the arm appears to have set without mortification, but I am sure he could benefit greatly from a leeching, if your man has the facilities . . . ?"

Gisbourne smiled. "I assure you, we have the finest facilities for prolonging . . . or expediting life. Now please—" He clapped his jeweled hands and called forth a pair of varlets waiting nearby with chairs. "Come and sit by the brazier where it is warmer and tell me all the news of your uncle, William the Marshal. God abide me, I met the man not two summers ago when he came to oversee some communication or other with the two Scottish brats the king had trusted to our care. In truth, they were not so much trouble as they seemed in the beginning. Once I tossed their bagpipes and the skirted fiend who played them over the walls . . . they were reconciled quite nicely to their habitats. Gallworm! Fetch ale and wine for our guests."

Gallworm relayed the order to a wench who hastened forward with the refreshments. Having been dismissed already, Eduard and Sedrick showed no reluctance in following Brevant out of the great hall. FitzRandwulf paused before he exited the room, aware of eyes burning into the back of his neck and when he looked back, he was not surprised to see Ariel staring after him. She was standing on the dais, waiting while the varlet fussed with her chair, and was caught in a spill of hazed light that streamed down from the single window overhead. Swathed in lustrous green velvet, with the gold barbettes trapping the fire of her hair, she looked as regal as any queen who might have stood there. As regal as any queen accusing one of her avowed champions of abandoning her.

Eduard ducked through the low doorway behind Sedrick and Dafydd. Brevant was leading them down a long stone corridor that connected the great hall to the barracks. The passage was confining in width and height, forcing the tallest to walk stooped over.

"The physic has been told to look beneath the bandages on your man's arm," Brevant warned under his breath. "If the bones are not genuinely broken, they had better be before the linens are unbound."

"He will find what he is looking for," Eduard said. "The question now is, will we?"

Brevant deigned not to acknowledge or answer the question until the barracks had been left behind along with Sedrick and Dafydd. They did not return to the great hall at once, but took a more circuitous route by way of the tower rooms where Henry and Ariel would be housed for the night.

"I suggested to Lord Gisbourne, what with the marshal's niece probably being accustomed to somewhat different ser-

vices than what our castle sluts are skilled at supplying, some
other arrangements might be made."

Eduard glanced sharply at Brevant. "He has given permission for Marienne to serve Lady de Clare?"

"She will be summoned before supper to draw the lady a
bath and tend her needs. I suggest you be there yourself to say
what you have to say while you have the chance." The captain
turned and the plates of his armour winked with reflected
candlelight. "I would also warn you that if the wrong ear picks
up a whisper, I will be the one chaining your ankles and wrists
to the rack—and I will do it, by Christ's cross, with an extra
twist of thanks for all the trouble you have given me."

Chapter 18

✝**M**arienne stood on the threshold of Ariel de Clare's chambers, her slender body trembling so badly the buckets she was carrying sloshed water over the lip and down the sides of her skirt.

Gisbourne had kept Ariel and Henry in the great hall until well past dusk and when Ariel had finally been escorted to her apartment, she found Eduard was already there, waiting.

There were two rooms set aside for Ariel's use and privacy, occupying the upper floor of the Queen's Tower. Neither were very large, with one barely more than an anteroom holding the garderobe and a pallet for a page or maid. The inner room contained the bed, a chest for clothes, an iron candle stand, and because it was the upper level, a small hearth with a crib for burning logs. Henry's rooms were identical in size and shape, located down a twist of stone stairs. There were no windows, as such, on either level, only deep, narrow vents cut high on the walls, and in Ariel's room, a cat's climb to the roof.

Only a couple of minutes passed, with Ariel too busy recounting Gisbourne's more obnoxious qualities—he liked to pick lice from his scalp and beard and crunch the shells between his teeth—before they heard the soft knocking on the outer doors. Robin, who had remained vigilant by Ariel's side throughout the afternoon, opened the door and stood there like a fool, gaping at Marienne as if she had grown three eyes and a pair of horns.

"Marienne?" he said on a breath. "Is it you?"

The smile that came slowly, disbelievingly to the young maid's lips (in truth, she had lost hold of her wits for a long, startled moment as well) grew inconceivably wider and brighter as she looked up into Robin's face. She blushed and lowered her lashes quickly, then raised them again, staring into his face as if she could have devoured him whole.

"Aye, Lord Robert," she whispered. " 'Tis me."

"You look . . . well," he said awkwardly, flushing to the roots of his hair.

"You look . . . a welcome sight, forsooth. I had given up hope of ever seeing the face of a . . . a friend again."

Her dark brown eyes were attracted by movement over Robin's shoulder, and she saw Eduard FitzRandwulf standing by the hearth. Her fingers lost their grip on the jute handles of the buckets and both crashed to the floor. With a cry of unself-conscious joy, she ran across the room and threw herself into the dark knight's arms. The mature, resolute facade she had been determined to maintain these past months for her princess's sake, crumpled into a child's sobs as she buried her face against his shoulder and clung to him for all she was worth.

Ariel was helpless to do much more than stand in the shadows and watch. She thought to signal Robin to close and bolt the door, but one look at his face, straining not to crack and fold in on itself, betrayed how close his own emotions were to the surface. She moved on silent feet and lifted the buckets herself, setting them down again inside the door before she closed it and stood with her back pressed against the banded oak.

"My lord, my lord," Marienne sobbed. "I confess we were still afraid it was not you."

"It is me," Eduard assured her gently. He smoothed a hand over her hair and tilted her head enough to press a kiss on her forehead, wiping a thumb across her cheek in a futile attempt to staunch the flow of tears. "Did you honestly doubt I would come?"

"N-not I," Marienne declared. "I never doubted it for a moment. I just never thought you would come *here*. H-how did you . . . ?"

Eduard shook his head. "It is of no consequence *how* we came, only that we have come, and that we have come to take you and Eleanor away from this place."

"Would that it were possible," she said in a whisper.

"Anything is possible if the heart is willing," Eduard insisted. "Now, what is this tripe the captain tells me? What is this nonsense I am told that the princess does not want to escape this place?"

"Oh . . . my lord—" Marienne sniffed and wiped her cheeks, then dragged her sleeve across the wetness streaming from her nose. "It is true. She has sent me here tonight to beg you to leave Corfe, leave England before the king's men catch wind of your presence here. You would be a grand prize to offer as hostage against my lord La Seyne Sur Mer's actions. A grand revenge for the king to hold you ransom."

"Think you either I or my father care one wit for the king's men or for the king's petty retributions against us? It is Eleanor whose safety must come before all else. Eleanor whose future must be protected against those who would harm her."

Marienne swallowed hard. "She is . . . convinced her uncle will keep his word and merely banish her. She is convinced his guilt over . . . over her poor brother Arthur will protect her from farther harm."

Eduard frowned. "He must have twisted her mind if she believes this. I cannot fathom how she would, after all that has happened."

"After all that has happened," Marienne said softly, "her beliefs are all she has left."

"She has me. And I will not allow her to remain an hour longer in her uncle's web than is necessary. I have come to take her away from here, and by God, I will take her away, willing or not."

"My lord . . . she loves you very much; surely you must know this."

Eduard's face remained taut and Ariel's drained to a paler shade of gray as she bowed her head and stared at her twined fingers.

"Just as I know you love her," Marienne continued. "She asks you . . . nay, begs you . . . because of this love, to heed her pleas and do nothing more to endanger yourself."

"And she expects me to obey? To simply ride away and leave her in this damp-ridden, pestilent prison governed by drunks and lechers? What happens when John's guilt over Ar-

thur's death fades—if, indeed, it ever affected him? What is to
stop him from ordering a more permanent means of ending any
further threats to his throne, for as certain as the day is long,
Eleanor remains a threat to him. A threat he will not bear
reminding of too many times.''

"My lady is no longer a threat to King John," Marienne
insisted softly. "He has already taken measures to ensure she
can never be a threat to him again."

"Measures? What measures? Even if he intends to make
her swear fealty to him in front of every baron in the kingdom,
there will come a time when he breaks into a cold sweat and
wonders if there were any rebel lords he missed."

"She is no longer a threat to the crown he wears," Marienne said again, a little more desperately this time. "She is no
longer a threat to his rule over England, Normandy, or Brittany. The only threat that exists is against her life if you attempt to take her away from this place, for she will surely die,
if not by the king's hand, then by her own."

"By her own?" Eduard sucked in a harsh breath. "What
manner of horror has the king promised to make her contemplate such a thing?"

Marienne lowered her chin until it rested on her chest. "I
am sworn to say only what I have said to you thus far, my lord.
I am sworn to say it and to exact a promise, sealed on the
holiest of vows, that you will pursue this thing no farther."

Eduard offered a short, remonstrative laugh. "God on high
should not test my patience with any more vows! How can she
expect such a thing from me without my knowing the reasons
behind it?"

"Her love is the reason behind it. And if your love for her
is one tenth . . . one *hundredth* as strong as her love for you, it
would be enough."

Eduard shook his head. It was beyond his comprehension
to accept defeat so easily and Marienne recognized the gesture
for what it was. But there was nothing more she could say or do
to explain, or even to ease the torment of her Eleanor's decision, not without breaking a most solemn vow of her own.

"Perhaps . . . I should go away and come back later, when you have had time to think on my lady's request."

Eduard did not answer. He gave no sign of any intent to do so, and Marienne turned away, her shoulders slumped under the weight of more misery than she could bear. Robin was standing where she had left him and she tried to smile again, but the threat of more tears was too bright in her eyes.

"Marienne . . . you must let Eduard help," he stammered. "You must convince the princess to *let* him help."

The sweet, heart-shaped face lifted to his. At fourteen she was more than capable of turning heads—Robert d'Amboise's had been most thoroughly swivelled since the first moment he had met her. A smile was enough to tie his tongue in knots, and a tear . . . A tear was enough to wrench his heart into his throat and nearly smother him.

"You have already helped more than you can ever know," she said. "Just the fact that you came for her, that there is still something good and fair and noble left to rise out of the sorrow and heartbreak . . . well . . ."

Robin was too devastated to reply and Marienne looked at Ariel for the first time.

"Forgive me, my lady. I was to assist you with your bath, and here we have talked the time away instead."

Ariel shook her head. "Think nothing of it; the time was better spent."

Marienne offered a small curtsy and was reaching for the latch of the door when she stopped and glanced back. "Be very careful of Lord Gisbourne. He plays the role of amiable host well enough, but he is cut of the same mold as his liege and master, who loses his charm to madness with a swiftness that can take your breath—and your freedom—away. Even our bold captain treads lightly around the governor's moods."

"I thank you for the warning," Ariel said, answering for them all.

Marienne cast a final glance at Robin and Eduard, then left. No sooner had the door eased shut behind her, however, than Eduard was moving toward it, his face set and grim, his hands taking an instinctive inventory of the knives, daggers, and sword comprising his personal arsenal.

"Where are you going?" Ariel asked. "What are you planning to do?"

"I am going to follow Marienne back to the tower and I am planning to find a way to talk to Eleanor myself, if I have to fight my way past every blasted guard in this castle."

"Eduard—no!" Ariel gasped, grabbing at his arm. "If you are caught—!"

"Leave go of me, woman," he snarled, yanking his arm free. "It may be all I can do to find the right cell in the right tower, and if that proves true, then so be it. But I must do something. Surely you can see . . . *I must do something!*"

Ariel saw. She saw the rage and anguish in his eyes, put there by the challenge issued against the strength of his love for Eleanor of Brittany. There was nothing she could say or do to ease it; nothing she could do to fight it, and she stepped aside, clearing his path to the door.

"Be careful," she whispered.

But he was gone.

Eduard nearly missed the first junction; would have if he had not heard a faint sniffle echo along a dimly lit passageway. They were in the labyrinth of tunnels carved beneath the keeps and towers to join each building to the next. It was almost pitch dark, with torches kept alight and smoking blackly at each exit to mark a flight of steps upward. He had to watch where he placed his feet so as not to scrape a heel on a loose bit of earth, and he kept his hand on the hilt of his sword to guard against the tip of the blade striking stone. Once he had to stop and flatten himself into a niche in the wall as two guards laughed their way through an archway and up a flight of stairs. One of them saw Marienne and shouted an invitation for her to join him in his bed later, but she ignored him and kept walking, and the two guards moved on, discussing what they might like to do with her should her nose ever come down from the ceiling.

Eduard pushed away from the shadows and made swiftly

after Marienne's ghostly shape far ahead. He was vaguely surprised he had not encountered any sentry posts between one building and the next, but then, on further reflection, he understood the reason why. Where was the threat? Corfe did not support a sprawling, bustling community like Amboise. It was a prison, a barren and self-contained stronghold populated by soldiers, whores, and wretches who would have nowhere to go even if they did escape their chains.

Eduard stopped again. He heard voices and tried to see through the gloomy smudge to identify the source. There was a table up ahead, outlined by the weak glow of a horn lantern. A guard sat on a three-legged stool, his arms folded over his chest. Beside him was a half-eaten loaf of black bread and a leather costrel of some unwholesome elixir that had rendered his eyes glazed and his mouth wet and slack.

Whatever Marienne was asking him was met with a belch and a thumb jerked over his shoulder. She passed under a low archway and through a narrow door, closing it behind her with a muted thud.

While Eduard debated what to do next, the guard stood and scratched vigorously at his crotch. He belched again and waddled like a penguin to where a crack in the stone blocks rose black and jagged through the slime. A hand groped beneath his tunic a moment and he leaned against the wall, grunting with relief as he aimed a jet of liquid into the crevice.

Eduard used the sound to muffle his approach and while the sentry was still occupied with shaking and tucking, he struck out hard with the heel of his hand, driving the man's head into a violent meeting with the stone wall. Eduard caught the body under the arms and dragged him back to his stool propping him in place between the table and wall. After giving the contents of the costrel a wary sniff, he tipped a quantity of the sour-smelling wine over the guard's chin and down the front of his tunic. It was a makeshift tactic at best, but he was fairly certain the sentry had not seen or heard him and would waken to suppose he had stumbled and knocked himself out in a drunken stupour.

Eduard opened the door a crack, half-expecting to see

another guard on the other side. But the passage was empty,
black as sin, and he retreated long enough to search the tabletop for the stub of a candle he had spied beside the loaf.

With his hand cupping the newly lit flame, he passed
through the door and drew it shut behind him. He could not
see much beyond the weak yellow flare he held in his hand,
and he went so far as to curse himself for blinding his own
eyesight by trying to stare through the light. He raised the stub
over his head and found he could see modestly farther. The
stone walls, cracked and slimy mortar looked no different from
the passages he had already traversed, yet he felt a quickening
sensation come over his body, a sense of expectation as if he
was very close to what he sought.

A mere dozen paces brought him to a solid wall. The
passage ended here, with no visible means for Marienne to
have exited.

Eduard whirled around and retraced his steps . . . and
saw it. A large black maw yawned in the passage wall and as
Eduard moved the light toward it, he had to quell another
flush of excitement as the shape of stairs emerged from the
blackness. Marienne had not troubled herself to take a candle
into the darkness; she must have known the way well enough
to dispense with lighting the stub that was obviously kept at
the guard post for that purpose. There was waxy evidence
spattered around the floor to prove that others saw a greater
need, and Eduard remembered Brevant saying the princess
was allowed to descend out of her tower twice a day to see her
confessor.

He started up the spiral staircase, taking the steps two at a
time. There was no change in the quality of the darkness until
he had climbed a goodly forty feet into the tower. When the
walls higher up began to take on shape and substance, he
doused his own candle and slowed his steps, taking caution
with his boots and his creaking leather belts again as he rose
steadily toward the soft bloom of light.

Marienne, unaware of the shadow that had stalked her
through the underbelly of the castle grounds, had gone directly
to where Eleanor was kneeling in prayer before the nave.

A hasty amen ended the devotions as the princess turned and grasped her hands.

"Did you see him? Did you speak to him? Is he well? How did he get inside the castle walls? Tell me all. Everything. Word for word."

"I saw him. I spoke to him . . . and . . . and I am shamed to say I wept like a child when I first went into the room."

Eleanor smiled and drew the girl into her arms. Marienne *was* barely more than a child, but she did not point this out. Instead she gave quick thanks that God had given her such a brave, dear friend. She could not have endured these months alone. Nor would she have had the courage to face the future alone and for that she would be everlasting grateful.

Eleanor stroked her hand down the curly tousle of Marienne's hair. "How does he look? Is he as handsome and roguish as ever?"

Marienne sighed. "He is even *more* handsome than I remember. Lord Robert is with him too, and he . . . he . . ."

Eleanor smiled and rested her cheek on the top of Marienne's head. "He is as big a rogue as his brother when it comes to stealing hearts. And as big a fool, I warrant, for following him here."

"Lady Ariel was with them, and in truth, she is not what I expected."

"How so?"

Marienne frowned. "Well . . . perhaps because she is the niece of William Marshal, I thought she might look somewhat like him—gruff and comely, big-boned and leonine."

"You are the marshal's daughter and *you* are none of those things," Eleanor pointed out.

Marienne considered it a moment. "She has a stubborn jaw, however . . . and her hair is a most shocking colour of red. Because she is the marshal's niece, does it not mean she and I are cousins of a sort?"

"Cousins," Eleanor nodded. "Which means you must not judge her bravery and courage on appearance alone. She must have a good deal of both if Eduard trusts her."

"She is very beautiful," Marienne allowed. "And she could scarce keep her eyes off him all the time I was there."

"Eduard? And the marshal's niece?" Eleanor leaned back. "Perhaps you should, indeed, start at the beginning. Marienne? Marienne . . . what is it?"

The maid had gone suddenly rigid in the princess's arms. She was staring past Eleanor's shoulder—a shoulder that had moved a moment ago to reveal the black-clad figure standing in the doorway.

Eleanor sensed a presence behind her and stiffened, her hands dropping and clasping together over her belly. "Marienne . . . please . . . ?"

"I am sorry, my lady," she whispered. "I did not know . . ."

"It was not Marienne's fault," Eduard said quietly. "I followed her from the Queen's Tower."

Eleanor reacted visibly to the sound of his voice. She gripped the maid's hands with a desperation that brought more tears flooding into Marienne's eyes, and for the first time in memory, she wanted to curse Eduard FitzRandwulf d'Amboise.

"Why?" Eleanor asked in a forced breath. "Why did you come here?"

Eduard took another step into the room. Eleanor's back was to him, but he could see how thin she had become, how shabby her tunic was, how dull and listless the long golden stream of her hair. "I wanted to know the reason why you would turn me away. I wanted to hear it from your own lips."

"Eduard, please," she whispered. "Please . . . go away. I cannot bear for you to see me this way."

Eduard moved closer, his hands balled into fists by his sides. "Whereas I cannot bear to see you shunning me as if you put a greater faith in John's promise of protection than you do in mine."

"Eduard—"

"If you still want me to go, I will . . . but only if you look me in the eye and tell me it is what you want above all else."

Marienne stifled a sob as she leaped to her feet, and only

Eleanor's strong grasp on her hands stopped her from throwing herself on Eduard. It was still without any inkling of anything amiss that Eduard watched the Pearl of Brittany square her shoulders and pull herself up. It was without any sense of foreboding at all that he saw her turn slowly to face him, saw the candlelight and shadow cast a confusion of images over the face renowned as being the most beautiful in all of Christendom. Indeed, it still was. And Eduard's heart soared for all of the two shocked, disbelieving gulps of air he needed to fully understand the reason she had not wanted to see him.

Eleanor had refused to see him because she could not see anything at all; her eyes had been gouged from the sockets and the lids cruelly seared shut.

Chapter 19

✝ **A**riel de Clare sat on the edge of her seat during the nerve-wracking eternity that was supper. She flinched at every sudden sound and caught herself staring at the entrance to the great hall more times than she cared to recall. FitzRandwulf had not returned to her chambers before the summons had arrived calling her to the evening meal, nor had he made an appearance during any of the various courses of soups, stews, fish, fowl, or meat. Any moment she expected to see his bloodied, battered body thrown down the stairs. She only wished it would happen soon and be done with so she could at least put her eating knife to good effect and slice it through Gisbourne's scrawny neck before she too was dragged away and thrown into some dark, vile donjon cell.

She had barely touched a morsel of food to her lips, and not just because everything swam in puddles of mustard seed and garlic. She had been accorded the honour of sharing Guy of Gisbourne's trencher, and even under normal circumstances she doubted she could have held her appetite past the first mouthful of partially chewed food that exploded across the table on a hearty guffaw of laughter from the governor's lips. The man was a pig. His hands were everywhere—in the platter of fish, in the round of bread, in the bowl of lentils, in the crux of his armpit, scratching savagely.

The company below the dais was even worse. They roared filthy epithets from one table to the next, followed by a volley of food if the remarks won no response. The men fondled their whores between courses of meat and pasties, and thought nothing of puking or pissing in plain sight of those above the salt if the urge came upon them. The women were coarse, black-toothed trulls who provided entertainment by clawing, pulling hair, and fighting with fists or knives if another trull looked too closely at a bulging groin. By meal's end, most were drunk and oblivious to who or how many carried them off to a musty corner of the hall. And through it all, Gisbourne picked his teeth with the tip of his knife, or belched vaporous remains of the meal across Ariel's face.

She had decided, long before the first course had congealed on the wooden platters, that Gisbourne would lose the ability to void himself with any degree of comfort if his greasy fingers dared to stray anywhere near her lap. She gripped her knife like a weapon, wary of every smile and squinted glance that slid her way, not really aware until halfway through the meal that it was Robin earning the furtive glances, not her.

The young man stood in loyal attendance by the side of Ariel's chair, clearly appalled, to judge by his expression, that a castle directly under the control of the king of England could be peopled by such misfits and brutes. He did not know he was the object of such close, feral scrutiny. He thought it was accidental when Gisbourne's hand brushed his thigh, even unto the third and fourth time it happened.

Henry was not so naive, nor so patient with the governor's growing interest in the squire. He tried distracting his host with questions and conversation, and when that failed to cool the hot stares, he sent Robin down to where Sedrick was on the verge of cracking heads, ostensibly to inquire after Lord Dafydd's condition.

Early on in the evening Gallworm had made a point of reporting to Gisbourne that the Welshman's arm was indeed broken. The cut from the sliver appeared to be healing well enough, but the barber had recommended bleeding him to drain away the imbalance of body fluids collecting in the healthy arm, as well as a strong nostrum of inflammable water to rid him of any lingering fever. Thus, the Welsh knight was the luckiest member of the group, for though he was hung with leeches and forced to drink nostrums, he was left in the relative peace and quiet of the barracks.

"You have another man in your party, do you not?" Gisbourne asked, his gaze following Robin over to where Sedrick sat. "Where is he?"

Henry lowered his goblet and dried his lips on his cuff. "He . . . prefers his own company, my lord, and I have granted him leave to enjoy it."

Gisbourne's head turned slowly toward Henry, his eyes as cold and flat as glass. "He does not appreciate our hospitality?"

"On the contrary, he is most appreciative, as are we all. But if you will forgive my bluntness for saying it, I have developed a certain hesitancy with regards to leaving our possessions unattended. We have already had one unpleasant experience in our sojourn. Another would cause my uncle to question my capabilities."

"You think one of my men would dare to steal your valuables?" Gisbourne demanded. "That you would sit as an honoured guest at my table while some churl ransacks your belongings?" The dark eyes remained slitted through an ominous silence, then widened under a hearty laugh. "You are probably a wise man, Lord Henry, to take the precaution. I would not trust a single one of them not to steal the teeth out of my head if I were foolish enough to sleep with my mouth open. All except Brevant, of course. He would still steal them, but only to polish them and sell them back at a profit."

"In any case, I will have Robin send my man down when he escorts my sister back to her chambers."

"You are leaving us so soon, Lady Ariel?"

"It has been a long, tiring day, Sir Guy. A tiring fortnight, to be sure, and I have been struggling to keep my eyes open since Compline. With your leave, of course, I would beg to be excused."

Her best, most obsequious smile, usually so effective against pretentious dolts like Guy of Gisbourne, was squandered to no effect, for he offered his own—equally transparent —and rose to his feet.

"It would be my honour and my privilege to add mine own sword arm to your defense, my lady. We would not want to lose you to some villainy along the way."

Henry pushed to his feet in complete agreement. Unfortunately, the edge of his spur caught on a leg of the chair, sending it tipping over sideways so that it appeared as though he arose with far more haste and urgency than was his intent.

"There, ah, is no need to trouble yourself, my lord. I shall accompany my sister; I am feeling the effects of a long day myself."

Gisbourne looked at him speculatively. A servant was righting the chair and it gave him an extra moment to note the glance Henry exchanged with Ariel. "You do not trust *me* to safeguard your sister's virtue? Perhaps I *should* take insult, my lord. Perhaps I should indeed be questioning the whereabouts of your man, but for different reasons."

"Different reasons?"

Gisbourne's eyes glittered and dropped slowly down to the Pembroke lions emblazoned on Henry's sleeve. He seemed to grow very still, as if he himself could not quite believe the connection his mind was trying to make, and when he glanced up again, it was to a point high on the wall of the great hall, undoubtedly in the general direction of a certain tower room.

"You will forgive *my* bluntness for saying it, but I also have valuables that must be safeguarded," he said evenly. "Captain Brevant! Yourself and four of your best, if you please. We will *all* escort Lady Ariel to her chambers and ensure no harm has befallen your man."

Trapped, Henry and Ariel could do nothing but allow themselves to be accompanied from the dais. Out of the corner of her eye, Ariel saw Sedrick surge to his feet, but on a sharp glance from Gisbourne, he was suddenly surrounded by the same guards who had been in jeopardy of having their heads crushed moments before, only now they were not laughing. Robin stood uncertainly by the table, his face pale and taut as he watched the De Clares being led away under armed guard.

Gisbourne paused and looked back. "By all means, call your young man to accompany us," he said to Ariel. "If the walls do indeed seethe with infamy, he would be better in our company."

The easier to lock us all together in the same cell? Ariel wondered.

With her heart thudding in her throat, she attempted to smile at Robin as he joined them. She could tell by the look in his eyes that he was as anxious as she to know what Gisbourne

would do when it was discovered Eduard had not been left
standing guard. Would he sound the alarm and search for him?
Would they search the princess's tower and find him there,
condemning them all to donjon cells deep beneath the bowels
of the keep?

Ariel had pondered, during the ride to the castle, if that
was to be her last glimpse of the outer world. She wondered
now if this was to be her last long walk without the weight of
chains dragging at her ankles and chafing her wrists.

There was no one standing guard at the entrance to the
Queen's Tower. No one stood outside or inside the door to the
chambers assigned to Lord Henry. Gisbourne's face betrayed
no emotions as the inner bedchamber was searched and pro-
claimed empty; if anything, his expression became more
thoughtful by the footstep, as if he was envisioning which
methods of torture would loosen their tongues the quickest.

"In the solar, perhaps," he suggested magnanimously,
waving to Brevant to lead the way up to Ariel's apartments.
The door was flung wide and he strode across the threshold of
the small anteroom like Caesar striding over the seventh hill of
Rome.

"Such diligence," he mused, casting an acerbic eye
around the obviously dark and vacant chamber. "Where could
he be, do you suppose?"

"Perhaps he was called away," Henry offered lamely.
"Or—"

"Or perhaps he had more pressing matters to attend to?"

Gisbourne was watching both Ariel and Henry, like a cat
waiting to pounce. So intent were all three not to be the first to
falter under another's stare, they did not see the door to the
inner chamber open quietly beside them.

Eduard FitzRandwulf was suddenly upon them, halted by
the same look of surprise that jolted the others in the room.

"My lords," he said, his hand falling instantly to the hilt of
his sword. "Is something amiss?"

"Where have you been?" Gisbourne demanded, craning
his neck to see past the knight's broad shoulders. "What have
you been doing?"

Eduard's eyes narrowed. "I assumed the Lady Ariel would appreciate a fire in her chamber, and since none of the castle servants appeared to hold the same considerations, I tended it myself." He paused and addressed Henry as any indignant vassal might. "My lord, I can assure you no one has ventured near these rooms without my knowledge."

"I have every confidence this is so," Henry said, his smile not quite as jaunty as normal. "And now that we are returned, you may avail yourself of the bountiful repast Lord Gisbourne has so graciously provided."

"I have already supped, my lord," he said brusquely. "I would better spend the time in the stables ensuring the horses are readied to continue our journey."

"Continue?" Gisbourne frowned. "But you have only just arrived."

"We have been in Corfe three days now," Henry said. "Which has put us three days behind in travel. My sister's groom will be stalking the ramparts of Radnor like a hound in heat. And then there is the king himself, who will not be overly pleased to hear his orders have been delayed by a broken arm. He was most adamant the wedding should take place before month's end."

"He is not known to go into rages at the sight of a pretty face. More's the like, he would fly into a rage with me if I were to send you away in such miserable weather, under such haphazard conditions, and without benefit of a proper escort."

Henry paused, debating some inner point with himself before he took the governor's arm and led him far enough away from the others to muffle the context of what he was about to confide in his ear. Gisbourne at first looked annoyed, then startled. He stared at Henry, whose flush of anger was not entirely put upon, then at Ariel—or, more specifically, Ariel's belly. This time, when they bowed their heads together again, it was Gisbourne who did most of the talking, and Gisbourne who drew Henry further aside until they were out the door and on the landing. Eduard took Ariel by the arm and steered her gently, but firmly, toward the inner bedchamber. Robin was right behind her, showing a maturity that startled her as he drew a sword and made ready to shield her with his own body if necessary.

Thankfully, it did not prove necessary, for after more muted conversation, only Henry and Eduard joined them in the chamber, with Henry delivering Gisbourne's kind regards for a good night's sleep.

"He is gone?" she whispered. When Henry nodded assent, she felt the relief flood her entire body. "And will he let us leave without conditions?"

Henry nodded again and Ariel slumped against the wall. "God in heaven, I thought sure he was going to insist we remain until the king arrived. What did you tell him to change his mind?"

"I told him the king would not be too pleased to see you here, since the two of you had seen quite enough of each other already. So much so, in fact, you needed a husband right away. Thus the haste. Thus the furtiveness."

Ariel's mouth dropped open. "You told him I was carrying the king's bastard?"

"It was the best I could think of on the moment," Henry protested. "And not something he would find difficult to believe, especially since he said he found you to be testy and irritable company through supper."

Ariel spluttered, swore, spluttered again, and looked to Eduard for some support, but he was not even paying attention. He was standing in front of the hearth, one hand propped against the stone, his face bathed in the flickering glow from the fire. It was only then she remembered where he had been and who he had seen.

"Were you able to find where the princess is being held? Were you able to speak to her?"

Eduard did not take his eyes away from the flames. "I saw her. I spoke to her."

"And?" Henry demanded. "Have you discovered some clever means of removing her from this pesthole?"

"I have discovered . . . she does not want to be removed. She . . . has expressed a heartfelt desire to stay."

"To stay?" Henry gasped. "Here? In Corfe?"

Eduard seemed to require a few moments to steel himself before turning and meeting Henry's astonished stare. "She claims the king has promised no further harm will befall her . . . and she claims she has no reason to doubt him."

"And you believe her?"

"I believe . . . she does not want to run the risk of having us all stay here with her, in cells adjoining her own."

Henry took a moment for deliberation himself. He would not be the first to admit to a keen liking for the Wolf's cub, or the first to eagerly present himself as a friend to the cool, distant knight. Notwithstanding this, he was genuinely firm in his respect for FitzRandwulf's loyalties and convictions. He could see the man smashing tables and blackening eyes over an accusation of cowardice; he could see him spitting in the face of any man who dared question his concerns over his own personal safety. He could *not* see Eduard FitzRandwulf d'Amboise, the man, the knight, the silver-eyed warrior so calmly reporting the princess's suggestion of a hasty retreat unless something else had happened. Something so terrible, so horrible, so frightening as to render even his considerable capacity for rage, impotent.

There were ways, Henry knew, of utterly demoralizing and smashing the spirit of captives, making them come to regard their captors as saviors.

"Has the king . . . done something to her mind?" Henry asked gently.

Naked pain filled the daunting gray eyes, like blood filling an open wound. "If you are asking if he has done something to guarantee she is no longer a threat to his claim on the throne . . . the answer is yes. Moreover, he has also ensured she is no longer a consideration to anyone's plans to incite a civil war in her name. If John were to choke on his own guilt, or fall on his own sword a dozen times, and if all other claimants as far removed as a tenth or twentieth bastard cousin suddenly fell ill and died of St. Anthony's Fire . . . Eleanor of Brittany would not be the chosen candidate for queen."

"Why?" Ariel blurted on a soft gasp. "What has the king done?"

Eduard turned back to the fire without answering. His shoulders hunched forward as he lifted his other arm and braced it against the wall, allowing him to hang his head between. There was tension in his jaw, and tension in the veins that rose and throbbed like blue snakes in his throat. Tension enough to cause beads of sweat to form across his brow and temples and to glisten where they ran in a thin trickle down the side of his face.

Ariel's throat went dry. Without knowing why or how she bade them do so, her feet carried her slowly toward the fireside. He did not look up, although he must have been aware of her presence beside him. Nor did he acknowledge the pale, slender hand that reached out and touched his arm.

"Eduard . . . ? How can we help if we do not know what has happened?"

He bowed his head and squeezed his eyes tightly shut. Henry tried to get his sister's attention from across the room, but she ignored him. She ignored everything and everyone as she realized, with a shock of incredulity, that the wetness dripping from Eduard's chin was not all caused by sweat.

She had never seen a grown man cry. Had certainly never imagined she would live to see evidence of such weakness in Eduard FitzRandwulf.

Her own eyes blurred behind a stinging hot liquid and she moved her hand closer to his. "Eduard . . . ? Can you not trust us?"

The long, dark sweep of his lashes remained closed and Ariel could see there were two emotions waging war within him—unmeasurable anguish and boundless fury. The one was causing the uncharacteristic flow of tears; the other had caused him to smash his fists into something hard enough and repeatedly enough to open the flesh on some of his knuckles to the bone.

"My God," she gasped, touching one ravaged hand with the tip of her fingers. "Eduard . . . *what has happened*?"

The heavy fringe of lashes lifted slowly.

"He has blinded her," Eduard whispered raggedly. "He has had her eyes put out like those of a common beggar."

Ariel's shock was complete. Behind her, she could hear Henry's half-formed exclamation and Robin's stunned cry, but the best she could manage, locked in the deathlike grip of Eduard's eyes, was the slow, hot release of her breath.

"He . . . the king . . . has *blinded* her?"

"He had her eyes plucked out and the lids seared shut," Eduard said harshly, "knowing full well the barons of England, regardless how loyal and sympathetic they might be to her plight, regardless how desperately they might search for a claimant to challenge his power . . . they would never put a blind, mutilated queen on the throne."

"My God," Henry muttered. "We should have suspected something was amiss. He could not have her killed without raising a hue and cry, but by the same token, he could not have let her live as a threat. Is she . . . otherwise well?"

FitzRandwulf sucked a deep, shaky breath into his lungs and straightened, taking Ariel's hand into his own without thinking. "She is thinner, as is to be expected. And sadder. But her concerns are for our safety, not her own, showing her courage and spirit are still as strong and true as ever. She is also adamant about not returning to Brittany. She would prefer death by the king's hand—or her own—before she would suffer the pity of her people or put them in the position of having to shun her."

"Then . . . is this to be the end of it?" Ariel asked. "Are we just to leave her here to rot in the king's prison?"

Eduard stared down into Ariel's face, but it was Eleanor he saw standing before him, her beautiful, ravaged features tilted upward, her voice laden with the tears she was no longer able to shed.

"There is no other way, Eduard. You must leave me here. You must forget me. You must all forget me and leave me to God's will."

"God's will," Eduard rasped, crushing Ariel's hand in his, "will not be done in this place. Not while I have a breath in my body."

"You will need more than breath, my lord," said a gruff, grating voice from the doorway. "You will need guts and heart and more courage than I was able to gather."

Eduard dropped Ariel's hand and reached for his sword, but Henry and Robin were both closer and quicker, their blades slashing through the air in streaks of gleaming steel.

Jean de Brevant stood in the doorway, his massive shoulders almost touching both jambs, his head bent to avoid the lintel. He made no move toward his own sword, raising his hands deliberately away from his sides to prove he had no such intent.

"What the devil are you doing here?" Henry demanded. "Have you come to gloat?"

Brevant took a half-step inside the room, wanting only to straighten the crook in his neck, but Robin misread the action and moved in front of him, his sword raised to bar the captain's path.

The gesture earned only a scowl. "I came because I knew, by the look on the Scarred One's face, he had been to the tower."

"You knew?" Henry spat. "You must also have known what he would find. Why did you not tell us? Why did you not forewarn us?"

"Would you have come calmly over the draw if you had known, or would you have stormed it with blood in your eyes? Would you have humoured Gisbourne's airs of grandeur or would you have treated him like a boil and lanced him at the first opportunity? As God is my witness, I did not think you would get this far. I never thought you would have the ballocks to ride through the gates let alone make plans to ride out again with Gisbourne's prized possession in your grasp."

"Are you suggesting there *is* a way to ride out of Corfe? There *is* a way to steal the princess out of here?"

Brevant's mighty chest swelled with the makings of a ripe curse, for Robin's sword was still hovering near enough to threaten the hump of his Adam's apple.

"Not with two broken legs and a cracked skull, there isn't," he snarled, "and that is what this fine-tempered lad will have if he waves his blade a hair closer."

"Robin," Eduard ordered quietly. "Let us hear what he has to say."

Reluctantly, and slowly enough to cause the reflected spires of firelight to dance and leap along the length of the polished steel, Robin obliged. He did not sheath the weapon, however, nor did he remove his eyes from the captain's bullish face.

"*Are* you suggesting there is a way to break a prisoner out of Corfe?" Eduard asked again.

"No," Brevant said flatly. "I am suggesting no such thing. You try to break her out, you try to make a run through the gates, and your backs will be as prickled as a porcupine with crossbow bolts."

"Then what can we do, Captain Littlejohn?" Ariel asked softly. "Can you help us?"

Glittering black eyes went to her face as if he was acknowledging her presence for the first time. "I can help you mount your horses so you can ride out of here, my lady. Calmly and openly under the eyes of the castle guard. I would stress the word calmly, for you would have an extra two riders in your group, but if the timing is right and the guards preoccupied with other matters . . . which they will be with all the preparations for the king's arrival . . . you might just be able to get a league or two beyond crossbow range before an alarm is sounded."

"Explain," Eduard demanded.

Brevant nodded and pursed his lips. "Gisbourne has ordered the castle guard doubled—not unexpected after the fright you tickled him with tonight. By tomorrow night, he will double it again, leaving very few heads lying abed for too many hours at a time. I know these men. Ask too much of them, press too hard, and they start fighting among themselves, missing their whores and ale, not giving a hell-fired damn if God himself was expected to ride across the draw."

"Are you saying they would not question the appearance of an extra rider in our group?" Henry scoffed.

"*Two* extra riders," Brevant said. "The little maid goes too."

"Marienne!" Robin gasped. "Of course she goes with us; we would not think of leaving her behind."

Henry looked as if he was about to scowl an objection but Robin and his sword had suddenly allied themselves in the camp of Jean de Brevant. "You cannot just leave her behind to suffer the governor's wrath alone," he protested. "I would sooner give her my place and take my chances here, with the captain."

Brevant glanced down and over his shoulder. "The captain will not be here, lad. He has had more than enough of the smell of this place. Besides"—the black, bottomless eyes looked at Eduard again—"as soon as the king discovers his castellan has been host to the son of the Black Wolf . . . he will undoubtedly loose the hounds of hell upon you. You will need an extra sword arm."

Startled, Eduard returned the calm stare. "You knew?"

The giant offered a rare, wide grin. "I saw you run the lists once, in Bayonne. It brought me back to England with a healthy respect for the training grounds of Poitou and Anjou. Yours is a face hard to forget, despite the bearding and the armour of a humble graycloak."

"You could have earned your own weight in silver marks had you sold your knowledge to Gisbourne."

Brevant's grin widened. "Aye, well, call me a fool. I would pay twice as much to see the look on Gisbourne's face when he finds the lady's cell empty."

Eduard nodded. "That makes nine of us all told. Exactly how belligerent do you think the guards will be?"

"You leave them to me. Just be ready, within an hour's notice, to be on your horses and waiting in the bailey."

"There is one other small problem," Henry pointed out. "Gisbourne has insisted we have an escort as far as the Salisbury road. Will *they* not notice the addition of two extra members to our party?"

"You are speaking of the king's finest," Brevant snorted disdainfully. "Find one among them who can count and I will find you a whore with three titties."

Henry's brows lifted gently. "Have they no sense of direction either? Once we leave Corfe, we can have no witnesses to say which road we took or which direction we favoured."

"Have you ever seen a dead man point his finger one way or the other?" Brevant demanded.

"Ahh. Indeed." Henry glanced at Eduard and shrugged. "So much for leaving any doubt as to who has plucked the Pearl from the gilded cage."

"If you are squeamish," Brevant grunted, "you can stay here and protest your innocence to Gisbourne. A day or two on the rack, if you are pitiable enough, he may believe what's left of you . . . enough to toss you over the sea wall, where he disposes of most of *his* unwanted witnesses."

"How will we get the princess out of the tower?" Eduard wanted to know.

"How will you convince her to come along?"

"I will convince her," Eduard promised steadfastly. "I will offer her something I know she cannot refuse now. Something she has wanted, needed, for a long time and is only now free to grasp with her whole heart and soul."

"Aye, well. If luck and God be with us, I can bring her here under the guise of taking her to the chapel. Once she is here, though, it will be up to you to either persuade her to come peacefully, or to knock her cold and pack her on a rouncy with the rest of your provisions."

Chapter 20

Ariel hugged the folds of her cloak close around her shoulders, barely aware of the cold gusts of wind tearing at her hair, or the wet spray of rainwater blowing through the squared teeth of the battlement walls.

She had taken the cat's climb to the roof, needing time alone with her thoughts and her feelings, hoping to cleanse both with the cold, crisp air. On a sunny day, the view of the sea below would be breathtaking. This night, against stormy skies and the gray-green luminescence of a turbulent sea, she saw nothing but nature's anger and frustration shadowing her own. Each howl of the wind, each hard tattoo of rain that beat on stone and mortar, each rumble and crash of the sea hurling itself against the craggy coastline found an echo in her own battered emotions.

Not that anyone else cared.

Henry had gone back to the great hall with the captain, hopefully to find Sedrick still in one piece. Robin had gone somewhere with FitzRandwulf . . . something about a rendezvous he had arranged earlier with the maid, Marienne. They had all gone, leaving her alone. Assuming she preferred it that way? Or assuming she knew they all had better things to do.

FitzRandwulf obviously did, now that his Eleanor was on the verge of being his.

I will offer her something I know she cannot refuse. Something she has wanted, needed, and is now free to grasp with her whole heart and soul.

He would offer Eleanor himself, of course. As husband, lover, protector. And in truth, the Pearl of Brittany would have no reason to refuse him. She was no longer a claimant to the throne. The royal blood of kings and queens still flowed through her veins, but the work of a glowing hot iron had stripped her of her birthright, stripped her of any obstacles standing in the way of a union between her and the bastard son of the Black Wolf.

How the sight of his beloved Eleanor must have shocked him! Eduard's love for her was so pure, so noble; it went deeper than any emotion Ariel could ever conceive of a man having for a woman. Deeper than anything she could in any honesty ever hope to experience herself.

Eduard FitzRandwulf d'Amboise had never professed to love her. He had never even led her to believe he *liked* her. He may have *lusted* after her a time or two, may even have had moments when the lure of soft female flesh had been too overwhelming for his rigid code of honour. But that was not love. It was a kiss stolen under the moonlight, or a challenge answered in kind. It was the effect of too much ale and a virile male body left too long craving something it thought was too far out of reach.

Well, he could reach Eleanor of Brittany now. He could reach her and hold her and love her . . . and probably never spare another thought for Ariel de Clare, wife of some distant Welsh prince.

Ariel leaned her brow against the cold, wet stone and knew the ache she was feeling inside would not as easily be forgotten, nor would it be assuaged by just any man. Most certainly not a man like Rhys ap Iorwerth, slayer of fawns.

"Sweet Mary, Mother of God," she whispered. "Why has this thing happened to me? Why now? Why with this man? Of all men . . . why did it have to be *this* one?"

A gust of wind whipped the wet ribbons of her hair out behind her, snatching at the folds of her cloak and belling it like a sheet of canvas under full sail. Breathless, gulping air and tears and misery, she turned to seek the shadowy protection of the covered stairwell . . . and slammed abruptly into the wall of Eduard FitzRandwulf's chest.

"There you are," he said, steadying her on her feet. "I know you told me you like storms, but is this not a little mad, even for you?"

With a gasp, Ariel sobbed something unintelligible and spun out into the rain and wind again, running farther along the catwalk until she came to an arch of stairs that bridged the roof of one tower to the next. Before she could cross it, however, Eduard's hands, then his arms circled her waist and brought her unceremoniously down again, pinning her against his body until she had kicked and squirmed and thrashed herself half into a frenzy.

"Ariel? What in damnation—?"

"Let me *go!* Take your filthy bastard's hands off me and *let me go!* You have what you want now. You have your Eleanor, your precious Pearl. You have your princess and I have my prince, and by God, we shall both be happy now because it is what we *both* want!"

She was strong and lithe and was able to wriggle free, breaking for the steps again before Eduard could fully absorb the thrust of her words. He made a grab for her and missed, but her foot caught in a wet twist of her cloak, sending her down on one knee before she could recover and lunge for the steps. It was long enough for him to catch up to her and when he did, he lifted her bodily against his chest and held her there until he could turn and trap her between himself and the battlement wall.

"Listen to me, Ariel," he hissed against her ear. "You have to listen to me."

"I *have* listened to you. I have listened and I have watched and I *know* how much you love her. I do not need to *hear* the words to know it."

"Ariel—!"

"No!" She covered her ears with her hands and crumpled her eyes tightly shut, refusing to acknowledge his command for attention.

The rain beat down on Eduard's unprotected head and shoulders, soaking his hair, running in chilling rivulets down his throat and under his clothes. His hands gripped her shoulders and trembled with the desire to shake her, but instead, with a deliberate, gentle strength, he took hold of her wrists and pried her hands away from her ears.

"Is that what you think? Do you think Eleanor and I . . . ? That we are lovers?"

Ariel kept her eyes adamantly shut against the lure of his voice. "I do not have to think anything. You *told* me you loved her. You said you had pledged your life to her. You carried her ring next to your heart just as she carried yours. And now you are risking all . . . everything . . . to save her! What else should I think?"

Eduard found himself at a loss. His grip on her wrists tightened a moment, then sprang free entirely as he shoved his fingers into the wet, tangled mass of her hair. He forced her to tilt her head up, forced her to open her eyes, and meet the silvery gray intensity of his own.

"You should think . . . *hard* . . . about the difference between loving someone you regard as a sister, or a cousin, or a sweet and gentle friend"—his fingers raked deeper, lifting her face higher—"and loving someone who burns their way into your heart and soul like a flame. I love Eleanor, yes. With all of my heart. She was the first true friend I ever had, and I am probably the only friend she has ever had. We traded rings a thousand years ago when she exacted a childhood promise from me to always be her champion, to always slay dragons in her name. We traded again tonight"—he paused and fished angrily beneath his tunic—"when she made me swear to let the one true beast who is her uncle live."

Ariel stared at the delicate filigreed ring and noticed where his own skinned thumb was once again bare. Her gaze rose slowly to his but she could not see him clearly for the sudden film of bright, hot tears.

"The way you acted," she whispered raggedly. "The things you said . . ."

"I have acted like a fool," he agreed tersely. "And I have said things I never should have said. What is more, I am probably going to do it again, now, when I confess the hunger—the *love*—I feel for you is neither brotherly nor based on friendship. It is like an open, raw wound I cannot seem to heal. It only grows wider and deeper each time I touch you, or hold you, or . . . dream of holding you even closer."

Ariel's lips quivered apart. "Me?" she gasped. "You love . . . me?"

His fingers threaded into her hair again, tenderly this time, more of a caress than a punishment. "If this ache I feel every time I look at you is love . . . then aye, I must love you. If this *need* I have to hold you and kiss you until you have not the will or the strength to refuse me what I would take from you . . . if this is love, then aye, my lady, I am floundering in it . . . and have been since the moment I saw you tilting at shadows in the armoury at Amboise."

Ariel thought the walls and rooftops took a sudden swift dip downward and she had to curl her hands into the thickness of his surcoat to keep from staggering to her knees.

"The other night . . . at the inn . . . ?"

"I should never have gone near you," he said huskily. "Never. It only made me want you more."

"But . . . you pushed me away."

Eduard shook his head slowly. "I did not push you away; I pushed myself away."

Ariel knew she should say something. She knew she should. But the quivering in her lips had spilled downward, had spread and become a trembling, throbbing heat that shivered into her belly and between her thighs, rendering her speechless. And because she could not speak, her eyes implored him for the truth, eyes that were wide and dark and so completely stripped of pride, they left him no choice but to answer.

He made a sound deep in his throat—a groan or a curse, she could not be certain—and his lips crushed down over hers, his response delivered so fiercely, so possessively, the shock of it left her breathless, drowning in her own heat.

Rain beat on their shoulders and splattered on the stones. The sea and sky rumbled like shifting boulders, offering a final warning, but it went unheeded. Eduard's good and noble intentions were lost in the consummation of taste, touch, and desperately clinging mouths.

His body crowded hers against the rampart and their mouths slanted this way and that, their tongues lashing together, their breaths raging hot and fast. Their heartbeats clamored a challenge to the storm unleashing itself around them and the trembling needs in their bodies rivalled the tumultuous, recoiling shocks that echoed off the stone walls.

"Eduard," she gasped. "Eduard . . ."

Rainwater bathed her face, made her hair cling to her temples and throat in dark, wet streaks. Eduard tore his mouth away and searched the shadows like a wild man, seeking a sheltered corner, an archway, a protected lee . . .

"Here," she demanded. "Now. With God watching, we shall defy the oaths made in His name. I am not afraid, Eduard. If you love me, I am not afraid."

Eduard blinked the rain and wind out of his eyes. He lifted his hands away from her long enough to loosen the buckles at his shoulders and to shrug his belts and baldric aside along with the heavily quilted surcoat. Within seconds the rain began to soak the linen of his shirt, plastering it to his skin, molding it to the hard slabs of muscle across his chest and shoulders. Seconds more and he might as well have been naked for all that the mysteries of his body were revealed in bold, rising magnificence.

He made short work of removing Ariel's cloak and loosening the green velvet tunic. His hands caressed her through the gaping layer of velvet before his fingers curled around bunches of fabric and tore the two halves asunder. Ariel arched her head back, her neck and throat glistening under the sheeting rain, her hands cradling the heat of his mouth to her bared flesh as he buried his face between her breasts. He reached for the hem of her skirt and pulled the crush of velvet up over her hips, his fingers greedy and searching as he sent them delving into the moist, deep heat of her.

A jolt of lightning traced across the sky as Ariel opened herself to the pressure of his stroking fingers. She was wettest there, where the rain had yet to find her, and hot . . . so hot he groaned and dragged her down onto the spread folds of her cloak, his hands moving swiftly, feverishly to free his own pounding flesh from the confines of his clothes.

With a mindlessness fueled by passion and long-denied hunger, he was between her thighs, he was pushing himself forward, he was thrusting into the lush folds of her body and stretching up inside, furrowing into her with a sense of urgency echoed by her long, shivering cry of fulfillment.

Ariel's mindless need forgave him his haste. Indeed, she revelled in the obvious agony of his own blinding demands, for there was but a moment of resistance, gone in the passing of a heartbeat, leaving only the more astounding awareness of being filled, impaled, glutted with hard male flesh. She groaned and arched her hips instinctively, straining to feel even more of him inside her. He obliged by thrusting again . . . and again . . . by plunging his hands beneath her bottom and lifting her until she learned how to lift herself, how to twine her legs around his waist and lock them there so that she could move with him, move against him, move for him.

Lightning bathed their bodies in a blue-white lustre, the rain causing their exposed flesh to gleam like marble. The sound of the wind and the sea drowned out the groans, muffled the ragged gasps of ecstasy that sent Ariel's hands clawing into the rapid rise and fall of his hips. Something burst within her. Something brilliant and beautiful, something bright and fiery hot that sucked the breath from her lungs and set her body moving in a blur beneath him.

Eduard threw his head back and gave one last mighty thrust into the convulsing softness. His eyes squeezed shut and his lips drew back over the slash of his teeth, but there was no withholding, no controlling the passion that erupted within him. He plunged himself into her, poured himself into her, trembling, quaking in the grips of a pulsating white heat that left him with nothing in reserve, not even his pride.

Ariel shivered.

It was only once and only the tiniest of gestures, but Eduard noticed and was quick to crouch before the fire and add another log to the iron crib. His hair was still wet, smooth and inky, pushed back from his brow by an impatient hand. As she watched, a sparkling bead of water gathered at the tip of a curl and was shaken free with the movement of his arm, hissing when it splashed on the hot stones.

He had just finished helping Ariel towel the excess moisture from her own hair and it was spread around her shoulders, little better than a wild froth of curls for all the vigorous rubbing. He had insisted she strip out of the remnants of her wet clothes and he had bundled her into a warm, dry blanket before seating her in front of the fire. He had not, as yet, spared a thought to his own comfort. His shirt still clung in wet patches to his shoulders; his hose were stained dark from the soaking. He had retrieved his surcoat and her cloak from the rooftop and both garments were hung over a chair, steaming and dripping into the silence.

Ariel studied his broad back, wondering what was going through his mind. He had not spoken more than a word or two since carrying her down out of the rain and she knew she was partly if not wholly to blame for his closed expression. She had caused him to break an oath of honour—no trifling matter to a knight at the best of times. This, however, must surely have been one of the worst, what with the shock of discovering Princess Eleanor's blindness already playing havoc with his emotions.

Ariel was not entirely guiltless herself, now that the heat of passion had cooled somewhat. She had behaved like a wild woman, clawing and spitting one minute, tearing at his clothes and keening like a hoyden the next. So much for nobility and breeding. So much for ever thinking she could hold herself aloof, unaffected by something so coarse and debasing as the physical act of coupling.

The experience had left her feeling anything but aloof and unaffected. She felt warm and slippery inside, acutely aware of a new tenderness between her thighs that throbbed and ached as if he was still there, strong and vital. Her skin tingled and her body hummed with a shameful restlessness. In spite of the rain, in spite of their haste and surroundings . . . in spite of everything, their joining had been a thing of immeasurable joy and beauty. Nothing quite so trivial as the word *coupling* could ever describe it, for far more than just their physical bodies had been joined. It was as if he had reached inside and touched her soul.

The new log had caught fire and Eduard ran out of excuses to poke and prod and rearrange the bed of hot coals. There was nothing else to be gained—or lost—by continuing to avoid the haunting green sparkle of her eyes, and he turned to face her, not quite knowing what he would see . . . or what he wanted to see.

She was beautiful: that was his first thought. Lushly, erotically beautiful with the flush of newfound awareness glowing soft and pink in her cheeks. He had only caught a glimpse of slender white limbs and a shiveringly cool body when she rid herself of her sodden clothing, but what he remembered caused his throat to close and his eyes to slip down to the edge of the blanket where it had begun to droop over her shoulder.

The enormity of what he had done kept his jaw tensed and his tongue stuck to the roof of his mouth. He had ravished the intended bride of a prince of Gwynedd. He had ravished the niece of William the Marshal, Earl of Pembroke, the most feared and respected knight in all of England, Normandy, and Wales. To a lesser degree, but of no less importance, he had ravished the sister of Lord Henry de Clare, a stalwart young lion in his own right who would no doubt take grave offence to FitzRandwulf's lack of control.

Silence stretched between them for another awkward moment before Eduard sighed and looked down at his hands.

"What we did . . . what *I* did—" he said quietly, "was an unconscionable breach of trust, my lady, and I take full blame for it."

"*Full* blame is not yours to take, my lord," she replied softly, "for I do not recall fighting you overmuch. Challenging you, aye . . . but not fighting you. Thus we shall have to share the blame in equal parts."

Eduard was adamant. "I took advantage."

"I was a willing partner."

"You were innocent."

"I may have been a virgin, but I was hardly innocent."

"My fault again," he said with a frown. "For you still would have been innocent had I managed to keep my hands off you in St. Malo."

"In body, perhaps. Not in thought." She waited until the

silver-gray eyes rose to hers before she added to her admission. "Had my thoughts been actions, I would have lost my innocence in the armoury at Amboise."

"To a brute and a lecher, and a"—he paused and smiled faintly—"a great gawping ape?"

"You were the first man who looked at me as if I was a woman and not just the means to an alliance with the Marshal of England."

"Had I known you were the marshal's niece, I would not have looked at you at all," he said dryly.

"See then, what we would have missed."

Eduard's mouth turned grim and she could almost see him withdrawing into himself again, closeting his emotions against any more displays of weakness.

"You act as if we have committed some terrible crime," she mused.

"In the eyes of the king . . . and God . . . it will undoubtedly be regarded as such."

Ariel turned her gaze to the fire. "For the king's laws, I care nothing. As for God . . . He had ample opportunity to drown us on the rooftop if He was truly angered by what we were doing."

"You feel no regret? No sense we have betrayed those who trusted us?"

She looked at him and her fists clenched around the folds of the blanket. "I trusted my heart, and it does not feel betrayed. Unless, of course, you did not mean it when you said you loved me."

A tremor passed through Eduard's body, but it was not caused by the chill of wet clothes. It was a stab of fear that slashed through him—the fear of a child who has suffered the darkest, blackest of nightmares and survived only because he has been able to put all hopes of love and being loved well behind the armoured plates surrounding his heart. He recognized some of that same fear in Ariel's eyes as she watched him and waited for his answer . . . an answer that would either destroy them both or bring them out into the light.

"I meant what I said," he whispered tautly. "I do love you."

She seemed to wilt a moment, though there was not a flicker or shiver of visible motion anywhere in her body. "In that case, my lord, I have only one pressing regret."

Eduard held his breath. "Yes?"

"My only regret," she said, moistening her lips with the tip of her tongue, "is that when I was so insistent with the words *here* and *now* . . . I had no idea the roof would be so . . . so unyielding."

Eduard continued to stare at her as if he expected impalement at any moment, and he was as slow to follow Ariel's hand down as he was to follow the hem of the blanket up over the hip she laid bare before him. The skin was chafed an angry red where it had come in contact with the coarse pebbling on the roof. In places the scratches were deep enough to have brought blood to the surface.

The swift, instinctive bracing of Eduard's defenses still required a final, long look into her eyes before it drained from his body on a sudden rush of breath. The rush became a halting laugh, and the laugh a deep, comfortable rumble of helpless surrender that turned Ariel's complexion an even deeper shade of pink.

"A rather unchivalrous response, my lord," she grumbled. "Especially since you show no such ill effects yourself."

Piqued, she started to push the blanket down, to cover herself again, when Eduard's hand reached out and caught her around the wrist. While the words of a protest were forming on her lips, he leaned forward and bowed his dark head over her thigh, his mouth bestowing a warm, gentle rain of kisses over the scraped flesh.

"For this, I *do* take full blame," he murmured, nudging the blanket higher, extending the path of his caresses to cover more than just the blemished area. "I would beg your forgiveness and ask, in my most humble mien, what form of penance might be acceptable?"

"What you are doing now will suit quite nicely," she said on a stilted breath.

He lifted his head a moment and his eyes narrowed. His hands skimmed up beneath the layer of wool and circled her waist, drawing her forward, almost to the edge of the chair.

It was so sudden—to be cocooned in a blanket one minute and in the next, naked and gaping down in shock and surprise at the head and hands determinedly easing her limbs apart. And when his mouth began to trace a sensual path over the top of her thigh, it was all Ariel could do to grip the sides of the x-chair and keep from tumbling off in a dead faint.

"What . . . are you doing?" she gasped.

"Proving how innocent your thoughts really were compared to mine."

"Oh . . . Jesu . . ."

His mouth explored the silky flesh of her inner thighs, coming just close enough to the fiery delta of curls to feel her body stiffen in apprehension. He kissed the rounded softness of her belly and let his tongue play havoc with the indent of her navel; he kissed her breasts and enticed her hands to abandon their grip on the chair, to show him, by means of twining her fingers around the wet locks of his hair, where she wanted him to kiss her, where she wanted his mouth to roam next.

Each rolling, fluttering stroke of his tongue drew a soft hiss of pleasure; each wicked pull of his lips tautened her skin and sent needles of heat slivering through her body so that she could not have denied him anything, did not deny him anything even when his mouth took absolute possession of the glistening, pearly folds of her womanhood. Her back arched and her hair rippled in coppery flames. Her mouth gaped open in shock, in stunned surprise, as the first of many sweet, shimmering implosions responded to the sinful intimacy. She stared down at the top of his head, at the gleaming waves of hair she clutched so tightly, and she whispered his name, she gasped his name, she shuddered his name free on the writhing, curling spirals of heat that wracked her body on each knowing thrust of his tongue.

The brightest peak was yet to crest within her when she was lifted off the chair and carried to the wide, raised bed. Smaller peaks, breathless shivers, were racing through her

limbs as she felt herself sinking back into the soft fur cover-
ings. With shaking hands she tore at Eduard's shirt. She peeled
it up his back and, with his help, tugged it up over his shoulders, baring the incredible expanse of virile male flesh that was
hers to explore. She did so eagerly, restlessly, skimming her
hands over the sculpted muscles, running her fingers through
the tangles of soft, thick hair that covered his chest. Not surprisingly, she had lost a good deal of her shyness somewhere
between the rooftop and the hearth, and she dragged his
mouth down to hers, kissing him with an open-mouthed boldness that demanded all the skilled expertise of his lips and
tongue.

While Eduard kissed her, he loosened his braies and
pushed them down over his hips. In a brief tumble of arms,
legs, and glossy red hair, their positions were reversed long
enough for him to kick the final encumbrances free, long
enough for Ariel to rise above him and gaze in awe at the long,
thick spear of flesh rising so proudly from the juncture of his
thighs.

They rolled again, his body naked, warm, and hard as he
pressed her deep into the bed of furs. His palms smoothed
over her breasts, cupping the supple flesh as he drew it into his
mouth and suckled each nipple to a crinkled tautness. Ariel
arched her back repeatedly, feeling the tug and pull of his lips
all the way down to her toes. His heat was between her thighs
and she moved with frantic little whimpers to entreat him
closer. She raised her knees and dug her heels into the bedding, tilting her hips up and forward so that he slid against her,
teasing her with both a threat and a promise. Again and again
he simply slid against the dense, glistening curls, denying himself, denying her until she was so wet and he so hard they
could not have stayed apart a moment longer, even if they had
wanted to.

Eduard groaned as he buried himself inside her. He
groaned and he gasped and he pressed his head into the curve
of her shoulder, stunned by the tightness and the heat she
wrapped around him. Ariel's hands shook where she clutched
him. She felt him plunging, stretching, pushing himself to the

limit, and then more . . . more . . . until she was filled, swollen, aching with a deep, saturating pleasure.

Her cries of awe fevered his blood and his first few thrusts were fast and powerful, more for the benefit of his sanity than anything else. Her body quickened against him in response, making his every muscle strain and beg for release. But Eduard was determined. He braced himself on outstretched arms, his lips moving in a silent litany of prayers to hold on, hold on, hold back even as Ariel flung her arms around his shoulders, her legs around his waist, and stiffened convulsively through wave after wave of intense, protracted ecstasy.

His eyes closed, his neck arched. His breath came harsh and choppy and his body gleamed under a sheen of moisture, his muscles quivering, his whole body feeling like a raw, chafed nerve. The fierceness of his impending climax stole his breath away. He shuddered and rolled his hips faster into hers, letting the pleasure come, letting it overwhelm him, letting it burst, throbbing and flame-hot into the wild and violent friction of Ariel's own continuing, continuous orgasm.

Flushed and panting, they rocked together in a crush of damp, steamy flesh. Ariel was numb, dazed, and still beset by the tiny, shuddering bursts of liquid heat that pulsated from his body to hers. She kept her legs locked firmly around his waist, kept her hips moving, arching gently to glean every last drop, every last shiver from his flesh. The incredible fullness diminished inside her, but he made no move to pull away, not even when he thought to ease the burden of his weight by turning onto his side. He turned, keeping her close, his hands cradling her thighs so that there could be no thinking he wanted to leave her, no allowing it if she wanted to leave him. Luxuriantly slippery inside and out, Ariel was flushed with the knowledge that she could give as much pleasure as she could take—pleasure she would have thought to be commonplace to a man of such careless might. And yet, if the fiercely possessive pressure of his hands was anything to judge by, he was just as shaken as she by the intensity of their expended passions.

Her head found a natural, comfortable pillow in the hollow of his shoulder. Her hair was stuck to the dampness on her temples and throat, and she gave a little sigh of thanks as he gathered it back into a single, thick tail that he spread beside her. It left his hands free to roam over the naked flesh of her back and shoulders, and he did so until the audible pounding of her heart slowed, and she could think and feel beyond the flush of carnal gratification.

It was a soft, fuzzy, engorged contentment that replaced the urgent restlessness of wanting. It made her very much aware of the shape and texture of their bodies, of the heat he radiated even in repose. She wished she could stay like this forever and wondered if every woman felt this way, or if it was only the foolish ones, the ones who had been too stubborn to admit this was something they could not accomplish on their own.

Ariel sighed and traced her fingertips over and around the contours of his chest. She could fire a bow, wield a sword, ride a horse, even swing a quarterstaff the equal of most men. And because she could, she had never felt any pressing need—or desire—to prove she could be just as soft and yielding as any woman. Eduard FitzRandwulf d'Amboise had wrought a change in all that. He had shown her, precisely and exquisitely, just how much of a woman he wanted her to be, how much of a woman she could be in the arms of the right man.

This man, she realized dreamily.

With this newfound pride in her own femininity bristling through her like a rash, Ariel lifted her head out of the snug cradle of his shoulder, intending to share the discovery with him. But Eduard was asleep. Soundly, deeply, blissfully asleep, with just the vaguest hint of a smile on his lips to suggest she did not have to tell him anything. He already knew.

Chapter 21

✝**E**duard was still asleep several hours later when a loud, urgent knock sounded on the outer door. The room was dark save for the low flame of the night candle, and it guttered to the brink of extinction as a sudden draft rushed across the bed. Eduard, quick as a cat, was on his feet and melting in the shadows as Henry came barging through to the bedchamber.

"Ariel? Ariel—are you awake?"

Ariel, scrambling to pull the bedsheets up to shield her nudity, pushed her hair out of her eyes and stared at her brother as he drew near the bed.

"Ariel . . . rub the sleep out of your eyes," he hissed urgently. "We have trouble. Brevant has just been to see me. A man was admitted to the castle not an hour ago bringing news that the king's ship has dropped anchor in Christchurch. The Leopard himself will be upon us before noon."

Ariel was struck dumb—by the news, and by the sight of Henry standing beside her bed, superimposed in front of the naked, amber-lit spectre of Eduard FitzRandwulf, his back against the wall, his sword gleaming in the revived light of the candle. Her vision clouded briefly with the threat of a faint, a faint that grew proportionately stronger as Henry's nervous pacing carried him around to the foot of the bed.

"If we are to have any chance to steal the princess, it must be done now, before the rest of the castle is awakened to make preparations for the king. Brevant has looked high and low for FitzRandwulf, but he is nowhere to be found. In the process of looking, however, he found something else. He—" Henry stopped and his breath huffed from his lungs on an angry curse. His foot had become tangled in something, and, thinking it to be an article of Ariel's clothing, he bent over to pick it up. While he was down there, his eyes were drawn to another crumpled heap . . . and another. He was able to identify each without too much difficulty once he recognized the black studded surcoat he clutched in his hand. A man's belt, a shirt, a pair of braies . . . a pair of cuffed leather boots . . .

It took another moment of stunned disbelief while he gaped at the bed, at the obviously naked and dishevelled figure of his sister, before he could straighten completely and turn slowly to acknowledge the glint of reflected light coming from the shadows.

Eduard lowered his sword. He was still in the half-crouched position he had assumed when he thought it was Gisbourne's men bursting in on them. To judge by the look on Henry's face, he was not all that sure he would not have welcomed the sight of soldiers more.

"You . . . *bastard!*" Henry exploded.

"Henry," Ariel gasped. "Please . . . I can explain . . ."

"Explain?" The hot fury of her brother's eyes shot back to the bed. "Explain *what?* Explain what you are doing naked in bed together? Christ Jesus, girl, I think I can guess that much by myself. Or perhaps you were going to explain *why? Why* you are naked in his bed, stinking of sweat and lust, when you were supposedly so eager, so determined to savour these fleshly delights with your intended *groom!*"

"Henry . . . I know it comes as a bit of a shock——"

"A shock? A shock to find you spreading your charms for the Bastard of Amboise? Nay, nay, sister dearest——" He paused and folded his arms across his chest. "It comes as no shock. A surprise, mayhap, that it took you so long to cull the stallion out of the herd."

"Henry, I would have a care," Eduard began, his voice low and held in check with an obvious effort.

"No!" barked the enraged lord. He held out a hand and thrust his finger up in warning. "*You* should have a care, sirrah. You should not speak yet. You should not utter one bloody word until I fetter this overwhelming desire to tear your heart out through your throat. What," he demanded, turning back to Ariel "were you thinking? What could you possibly have been thinking?"

Ariel glanced at Eduard, then met Henry's accusing glare. Strangely enough, now the initial shock was passed, she started

to feel quite calm. And not a little resentful that a man known
to have cuckholded many a groom and husband himself could
be standing so righteously before her now.

"I obviously was *not* thinking, brother dear. I was just
doing."

Henry hissed the air out from between his teeth and raked
a hand through his hair, grasping the tawny ends in his fist as if
he would have liked to rip it out in chunks.

"Ariel . . . ! *Damnation*, Ariel . . . do you know what
you have done?"

"I have a fair idea," she answered coolly. "I have greatly
reduced my value as a virgin bride."

Henry blinked. A few blond threads came away between
his fingers as he lowered his fist and leaned it on the foot of the
bed. He blinked again and seemed to gather his wits enough to
force a sardonic smile. "Well, I am sure the donjon guards here
at Corfe will not rue the loss overmuch; they seem to prefer
their doxies experienced. And once they are finished passing
you around, you might just want to have a fond memory or two
to savour. I doubt the same may be said for your brother," he
added, casting a cold eye in Eduard's direction. "After tonight,
he will not have too many pleasant memories at all."

"What does Robin have to do with this?" Eduard asked.

"Gisbourne has him," Henry said succinctly. "*How* he got
him, I do not know, but according to Brevant, when he went
with Gallworm to announce the king's imminent arrival, the
boy was trussed like a hog and unconscious in the corner of
Gisbourne's anteroom awaiting the governor's pleasure."

Eduard's face blanched for all of the two breaths it took
him to funnel his rage into action. He crossed the room in
three long strides and started snatching up his clothes, donning
his braies and tunic as fast as he found them, not troubling
himself with any belts save the one that sheathed his sword.

"Where is Brevant? How long ago did he see Robin?"

"Brevant is below, in my chambers. He came straight here
from the Constable's Tower, uncertain of who you would want
to see rescued more—the princess, or your brother."

Eduard stamped his feet into his boots and strode out of

the room without another word. Ariel, who had made haste to pull on a shapeless bluet, was not far behind him, running down the stairs, all flying hair and whiplashing linen.

Henry caught her before she flew through the doors to his chamber, his fingers like iron bands around her arm.

"We have not finished saying all there is to say; we have only delayed it."

"Fine! Good!" she cried furiously. "It will give you time to see how"—she grit her teeth and wrenched her arm out of his grasp—"*happy* he has made me!"

Brother and sister entered the chamber in time to see Eduard selecting an arsenal of daggers out of the belts and bucklers lying amidst their armour.

Brevant stopped speaking and looked up sharply, but a brisk order from Eduard started him talking again, low and swift.

"—on the upper floor. There will be guards in the passage below the tower and two more posted at the bottom of the stairs. He had his favorite whore in the room with him, probably to prime him and share the fun."

Eduard glanced up and a muscle jumped in his cheek. "How long before he will be missed?"

"Gisbourne? With the king coming—" Brevant's eyebrows bunched together in a deep, hairy vee over the bridge of his nose. "Not much past dawn. Gallworm will be pissing himself to prove how efficient he is, so he'll not let his master sleep until his usual midday debauch."

A quick look told Eduard there were only two scored lines remaining on Henry's night candle to mark the proximity of dawn, and he had to stop and peer again as if he could not believe he had slept so long.

Grimly, he tucked the last blade into the lethal array in his belt and clasped a hand around Brevant's arm. "Can you still get to the princess? Can you bring her here *now?*"

"Now?"

"Did you not just say we have until dawn?"

"Aye, but—"

"But what, my friend? Are you turning squeamish—or do

you have a better use for your ballocks at the moment than testing the mettle of your own plan?"

Brevant stared intently. "You see to the boy, I will see to the lady."

Eduard gave the captain's arm an extra clap and turned to Henry. "Sedrick and Dafydd will have to be rousted and told what we are about. The horses will have to be saddled, including the extras."

"Consider it done," Henry nodded.

Eduard's gaze found Ariel. Her eyes were rounded and dark, set in a face so pale it glowed in the candlelight. Her hair . . . Jesu, God . . . her hair . . . the creamy smooth slope of her shoulders . . . the *change* . . . the noticeable look of a woman who has discovered passion . . . all these things combined to stall his ability to think past the danger he was putting her in.

"Tell me what I must do to help," she prompted determinedly.

"Go through the packs and find all the extra clothing you can. When the princess and Marienne are brought here, they will have to be dressed, quickly and warmly, to look common enough to pass as varlets. See to yourself as well and remember: warmth above all. It would raise suspicions if we were to leave without the packhorses, but we will be moving too fast to take them much farther than the first bend in the road. We can forage for food, but blankets and clothing . . . we must take all we can carry."

"But . . . the princess? What if she still refuses to go?"

"She will go. Once Brevant has brought her from the tower, she will have no choice but to go. In any event"—he rested his hand briefly on her cheek—"Robin and I will be back here in plenty of time to tup her on the head and sling her over the rump of a rouncy if that is what is required."

"Be careful," she whispered.

"Be safe," he murmured. "And until I get back, do whatever Brevant tells you to do. Promise me this."

Ariel's lips trembled apart and the best she could manage was a nod. He planted a swift, hard kiss over her mouth and walked out of the room. Henry and the captain were a beat behind, her brother passing a final, troubled frown over his shoulder before he dashed out into the stairwell.

Ariel held her breath until she could no longer hear their footsteps pounding down the stairs. The feelings of contentment, well-being, and self-confidence that had made her so boldly reckless during the night dwindled away with the last echo, leaving only an erratic heartbeat and a certain, chilling sense of dread in their place.

Robin concentrated hard on keeping his grip on consciousness. Twice it had slipped away from him and twice he had wakened no better off knowing where he was or why he had been brought here. Once, it had been the sound of voices that had blown away the suffocating clouds of insensibility, one of them gruffly familiar.

"What is he doing here?" Brevant had asked.

"The master was intrigued," was the whispered reply. "So strong, so lean, such a handsome young Adonis. He had his guard watch for an opportunity to . . . ah . . . invite him along for the evening's entertainment. The opportunity happened late, but happened, and, together with the news of the king's arrival, you can see my lord is in a fine mood to celebrate. Of course"—a cackle of laughter brought the grating voice low enough to imply a delicious irony—"as always, he has to prove himself a man first. He is with his whore now, determined she should be able to bear witness to what an extravagant stallion he is in all ways. Alack, he will not be able to prove much if the boy refuses to come around. Curse those louts for being overly enthusiastic . . . I hope they have not killed him."

Robin had forced himself to lay very still and not to react to the bony finger that prodded his arm, or the vile stench of the seneschal's breath as he leaned close to check for signs of a return to consciousness.

"Mmm. I suppose as long as the flesh is warm, it will do."

"Gallworm," Brevant snarled, "one day someone will squash you like a bug."

Another period of blackness had followed, not quite as deep or as long, for Robin had been aware of periodic bursts of laughter coming from nearby, and once . . . a woman's clammy hand had smoothed over his brow, wiping his hair off his face.

The gesture, repulsive in the one sense, made him think of Marienne, and the way her soft white hand had reached up to tuck an errant lock behind his ear. His skin had prickled all over at her touch, and had made him desperate to kiss her. He wished now that he had. He wished it with all of his heart and soul. But he had more to thank, with his heart and soul, that she had already left him to return to the princess's tower when the two men had stepped out of the shadows and cornered him.

It had happened so fast, he had barely put a hand to his dagger when the blow to his head had knocked all of the fight and most of the sense out of him. He had been aware, in a dim, sickening sort of way, of being slung over a pair of shoulders and carried like a sack of flour down a few turns in the corridor. He remembered stairs and he remembered coarse laughter. He remembered being dumped on the floor hard enough to hit his head again, and when he had awakened, he had been bound hand and foot, blindfolded, and had a sour rag stuffed in his mouth.

The voices of Gallworm and Brevant had come later, as well as another drifting slide into blackness. Now he was fighting nausea, anger, and frustration in equal parts, chafing his wrists raw in an effort to loosen the ropes twisted around his wrists.

There was only one man in the castle Gallworm would address as master, and that one person had eyed him with a distinctly carnivorous hunger all through the evening meal. Robin was not a fool, nor was he completely naive. He had heard of men like Gisbourne who harboured secret perversions. He had even heard the rumours about King Richard, but having met the godlike warrior once, he had found it too horrific to believe.

Robin strained so hard to pull his knots apart, he could

feel the sweat beading across his upper lip. He sawed his ankles back and forth, winning some slackness there, but whoever had caught and tied him had taken no chances in losing him.

He collapsed a moment, wheezing noisily through his nose. His back was up against a stone wall but he could find no rough edges, nothing that might snag or pick into the cords. His knife and falchion were gone, naturally. He had his teeth if he could get to them. And if he could get to them in time.

Surely someone was due to come out and check on him again. With sweat on his face and a heartbeat that banged like an ironmonger working on his anvil, he could not hope to trick the next clammy hand that poked and prodded.

A volley of muted laughter spurred Robin into a burst of furious activity. He stretched his arms down and rounded them as much as they would go in an effort to wriggle his hips through the loop they made. He got stuck halfway through and rolled hard enough to bang his knee on the wall, but he persevered, grunting, straining, sweating his hips, then his legs and feet through.

He tore at the blindfold first and tossed it aside, then uncorked the filthy gag from his mouth, hawking and spitting twice to rid himself of the spurious taste. He had guessed—correctly—that he was in a small room adjoining Gisbourne's main quarters. It proved to be no larger than a hound's room, and indeed, from the smell of the floor and stains in the corners, he half-expected to see the bristled face of a wolfhound standing guard over him.

Wary of the closed door only a few paces away, he brought his wrists to his mouth and started chewing on the knots in the jute, widening his visual search as he did so, hunting for anything that could be used as a weapon.

There was nothing. Not even a stick of furniture to break over someone's head. The walls were bare stone with iron cressets bolted into the mortar. The room was lit by thick wax candles, not torches, one on either side of the doorway. The ceiling was high, rising in an arch that was probably continued in the main chamber. No door blocked the exit to the stairs, which were wide and well lit to ensure a safe descent. The upper reaches were naturally gloomier, with the walls and beams mossed with the ghostly weavings of a colony of spiders.

Robin was gaining some success with the knots when he heard a dull thud on the far side of the door. It swung open a few seconds later and a woman came staggering out, a hand massaging the shoulder she had just bounced off the wall.

"Well then? Awake at last, are ye? Oooooo"—she stumbled closer, squinting her eyes to see through the drunken haze—"ee said ye were a pretty one, and so ye are. Pretty enough to eat," she added, grinning lewdly around a slick set of gums marked by a few stubs of teeth.

Robin pushed himself upright and sat with his back braced against the wall. The woman was big and blowsy, naked as the day she was born, with breasts like great heavy dugs that hung to her waist and juddered with each move she made.

Robin found enough spit to moisten his lips. "Untie me," he whispered. "Untie me and I will make it worth your while."

"Untie ye?" she screeched. "Nowt bluddy likely, sweet. Truth is, ee's going to want ye tied even more, hand and foot to the bed posties so's ee can do his best and his worst all of a time. When it's my turn, though, mayhap then I'll untie ye. But only if ye make it *well* worth my while."

Robin muttered something under his breath and she swayed closer to hear, close enough for him to reach up and grab her by the greasy shanks of her hair and bring her head slamming forward into the stone wall. A grunt brought her down like a felled tree and set her mountainous rolls of soft white flesh sprawling over Robin's legs. He struggled and kicked to free himself, and in doing so, slipped his ankles loose of their binding.

He was up on one knee and set to run for the stairs when another naked body appeared in the open doorway. It was Gisbourne. Once a formidable champion in the lists, he could still boast a muscular toughness; the sword he held to Robin's throat did not waver by so much as a hair's breadth even as he increased the pressure upward, forcing Robin to scrape and push himself to his feet.

"Surely you were not planning to leave so soon, were you?" he asked silkily. "And what have you done to poor Grisella? She was *so* looking forward to your company . . . as was I."

"Not in this lifetime, my lord," Robin hissed through a clenched jaw.

Gisbourne's eyes widened and the point of his blade dug deeper, forcing Robin to stretch his neck to the limit.

"A lad with spirit," he said, shuddering over the words. "I like that. So many come to me wailing and weeping . . . they bleat like little lambs and keen for their mothers . . . and usually spoil it all by falling into a dead faint. You do not look like the fainting type, Robin-in-the-hood. You look like the type who will fight me, aye"—he grinned—"right to the end. It would be a shame if I had to curb some of that fight from the outset. It would have to be a shame to have to slit a hole in your belly and lead you inside by your entrails . . . but I assure you, I will do it. And if I do, I can also assure you, you will come with me most willingly."

Robin swallowed against the pressure of the blade and felt the edge nick into his skin. The thought was there, as pure and clear as the blue of his eyes, that all he had to do was lunge forward and the blade would open his jugular. But his eyes flicked briefly to the open landing at the top of the stairs, and the thought of death was replaced by the need to live. He met Gisbourne's lazy stare again and offered a small nod of assent.

"How very astute of you," Gisbourne breathed. He drew the sword back enough to challenge the look in Robin's eye, and when nothing came of it, he withdrew the threat further and waved it toward the door. "After you, cheri."

Robin took a step, then brought his hands up in front of him, reaching to catch the hilt of the dagger Eduard tossed him.

Gisbourne swung around to block the throw, but too late. As startled as he was to see the flash of steel streak past him, he was doubly staggered to see Eduard FitzRandwulf looming at

he top of the stairs, his dark hair thrown forward over his
brow, his scarred cheek pleated with a menacing grin.

"What the—? Guards! *Guards*!"

Sir Guy looked expectantly down the stairwell but Eduard
only shook his head. "Shout all you want, Gisbourne. They
cannot hear you."

The governor slashed his sword toward the landing and
met cold steel for his trouble. Another thrust and sparks flew
the length of both blades as they sliced together, venting fury
to the hilts. Gisbourne whirled on the balls of his bare feet, his
sword gripped in white-knuckled fists, swinging it like a
hatchet at the level of Eduard's knees. FitzRandwulf cleared
the arc easily and parried with a backhanded cut that turned
the governor far enough off balance to allow Eduard to kick
out and plant a boot in the back of Gisbourne's thighs.

Sir Guy's legs went out from under him and he landed
heavily on his knees, skidding several feet on the rough stone,
leaving two streaks of skin and blood in his wake. He roared
with the pain and scrambled back onto his feet, but by then
Robin had severed through the rest of his bindings and was
able to put the dagger to better use, jabbing it up and under
Gisbourne's chin, reversing their positions of only moments
ago by making him dance backward to the wall and stand on
tiptoes, his neck strained in a painful arch, his eyes bulging.

Gisbourne's hand sprang open and he dropped his sword
with a metallic clang that bounced a time or two off the stone
walls before fading to a dull ring.

"How *dare* you raise a knife to me, *boy*. Move it now. At
once. And perhaps I will let you live."

Robin nudged the steel tip higher. His face took on a
terrible maturity; his eyes burned with blue flames, contempt
and revulsion aged him swiftly and savagely beyond his fourteen years. Having looked death in the face and knowing there
was nothing to fear there, he could look a paltry creature like
Guy of Gisbourne in the eye and scorn him. He could hate him
too, not just for what he'd almost done to him, but for the
delight he took in doing it to others.

Eduard was not unaware of the changes that had come

over his young brother. If anything, he saw himself standing
there, his thigh opened to the bone by the Dragon's blade, and
he knew Robin was angry enough, sickened enough, to kill
Gisbourne just as he could have killed Etienne Wardieu. He
also knew that killing Gisbourne would make the loss of
Robin's youth irretrievable, and for that reason alone, Eduard
reached out a hand and laid it on his brother's arm.

"See if you can drag yon hub of womanly beauty into the
bedchamber while I settle a few matters with Sir Guy."

Robin swallowed, brought the tremors in his arm under
control, and nodded stiffly, lowering the knife by slow degrees
as if it was the most difficult thing he had ever forced himself
to do.

Gisbourne waited until the knife was safely lowered to the
boy's side before he straightened and glared fiercely at Eduard
—a difficult thing to do stark naked and grayer than the cobwebs that floated overhead.

"Enjoy this moment while you can," he spat, "for you are
both dead men."

"But still able to walk and talk," Eduard said with narrowed eyes. "Which is somewhat more than you will be able to
do with"—he glanced askance at Robin—"what was it Littlejohn said?"

Robin looked startled a moment, then quoted, "Not with
two broken legs and a cracked skull."

"Ahh. So it was. And so it shall be," he added softly.

Gisbourne saw FitzRandwulf lift his sword and watched in
horror as the mighty shoulders put their all into a swooping
swing. An instant later, Gisbourne's senses exploded in a
starburst of pain as the flat of the heavy blade smashed across
both bleeding kneecaps. Robin had adroitly stepped aside to
avoid the blur of steel, but as Gisbourne's arms flailed and his
body began to pitch forward, it did so in Robin's direction. A
reflex action brought the lad's hands upward to fend off the
possibility of catching Gisbourne and saving him from an unchecked fall. The dagger he clutched came up at the same
time, and as Sir Guy plunged forward, the well-honed edge
slithered between his thighs, met a limp protrusion of unresist-

ng flesh, and sliced it off without undue strain on Robin's
wrist or . . . after the fact . . . his conscience.

Sir Guy's scream was bloodcurdling enough to prompt a
curse from Eduard's lips as he swung his sword again, this time
bringing the blunted end of the hilt smashing against Gisbourne's temple, with enough force to send the black eyes
rolling up beneath the lids, vouchsafing his inability to sound
any alarms for the rest of the day.

The two brothers stood side by side, staring down at the
broken sprawl of Gisbourne's body, both of them wincing at
the damage wrought by Robin's dagger.

"Killing him *would* have sufficed, little brother," Eduard
mused.

Robin drew a shaky breath and flung the bloodied knife
onto the floor. "At least he will have something to remember
me by."

"Remember you? I would hasten to suggest you never
cross his path again. I would also suggest we waste no more
time in pleasantries. Hopefully, by the time we hide these two
and return to our own chambers, Eleanor and Marienne will be
here, waiting for us."

Robin nodded, managing to hold down his gorge while
they dragged Gisbourne and the whore into the bedchamber
and arranged them under blankets and furs to look as if they
slept in blissful exhaustion. There was a deal of blood on the
floor of the anteroom, but it could not be helped. A last glance
and Eduard pulled the door shut behind them, clapping his
arm around Robin's shoulders as they headed swiftly for the
stairs.

Chapter 22

✝ **A**fter Henry, Eduard, and Brevant had left her, Ariel made a quick search for spare clothing and came up with what she supposed would have to do for two complete outfits. She took Eduard's only extra shirt back to her chambers with the rest of the bundled clothing, and for some inexplicable reason, felt better for wearing it in place of her own long linen bluet. She did not have much in the way of spare belongings herself, only the velvet gown and silken undertunic she had ruined in the rain last night. Both had been torn by haste and rough treatment and, rather than simply leave them by the hearth or pack them to have to explain their condition at a later date, she rolled them in a tight ball and thrust them into the fire. A few sticks of kindling and a spill of candlewax supplemented the curling heat from the bed of coals, and she finished dressing in the bright blaze of the burning garments.

Her hair required the perseverance and vocabulary of a Flemish foot soldier to unsnarl and tame into a manageable braid. The heat of sheer frustration was still fuming in her cheeks when the outer chamber echoed with the sound of hurried footsteps. Henry was back to collect their equipment and, barely a minute later, Captain Brevant arrived, striding into her bedchamber with two slender, clinging shapes in his shadow.

"My lady; I see you have responded well to the need for haste. As you can see, I have accomplished the first half of my task. My lord"—he looked to Henry—"you have seen to the horses?"

Henry nodded. "Sedrick has it well in hand. I came back to see if I could be of further use."

"You can," Brevant grunted. "You can guard our charges until the final preparations are made. My lady—were you able to find suitable clothing?"

Ariel moistened her lips and glanced at the bed, where she had deposited her scavenged findings.

"Good," Brevant nodded. "I will leave you to it then. As soon as all is ready below, I will return to fetch you. Remain here until I do so."

Marienne, hailed from a troubled, anxious sleep, flinched aside as Captain Brevant exited the room as abruptly as he had entered. She looked even younger, paler than she had the first time Ariel had seen her, and the folds of her worn, patched night tunic trembled visibly against her body.

The second figure could not flinch from what she could not see, but she shook with equal vigor, her fear the result of being roused from her tower and led she knew not where for a purpose which had not yet been explained. She knew it had been Jean de Brevant coaxing her to haste and silence, and she knew Marienne was blatantly terrified. Part of the reason for their terror and uncertainty was that they had not made their way to this place without incident. Twice they had been cautioned to press into a corner of the passageway while Brevant's sword had made short work of queries by other guards as to where they were going at such an ungodly hour.

Eleanor could also smell the rank odour of scorched velvet, mingled with the vague, distinctly feminine scent of rosewater.

"May I presume . . . I am in the company of Lady Ariel de Clare?" she asked tremulously.

Ariel's first response was to nod, since her tongue had decided to remain stubbornly clamped between her teeth. It was difficult to find the words to say, having at last come face to face with the woman she had regarded as her strongest competition for Eduard's affections . . . the woman widely acclaimed to be the most beautiful creature in the realm.

She could see why. Regal, noble features bespoke the bloodlines of kings and queens. All of mankind would have had to be blinded not to recognize the golden-haired niece of Richard the Lionheart, granddaughter of Henry Secund and Eleanor of Aquitaine, last of the true Angevin princesses, and, through no misfault of her own, the rightful queen of England. Despite her eyes being so hideously sealed shut, Eleanor radiated delicacy and grace. A man would have to have been a fool not to love her and a king equally foolish not to envy and fear her.

Even Henry, who was handsome enough to rarely find himself wanting for the company of a beautiful woman, stood mute in the shadows, awed by the light that seemed to emanate from within the slender form of Eleanor of Brittany.

"Your Highness," Ariel murmured, forcing her legs to carry her forward. She started to drop down onto her knees, but Eleanor was quick to halt her.

"Please. There is no longer any need to kneel before me. I am a charity ward of mine uncle's now, due nothing more than a common greeting."

Ariel glanced at Marienne, who was bravely trying to hold back the watershed of tears brimming along her lashes. The task was rendered impossible as Robin came bounding through the door with the impact of a gust of wind, sweeping the young maid off her feet and spinning her so high, her legs were bared to the thighs. He was out of breath from running up the stairs, but as he brought Marienne to ground and held her close against his body, he beamed a wide smile over the top of her head.

"Highness . . . Lady Ariel . . . Eduard and I met Captain Littlejohn on the stairs."

"You are both . . . all right?" Ariel gasped.

"Aye, my lady. Right and ready."

"Ready for what?" Eleanor pleaded. "What is happening? Why was I brought here?"

"Your Grace," Robin explained, "we are taking you away from this hellish place. Eduard tells me Lord Sedrick is in the yards now, saddling horses. Lord Dafydd is purloining foodstuffs, and—"

"What do you mean you are taking me away?" Eleanor recoiled with surprise, stumbling back until she met abruptly with the wall. "And who are these lords you mention? I am familiar with none of them."

Henry was bestirred to step forward. "If I may, Highness . . . my name is Henry de Clare, and I am brother to Lady Ariel. Lord Sedrick of Grantham is a loyal vassal of our uncle,

William the Marshal, and Lord Dafydd ap Iorwerth is . . . is a Welshman, come with us from Pembroke to Paris and now to here. We are all here in the marshal's service and with Lord Eduard FitzRandwulf's guidance."

The princess raised a trembling hand to her temple. "But . . . I told Eduard . . . I wanted no part of a rescue. The king—"

"The king is docking his ship even as we dither and dally, Your Highness," Robin said. "And when have you ever known my lord brother to do aught he was told, especially if he was told it was impossible?"

"But . . ." Eleanor's hand fell from her temple and gripped the crucifix that hung around her neck. "I have accepted my fate. Marienne, yes, take her and leave if it is at all possible, but I must stay here. The king will never let me go free."

"We are not asking his permission," Henry said evenly. "And as the captain has said, we do not take one without the other. We all go together, or none of us go at all."

"Captain Brevant is helping in this madness?" Eleanor whispered.

"Willingly, my lady," Marienne said, her fear beginning to give way to excitement. "He is a good man, and as such, has surely had his fill of this place, as have we all."

"He has sworn to see you safely away," Robin added. "And to lend his sword as far as Nottingham if need be."

"Nottingham?" Eleanor's lovely face showed more confusion than ever. "Why on earth—?"

"It was Eduard's idea," Robin said proudly. "For the time being, at any rate, he reasons the safest place to hide you is right under the king's nose. Certes, the Channel will be watched and all ships searched that are bound for Brittany. Brittany itself will be scoured from border to border. It was originally planned to take you to Wales—"

"Wales!"

"Powys, Your Highness, but Eduard has reconsidered in light of your . . . your reluctance to test the king's mettle. His . . . *our* father, Lord Randwulf, held lands north and east of Nottingham. In Lincolnshire. He still has many friends thereabout, loyal to our grandfather, and among them is a certain prioress who owes a large favour to the House of Wardieu."

"My head," the princess gasped. "It begins to spin, Robin. Can you not speak in plainer terms?"

"Plainly said," bespoke a deep, familiar baritone from the doorway, "if you will allow us, Eleanor, we will fulfill your brother's promise to you."

"Eduard?" A slender white hand trembled over empty air for a moment until it was caught and held firm by the stronger, bolder grasp of Eduard FitzRandwulf d'Amboise.

"The priory is called Kirklees, and the abbess will welcome you to its cloisters without a qualm, I can promise you. Safely there, the king cannot touch you, even if he manages, by some wild mischance of fate, to determine your whereabouts. And though it galls me to say it, he will have no more need to fear you once he knows you have taken your vows to heart."

"A priory?" Eleanor whispered, raising the fingers of her other hand to her lips. "Can it be true?"

"It can," Eduard promised. "And it will, I swear it on my soul, providing you offer no more arguments."

"But the risks, Eduard! Nottingham is so far away!"

"It is closer than Wales, with fewer obstacles in our path. A week, no more, and you should be safe behind the walls of Kirklees."

"And you? What will you do then? How will you get back to Amboise?"

"By a somewhat longer route, I imagine," he answered casually. "I have sworn to bring my father word *personally* of your safe conduct, and I fully intend to do so, regardless of any kings . . . or dragons . . . who might stand in my way."

Mention of oaths made reminded Ariel of oaths broken, and she could not stop herself from glancing his way. He had donned his armour, his polished mail hauberk and chausses, and overtop wore the plain gray Crusader's gypon, slit at the sides for riding. His hair was hidden beneath the mail coif and his gauntlets were tucked into his belt, near the hilt of his sword. He looked every inch a man to whom failure was unheard of. An hour ago, she had been naked in bed with him, thinking everything had changed. Seeing him now, armed and defiant, she suspected nothing had changed at all. Eleanor's safety was still his first priority, as it should be. But by the time he delivered the princess to Kirklees, would Ariel de Clare be long gone on the road to Wales?

"My lady," Henry said gently, stepping forward to win the princess's attention. "We have come this far with no ill effects. God must have willed it, just as He has put the safety and solace of Kirklees within your grasp. How can you refuse Him?"

Eleanor's head was bowed. When she raised it, there were twin streaks of wetness streaming from the puckered scars across her eyes. The effect on Henry was likened to an iron hammer striking him across the chest.

"How odd," she whispered softly, her finger lifting from her mouth to her cheek. "To still be able to weep."

"Surely they are tears of happiness," Henry said. "To know God has found a way to bring you into His house."

Eleanor gasped at a breath, then surrendered with a small, fleeting smile. "It appears I cannot fight all of you . . ." She lifted her face. "Perhaps you will tell me what I must do?"

Robin refrained from letting out a whoop of joy, but just barely. Ariel and Marienne moved at once to sort through the variety of garments strewn on the bed.

"You must wear a disguise," Ariel said. "A squire's disguise is best, with a cloak and a hood to keep your head well covered."

"A blind squire," Eleanor mused. "Indeed, it might draw a curious eye or two."

"It was more the colour of your hair I was thinking of, Highness," Ariel amended. "Such a golden crown would not go unnoticed."

The faintest hint of chagrin pinkened Eleanor's throat and she apologized by way of a compliment. "Eduard tells me your own colouring is nothing shy of spectacular."

With Ariel's startled glance, FitzRandwulf cleared his throat and snatched up Robin by the sleeve of his hooded jerkin, ushering him out the door. "Come along, Henry, and help gather up the rest of the armour. Ladies . . . as swift as swift can?"

"Before you can blink an eye," Marienne promised, already shaking the folds—and dust—out of the chainse that would replace Eleanor's long tunic.

"What am I to do with this?" the princess asked, pulling Ariel's thoughts back to reality. In her hands she held a leather belt, strung with over forty rawhide strips.

Since it was the very article that had given Ariel so much grief on the journey through Normandy, she felt expert enough to offer instruction.

"It is worn thus, Highness," she explained, buckling it firmly around Eleanor's waist. "These ties are called points and are used to bind the hose snugly to the limbs."

"So many?" Eleanor exclaimed. "Can not just one or two suffice?"

"Men . . . especially *knights* are all vain creatures," Ariel announced grimly, catching up the first leg of the hose Marienne assisted the princess into. While she began to attach the points to the corresponding ring of eyelets woven into the top of each stocking, she kept talking, if only to keep her mind off the next and most dangerous stage of the rescue. "God and all the saints forbid there should be a wrinkle or a sag to mar the bold thews of such a fellow's thighs. For a woman to bare an ankle, it would cause the earth to tremble and monks to prostrate themselves by droves. But a man—ho! The tighter the hose, the shorter the tunic . . . the more likely he is to strut and stretch and boast of his wares. Why, I have even known my brother to pad himself with wads of linen for the benefit of winning a particular maiden's eye."

Eleanor's lips trembled with a smile. "Did he succeed?"

Ariel paused and thought back. "As it happened, halfway through the evening, the wadding shifted and started to creep down toward his knee. He had the maiden swooning, but not for the reasons he intended."

A small choking sound sent Ariel's gaze flying upward. Her expression changed from concern to relief to shared amusement when she saw that Eleanor was laughing. Marienne was laughing too—and fighting tears again, blessing Ariel with silent thanks for prompting what had been the first time the princess had laughed since the fiasco at Mirebeau.

Chapter 23

✝ **A** gray and sinister dawn was seeping through the teeth of the outer battlements as FitzRandwulf's party assembled in the courtyard. Few of the lower windows showed any signs of light; most were still shuttered against the wind and the rain that came and went in waves, sweeping across the bailey, soaking and resoaking everything in its path. The walls were silvered with it and the gutters overflowed, sending swift rivulets of water running through the cracks and crevices in the cobbles.

Ariel walked into the circle of horses and hissing torchlights, looking neither to the right where Henry was conferring with Brevant, nor to the left where Eduard and Sedrick were rearranging their saddle packs with exaggerated care as they kept a close watch on the doors and windows that opened on to the bailey. Ariel was more conscious of the two cloaked and hooded figures who followed steadfastly behind her. So engrossed was she in worrying how Eleanor would cope with the uneven cobbles, she stubbed her toe on one and nearly launched herself headlong into her palfrey. The princess did not miss a step, however. She kept her head tilted forward and a hand grasped around a fold of Marienne's cloak, gauging each footfall to precisely match her maid's.

Six grumbling, grousing guardsmen stood in a huddle beating their arms for warmth and cursing in unbroken waves over Jean de Brevant's lack of concern that none of them had laid their heads on their cots more than an hour. The captain had insisted the ruse was still necessary, to give the appearance of leaving Corfe under protection of Gisbourne's guard, otherwise the sentries on duty at the gates might question the reason why only he accompanied them.

Collectively, they looked as nondescript as when they had ridden through half of Normandy, yet their swords were within easy reach. They all wore their helms and carried their shields slung across their backs on leather straps, rubbing an assort-

ment of arms that might otherwise have been relegated to the
packhorses. Even Ariel, when she mounted her palfrey, found
both a falchion and a bow looped over her saddle, placed there
by a man whose gray eyes acknowledged her glance and expressed confidence in her ability to put the weapons to good
use if it became necessary.

Brevant, cursing the rain in a loud enough voice to earn a
partial grumble of agreement from the guards, ordered the
knights to mount and waste no more time dallying. He had
better things to do, he said, (eliciting another round of sly grins
from Gisbourne's men) than to squander the morning pointing
them onto the right road. He assumed the lead on his enormous rampager and set a belligerent pace through the inner
bailey and over the first draw. The outer bailey was just as
deserted and bleak; the ground was mud underfoot and the
horses made deep sucking sounds as they approached the huge
barbican. They rode in pairs and threes, with the guardsmen
remaining in a glum pack in the rear, preferring to keep to
their own company.

Ariel, despite the rain and the chill, found she was sweating uncomfortably beneath her layers of linen and wool. The
skin between her shoulder blades was clammy and her hands,
inside her gloves, were sticky with a dampness that had nothing to do with the wetness that leaked under her clothes.
Henry rode beside her, and although his face was naught more
than a dark blot beneath the steel nasal of his helm, she
thought she saw a puff of breath after one sidelong glance,
accompanied by the whispered words: "Courage, Puss."

Behind them, riding three abreast were Sedrick, Eleanor,
and Eduard. Iorwerth, with his arm cradled in a leather sling,
rode behind them with Marienne and Robin completing the
threesome.

Twenty paces from the main gates, a shadow detached
itself from the guard tower, prompting Brevant to hold up his
hand and signal a halt. He rode forward alone, supposedly to
identify himself and explain what they were about. Ariel could
hear nothing but the loud pounding of her heartbeat. Her
palfrey took a nervous half-step sideways and skidded on a

hump of mud, righting itself with an indignant snort. Somewhere off in the rain-soaked distance she thought she heard a
bell ringing, but since she had no idea of the hour, she could
take no comfort in knowing if it was a church bell or an alarm
bell being sounded.

Beside her, Henry cursed softly into the drizzle. His helm
creaked as he turned his head to glance over his shoulder, but a
hissed warning from FitzRandwulf stopped him before the
gesture could be completed.

Brevant had been swallowed into the gloomy base of the
barbican tower, and the expectation of hearing a scream or a
shout grew proportionately with each agonizingly slow minute
that ticked past.

When the shout did come, it brought all of them jumping
out of their skin. Barely had it tightened around their bones
again when the grate of rusted iron links winding through a
winch sent spidery clawmarks of relief scratching down their
spines. The spiked grate of the portcullis seemed to take another eternity to lift high enough for Brevant to stalk out of the
shadows and remount whereupon an impatient wave of his
hand brought them moving forward again.

The horses hooves, clacking over the wooden draw,
sounded like the rumble of thunder. Ariel was certain a mo-
mentary shout would bring a hail of crossbow bolts raining
down upon their heads, and she rode as stiffly as a wooden
marionette at a fair.

The village seemed to be leagues away, the forest beyond
might have been on the other side of the world. On their right,
the sea shone dully through the rocky hillocks that shaped the
coastline; landward, to the east, a receding mountain range of
low-lying black clouds still bristled with night evils.

Evil, in another form, sent a second shock to test the
strength of Ariel's heart and nerve. They were barely through
the village and taking their first cleansing breaths of forest air,
when the unmistakable blast of a horn trumpeted an alert to
anyone venturing along the road: the royal cavalcade was approaching and expected to encounter no obstacles in its path.

Eduard and Henry exchanged a hard glance.

Their first instinct was to order everyone into concealment behind the wall of dense underbrush that lined the road. With the poor light and the rain, there was a chance the cavalcade would pass by without paying too close attention to the forest shadows. It was Brevant who kept a leveler head and drew the knights' attention to the guardsmen who, though resentful of being out on the road in such miserable conditions, were already in the process of dismounting and smoothing their tunics lest the king's eye happen to fall upon them as he passed by.

"Now we'll see what stuff your balls are really made of, my lord," grunted the captain, grinning.

He took command, ordering his men to form a straight line along the side of the road. Following their example, the De Clare party dismounted and led their steeds clear of the road, subtly forming a second line opposite the captain's men. Eleanor, Marienne, Ariel, and Robin were put well back with the horses, while the knights prepared to give proper salute to their liege.

The next blast of the horn went right up Ariel's spine. Robin was beside her and she took some courage from the wink he gave before he bowed his head deeper into the shadow of his hood. All of the knights and guards went down on bended knee and lowered their eyes as the first of the king's horsemen came into view. He, in turn, saw the troop of graycloaks and men-at-arms kneeling in the rain by the side of the road and gave two brief blasts on his horn to alert the others behind him.

Only Brevant remained afoot, his lance held high to display Gisbourne's pennons. One of the heavily armoured guards in the king's troop rode forward with brisk authority to exchange a few words with Brevant, and, seemingly satisfied with the answers he received, barely glanced at the bowed helms of the others before he wheeled his horse back onto the road and rejoined the rest of the guard.

Ariel, her view partially blocked by her brother's broad shoulders, risked a few peeks as the cavalcade moved past. A guard of perhaps a dozen foot soldiers marched in the van, carrying the pennons and banners that normally would have

fluttered colourfully and boldly to celebrate the approach of
the king. Rain and wind had wrapped most of them to the
lance poles, but here and there, a snap of wet silk revealed
John's device of stalking leopards. Behind the footmen came
archers, and behind them, a single horse with the king's personal confessor, who glared through the rain with a mean and
unholy expression, probably thinking of a warm bed and a
blazing fire. Fully a score of mounted knights splashed by
next, their faces almost completely obscured by visors or long,
wedge-shaped nasals. Heavy suits of chain mail were supplemented by baldrics and belts holding swords, daggers, and
battle-axes; all creaking and sawing back and forth with the
motion of the heavy destriers. Most of the animals looked wall-
eyed and balky, having spent the past two days in the bowels
of a transport ship.

Riding in the middle, surrounded by this armoured pha-
lanx of mercenaries, was the king. Ariel might have missed him
entirely, so swathed and caped was he against the elements,
but for a turn of the head and a glimpse of the long, pointed
face. There was nothing regal about him. Nothing to set the
heart aflutter or the lips moving in a prayer of exhaltation.
Certainly nothing that would bring to mind his brother, the
glorious golden-maned lionheart who had ruled before him.
John's features were dark and mean, his face starting to look
bloated under the vee-shaped beard and prickling brows. His
body was swollen from his overindulgence in rich foods and his
legs stuck out, short and stubby, from the sides of his horse.

Ariel lowered her lashes again. Another raised his and
stared at England's king through flint-gray eyes as cold as ice,
as hard as steel. The bitter taste of gall rose in Eduard's throat
as he watched the pompous, gloating fool parade past. It would
have been so easy—an arrow in the back and damn the consequences—to end all of Britain's woes then and there.

Eduard felt the hatred burning through his veins like acid.
He saw the faces of the knights taken at Mirebeau who had
been brought here to Corfe in chains and left to starve to death
in darkness and unimaginable agony. He saw the proud, handsome face of Arthur, and the tormented features of the dowa-

ger queen so utterly devastated by the need to choose between a son and a grandson.

And there was Eleanor. A casual word from John had crippled her forever. Eduard had not allowed himself to think about it until now, but he wondered if her uncle had watched while his torturer stuck his thumbs in Eleanor's eyes and gouged them from the sockets? Had he savoured the pain she must have endured, the fear and incomprehensible terror she must have felt being strapped to a chair, her head held rigid while she suffered through the appalling disfigurement? Was her last sight that of John smiling, gloating over his cleverness and cruelty?

Sweat broke out across Eduard's forehead and the muscles in his belly tightened in spasms. He was thankful he had not broken his fast that morning, for he was having difficulty combating the surges of bile. The nausea fueled his hatred until it pricked and stung behind his eyes and in truth, he was not surprised to see the king's head swivel slowly around, as if he had felt the threat and searched for the source.

With an almost superhuman effort, Eduard lowered his head. The shape of his helm shielded most of his face from view, and luckily, with Brevant's impressively huge frame overshadowing all others, FitzRandwulf's own formidable presence earned no more than a cursory glance.

And then the king was gone, swallowed into a green and gray miasma of rain and sagging pine boughs. More foot soldiers and servants formed the straggling rear of the cavalcade, and when they had safely passed and the last sucking footstep had faded along the forest road, Brevant released a long, slow hiss of breath.

"There you have it then, my lords," he said as he walked back to join Eduard and the others. "If I were a generous man, I would give us an hour before all hell descends upon us."

"The rain will slow that descent," Henry said.

"The rain will slow *us*," the captain countered smoothly. "More so if we do not rid ourselves of extra baggage now."

So saying, he walked straight to where his men were grouped together and, without a change in stride or expression, swung his wickedly barbed scimitar with both hands, catching the first man high under the chin where the narrow gap between the hauberk and hood left a strip of skin exposed. The edge of the glaive slashed through the man's throat, tearing out bone and gristle, shattering the jawbone and silencing the startled scream under a gout of bright red blood. The remaining five guards fanned back in shock and surprise. The horses smelled blood and reared, pawing the air with muddy hooves.

FitzRandwulf unslung his shield and hooked it over his forearm in a single fluid motion. He drew his sword with a hand that offered no apology for wanting blood, and he lunged for the nearest guard even as Brevant's terrible weapon was laying open the chest of his second victim, throat to gut.

The shrill clash of steel on steel sent the women scrambling clear of the sudden outbreak of violence. Two more guards were writhing face down in the mud before they could unsheath their weapons; a third gave Eduard a few screaming steps worth of resistance before his blade was scraped aside and cold steel punched through skin and rib and spine to emerge bloodied on the other side. The sixth man managed to grab his horse and swing himself onto the animal's back, kicking and shouting at the beast to retreat before he was fully balanced. He gained no more than a pitiable few paces when he stiffened suddenly in the saddle and threw his arms wide. The air caught him and tossed him backward. He landed spread-eagled in the mud, a small six-inch iron quarrel jutting from an eye socket, leaking crimson tears down the side of his face.

It was all over in less than a minute. Marienne was screaming and Lucifer was dancing in a thunderous circle, his gleaming black coat spattered in mud and blood. Henry, Dafydd, and Sedrick had only just managed to draw their swords and were crouched at the ready—ready for a fray that was finished before they had realized what Brevant had begun.

"God's grace!" Henry gasped. "You could have given a word of warning!"

"The warning," Brevant grunted, "is this, my lord: the king's men will be riding up our heels quicker than you can spit, and we have no time to waste on niceties. Linger here awhile if you doubt me and—saints and God above! What's *that?*"

That was the diminutive green and brown clad shadow who came swooping down out of the treetops and landed almost on top of Sedrick. Brevant moved with lightning reflexes, thinking it to be some winged creature from hell come to avenge the slaying of the king's men, and if not for Eduard's equally swift reaction in cutting his blade across the path of Brevant's sword, Sparrow would, in all likelihood, have found his head parted from his shoulders before he could finish chuckling over his timely arrival.

As it was, he found himself sprawled flat in the mud, where he had flung himself to avoid the cold slick of air disturbed by Jean de Brevant's sword. Being unaccustomed to flinging himself anywhere, let alone in a stinking quagmire of mud and rotted leaves, Sparrow lay there for a long, stunned moment, the air huffed out of his lungs, and only the whites of his eyes free of brown sludge.

"The great, lubbering suet-gut!" he exclaimed syllable by syllable, extricating one arm, then the other from the oozing mess. Sedrick leaned over and grasped a fistful of Sparrow's fur vest, hauling him up and setting him on his feet again with a grin as broad as his belly.

"Nice of ye to join us again, Sprite. Bit off the mark, though, weren't ye?"

Sparrow still had hold of his arblaster, and at the sound of Sedrick's chuckle, whirled around and drove the tip of the wooden bow into the toe of the Celt's boot. The knight leaped and gave a howl of pain, which barely dented the wood elf's craving for revenge. He rounded on Brevant and drew the two bone-handled daggers he wore at his waist, filleting the air in a promisory blur as he stalked the armoured giant.

"Sparrow! Hold up!" Eduard shouted. "It was an honest mistake, with no harm done."

"No harm? No harm!" The little man puffed up like a quail in moult. "Two full days have I paced and pondered, fretted and feared, and now I am come back to join you only to

have this lumber-nose send me arse over gob! Not likely I will
hold up, sirrah! Not likely."

His daggers flashed again, but the point of Eduard's sword
sent them both spinning away into the mud. Undaunted, Sparrow drew a wicked-looking hatchet from a sheath in his belt
and was about to fell a limb or two when he caught sight of the
four cloaked and hooded figures by the side of the road. Robin
was trying desperately to catch and calm the horses, Ariel and
Marienne stood with Eleanor sandwiched between them.

The two women had remained steadfastly by the princess's side, relaying everything that happened, reassuring her
in the calmest tones possible that the fighting had gone in their
favour. Sparrow's arrival and subsequent mud bath had eased
some of their terror; seeing a long thread of silver-blonde hair
blow free of the dark hood put a broad smile on the seneschal's
face and made him forget abruptly about Jean de Brevant.

"Our Pearl!" he cried. "Our Little Pearl has been saved!
Good St. Cyril, I offer thanks to all the . . . the . . ."

Eduard had not been able to warn him. He had seen
Sparrow's black eyes dance with delight as he recognized the
princess . . . and a moment later, widen with shock and horror as he caught sight of the face beneath the hood.

"Oh." Sparrow cried softly. "Oh . . . sweet Jesu . . ."

"There is no time for an accounting now," Eduard murmured tautly. "All will be explained to you later, when we
have put some distance between ourselves and Corfe. In the
meantime, it is enough for you to know we have barely
skinned our way out of the castle keep; even now, I should
think the castellan is trying to waken the governor and is discovering Sir Guy is not all that he should be."

"Dead, then, is he?" Sedrick asked.

"Not when we left him. But he may wish he was when he
comes around again. Once more I say, all will be explained
when the breath of the leopard is not so close upon our necks.
Robin! Dafydd! Gather up the spare horses . . . strip them
down and string them together; we will take them along until
we find a sweet enough meadow to deter them from running
back to Corfe too soon. Sedrick, Henry, Jean . . . give a hand

with these bodies. The longer it takes John's Brabançons to find them, the longer they will think we move with caution. Sparrow . . . did you find us a safe route away from here?"

Sparrow's round, dark eyes lifted to Eduard's. Pain and grief swam in their liquid depths, for he had known the princess since she was but a twinkle of silver light on a swaddling board. But he nodded and pointed a shaky finger down the road.

"A league more and you will see an oak scarred and split in half by lightning. Veer off the road and follow the cut in the trees until you find the river. Follow this as far as you can, keeping to the middle in case they bring hounds." He gave the thought a mild shudder and added, "Where the river widens and breaks in two, follow the north branch, again as far as far can take you . . ." His voice faded and his eyes slid back to where Eleanor stood.

"Sparrow?" Eduard prodded gently.

"Aye. Aye, as far as far can take you . . . then—" The curly head snapped forward again and a ridge of grim determination hardened his jaw. "Wait there until I come and fetch you, for though the lot of you might fancy yourselves great and glorious huntsmen, you will have your feet walking in circles without someone to shew you the way."

"Ye're not coming with us?" Sedrick asked.

"I will dally here a bit and see how many bees come out of the hive to search for us."

"Aye, and if the weather holds at this much misery and no more, it should help us a bit," Jean de Brevant remarked, squinting up at the gray, shifting mass of cloud above them. "If it turns, though, and gets any colder . . ."

Eduard followed his gaze to where the three women stood huddled together. They were soaked and frightened and could not be expected to last too long without heat and shelter.

"At the end of the path I have given you is a waterfall," Sparrow said, reading the concern on Eduard's face. "Beneath it is a cavern, large enough to build a fire and heat a pan of food. It will take three, four hours to reach it in this mort of

English hospitality, but once reached, will give shelter for as long as it takes to bolster any spirits, should they be flagging."

"You'll not dally here too long," Eduard said by way of a warning.

Sparrow looked down the road toward Corfe, then up into the thick boughs of the pines that lined either side of the tract. "Only long enough to delay them," he said narrowly.

Eduard nodded and sheathed his sword before turning and walking back toward the bodies of the dead guardsmen. Jean de Brevant was close on his heels, a frown pleating his face.

"What can one elf hope to do against a score of the king's men?" he asked, helping Eduard lift and carry the first body into the brush.

"You would not have to ask if you knew the elf," Eduard answered.

Sparrow asked himself, a dozen times, what he was doing wedged up in the boughs of a tree with rain drizzling down his nose and the occasional squirrel sniffing at his rump. He stank abominably. His vest was still thick with mud and his face streaked with grime, but he reasoned it helped in concealing him . . . if only the squirrels had not started thinking of him as a large brown nut. A troop of them squatted on an adjacent branch, bickering and debating amongst themselves how best to drag their discovery into their hidey-holes, and Sparrow was forced to heave the odd pine cone across the gap when their numbers grew bold enough and shrill enough to sound like a gathering of fishwives.

He had been cleaved to the crotch of the tree for nigh on three hours, as best as he could figure it from the distant tolling of church bells. The oppressive drizzle had kept travellers off the road and no one had passed either way. The tracks left by the men and horses had lost their sharp definitions and the hollows were filled with puddles of water, spotting the road like a leper's skin. Behind and beneath him, out of sight of anyone riding or walking by, were the bodies of the six guardsmen slain earlier. Sightless and soundless, they watched Sparrow with an equally unnerving diligence.

He adjusted his collar and lowered the jaunty brim of his felt cap, scowling at the water that ran free. He would give the king's blundernoses until the next bell hour to show themselves, or he was leaving. Two days and nights' worth of not knowing what was going on was two days and nights more than his patience could be expected to tolerate. He had only offered to stay behind now because he knew the Wolf would have expected it of him. He was the only one small enough, agile enough, clever enough to outwit any would-be hunters long enough to buy Eduard the time he needed to hie the princess out of immediate danger.

Still, it was too long for them to be on their own in this accursed, foul, damp country. They would need his, Sparrow's, uncanny knack of knowing exactly where he was going—even if he had never passed that way before—if they were going to steal the Pearl safely away.

On the other hand, it was possible the king would be in no great hurry to have her back. He had done his worst already (and with this thought, Sparrow's face flushed a venomous red). He might not consider a blind princess worth the effort of retrieving. Why . . . he might even *want* her to be stolen away, hoping she might fall victim to the cold and rain, thereby relieving him of the burden and guilt of having her expire while in his care!

Had Eduard considered this?

Not that Sparrow would have ever sanctioned leaving her behind, but had Eduard considered if Eleanor died while in his care, the king could protest his own innocence, deny his own culpability, and blame whatever fate befell the Pearl squarely on the heads of William the Marshal and Randwulf de la Seyne Sur Mer?

"God save us all, lads," Sparrow said to the clutch of squirrels. "It seems we are swivved either way, should they catch us now."

Deciding not to wait for any more bells, Sparrow slung his arblaster over his shoulder and made preparations to leave his

perch. He was about to leap to another branch when he was
drawn back against the trunk by the faint but unmistakable
braying of dogs. A large pack of them, he guessed, followed by
an even larger pack of galloping hooves.

He swung his bow around again and nocked a quarrel to
the string. He drew half a dozen more from his quiver and
jabbed their tips into the soft bark of the tree, ready and waiting to be quickly snatched up, loaded, and fired when the
troop came into view.

He did not have long to wait. The sound of the hounds
drew beads of sweat across his brow but he steadfastly ignored
the memories and the itching of the scars brought on by youthful encounters with the salivating beasts. He closed one eye
and sighted carefully along the shaft of the arrow as he drew
back on the string . . . and chose his target.

The soldiers rode two abreast, their lances festooned with
the standards and pennons of the king. At least a score,
mayhap more, comprised the double column of bobbing conical helms and flapping red mantles. All were fully armoured
and bristling with business. A toady, hook-nosed hunchback
was in the lead, bristling somewhat more than the others in his
newly assumed position of authority.

It ended as ignobly as it had begun as Sparrow's bolt
caught Gisbourne's seneschal high in the chest. A second bolt
sent the man beside Gallworm slewing off his saddle with a
scream of agony; a third and fourth jerked back on their reins
as they felt the punch of steel through armour and bullhide.
Their horses reared and skidded back in the mud, causing
those behind to scatter and buckle into one another in a sudden crush of screaming horseflesh and shouting men.

Sparrow snatched up the last two bolts and loosed them
randomly into the fray, then slung his bow over his shoulder
and moved nimbly to another tree farther along the road, one
with an equally clear vantage over the scene below.

Several of the soldiers had drawn their swords and were
bracing themselves, wild-eyed, for the expected ambush to
erupt from the bushes. Sparrow picked off three more as easily
as skewering melons off a wall, then moved again, careful to

keep a thick shield of pine boughs between him and the searching eyes. Some of the mercenaries carried crossbows and fired bolts into the trees, but Sparrow struck and moved, struck and moved, never remaining in one place long enough to present a target.

It was sheer misfortune—or utter stupidity—that made him stop and draw one last bead on the retreating crush of soldiers. He loosed an iron quarrel and a curse at the same time, rewarding himself with a small leap of glee as the keeper of the hounds clutched his throat and fell backwards into the mire-muck, releasing the yelping, braying pack of fur-muzzled devils to set off at a run back for the castle, their tails curled low between their legs. Unfortunately, Sparrow's glee momentarily overrode his sense of caution, and even as he realized he had sprung up in full view of a crossbowman, he could see the lout's finger pull the trigger and launch the bolt straight at him.

It was odd how he could see it so clearly. So distinctly. It moved as if it cut through liquid, not air, the barbed iron tip rotating slowly as it found the gap in the trees and struck its target with a solid *whonk!*

Chapter 24

✝ The rain stopped around mid-afternoon but the sky never grew any brighter. It grew colder, however, and by the time the sodden, shivering travellers arrived at the waterfall, there were ice crystals forming on the ground and on their clothes. Building a fire and drying themselves off was a priority and while Dafydd and Robin searched for a modest shelter for the horses, Eduard located the tunnel-like entrance to the cave that led behind the wall of water and opened into a large, musty hollow formed in the solid rock. There was evidence it had been used by both two- and four-legged creatures in the past, and proof that Sparrow had thought well enough ahead to stock an ample supply of dry kindling and wood.

Since there were no dry clothes for the women to change into, a wall of wet cloaks was strung up, dividing the cavern in two halves. The women waited, blue with cold, while a fire was built, then eagerly and willingly stripped down to their tunics, which would dry the fastest, and sat almost on top of the flames, enjoying the sensation of wrinkled toes and icy fingers drying in the heat.

Marienne fussed and fretted over Eleanor, unplaiting her hair and spreading it to dry, coaxing her to drink some broth the handy Welshman brewed out of the assortment of purloined foodstuffs he had carried away from Corfe. Marienne did not have to coax hard, for Eleanor found the broth delicious and her appetite ravenous. Warmed inside and out, cocooned by walls of steaming clothes, the princess was persuaded to rest her head on Marienne's lap, whereupon she fell fast asleep despite her protestations against being pampered.

Ariel fought to keep her own eyes open but she too was lulled by the heat and the bright glow of the fire. Her eyelids drooped and her head swayed forward, burdened by the weight of her hair. The sound of the river rolling by overhead vibrated the air and even though the men had to talk loudly to be overheard, Ariel found herself drifting to the sound of their voices, sliding sideways, and finally curling up asleep on the floor.

When she wakened—she knew not how much later—the fire had been robustly restocked. Marienne and Eleanor were both asleep, covered by blankets. Ariel had been covered as well, though the folds of the wool cloak still gave off a slightly damp smell.

She pushed herself up on one elbow and rubbed her eyes to remove some of the fuzziness. She could hear nothing over the rumble of the river, no voices coming from the other side of the blanket—were they all asleep?

Creeping to the woolen wall, she poked a finger between two overlapping edges and inched them apart. Lord Dafydd was the first one she saw. He was sitting with his back propped against the cavern wall, his head tilted to one side, his complexion pale beneath the beard. He had not complained throughout the long, wet morning, not when river water rose as high as the bellies of their horses, not when brambles and briers tried to drag them out of their saddles. His arm must have given him nothing but pain, but he had drawn his sword alongside Henry and Sedrick, prepared to fight to their defense on the roadside, and he was first out of his saddle to help with whatever task was asked of him. He had not asked to become involved in any of this madness. He had only gone along with it because of her, because she was betrothed to his brother. What would he do when he discovered she had deceived them both by falling in love with Eduard FitzRandwulf?

Robin was curled in a tight ball, his back to the small fire they had built on their own side of the wall. Henry and Sedrick were dozing lightly, their experience and training telling them to take advantage of what time they had to rest and restore their strength.

Sedrick managed to pry an eyelid open and offer a weak smile as Ariel tiptoed past, but he did not ask her where she was going or why. He had enough to do to keep his eyes and ears on Jean de Brevant, for he still did not trust the man not to turn on them all and slit their throats for the gold they carried in their money belts.

Captain Littlejohn was soundly asleep, his massive chest rising and falling like a farrier's bellows. He had stripped out of his armour, as had the others, and was sprawled comfortably in a linsey-woolsey chainse and hose, looking no less formidable now than when he was wearing several layers of padding and chain mail.

Ariel drew the edges of her cloak around her shoulders and ventured into the much cooler tunnel that led to the opening beneath the falls. A shiver was about to send her hurrying back to the warmth when she saw a shadow detach itself from a niche in the wall and come forward into the light.

"There is no sign of Sparrow yet?" she asked.

Eduard shook his head. "It has only been a couple of hours. I will allow him a couple more before I worry him into an early demise."

"You are not worried now?"

"Not about Sparrow," he said. "In all the years I have known him, he has never overstayed his welcome anywhere his feathers might get clipped. He comes and goes like a ghost in the night and . . ."

The words just stopped, the thought simply ended. The need to talk was suddenly, overwhelmingly surpassed by the need to gather Ariel in his arms and hold her so close he feared he might crush her. To kiss her so hard, it all but took his breath away.

Ariel clung to him and did not protest his roughness. She welcomed his urgency and matched it with her own. His body was cool through the thin layer of his tunic and hose, but it smouldered quickly when she spread the folds of her cloak around him and pressed her own scantily clad body next to his, warming them deeper than any man-made fire ever could.

"I was so frightened today," she confessed on a gasp. "I wanted so desperately just to touch you . . . hold you."

"You were brave beyond measure," he countered. "And in truth, I longed to do more than simply touch you, or hold you.

When I saw you sleeping in there, curled up like a kitten . . ."

"You covered me?"

"It was either that or join you," he said huskily. "And I
doubt the others would have survived the shock."

"The others are all asleep now," she said, breathing just
as huskily in his ear. "Only you and I are awake, my lord. And
quite alone."

He groaned and pressed a muffled curse into the tender
crook of her neck. "You play unfair, wench, to tease a man so."

"Unfair," she agreed, her mouth molding eagerly to his as
he kissed his way from one side of her neck to the other. "But
I do not tease."

His hands pushed savagely into her hair and he held her
away from him for a long, long moment of melting contempla-
tion, his gaze roving from her moist, swollen lips, to where the
exquisitely peaked crowns of her nipples strained against the
cloth of her tunic. His tunic, he realized with a jolt, and was at
once irrationally jealous of its intimacy.

His mouth covered hers again, this time with a bold intent
that sent tremors racing through the length and breadth of her
body. His hands slipped down to her waist, then her hips, and
he pulled her against him, heat to heat, flesh to flesh, groaning
deep in his chest when she responded with a shuddered,
breathless plea. His hands skimmed up beneath the hem of
the tunic and cupped the heavy coolness of her breasts, and
she shuddered again, unable to keep the wildness from flowing
into her limbs, making them part brazenly over the growing
bulge in his loins.

"Someone could come—"

"Someone could," she agreed again, panting lightly as his
thumbs abraded her nipples with small, torturous brushstrokes
then trailed deliberately down and around to cup the softness
of her buttocks. The challenge was there, gleaming in the
smokey gray eyes, and Ariel's hands answered it, moving down
to his waist and unfastening his belt, casting it away in the
shadows. A second assault, launched beneath the hem of the
loosened chainse, met with a hissed curse when she discovered

the rows of infernal rawhide points that bound his hose to his thighs.

Undaunted, she tugged only the front few thongs free so that the surging flesh that was already halfway clear of the slash in his braies, leaped through the widened gap and pushed forward to fill her questing hands.

Eduard shuddered and bent his head forward. Her lips were there to savour his soft oaths even as she guided his heat between her thighs.

"Help me," she implored. "Lift me."

"Madness," he gasped.

"Yes. Yes. Yes . . ."

When she felt her feet leave the ground, she drew her knees high and hooked her legs around his waist. A shallow cry, stifled against the curve of his shoulder greeted the straining spear of his flesh as he lowered her over him; a gasp of splintered wonder sent her teeth sinking into the ridge of solid muscle and her hands threading into the dark mane of his hair.

Eduard stood motionless. He had heard her cry and had felt her stiffen against him and he was afraid—because he had never needed or wanted a woman as badly as he needed and wanted Ariel now—that he was too big and too hungry to cause her anything but pain.

The next few gasps he heard dispelled those fears, for they were accompanied by such greedy, undulant urgings of her hips, he was compelled to lose all sense of caution and reason, and thrust himself so deep inside her, it was all he could do to keep his pleasure from spilling then and there.

He *was* big, but Ariel only rejoiced in the hunger and stretching thickness. There was no pain. Sweet Mother Mary, there was no pain, only pleasure—deep and shaking, all-consuming, ravaging pleasure.

Something cool and damp was against her back and she realized he had moved into the darker shadows near the mouth of the tunnel where moss grew lush and soft on the walls. The contrast of thrusting heat and cushioning coolness sent her fingers clawing into his hair. The sound of the water roaring only an arm's length away, the sight of it blurred and luminescent plunging past them with such power, such might, only made the power plunging within her seem all the more shattering and intense.

Ariel's ragged gasp of warning brought Eduard's mouth back over hers in time to swallow her hoarse, gusting cries of rapture. He felt her begin to convulse around him and he weathered the stunning ferocity of her climax as long as he could before his own tempest broke within him, causing them both to cry out against each other's mouths and writhe through the deluge of ecstasy together.

Eduard held her with bruising desperation. He held her with a body that continued to press her into the moss, continued to move with each of her soft, mewling cries until the last thudding pulsebeat of pleasure had shivered from their flesh. Neither wanted to be the first to move or the first to break the spell. Their mouths were still together and the need to muffle each other's cries changed without thought or notice to a need to acknowledge the flamboyant excesses of their passion.

"Shameless," he breathed against her lips. " 'Twas not a position I would have thought a lady yearned to couple in."

"I was not thinking, my lord," she admitted with a slow sigh. "I was only . . . needing."

"Even more shameless then," he whispered, his hands continuing to cradle her against him. He kissed her again, and this time, Ariel's legs—utterly depleted of strength—began the long slide down from his waist. She looked up at him, her lashes spiked with tears, and after a moment, raised a hand from where it rested limp on his shoulder and traced cool, trembling fingers over the hard ridges of the scar on his cheek.

"My only shame is remembering the things I have said to you in cruelty and ignorance. My shame is my pride and I gladly lay it at your feet, my lord, to trample upon, discard, or scorn as you will."

Eduard covered her hand with his own and drew it from his cheek to his lips. "How could I possibly scorn that which I possess too much of myself?"

Her eyes were like dark mirrors to her soul and he could see each brush of his lips, each flicker of his tongue reflected there. She was still aroused, still peaking delicately, languidly, in a way that made him acutely aware of where they were still joined together.

Ariel was aware of it too and her lashes fluttered down and her teeth caught her lower lip, curling it between them in a sharp bite for courage.

"Have you . . . given any thought as to what will happen at Gloucester?"

He had given a good many things a great deal of thought over the past twelve hours; he had not anticipated the need for outright answers so soon.

"I . . . know I have no claim," she stammered, swallowing to cover the awkward gap caused by his silence. "Nor do I expect you to feel any obligation to marry me, but . . . I would ask . . . *beg* . . . that you do not cast me aside altogether. I w-would stay with you as your mistress, your cook's helper, your boot scrubber if that is what you would make of me, but only . . . do not . . . banish me—" she sobbed, "—to Wales. Do not . . . m-make me wed a man . . . I do not know . . . or . . . do n-not care to know . . . or . . ."

She dissolved in tears and buried her face against his throat, too mortified to see the look of shock which she was certain must be widening his eyes as he beheld the ultimate proof of her brashness. He still cupped her hand over his lips—it was frozen there by horror, she supposed—and she could feel his breath, hot and stilted, gusting into her palm.

She reclaimed it with yet another sob and clenched it into a fist, fighting the urge to strike out at something, anything, but most especially the motionless, unresponsive wall of muscle that held her trapped against the moss.

"I . . . have no need for a boot scrubber," he admitted finally. "And I have already sampled your talents as a cook's helper, only to find them sadly wanting. As to a mistress . . . aye." He paused consideringly and ran both hands down the curve of her back. "You show promise of a distinct knack there, my lady, but alas . . . no. I have no need for a mistress either. I have neither the time nor the energy to spare on such things."

Ariel's hopes sank and her shoulders sagged, but it seemed he was not finished chastising her yet. Nor would he let her escape without tilting her face up and forcing her to meet his gaze.

"It will have to be as a wife, or nothing at all," he said quietly.

Ariel's breath stopped in her throat and her heart missed a noticeable beat.

"Your . . . wife?" she whispered.

"If you will have me: a scarred and saddle-galled beast, arrogant and ill-mannered, brutish, unfeeling—" He pursed his lips and frowned. "My memory fails me, was there more?"

She studied his smile intently. "You mock me, sir."

"I love you, my lady. God Himself could be waiting for you at Gloucester and I would not relinquish you."

Stunned, she barely responded as he bowed his head, kissing her with all of the tenderness she could have longed for and more than she deserved.

"Of course . . . your uncle is another matter. He will not be pleased to hear how you have spurned another groom."

"I have not spurned Rhys ap Iorwerth," she protested softly. "I have simply made a wiser choice."

"Nonetheless, you have broken your contract with him. A contract your uncle signed and sealed in good faith."

"The contract is void if I marry another—Lord knows the Welsh have stolen enough brides away from their intended grooms to be well acquainted with the law. As for Uncle Will . . ." She paused and the relief she felt brought forth a giddy question. "Are you afraid of him?"

"Me? Afraid of the Marshal of England? The greatest champion of all time? Only from the ankles up, my love; only from the ankles up."

"But he likes you. He *admires* you; this he told me himself."

"Aye, well, his admiration might dim somewhat once he learns how sadly we have botched things."

"Botched? But you have saved the princess. You have stolen her out of King John's clutches."

"That we have," Eduard agreed grimly, disengaging himself as gently as possible. "But in such a way as to leave no doubt who was responsible. Part of your uncle's plan was to keep the king from having positive proof of your involvement. Gisbourne may not yet know who I am, but he will surely waken with blood in his eye and the name De Clare screaming from his lips."

"Whatever did you do to him? Furthermore, what did he want with Robin?"

Eduard glanced up from refastening his points. She still stood against the moss, her cloak skewed to one side, her tunic raised in a crush above her thighs. The stone walls of the tunnel were damp from the mist and the tiny, glistening bits of minerals in the rock reflected the opalescent wash of light that came through the falls, seeming to form a glowing nimbus around her. Despite her obvious and magnificent look of debauchery, Eduard thought it best to guard a small part of her innocence, for a while longer at any rate.

"Suffice it to say he wanted Robin for no good reason and that Robin himself offered his refusal in a way Gisbourne will not likely soon forget—or forgive."

"Meaning he wanted Robin in the same way you wanted me . . . and Robin responded in a similar fashion as Alan of the Dale."

"Alan of the . . . who?"

"The outlaw who ambushed us on the road to Rennes. He said the guards wanted to use him as a whore, and he butted them, all right, but—"

Eduard's mouth came down swiftly, perfunctorily, over hers, muffling her recollection along with the small laugh she accorded the look of surprise on his face.

"I have an excellent memory," she said when she was able.

"Aye, and a knack of drawing on it at most inopportune moments."

Ariel's expression sobered. "Is Robin . . . that is, he was not hurt in any way, was he?"

"Only in the way he views the meaning of being in the

'flower' of knighthood. He, my lovely, is not quite so worldly-wise as you. Or me, alas. He is still convinced there is no true evil in the world, only slightly misguided fools who need a strong hand to show them the way to gaining purity of soul and goodness of heart."

"But you do believe it? You believe true evil exists?"

"I am a product of it," he said quietly. "And because of it, or perhaps in spite of it, I have tried too hard to protect Robin from the blacker side of humankind."

"Because of it . . . because of *you*, my lord," she insisted, "and the man you have become *in spite* of everything, he will make for a braver and bolder knight one day, for he will want to be just like you."

Eduard lost himself in the drowning green of her eyes for a long moment and saw the pride and love shining there. It was pride for him, love for him, intense enough and honest enough to make him bow his head slightly, overwhelmed by the smothering tightness that took hold of his chest.

The same tightness was etched on his face and Ariel recognized it for what it was. She had been suffering it herself, the whole blessed day long, each and every time she glanced his way. The worst of it had been eased and was still wet and slick between her thighs, but she knew it would happen upon her again and again until they were out of England and could shout their love for each other to the world.

Until then, however, they would have to be content to shout it to themselves, in quiet ways. On darkened rooftops and in watery caves. With a look or a touch, or a few fleeting moments of intimacy that were over too soon. Too soon.

"Did you really mean what you said?" she asked softly. "If God Himself were waiting at Gloucester, you would not relinquish me?"

He did not meet her gaze, but the muscles in his arms bunched beneath her hands as he pulled her close again.

"I meant it," he whispered, burying his lips in her hair. Ariel pressed herself into his heat and her hands climbed up to his shoulders, then slid around, lacing together at the back of his neck. She was aware of his heartbeat hammering in his chest and of the tension coursing through his body. The tumbled waves of her hair framed the expectant face she raised to him; her lips, soft and moist, traced a warm, seductive path up his throat.

"Absolutely shameless," he murmured.

Ariel sighed. And agreed.

Henry de Clare heard a woman's muffled cry and opened his eyes. It took a minute to register the scene: the cavern, the wool blankets hung to dry, the fire throwing shadows and shapes on the walls.

The others—Sedrick, Dafydd, Robin, and Brevant were asleep. FitzRandwulf was standing guard at the entrance to the tunnel and the women were . . .

Henry pushed to his feet, a curse forming on his lips as he jerked aside a corner of the blankets. Marienne and the princess were lying by the fire but the place where Ariel should have been was glaringly empty.

Henry dropped the blanket and started to reach for his baldric when he heard the cry again and realized it had indeed come from the other side of the blankets. Without thinking, he lifted the edge again and saw what he had missed before. Eleanor's long, slender legs had thrashed most of her blankets free. Her face was bathed in sweat and her hair was a blonde tangle, matted to her temples and throat in tight, wet curls.

"No," she gasped. "Please . . . *please!*"

Henry ducked beneath the curtain and stretched out a hand to touch Eleanor's shoulder, but a small white fist grasped his sleeve first, preventing him.

Shocked, thinking Marienne might have misinterpreted his gesture as something other than concern, he folded his fingers into his palm and withdrew his hand immediately.

"I was only wanting to see if she was unwell. A fever, perhaps—?"

"It is no fever, my lord," Marienne whispered. "Save the one in her heart."

"*Please,*" Eleanor cried, thrashing in torment. "Arthur . . . my God, Arthur . . . tell him what he wants to hear. I was wrong. *I was wrong.* Tell him. Tell him anything. Tell him—" She stiffened and her back arched up off the floor. Her arms started to tremble and flay the air and Henry, helpless to do more than watch, saw Marienne move calmly to where Eleanor's head rolled back and forth on the hard stone. She quickly folded a blanket and tucked it beneath the princess's head, then crouched and took hold of her wrists, gently keeping them from striking the wall or the rough floor.

"Forgive me, my lord," Marienne cried softly, "but if you could hold her ankles, she might be stopped from doing herself an injury when the worst of it comes."

Worse, Henry thought, doing as he was bid. How much worse? And why did the girl not simply waken her?

" 'Tis the Angevin curse," Marienne explained over the tears that started to well in her eyes. "It only happens when she is very weak, or very tired . . . or very frightened. And 'tis more like a trance than a true fit. A nightmare from which she cannot be wakened until it runs its course. She . . . feels guilt over her brother's death. She thinks . . . it was because of her, because he did not want to appear weak or unworthy in front of the courage she displayed . . . that he refused to accept the king's offer of exile. And because he kept refusing, the king became angrier, and . . ."

"Arthur!" Eleanor's shivered cry drew Henry's shocked gaze downward again. "Arthur . . . sweet, merciful Jesus, where is Arthur? Not dead. Not dead! *Not dead!*"

Eleanor twisted so suddenly, Marienne lost her grip. The princess reared up, flailing her arms, sobbing and screaming soundlessly as she went through the horrific motions of trying to escape some torment from which there was no escape.

Henry caught one wrist, then the other, surprised by the strength of her pain. He crossed her arms over her chest and drew her back against him so that she was pinned firmly against his body. He held her there, through one tremendous struggle after another, until they were both panting and running with sweat.

Marienne watched, her hands covering her mouth, her cheeks wet with tears. She knew it was over when Eleanor shuddered and went limp in Lord Henry's arms, and she knew this episode had been worse than many others because of the anxieties roused by the escape. She was thankful Lord Henry had been there to help. Thankful he was helping still by holding the princess and rocking her gently as he smoothed the silvery web of hair back off her face.

His hand shook visibly when he lifted the last few tendrils away, for the shadows in the cavern had almost made it seem as though her eyes were simply closed against the intrusion of the firelight. A further heart-stopping illusion made him imagine the scars were crescents of golden lashes and that any moment they would lift over eyes so blue they would sparkle like a deep clear lake.

"Does FitzRandwulf know about this?" he asked quietly.

"He knew she suffered them as a child. It was one of the things they had in common."

Henry's head shot up. *"FitzRandwulf suffers fits?"*

"Oh no, my lord. Not fits." She hastened to explain, "I am told he . . . used to suffer nightmares. Terrible nightmares, and when my lady first happened to see him in the midst of one—she was but a child then—she thought it a common bond they shared. Truly, 'twas only nightmares. And my lady's fits are so very mild, they could almost be mistaken as such themselves. Indeed, there were a number of years when she suffered none at all. But now, with Arthur . . . and all else . . ."

Henry looked back down at the Pearl of Brittany. She was sleeping deeply; exhausted. One of her hands was curled around his neck and her body was burrowed against his for warmth. She was so thin and fragile, so pale, so lovely, so . . .

"My lord—?"

Henry shook away Marienne's worried frown. "She is asleep. Soundly now, I think."

Marienne offered a tremulous smile of thanks as she helped him ease Eleanor down onto a bed of cloaks. He waited until there was no longer any excuse for him to remain on this side of the blankets, and when he turned awkwardly to leave, he felt Marienne's hand on his arm again.

"Thank you, my lord. Not just for this, but . . . for everything. I am quite certain, you see, that the king was come to Corfe to settle things with my lady once and for all."

"Settle things?"

"He has tried so hard to break her mind and her spirit, I have no doubt he was counting on her to succumb long before now. I have even less doubt he had decided to have Gisbourne arrange an accident, so you see"—she folded her hands tightly in her lap—"whatever happens now can only be better than what would have happened had we stayed behind. And if it is true, if it is at all possible for my lady to find safe haven at Kirklees . . . I . . . I know she will find peace. I know she will be released from these demons that haunt her."

Henry felt, suddenly, as if his whole body was on fire. His arms burned where they had held Eleanor and his heart pounded in his chest with such force as he had never felt before, in the heat of battle, or passion.

He gently pried one of Marienne's hands free and sandwiched it between his with a fierce promise. "She will find haven at Kirklees," he rasped. "You have my word on it . . . and my life."

He sealed the pledge by raising the young maid's captive hand to his lips. A last glance at Eleanor of Brittany sent him ducking quickly between the blankets; the need for cool, clean air sent him across the cavern and out into the gloom of the tunnel. Confused by too many new, emerging emotions, his composure took a sharp plunge downward when he rounded a curve in the tunnel and saw more than just the rushing gray-green wall of water.

Ariel leaned into the warmth of Eduard's body, her own beginning to display amazing recuperative powers by moving eagerly against the rhythm of his caressing hands. A few minutes ago, tottering on legs as weak as those of a newborn fawn, she would not have thought it possible to feel her blood racing anew and yet it was. Racing and flushing through her limbs so adamantly she heard Eduard press a deep, throaty chuckle into the soft pink curl of her ear.

"Once, Vixen, is shameless," he murmured. "Twice would be . . ."

Ariel lifted her mouth to his and silenced his censure with a kiss that left them both short of breath and caution. Ariel moaned in assent as he started to lift her again, but a movement in the shadows turned her passion to shock as she pushed herself out of Eduard's arms and scrambled hastily to pull her tunic down over her bared thighs.

Eduard saw the look of horror on Ariel's face and turned, alerted to the presence of someone behind them. His hand moved instinctively to his waist, to the sword that was not there but leaned against the stone wall more than two full strides away. His second instinct was to shield Ariel with his body, which he did by turning to meet the threat face to face.

Lord Henry de Clare, his tawny hair glinting gold against the flare of light emanating from the cavern, moved forward with slow, measured steps. Neither Eduard nor Ariel had heard his approach over the rush of the waterfall, nor did they know how long he had been standing there observing them. To judge by the rigid look on his face, he knew they had not merely been enjoying a few minutes of private conversation. To judge by the way his fist opened and closed around the hilt of the dagger he wore thrust in his belt, he was not amused by what he had seen.

It was a reflex action that sent Ariel's hands down to further smooth the wrinkles in her tunic and to draw the edges of her cloak over the sudden chill in her flesh. Henry's eyes scorned the gesture as much as the grim lines of his mouth suggested such modesty was late in coming.

"Here?" he asked coldly. "Without so much as a bed or haystack for comfort?"

Eduard fisted his hands. "Since your sister has agreed to be my wife, I would advise against offering too many insults."

Henry's hazel eyes held FitzRandwulf's for a few hard moments, then sought the pale sliver of Ariel's face where it peeped out from behind her lover's shoulder.

"Is this true?" he asked.

Ariel slipped her hand into Eduard's larger, warmer one.

"No. The *absolute* truth is that I offered to be his mistress if he would take me anywhere but to Gloucester . . . and he refused me. I had not even dared to hope he would take me to wife, but alas—" She looked up into Eduard's bemused eyes and smiled. "He said it was to be thus or not at all, and so dear brother, I have accepted."

Henry opened his mouth, but snapped it shut again. His gaze flicked from his sister's face to FitzRandwulf's, but when he realized they had eyes only for each other, he threw his hands up in the air and turned on his heel to glare at the wall of sheeting water.

"I know I have asked this before, but have you . . . have either of you . . . any notion of what you are doing? It is all very well and good to make dewy-eyed plans in the heat of passion, but . . . have you given thought to what you will do when the heat wanes? Where will you go? How will you live? Good God, man—" He swore loudly and rounded on Eduard again. "Half the king's men will be hunting for you and the other half for us. Your father and our uncle will have to publicly disown us and disclaim having any prior knowledge of our intentions if they are to have *any* hope of avoiding the king's retribution. They will have to declare us renegades and traitors and will no doubt have to make the gesture, at any rate, of helping the king try to hunt us down. Had you not crippled and castrated Gisbourne, we might have been able to exile ourselves to Navarre or Aragon—or even to Rome to plead our case before the pope. But Gisbourne will want our heads to stick on pikes and John will give him full rein to chase us to the edges of the earth."

"You *castrated* Gisbourne?" Ariel asked, glancing up in mellow surprise.

Eduard shrugged. "It was an accident. He fell on Robin's blade."

"Better he should have fallen on it with his heart," Henry remarked grimly. "And I should still be thinking seriously of ripping yours out of your throat for doing what you have done to my sister."

"Believe me," Eduard said quietly. "I had not planned to take a wife back to Touraine with me."

"And I had not planned to let the man live who despoiled my sister," Henry countered.

"Meaning you have changed your mind?" Ariel asked, barely daring to breathe.

Henry stared. He sighed and shoved his fingers through his hair, then sighed again. "Allowing that there are now two signed, legal contracts binding you to two different men in marriage . . . are you certain you will not change *your* mind again? Are you certain *this* is the man you want? The life you want?"

Ariel saw her life at Pembroke flash before her—the staid, noble existence that had somehow always seemed so empty, so lacking in purpose. She had been restless without knowing why, defiant without knowing what she was striving to defy. The suitors she had rejected, regardless of the reasons, had all been alike, all come in search of an heiress of good blood and hearty breeding stock. Love had never been a consideration. Affection had never weighed as they mentally checked her teeth, gums, width of hips, and declared her healthy enough, wealthy enough for their purposes. Life with any of them would only have meant more restlessness, more emptiness.

Whereas life with Eduard FitzRandwulf d'Amboise would be a life filled with passion and excitement and love. Bearing his children would be her joy, not her duty. Sharing his destiny would be a challenge, a pleasure, a headlong rush into the unknown that made her heart pound just to think of it.

"I love him," she said, answering Henry's question in the simplest terms she could apply. "Nothing will ever change that."

Henry's response took another full minute to form, and it did so with a slow shaking of his head. "In a way, I suppose this is all my own fault. I should never have agreed to plead your case before Uncle Will. I should never have agreed to take you out of Pembroke, and surely never have agreed to take you to Normandy. I should have just given you to the Welsh prince of thieves then and there . . . rapped you on the head and put you in front of the altar too dazed to concoct any more of your schemes let alone draw me into them. But alas, I have never been able to say no to you, Puss, have I?"

Ariel moved forward, skirting around Eduard's tall frame. She went to her brother and put her arms around him, resting her head briefly on his shoulder. "I am sorry about Cardigan. I know it meant a great deal to you to have the De Clare name restored to its proper place."

"It never meant as much as your happiness," Henry murmured, wrapping his arms around her in turn. "And I warrant" —his eyes rose and sought Eduard's across the gap—"if having a Wolf's cub is what will make you happy—?"

"Delirious," she whispered.

A glance passed between the two men, leaving each with a mutual respect for the other's commitment to Ariel's happiness. In its wake came the glimmering beginnings of a genuine friendship.

In its wake also, came another sigh of exasperation, for it had all become too much for Sparrow to bear in silence.

"St. Bartholemew and all his blundering acolytes look down upon us with mercy!" he groaned, staggering out of the shadows at the mouth of the tunnel. "I lived through this once, with that selfsame Wolf whose cub, methought, had an even thicker layer of armour 'round his heart. I swore then I would not survive it a second time, God aggrieve me if I did not. I swore it, and now look you here: I am dead."

With a dramatic flair that would have been the envy of a dozen swooning beauties, Sparrow clutched the shaft of the bolt that protruded from his shoulder and pitched face forward in a dead faint.

Kirklees Abbey, Nottingham

Chapter 25

†The moon hung bright and cold in a velvet sky. The light it cast was as strong as daylight, washing the stone walls of the abbey a ghostly gray. A rising wind sent little swirls of silvery stardust across the ground, for it had snowed earlier in the day, leaving a thin layer of crystalline powder clinging like hoarfrost to the frozen grasses and branches.

Kirklees sat upon the crest of a gentle roll of land. In summer, sheep grazed on the meadow below and a thousand birds built a thousand nests in the branches of the ancient apple orchard someone had planted a thousand years earlier. Behind the orchard, along a narrow gorge and beyond the crest of yet another graceful hillock, loomed the seemingly endless and impenetrable denseness of the royal forest known as Sherwood. Even in winter, with the huge oaks and ashes stripped of their glossy leaves, the woods were dark and forbidding. Spirits were known to dwell there. Demons and fiends, wizards and witches made the glades and gorges their homes and anyone with the wit or will to retain possession of his soul knew better than to venture into Sherwood alone.

Ariel huddled in the warmth of a thick fur robe, not so much chilled by the weather as by the proximity of Kirklees Abbey to the haunted glens of Sherwood. 'Twas a strong arm's bowshot away from the ivy-covered walls, and she wondered at the courage of the nuns who lived out their lives under the devil's eye.

She shivered under the weight of her own superstitions and deliberately turned her back on the first nagging uncertainties she had experienced since leaving the cavern under the waterfall five days ago.

Sparrow had not, in fact, died. He had roused from his faint as soon as he was carried into the presence of a larger, more appreciative audience, whereupon he had recounted his meeting with the king's men—near a hundred, he had estimated, with a goodly half of them gone to meet their maker, thanks to his keen eye and steady nerve. The quarrel in his shoulder had been the only thing hampering him from ridding the world of the lot.

"A pity, that," Brevant snorted, clearly cynical of Sparrow's tallies. "For their livers will be boiling now and they will be twice as thirsty for blood."

Sparrow had brushed off the captain's concerns with a lofty wave of his hand. "A pox on their stewed livers. By the time they strengthen their backbones and tip a toe onto the road again, we will be well on our way to Nottingham."

Dafydd ap Iorwerth scratched a hand through the black waves of his hair and looked askance. "Nottingham? But my brother awaits us in Gloucester."

Henry and Eduard exchanged a glance, with the latter pausing to scowl over Sparrow's loose tongue before he addressed the Welshman. "We will not be going to Gloucester, Dafydd."

"Not going?" The dark brown eyes lingered on Eduard's face a moment before seeking Ariel's in the glow of the firelight. "But . . . those were the arrangements, were they not?"

Ariel moistened her lips to speak, but it was Henry who drew the young man's startled gaze.

"Aye, and a fine way to repay a man's diligence and perseverance, by any measure. And we've no excuses to offer, my lord, save for a woman's complete lack of sensibilities, for it seems my sister has decided to follow her heart, not her head, and return to Normandy with Lord FitzRandwulf."

Over the sudden stillness that gripped the close circle of men, Ariel heard Sparrow mutter another curse to all the saints who had conspired to put him in service with madmen. Robin, conversely, seemed to come to life, his eyes widening and growing bright with dawning comprehension, his every romantic belief in chivalry, knighthood, and honour justified. Sedrick was giving his head a little shake, as if a faery had planted feathers in his ear, and Iorwerth . . .

Dafydd ap Iorwerth had stopped staring at Henry and was

instead staring intently at the floor, his hand studiously massaging his heavily bandaged forearm.

Ariel reached out and laid her pale, cool fingers over his.

"I am sorry, Dafydd. Truly I am. For you to have come all this way, to have acted in good faith and friendship as you have, only to be betrayed by a woman's fickle nature . . ." She hesitated and bit down hard on her lip. "You have every right to be furious with me. To hate me, even."

Dafydd's brow pleated in a frown. "My brother is the one who will be furious. The insult to his pride he might be able to swallow, but do not think, for all the heartfelt apologies or appeals to his human nature, he will so easily walk away from a promised alliance to the House of Pembroke. The fact that he has a contract, signed by the earl marshal—"

"*My* signature was never affixed to those documents," she interrupted quietly. "A small thing, I know, but—"

"Your consent was implied," he countered.

"Nonetheless, I swore no formal oath before witnesses, my lord, and in Norman England, if not in Wales, such an agreement is not binding without my written consent. Moreover"—she felt her cheeks warming to the challenge to defend her actions—"if your brother was so determined to wed himself to Pembroke, why did he not accompany us himself? Why did he not plead his case before my uncle in person? Why did he send you in his stead when he could have witnessed the contracts and taken me to wife then and there?"

Dafydd's head was still bowed and his expression was difficult to read aside from the muscles that flexed in his jaw.

"He sent me, my lady—" he lifted his handsome young face to the light, startling all present with the sight of a wide grin "—because he had the problem of his *other* wife to tend to before he could marry with you."

"His *other* wife?" Henry and Ariel echoed.

"Aye. A puling sop of a thing foisted on him by Llywellyn some ten years ago. Ugly as a dray horse as well, but she gave him deed to a goodly portion of Clun Forest in the bargain."

"Why are we just hearing about this wife now?" Henry demanded.

"Why was I only told about Eleanor of Brittany outside the walls of Corfe Castle?" Dafydd rejoined smoothly.

Henry sat back on his heels, stymied for an answer that would be taken as anything other than a challenge to the Welshman's honour.

Eduard rubbed his thumb along the lush growth of stubble covering his chin. "How was your brother proposing to deal with this small matter of an existing wife?"

"Annulment. He has huffed and puffed over her for ten years to no avail: she is barren. More's the like he will have tossed her over the ramparts at Deheubarth, for he would not want to lose Clun back to her father or brothers. The same fate, I might add, undoubtedly awaits me if I return, for Rhys has little patience for fools or failures."

"You are his brother," Eleanor said, her voice husked behind the wall of blankets.

Dafydd stared at the barrier a moment, then shrugged and sighed. "No more than an extra spill of our father's seed so far as either Rhys or Llywellyn are concerned. Rhys has only tolerated my presence this long because I have an honest face and gentle manner that makes it easier for a lord to believe his cattle have strayed rather than been stolen." He glanced pointedly at Henry, flushing slightly under the returned glare, then let his gaze touch briefly on Eduard, Sedrick, and Robin. "You have shown me more camaraderie in these past few weeks than my brothers have in all my years. Not that I consider myself in any way worthy or"—he bowed his head again quickly—"or deserving of the friendship of such men as yourselves, but . . . if I might say it without drawing anyone's scorn or wrath, I will guard the memory of these times for howsoever long I have left in this mortal guise."

Sparrow groaned again and rapped the palm of his hand against his brow. "I am besotted by a plague of fools. I suppose now we must trail this wet-eyed lambkin along with us? I do not suppose we could simply beckon yon Littlejohn to wield his steel pricker to good effect and solve the problem of an addled Welshman with one swarthy stroke?"

"I do not suppose we could," Eduard mused. "But you

assume, Puck, our fine young Welshman would be addled enough to want to throw his lot in with us after all we have not confided in him."

Dafydd's face was as honest in its relief as it was open in its disbelief. "You would allow it? You would allow me to return with you to Normandy?"

"If my wife will have no objections," Eduard said, turning to arch a brow in Ariel's direction.

"None," she said at once. "But what about Lord Rhys? How long will he wait at Gloucester before he realizes we are not coming?"

"Long enough for Llywellyn to plan a warm reception for him when he returns to Deheubarth," Dafydd suggested.

"No warmer, I troth," Sparrow declared, "than the one Lackland is planning for *us* ere we linger too long in these poxy woods—or am I the only one recalling we are but a half day's ride from the donjons at Corfe?"

"We have none of us forgotten," Eduard replied blandly. "And we will be on our way just as soon as we find a barber to pluck that arrow out of your shoulder. 'Tis wedged too deep in the bone for any of us to try to dig it free. Littlejohn—? You know the villages hereabout better than we; do any of them boast a skilled healer?"

"Bah!" Brevant drew out his eating knife and spit on the blade. "No need to waste time with such extravagances. I have separated my share of iron from bone."

Sparrow gawped. "I do not be thinking so, Lord Lubbergut. I would sooner dis-wedge it myself before I would let those great hairy paws have at me!"

"Then you had best dis-wedge it," Brevant growled, looming closer, the blade of his knife flaring orange in the firelight. "And do it fast, before these paws decide there would be more pleasure pushing rather than pulling."

Sparrow gave a yelp and yanked on the shaft of the arrow, surprising no one more than himself when it jerked out freely in his hand. He stared at the gleaming redness that dripped from the barbed tip, then at the gaping wet hole in his flesh . . . and his eyes crossed and rolled to the back of his head.

Eduard caught him before he could splat onto the hard ground, quickly ascertaining this faint was for real. It was just as well he remained unconscious for a time; without the benefit of needle and thread to close the wound, they had no choice but to staunch the bleeding by cauterizing it with a glowing faggot from the fire.

Within the hour, and under a cloak of darkness, they had been packed up and on their way. Sparrow, still oblivious, was strapped securely onto Robin's saddlepack and did not rouse again until they stopped on the far side of Salisbury. They rested during the day and at dusk took to the roads again, skirting well clear of towns and villages, breaking the pattern only when it became necessary to send one of their number to purchase foodstuffs they could not scrounge from the land.

On the morning of the third day, Sedrick announced his decision not to stop and rest with the others but to strike out due west and to keep pushing day and night until he reached Pembroke. Someone had to warn Lady Isabella before the king thought to dispatch a troop of men to take her and the children hostage in retaliation. Since he, with his gruff appearance and Celtic accent, could move more anonymously through the border Marches than Henry, Sedrick had elected himself to the task without any consultation or argument.

The marshal had not survived the various Angevin temperaments for over sixty years by being taken unawares. No doubt his spies had already informed him of the princess's escape and he was already taking steps, albeit reluctantly, to divert suspicion away from any personal involvement. They had discussed this at Amboise and Henry had, with his usual casual indifference, accepted the possibility of full blame falling on the De Clare name, and also that his presence might not be too welcome in England for some time. He had assumed Ariel would be safely hidden away in the wilds of Deheubarth, and he had assumed he would be equally isolated at Cardigan where nothing short of an armed siege would pry him loose.

That was, of course, before Ariel had announced she had no intentions of fleeing to Wales or of marrying Rhys ap

Iorwerth. It was also before he realized he was falling in love with Eleanor of Brittany.

"I do not think I will be returning to Normandy with you, Puss. Not just yet, at any rate."

"Not return?" She sought her brother's face, brightly lit under the wash of moonlight. Henry had said he wanted a private moment of conversation with her, and for all that they had stood apart from the others, admiring the walls of Kirklees Abbey for nigh on ten minutes, these were the first words he had spoken. "But why not? Where will you go? What will you do? You cannot go back to Pembroke; you said yourself the king will declare us outlaws and traitors. Where can you go, other than Normandy, where you will have less chance of someone recognizing you and bringing the royal hounds down on your heels?"

"Actually—" He paused and looked around them, his hazel eyes focussing on the black crust of forest that bristled across the horizon. "I was not planning to go far. Not until I can be sure the princess is safe and none of those same hounds have sniffed her out here."

"And if you are recognized? Will you not be *drawing* them to her?" Ariel asked gently.

"As Henry de Clare, aye, I might," he agreed. "Even as a solitary nameless knight, my presence might stir a rumour or two. But I have been listening to some of Robin's tales too (he had been regaling them all with more tales than a troubadour, hoping to distract Eleanor from her worries with more pleasant reminiscences). The one that stalls in my mind is the one about his mother's first meeting with the Wolf and Alaric FitzAthelstan—do you recall it?"

Ariel shook her head, too perplexed to think of tales told around a fireside.

"She had been kidnapped by Lord Randwulf and managed to escape briefly into the woods. Drawn by the bells of a monastery, she sought refuge there, unaware the grounds had been long abandoned. Lord Alaric, disguised as a humble friar, had answered her plea for sanctuary, and she had thrown herself at his mercy only to discover he was the Wolf's loyal captain."

"And so you plan to find a deserted monastery and disguise yourself as a monk?" Ariel asked wryly.

"Kirklees is cloistered," he said softly, ignoring her sarcasm. "The only men allowed inside the main gates are of the Holy Order. If I have to shave my head in a tonsure and wear the robes of a monk in order to see her, I will do it gladly and willingly."

Ariel's smile faded. "You are serious."

After a long, wind-rustled delay, Henry met her gaze. "I cannot just ride away and leave her here unprotected."

"What will you do? Tuck a sword beneath your cassock while you tend sheep on the hillside?"

"I will tuck a sword and tuck a knife . . . I will even tuck Littlejohn's glaive beneath my robes if need be, but I will not leave Eleanor alone and unprotected until either the king is dead or the barons come to their senses and find a way to prevent him from murdering his niece as he did his nephew."

Whether it was a trick of the moonlight or just the heat of his convictions burning through, Henry's eyes were glowing white-hot, like the core of a flame. Ariel had seen the same heated passion before, in Eduard's eyes, the stormy night on the ramparts of Corfe Castle. She had attributed it then to the lightning, and only later to love, but . . .

"Henry . . . ?" The unspoken question was snatched away on a frosted breath, but the answer was plain enough to see.

"Laugh if you like," he said stubbornly, hunching his shoulders against a chill. "It would be no less than your due after the way I reacted to you and FitzRandwulf."

"But . . . the Princess Eleanor . . ." Trying to think of the gentlest way to say it, Ariel was eased of the burden when Henry said it himself.

"Longs only to show her love for the Church, yes, I know. And I would not even try to dissuade her, for that love is as pure and shining as any I have seen. Nay, I would be content just to be near her, to see her now and then, to speak with her of harmless things." He looked away again, staring at the gray walls of Kirklees as if he knew they would soon be enclosing his heart.

"Have you told Eduard?"

"I have told him," he nodded. "I have also told him he has little say in the matter, little choice either, for he can waste no time returning to Normandy. The quicker he is known to have left England, the quicker the wind will carry the news and the name of his new bride to the king's ears. What is more, John will hear that Henry de Clare is in Normandy as well—a little darker in appearance and speaking in a broader accent than might be expected, but—"

"Dafydd?"

"He has agreed to play me for a while, if only to throw his own brother's hounds off the scent."

Ariel whuffed a soft, misty breath into the stillness. It was obvious he and Eduard had discussed everything most thoroughly and she could expect small success in trying to persuade him to reconsider. It was nonetheless a shock to realize he would not be returning to Normandy with them, and a greater shock to realize she might not see him again for a very long time.

"Are you certain this is what you want to do?" she whispered.

"I have never been more certain of anything in my life . . . except, perhaps, knowing that I will miss you."

Ariel went readily into his arms. "No more than I will miss you. You will be careful? You will do nothing foolish to draw attention to yourself?"

"I will be as careful as careful can," he promised. "And you . . . you will have to learn to obey this new husband of yours; he does not seem to me the type to tolerate your schemes and rebellions with as much humour as the other men you have managed to tame into mere shadows of their former selves."

"I have no wish to tame him," she admitted honestly. "Although I confess, the prospect of *being* tamed holds great appeal."

Henry held her out at arm's length and frowned. "By God, I believe you really do love him."

"Enough to forgive you for even doubting me."

The faint crunch of footsteps prompted them to turn and follow the progress of the cloaked figure of Eduard FitzRandwulf as he walked down the slope from the abbey gates. The small group waiting by the horses, comprised of the Princess Eleanor and Marienne, Robin, Littlejohn, Dafydd, and Sparrow, stirred as well, and together with Henry and Ariel, converged on the descending knight as he reached the bottom of the hill.

"It is settled. The abbess has agreed, most heartily, to welcome Eleanor into their midst. She has also agreed to guard her anonymity, even amongst the other sisters, who will be told only that the new novitiate is the orphaned daughter of a noble who fell out of favour with the king. A common enough story these days, it seems."

"What did you tell *her?*" Henry wanted to know.

Eduard responded with a smile. "That the lady was in fear of her life. That she was indeed an orphan, persecuted by the king, and if word of her presence here—even the merest hint of a whisper were to reach the royal ear, not even the cloisters of Kirklees would be sacrosanct. It tended to raise her hackles a little, as I had hoped it would. She was ever a fearless old grisette; the only one of my memory who dared to challenge the Lord of Bloodmoor Keep's *droit du seigneur* with the village maids who chose to marry themselves to the Church rather than submit to his lusts."

"Did she remember you at all?" Eleanor asked.

"If she did, she kept it confined to the gleam in her eye. And if she suspects our lady's identity, I have no doubt she will keep the secret with her unto the grave."

"Eduard . . ." the princess stretched her hand across the darkness. "How can I ever thank you? How can I ever begin to thank any of you?"

"Your happiness is more than thanks enough," Eduard said, pressing her slender fingers against his lips.

"And yours," she whispered, "is all that I could have hoped for."

"You still have the ring," Eduard reminded her firmly. "If you ever need me, for any reason—"

Eleanor smiled. "I will dispatch it to Amboise with all haste, I promise. But between Lord Henry and Marienne, I doubt if even so much as a flea would dare trouble me."

Robin's gaze burned through the gloom and held Marienne's for a moment, only to lose it in the next as she lowered her eyes. Eduard did not miss the pinched expression that came over the young squire's face. Nor did Eleanor, with her strangely heightened perceptions, fail to detect the sudden tension that quickened her maid's breath.

"Marienne is still young," she said to no one in particular. "But she is old enough to know the Church is not her life, as it has always been mine. A year or two from now, when she is convinced I am content and at peace, she will be able to choose her own way in the world."

Robin's expression brightened. "She will be free?"

Eleanor laughed softly. "She is free now, Robert. A convent is not a prison, it is a place of peace and tranquillity. Marienne will be free to leave any time she wishes."

Robin muttered a hasty pardon and, snatching up Marienne's hand, pulled her to one side where they stood with their heads together, a flurry of whispered promises passing between them.

Still smiling, Eleanor tilted her head slightly to acknowledge the source of another bemused sigh. "Lady Ariel?"

"Your Highness?"

"I must needs thank you as well, for more than you can possibly imagine. With the exception of Marienne, I have never had the pleasure of female companionship before—none that I would care to call 'friend' by any rood. And I would so like to think of you as my friend, and to know that you might smile with fondness sometime when you happen to think of me."

"I . . . *we* . . . shall think of you all the time, my lady,"

Ariel insisted, tossing protocol to the wind as she leaned forward and gave the last Angevin princess a fervent hug.

Startled, and overwhelmed to the verge of tears, Eleanor squeezed Ariel's shoulders just as tightly, her voice ragged against her ear. "I had almost forsaken all hope of Eduard ever finding a woman willing, or surely even able, to convince him he is worth loving. Indeed, the most fearsome opponent he ever defeated on or off the battlefield could have crushed him afterward by uttering but a single word: bastard. Love him, Ariel. Love him with all your heart and you will not regret it, not for one single moment."

"I do not regret it now," Ariel said earnestly. "Nor will I ever."

Beside them, Eduard cleared his throat and glanced up at the abbey. "The abbess is waiting to admit you."

Eleanor and Ariel stepped apart, and in a halting voice, the princess bade a final farewell and thanks to Dafydd ap Iorwerth, Jean de Brevant, and Sparrow, astonishing the diminutive seneschal by bending down and brushing his rounded cheek with a kiss.

"Promise me you will see them all home safely. It is a charge I bestow upon thee most solemnly."

Sparrow puffed a chest already wadded with bandages and gave the balance of his arblaster an imperious adjustment. "You may count upon me, Little Highness. As always."

"Give my love to Mistress Bidwell. Tell her I shall pray daily for her continuing perseverance."

Sparrow started to reply, realized it might be a veiled reference to his own recalcitrant nature, and accorded the request a muffled, "Harrumph!"

With Eduard on one side and Marienne on the other, Eleanor went willingly to her fate. She paused at the low, arched postern and, after a last word with Eduard, pressed something into his hand and walked through the portal with Marienne and was swallowed into the dark silence of Kirklees.

Eduard continued to stand alone, in the shadows of midnight, his head bowed, the dark waves of his hair blown forward over his temples. He turned slightly, angling his hand into the moonlight and uncurled his fist from around the object Eleanor had given him.

It was a pearl. A single white pearl, as large as a robin's egg, as lustrous as the smile of joy that had been on Eleanor of Brittany's face as she had walked to meet her destiny.

Epilogue

✝ The safe return of the Wolf's two sons to Château
d'Amboise was cause for a week of feasting the likes of
which the castle and village had not witnessed in years.
The arrival home of Eduard FitzRandwulf with a new bride by
his side sent waves of shock recoiling throughout the countryside, with tremors reaching as far as a cold, drafty room in a
castle keep in Falaise. There William the Marshal sat before a
crackling fire, a cup of mulled wine warming his hands, a wide
and (truth be known) not altogether surprised grin warming his
heart.

Behind him, snuggled under layers of fur to ward off the
winter chill, was his wife Isabella. The countess and their ten
children had arrived at Falaise only a few days earlier, led by
an exhausted Sedrick of Grantham, who had packed the gaggle
aboard a fast ship and sailed from Pembroke within hours of
his arrival there.

Jean de Brevant had accompanied FitzRandwulf back to
Amboise, claiming he had aught better to do than to pester
Sparrow into an early grave. He had heard of Eduard's famous
sire—who of warm blood and living flesh had not? He took an
oath of homage to Randwulf de la Seyne Sur Mer and was, in
due time, made captain of the Wolf's personal guard, a duty
which, in turn, would include protecting his firstborn son and
heir, Robert d'Amboise, when he gained his gold spurs of
knighthood and declared his intent to return to England to
fetch Marienne FitzWilliam home.

Dafydd ap Iorwerth played the part of Henry de Clare so
well, an assassin's arrow felled him not a month after their
return to Amboise. As it happened, he was in the village at the
time, pacing along the banks of the river Loire, trying to stoke
up the courage to cast a friendly smile in the direction of the
miller's widowed daughter. Luckily the arrow struck the meat
of a thigh muscle and the young Welshman was not only able
to loose off an arrow of his own to kill his attacker, but he won

the wide-eyed interest of his original quarry, Gabrielle, when she brought him back to her tiny cottage to nurse his wound. She proved to be an excellent care-giver, more so when she judged, by the frequency and intensity of his blushes, that he was yet a virgin.

Ariel had cause to suspect by the grin on her husband's face as he recounted Dafydd's plight that there was more to the story than met the casual eye, but she wisely kept her suspicions to herself. She had no reason to be jealous or envious of Eduard's past liaisons, not when she had the heat of his body to warm her every night, and his unflagging energy and passion to guide her breathlessly through every day.

Which is not to say their union was perpetual bliss and contentment. Their battles were monumental and the entire household came to be wary of the sight of flaming red hair and flashing green eyes stalking through the baileys and keeps. They came to watch, expectantly and with bated breath, at just what point during a meal or muted conversation the Wolf's cub would fling his patience aside and snatch up his bride by the hand or sling her like a sack of grain over his shoulder and carry her up to their apartments, there to remain until they both emerged, subdued and markedly weaker about the knees, their differences either resolved or forgotten.

They remained at Amboise until Ariel was delivered of their first child—a daughter, Eleanor, born with flame red hair and eyes so green they were like crystals plucked from the sea. The day of her birth marked the second time Ariel saw tears spill freely from her husband's eyes—no match for the flood that poured from her own when he presented her with the pearl their daughter's namesake had given him, mounted in a necklace of fine gold circlets, each containing a perfect cabochon emerald.

Eleanor was born in the late summer, the same time Philip's armies overran Normandy, Anjou, Maine, Touraine, and most of Poitou. He met no resistance from the black and gold devices of La Seyne Sur Mer, for in March of that year, the dowager queen had died at Fontevraud. Philip, relieved he would not have to face Lord Randwulf's army, nevertheless cut a wide berth around Amboise and its surrounding territories, preferring to leave sleeping wolves lying undisturbed.

With Normandy under French rule, John's search for Eleanor of Brittany effectively ended. It galled him to know she had been stolen out from under his nose, but it was not as if she could ever challenge him for possession of the throne. He reacted to the loss of his niece and the loss of Normandy by spending the next year in an orgy of feasting and debauchery. He was all but convinced William the Marshal was behind the rescue, but with no direct proof, he had to settle for seizing any and all estates deeded to the De Clare traitors. Most of these, he discovered to his further rage, had been placed in trust with the Countess Isabella of Pembroke, who was just as adamant as her husband in decrying the youthful passion and misguided zealousness that had led her niece and nephew astray.

As to Guy of Gisbourne's description of the scarred knight who had left him a cripple, there was little doubt in the king's mind it was Eduard FitzRandwulf d'Amboise, even before he heard of the marriage of the Wolf's cub to Ariel de Clare. Realizing he must have passed within arm's length of them on the road to Corfe threw the monarch into such a frothing fit, he was nearly a month in bed recovering his senses.

Having seemed to simply vanish into thin air, Eleanor of Brittany was referred to thereafter as the Lost Princess of Brittany. Stories, songs, and legends of what *really* happened to her were rekindled occasionally, each with eyewitness accounts of either her demise or her appearance as a ghostly spectre in the king's chambers. All of the stories were related by the tawny-haired monk who visited Kirklees faithfully each and every week for the next seventeen years. So familiar had he become to the peasants who worked the fields around the abbey, that after the first few months he rarely troubled himself to change out of the drab brown cassock he wore. A stranger passing through the greenwood might have thought it odd to see a monk practicing with a sword and bow, odder still to see the collection of outlaws and misfits he collected into his fold. But there were few strangers who ventured into the heart of Sherwood, and none who emerged if the forest residents did not like the look of them.

Occasionally, messages arrived from Normandy and were also shared in the sunny garden of Kirklees. News that Ariel and Eduard had moved to a fine castle of their own near Blois, where two strapping sons and another daughter were born in successive springs, put smiles on their faces and joy in their hearts. News of Robert d'Amboise's rise through the ranks of knighthood set a third face blushing more hues of red than a summer sunset.

Marienne FitzWilliam had blossomed into a beautiful young woman. Because she had not taken any vow of seclusion, she was often sent to the market in Nottingham to trade the linens woven by the nuns of Kirklees. It happened one day, she was caught in a circle of sunlight, frowning in concentration over a selection of needles and spindles, when the bored and lecherous eyes of a town official happened to settle on the abundance of glossy chestnut curls. His name was Reginald de Braose and he was in the service of the new sheriff of Nottingham . . .

But that, dear reader, is another story.